W9-CQR-607

MALDENE

Volume Two

by
Mark Anthony Tierno

PublishAmerica
Baltimore

© 2007 by Mark Anthony Tierno.
All rights reserved. No part of this book may be reproduced, stored in a retrieval system or transmitted in any form or by any means without the prior written permission of the publishers, except by a reviewer who may quote brief passages in a review to be printed in a newspaper, magazine or journal.

First printing

All characters in this book are fictitious, and any resemblance to real persons, living or dead, is coincidental.

At the specific preference of the author, PublishAmerica allowed this work to remain exactly as the author intended, verbatim, without editorial input.

ISBN: 1-4241-9030-4
PUBLISHED BY PUBLISHAMERICA, LLLP
www.publishamerica.com
Baltimore

Printed in the United States of America

Table of Contents

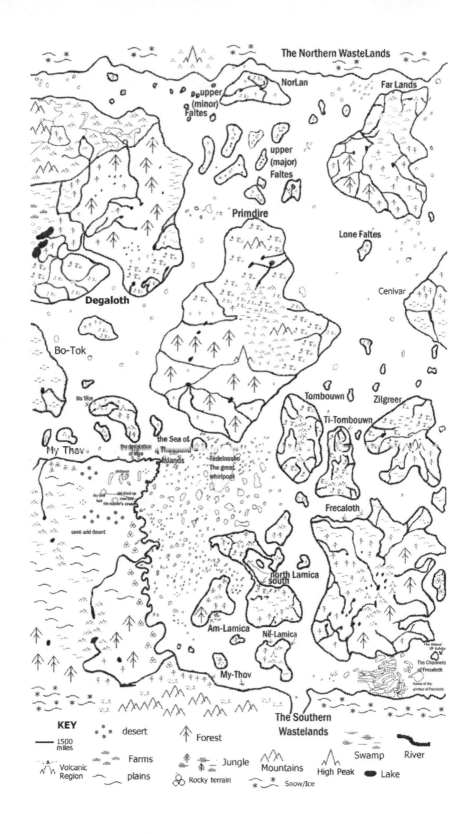

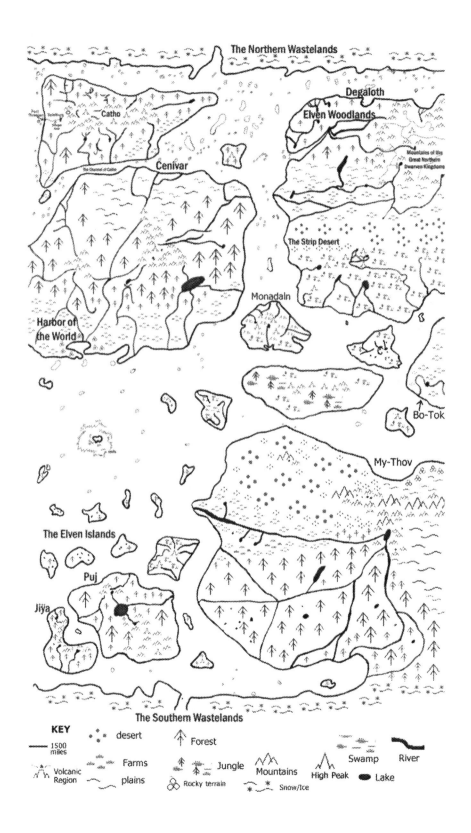

MALDENE

Volume Two

BOOK III:

In Search of Thïr Tÿorca

CHAPTER NINETEEN
Sydelburg

R.K.: 9,990, 23 Arüdwo:

We have been traveling along Threegan Road for over a thousand miles now and are well into the interior of Catho. We have had no major incidents impeding our progress and so have been making pretty good progress, even despite the sorry state of our mounts. With Lindel's help, though, our horses have been improving a bit.

Along the side of the road we have been traveling, there have been the occasional old stone road-marker. I believe these to be ancient leftovers from the old Kingdoms. Their markings would correspond with the language of the times, and their placement consistent with the Kingdoms' habits of maintaining road systems throughout their domains. I would have loved to study them more carefully, but both Eldar and Lindel reminded me of our goals by physically pulling me away from the markers.

Rather rude of them.

Especially since the next time we came across one, Lindel urged my horse into a sudden gallop past it.

We have encountered a few other travelers along the way, more than a few coming from the interior. Several of them have been fleeing raids from tribes of beast-man creatures coming from the nearby hills and mountains. Apparently these raids have been severe enough to force several families to flee and entire small villages to be abandoned. Quickfoot may have been right about our walking into a little war.

We have passed by several small towns poking out from the woods alongside this road, staying in some for the evening, renewing our supplies, and moving on. From such places we have been picking up information on our possible destination. The mountain range of Catho is some six thousand miles long and over fifteen hundred miles wide. While not the largest range in the world, this would be more than big enough to leave us searching until we'd died of old age. The dimenio-book of history has given me some information with which to narrow down the search, but we still need to learn more. We are told that Threegan Road ends at a town up ahead called Sydelburg; maybe there we can learn more.

R.K.: 9,990, 24 Arüdwo:

We are passing by some farms now, with Sydelburg just up ahead. I've seen some of the farms reduced to scorched plots of land, while others' crops grow but sparsely and weak, as if from poisoned ground. I've seen many people crowding both down the road and in from the countryside towards Sydelburg, their homes on their backs. As we near the edge of town, I see guards about in the streets in greater numbers than one would normally think sufficient. I've seen a makeshift graveyard with several freshly dug graves.

Definitely a city under siege.

The dirty streets were clogged with humanity; individuals who hadn't had time to wash in many rises of the sun, whole families carrying the remains of their lives with them, as well as the occasional rogue selling the necessities of life at over-inflated prices to the desperate. Bronto had to elbow his large frame through the refugees and the beggars, while Lorel had to wade through the needy as they pulled at him and begged for scraps of food. Lorel gave out what scraps he had on him as the dirty faces passed on by, but it wasn't enough; he realized that it wouldn't ever be enough for this horde of the dispossessed. He couldn't help even a small portion of them. Eldar, his instinct for cities never failing, lead them through the crowds, down smaller side streets, and around the maze that was the town, and out into the more spacious town square, its cracked and faded fountain not having seen water for some time now.

"We've got to find someone that knows the area, maybe even a local mystic," said Sabu as they walked past open-air cloth booths selling anything from fruits to personal ornamentation.

"Maybe I can speed up our search," Sindar offered. "I haven't been idle in the practice of my mental powers, after all."

"Okay mister psychic," Eldar mocked lightly, "which way?"

As Sindar concentrated, they walked out into the more open central area of the square, people buzzing about around them, as they held their own small island of safety next to the old cracked fountain.

"The East side of town, but a short walk from here," Sindar finally said. "I've just spoken to him, and he's expecting us."

"That was fast," Eldar remarked, "an appointment and everything."

"Then we're off," Shong said.

"Good," Lindel sighed, "this wash of refugees is a bit unsettling."

"Wait," Lorel stopped them as they were about to leave, concern on his face, "there must be something that we can do to at least alleviate the needs of these masses."

"That would do little good," Candol disagreed, "the raids will just produce more. The needs of Indra would have us onward to larger concerns."

"And does your Indra not care for the suffering of an individual, or of the impoverished masses before us," Lorel said, face tight with anger.

"Touchy, aren't we," Mauklo commented. "I think I'm going to like him."

Candol put a hand on Lorel's shoulder and calmly looked him in the eye before answering.

"Indra would have us look after the *cause* of all this about us, and not just cure its symptoms."

Lorel looked at the priest, gazed slowly out at the masses passing around them, then back at Candol, the truth of his words showing upon the priest's face. Lorel seemed to consider Candol's words, his face relaxing a bit.

"Still," Lorel said, more calmly, the pain of emotion still showing in his look and his stance, "there must be something that we can do to lessen their suffering."

"The strong among them will survive," Kilgar shrugged, "the rest should learn to fight better."

"You are so cynical for one so young," Lorel said, looking down at Kilgar. "But maybe I *shall* teach them to fight; or at least how to survive. I must do *something* while we are here."

"Good," Eldar interrupted, "then how's about you take Bronto, Shong, and Kilgar, and go work on that while we get our directions."

"That I shall!" Lorel brightened. "No help shall be refused while I am about."

"Then again," Mauklo sighed, "I may have spoken too soon."

"Kilinir and myself have our own errands to seek after," Kor-Lebear put in as he stood next to Kilinir, "maybe we'll join you later."

"One wonders what type of errands those two would have," Lindel commented.

"Then we'll meet back here at nightfall," Sabu said, "and leave tomorrow when the sun rises at mid morn."

A cloaked figure watched them from amongst the surrounding crowds as they left to their various errands.

The room they walked into seemed small, so crowded was it with all manner of books, vials, and odd implements of research and magic. Dust hung from the low ceiling in wispy cobwebs, the dim light leaking through the covered windows lightly illuminating them. The frail door slammed shut behind them, as they saw the only other exit to this room was a door-like opening on the opposing wall, covered over with a thin grey cloth. Sabu, Eldar, Sindar, and Mauklo had entered the mystic's small abode, the others with them having decided to stay outside. The mystic's place was at the very edge of the city's eastern side, being surrounded by a small slum area with a fair view of the outlying farms and the distant mountains beyond. It was an innocuous shack in an innocuous part of town.

"Are you sure he knows we're coming?" Eldar asked, as they looked around.

Before anyone could answer, a voice came from the area beyond the covered opening.

"Of *course* I know you're coming! I'm a mystic, aren't I?" came the irascible voice. "*Sotüva*, you young ones can be dense sometimes."

They looked over as, from behind the grey cloth, walked out the mystic. He was old and grey, his white hair coming down to his shoulders, his chin clean-shaven, his skin the white one gets from having seen no sun in too long a time. He wore a long night-shirt, its dingy off-whiteness coming down to his bare ankles. He walked with a slight stoop, and with small steps, but at a fast hurried shuffle that told of an energy that only true impatience can supply.

"I heard your friend's mind call," he said rapidly. "Dangerous thing, broadcasting your mind openly like that; no telling who else could hear you. Sit down anywhere."

They looked first at the source of this rapid tirade, blinking at him in mild befuddlement, and then looked around for a place to sit. The old man went over to a dusty old chair and sat down, while Sabu and Eldar tried to find a place for themselves.

"Just move some of that stuff aside," the old man said, "my name's Bathow."

Sabu gently moved some old books aside and sat down on what looked to be a chair, while Eldar just shrugged and, rather noisily, pushed a whole section of books, vials, and whatnot, off of a table and sat up on top of it.

"My name's Sindar, and I think I'll stand," responded Sindar, looking around doubtfully.

"I think I'll supply my *own* seat," Mauklo said, walking over to an open space.

Mauklo pointed a finger at the ground next to him and, with a short *pfft*, a clean, small, leather-bound chair appeared.

"There," he said, while sitting down, "definitely more dignified."

"Oh yeah," Eldar smiled, "never mess with his dignity."

"My name is—" Sabu began, offering his hand out to Bathow.

"I *know* who you are," Bathow interrupted impatiently, turning to shuffle through some papers on an old desk, "I'm the best mystic in Catho, so give me some credit. You want to know how to get to the Dragon Mountains and the Valley of Lights. A fool's errand if ever I heard one. Especially with all the raiding going on between here and there."

"The petty squabblings of some goat-herders and beast-men shall not deter us," Mauklo said calmly.

"If you are truly as good as you say," Sabu said, "then you should know why these raids will not stop us."

"I think he's just faking it," Eldar said, dangling his feet off the edge of the table. "Sindar told him our names when he made mental contact. The rest, he doesn't know from horse flop."

"I know enough to keep shut in front of my elders," Bathow growled.

"Ha," Eldar smiled, "I'm probably older than you are. I just don't show it like you humans."

"Older and twice as foolish," Bathow countered. "Yes, I have the information that you want, and it's enough to get you all killed. You should do what I do; hide from the forces of darkness and hope that they pass you by."

"I have little patience for cowards," Mauklo stated calmly.

"You may call it being cowardly," Bathow replied, "I call it staying alive long enough to pass my knowledge on to others, that it may not be lost."

"And then, what would you expect those others to do with the knowledge that you give them?" Sabu asked.

"Why, keep themselves safe and hidden so that they too may pass on the knowledge when their time comes." Bathow replied.

"But then, of what use," Sindar interrupted calmly, "is having power and knowledge if you can't improve the world with it? If you have such knowledge, yet hide away with it, then you do even less than the peasants outside. By not using your knowledge, it is as if the knowledge had never existed in the first place. What then do you preserve your knowledge for?"

Silence came down with Sindar's words, spoken with the calmness of truth, while Bathow seemed lost in thought. Finally, he looked up, his grey eyes now showing a purpose. He raised up his right hand, rolled it tight into a clenched fist, and muttered a few quick syllables under his breath. A quick flash of light discharged from his fist, and then he relaxed his grip, letting down his hand.

"We are safe from unwanted ears now," Bathow said more calmly, "and I can assure you, my young wizard, that I do what I can."

"Aside from acting so unpleasant, you mean?" Eldar observed.

"There are forces that seek after those who would boldly do right," Bathow said, "and knowledge and power are useless if one is dead. So, I hide. I do what I can for the world around me but…"

"Just not too openly," Eldar finished, taken aback, "I'm sorry."

"You seem kind of open to us." Sabu pointed out.

"Like I said," Bathow replied, "I'm good at what I do. I've been waiting for you all for a good number of rels now. It has been for the likes of yourselves that my knowledge has been passed down through the generations; ever since the time of the old Kingdoms. Here are the maps that you came for."

Bathow reached amongst the papers he'd been shifting around on his desk, and produced some rolled up into a cylinder. These he handed to Sabu.

"Since the old Kingdoms, you say?" Sabu asked. "From what source did it originate?"

"My ancestor was a high advisor for one of the Kingdoms," Bathow answered. "When the world collapsed around him, he sought to preserve some things for future generations, that his learning not be lost in the mists of time."

"Indeed some things worth learning," Sindar observed. "Perhaps you could serve as our teacher, maybe even travel with us."

"No; time is short," Bathow replied, relaxing back into his chair, "he hunts for you more than any. Be careful, for the game is his."

"Anyone know what he's talking about?" Eldar asked.

"Obviously," Mauklo said, "he's giving us some precognitive advice."

"It is never what it seems," Bathow quietly intoned, his eyes looking distant, "never. Don't spend a lifetime learning that the hard way; like I did."

"If you have been waiting for so many rels," Sabu asked, when Bathow had finally stopped and was beginning to loose his distant look, "why now, do you seem so rushed?"

"It is good that you do not yet have any family," Bathow said, seeming to ignore Sabu's question, "those that would be heroes should not have anyone close that can be threatened."

"I had a family once," Bathow reminisced, "A wife and two stout sons, at an age when I sought to change things. I learned the hard way how one can be broken. Now, I have no one to pass on my learning to; my knowledge shall finally be lost."

Bathow looked thoughtful, then suddenly shook himself out of his reverie.

"Ignore the ramblings of an old used-up man," Bathow said, a bit more briskly, "and pay attention to his advice. Time is short."

Before they had time to ask another question, the outside door flung open, a golden-haired elven figure standing in the doorway.

"A raid comes," Lindel said, notched bow ready in his hands, "a cloud of smoke rising up through the farmlands. There looks to be a lot of them."

"That's the trouble with that spell," Bathow said, getting up, "it not only protects one from being heard, but from *hearing* as well."

"Sounds like a reason to rumble," Eldar said, hopping up off the edge of the table.

"So much for our dose of altruistic advice," Mauklo said, standing up, the conjured chair disappearing in another short *pfft*.

"I'm sure we might be able to do something about this raid," Sabu said as he got up, "we've faced worse."

Bathow just smiled as they all went outside.

It was afternoon outside, Bathow was the last to leave his small home. They walked down the street, towards where the city suddenly left off, overlooking the farms beyond. They were on a slight rise, Candol and Quickfoot there waiting for them, a large cloud of smoke rising in the distance.

"Sounds like we might get a little workout," Eldar grinned. "After all, how bad can these beast-men be?"

Thunder, the sound of a hundred deep drums, come beating through the ground. Distant cracks of lightning, rumbling low and rhythmic.

"Someone tell me I don't recognize that sound," Eldar said.

Quickfoot dived behind Candol's fluttering robes, his face peering out from behind.

"I remember them!" Quickfoot whimpered.

They watched as the distant cloud of dust got closer, along with the thunderous hooves.

"It certainly *sounds* the same," Eldar said, looking less sure of himself than before.

"If you wish to have a look at our foe," Bathow said, coming up next to them, "there is a way."

With a wave of his hand, the air in front of him shimmered and shifted, quickly forming into an image, floating up in the air in front of them. They all looked at what the image beheld.

"Chupek; it can't be!" Lindel exclaimed. "You mean there's a whole *tribe* of these things?"

A cloaked figure crouched atop a nearby rooftop, observed them as they watched the conjured image. Horses danced through the vision, large horses, their hooves almost claws, long mangy hair covering their bodies, their breath snorting out angry dark smoke. On their backs were the beast-men, their twisted animal faces glaring out as their clawed hands tugged the reins ever tighter. Through the image their distant guttural cries could be heard, as they swung their twisted swords out in front of them.

"They're just like the ones we killed back when we met Lindel, Sindar, and the others," Candol said, peering at the image.

"That's okay," Eldar brightened, getting out his sword, "we killed them before, we'll do it again. And now we're better at it than before."

"We'll need to be," Lindel said, nodding towards the approaching cloud, "take a look at the size of that cloud."

Sabu bit his lip, looking at both the image and the cloud of dust, as if quickly calculating something. Finally, he turned to Sindar.

"Call the others," Sabu said in a serious tone, "there's hundreds of them out there."

"It would be in the best interest of the local rich to help these refugees," Lorel was saying as he, Bronto, Shong, and Kilgar walked up the street towards the large house. "If we could convince at least one of them to offer some assistance, then we will have helped."

"I guess so," Shong said doubtfully, "but diplomacy isn't among my skills. I feel much more comfortable in battle then with words."

"You and me both, my friend," Bronto chuckled.

"Words are a waste of time," Kilgar said, clutching his long curved knife, "politicians use words."

"Don't worry, comrades; if need be, I shall do the talking," Lorel said, as they went up to the door.

The door had a large ornate knocker, with which Lorel pounded twice, each thud echoing loudly throughout the large house beyond. Moments passed before the large door began to slowly creak open.

"We would speak with the good sir or madame of the house," Lorel began speaking immediately, "about the plight of the poor refugees that you have surely noticed about town."

The door opened fully, revealing a lady. Definitely into old age, yet still walking with the straight back of vigor and youth, her white hair seemed to stand straight up on its own, radiating out in all directions from her head like they were trying their best to launch themselves outwards. Her white wrinkled skin suggested tiny stringy muscles underneath. Her rich-looking, if somewhat old, clothes hung around her like a small tent protecting its young, if such a structure could indeed have any. She looked out at them, wrinkled face expressionless.

"I am the owner of this house," she said in a high cracked voice that sounded like broken glass.

"We would not trouble you," Lorel went on, "but it weighs upon the soul to see such numbers in so desperate a situation. Now maybe, with your own fine fortune, you could at least help feed some of the desperate that have..."

While Lorel prattled on, her eyes looked at each of them in turn, finally wandering over to Shong, who just gave a polite nervous smile. The lady then smiled broadly, her wrinkles slowly moving out of the way of her expanding mouth, as she interrupted Lorel's speech.

"Well!" she almost shouted, in a screech of a voice that could compete with fingernails on a chalkboard. "Aren't *you* just the cute one! Why, come in, come in."

Shong turned his head to look behind him and see who, in his direction, she was talking to. Unfortunately, there was no one behind him.

She opened the door wide, and motioned them in. Lorel lead the way in with an offered 'thank-you', followed by Kilgar, Bronto, and Shong.

"I think she likes you," Bronto whispered to Shong.

"Don't say that," he whispered back.

The interior of the grand house looked richly furnished, or rather would be if someone had bothered to clean it the last several rels. The ceiling high overhead boasted a dusty and cracked chandelier with several old candles in it. A carpeted staircase wound up to a second floor at the rear of the large greeting room. Dusty carpets lay everywhere, and the tall windows were all covered over with thick layers of tapestries. The door closing behind them, the rich old lady turned to face them.

"My name is Margo Courtneed," she said, staring directly at Shong, "but you can call me Margo. Do you know you're just the cutest young man to come in my home in a long while; ever since my fifth husband died."

"Miss Courtneed," Lorel interjected, "about the poor refugees, surely you have noticed——"

"Oh, there's always refugees," she said offhandedly, and then faced Shong again, smile on her face. "So, have you a wife?"

"Uh, no," Shong said doubtfully, "I've never been——"

"Ah good," she went on. "You know, you remind me of my third husband."

"Miss Courtneed," Lorel persisted, "the raids are a danger to all, they deprive one of their homes and lives. That is why they so need your help."

"You look just *sooo* strong," her voice screeched on, as she walked up next to Shong, putting a flirtatious wrinkled arm around his waist. "I bet you're pretty good with that sword. Care to show a mature lady how to use it?"

Her old dress hung loosely about her old skinny limbs. A smile cut through the crevices of her face as she batted eager old eyes at Shong.

"She scares me more than that first dragon did," Kilgar whispered to Bronto.

"You and me both kid," Bronto whispered back with a quiet chuckle.

"Uh, my friend here is right," Shong said, trying to politely squirm his way out of Margo Courtneed's grip. "The needs of the refugees are much more important than any personal ones."

"Oh, if *that's* all that's stopping you," she said, drawing her arm even tighter around Shong's waist. "I'll see that they're fed whatever I can spare. Will that make you happy?"

"Why may the gods of good thank you, my lady," Lorel said, though Miss Courtneed seemed oblivious to the others, "an act that shall surely reward the giver."

"Now, with business done," she continued, "how do you feel about large weddings?"

Shong looked imploringly at Bronto, helpless in the old withered arms of the assertive lady. Bronto grinned back at his friend's predicament before intervening.

"I am afraid that he already has a girlfriend," Bronto said.

"Oh?" she responded, looking up at the others for the first time.

"Three as a matter of fact," Bronto continued, "and he must already decide between them."

Shong looked like he had severe stomach pains, while Margo glanced back at him in surprise.

"Is this true?" she asked.

"Well, uh," he hesitated.

Shong looked up at the wrinkled face looming over him, the rich old clothes, and the hair trying to still launch itself outwards. He came to a decision.

"Why, uh, yes," he said, hesitantly, "there are these three young girls who—"

"Ha, is that all?" she said, resuming her smile and attempt at a seductive pose. "I can compete with any young girl. I can offer you anything they can."

"They're the King's daughters," Bronto said.

"They are?" she asked surprised, and then looked a bit downcast. "I suppose that's a bit hard to compete with."

"And, if there's one thing I would never want to do is offend a King," Shong said hopefully, as he squirmed his way out of her loosened grip, "especially the biggest King around."

"I suppose," she replied despondently.

Shong was halfway to Bronto when he looked on at the poor woman, feeling sorry for her.

"And besides," he added, "they're so young, if I were to refuse them all they couldn't take it nearly as well as one of your mature worldliness. You know how young girls are."

"Why yes," she brightened. "The poor dears, I mustn't be so selfish. They could get broken-hearted so easily."

Shong looked relieved. Then, Margo got a bright look in her eyes and looked over at Shong.

"Maybe, in a few rels, when they're over their infatuation with you…," she offered, in her cracked screech of a voice.

At that timely moment, Bronto's eyes got a distant look to them for but a moment. His face turned serious as called out.

"Sindar," he said, "he calls to us. The beast-men are making a raid on the town."

"Oh, then we must go to protect the town," Shong said, grabbing out his sword as he mouthed a silent 'thank-you' to whatever gods may be listening, "and to see that no vile beast comes near your precious self."

They all rushed to the door before Margo could think to stop them. Shong was the first one out.

"Thank-you, my hero," she called out after him, as Bronto and Kilgar quickly followed their comrade out. "I will not forget your gallantry."

"And thank-you, Miss Courtneed, for the gift to the refugees that you are to make," Lorel said, still standing in the doorway. "The gods shall smile upon thee for being so—"

Lorel's speech was suddenly interrupted by a large arm grabbing him around the chest and quickly lifting him out through the door.

"Oh," Margo Courtneed sighed, "it's always the cute ones that are so brave."

A hundred men were arrayed along the edge of town, each in his studded leather armor with his own sword ready for immediate use. Bathow stood with Sabu and the others at what seemed to be in the middle of their lineup, watching the cloud get ever closer. A dark-haired man dressed in metal scale armor approached them from the back ranks.

"No civilians in the front lines," he said. "Get back to town; you too, old man."

"The officer in charge, I take it," Sabu said. "Captain, we have fought these creatures before; we may be able to be of assistance."

"Now *there's* an understatement," Eldar said under his breath.

"And Bathow here is a great mystic," Sabu finished.

"I'll have no responsibilities for wet-behind-the-ears civilians and the local crazy man," the Captain answered. "I'm sure you mean well, but this is work for professionals. And, as for Bathow here being a mystic, if he is then where's he been hiding it all this time?!"

"He's right about that," Bathow said, his night-shirt flapping in the breeze, his white hair hanging about his shoulders, as the Captain shouted out orders to his troops. "I haven't been of much use in my life. Maybe it isn't too late to change that."

"In the eyes of Indra, it never is," Candol advised.

"Okay now," the Captain came back to them, "no priests, young pups, and old men at the front. They'll be here in moments."

"Since you refuse to listen," Sabu said, "then let me put it this way."

Sabu faced out towards the oncoming cloud, now easily discernible as contorted figures riding atop their mangy mounts of death, swords singing through the air in anticipation of blood and death. He raised up his staff, muttering several indecipherable syllables under his breath. The Captain just shook his head and stepped towards him, but was blocked by the point of Eldar's sword.

"Not a good idea," Eldar smiled, "just wait for it."

The top of the staff glowed a bright blue, as well did one watery-looking gem set atop it. Sabu pointed his staff at the oncoming horde.

Crack of thunder, ground splitting open. Sound of rocks tearing apart, the rumble of large masses of ground being moved aside as if by some large hand. The earth beneath their feet shook as the ground in front of the horde tore loose from itself. Mounts tumbled as the ground beneath their clawed hooves moved and buckled. Directly in their path, stretching all along their oncoming front line, a large crack opened up in the ground. Ten feet wide it opened, swallowing the first rows of screaming mounts finding themselves suddenly charging into its depths. But Sabu wasn't finished, for with the sudden bright glowing of the Water Hevon Gem, a wall of water soared straight up out of the pit, remaining as a standing wall of water ten feet thick, over a rent in the ground that still didn't know its own depth. Sabu lowered his staff, cocked his head to one side, and looked the Captain in the eye.

"Okay," the Captain said slowly as he took in the scene, "I guess you can stay after all."

"I knew you'd see it our way," Eldar said, lowering his sword.

"And you say old Bathow here's a mystic," the Captain asked hopefully, "for if he really is, then we sure could use him."

"The best," said Sabu, the hope and faith in his eyes staring straight at Bathow, as if by will force alone would he wake the old mystic up from his self-pity.

Bathow straightened himself up as all eyes focused on him. He straightened out his nightshirt as well as his stoop. He raised his chin, a defiant look taking hold of his face. Time seemed to peel itself off of him like an old rind, as a new determination seemed to youthen his entire self. He looked at the Captain, dingy nightshirt flapping in the wind, the roaring sound of Sabu's wall of water in the background.

"Yes, I'm the best mystic in all of Catho," Bathow said, in a voice more sure of itself, "and it's about time I started to act like it."

Bathow snapped his fingers, and his old dingy shirt changed into a deep purple robe, its dark color speckled with strange mystical symbols. Around his neck he now wore a glistening pendant, its purple gem set into a golden sunburst. The Captain's eyes opened wide with astonishment, several other nearby troops also staring at the wizards in their midst.

Bathow raised his hands up to waist level, palms upwards. He just concentrated a few moments, not even muttering a single syllable. Traceries of light seemed to flick across his palms then dance outwards, leaping first to the Captain and then outwards to each of the arrayed soldiers in turn, spreading like some bizarre wildfire of light. Bathow put his palms down and then looked up at the Captain.

"My powers are those of divinations and protections, as handed down my family line from the great Purple Wizard of the old Kingdoms, from a time now forgotten. You and your men are now protected from the bulk of what those beasts can deal out. But I suggest that you hurry."

The astonished Captain looked out at where the old mystic had nodded.

Through the wall of water now, the hook-hoofed mounts and their nightmarish riders were leaping, most landing in a fallen heap, but all quickly getting back up again. They stayed there as more of them came through, as if waiting for their numbers to grow before charging forth.

"Okay men," the Captain shouted, "come on, let's get them while they're down. Charge!"

As the Captain sounded his charge, the robed figure on the rooftop looked straight at the back of Bathow, a soft dry high-pitched cackle escaping from beneath the hood.

Bronto drew his immense sword from off his back as they ran down the crowded streets. The sounds of battle were in the distance as people scurried about to seek refuge in their homes and businesses. Shong was at his side as he rounded a corner to catch up with Kilgar and Lorel, also weaving their way through the panicking crowds.

"This city sure is…a lot bigger when you have to…*run* across its entire length…in but a few short diids," Shong commented between breaths as he ran.

"As Eldar would say, what fun would a battle be if we didn't have to work for it," Bronto said, without even breathing hard.

"How bad do you think it is?" Shong asked, as they rounded a corner, nearing the edge of town.

"All Sindar said was that we're in the middle of a small war," Bronto said, "and that was good enough for me."

"Given the circumstances," Shong replied, "having to rescue someone's pet cat would have been enough to get me out of there."

Bronto smiled at his friend's close escape from Margo as they finally came to where the buildings suddenly dropped off in favor of the surrounding farms. Kilgar and Lorel were standing at the edge of the small road, looking down the grassy slope at what lay below, when they finally caught up to them.

"I know not what type of vile creatures they fight," Lorel was saying, "but we must help those men down there that fight them."

"We know what they are," Bronto said, looking down over Lorel from half a foot higher, "and they're very dangerous."

"By the beard of my *koren*," Shong remarked, "there's so *many* of them this time."

"How is it that the city troops hold out so well against them?" Kilgar asked. "They should be torn apart."

"That'll be Sabu's doing no doubt," Bronto answered.

"We must fight by their sides to protect the city," Lorel decided as he then ran down the slope, sword in hand, to join the battle.

"Wait," Shong shouted, "you don't know these creatures!"

"Well," Kilgar said, pulling his knife, "that's one more we have to protect."

"Come on," Bronto said, as they all charged down the grassy slope.

The city's troops had met the creatures as they came through the giant wall of water, gaining the advantage as the beasts came plunging through. But the creatures were tough enough to still prove more than a challenge. The troops' swords had little effect on the creatures or their mounts, as the creatures in turn sliced through with their own steel-blue swords, shattering the troops' swords, slicing through their studded leather armor. But Bathow's magic was still serving its purpose: the troops were proving harder to kill than the invading creatures might have expected.

The weeds in the field became fiery tendrils, reaching up to grab at the clawed hooves of the creatures's mounts, as Sindar flexed forth his magic. Eldar was out in the field, his sword alight with deep red flame, slashing at nearby beast-men and their mounts. Lindel stood with Sindar, each carefully aimed dark-metal arrow sailing forth from his bow landing square between the eyes of an invader. Candol was with Bathow, lending the support of Indra in the protection of the troops, while Quickfoot had found a safe spot behind a wall from which to throw his precious daggers. Sabu was standing next to Mauklo and Sindar, lowering his staff after having just delivered a bolt of lightning at one of the creatures. Mauklo watched the battlefield with interest.

"We may be able to help them win this little war," Sabu commented.

"It isn't a war," Mauklo said, in a matter-of-fact voice.

"Maybe it's too small to be a war by *your* standards," said Lindel while notching his next arrow, "but it's big enough for these people."

"That's not what I meant," Mauklo said, "I meant that those creatures aren't fighting as if they're in a war."

"Sounds like you have an interesting observation to make," Sabu said as he thought about what next spell to use.

"Notice how they change tactics," Mauklo pointed out towards the battlefield. "They have no set battle or plan of attack. They try several different methods of combat, retreat, and then try again differently."

"I see what you mean," Sabu said as he studied the battle below more carefully. "If not a war, what then?"

"It's a training exercise," Mauklo said. "Some other force or commander of their's has sent them on these raids, and at this city, in an effort to train them in combat."

"What would they be training for, then?" Sindar wondered, as he finished up his latest spell.

Lindel's arrow sizzled through the air to impact in the skull of one of the creatures while they thought this over, its pointed tip protruding straight out the back of the center of its deformed head.

Bolts of blue flame shot out from the swords of some of the creatures, roasting a few of the troops beyond what the protections of Bathow and Candol could withstand. Eldar slashed away with his flaming sword as one of the creatures took aim at his back. The tip of the sword flashed blue as Eldar battled away unawares.

"Eldar, look out!"

The shout had boomed across the field, attracting the elf's attention like a blow to the gut. He turned to see flaming blue death racing through the air towards him, but a few scant feet away, and closing. He saw within its flames the death it had caused back on the island where he had first met Sindar, the death of Thorlan at its fiery touch. Almost instinctively, he raised his flaming sword as if to deflect it. The blue flame hit.

Like light hitting a mirror, the blue bolt deflected off of Eldar's own fiery sword, to slice through the air and hit, instead, another of the beast riders. The unintentional target had but a brief moment of shock before he was reduced to a shower of black dust drifting upon the wind.

"Hey great!" Eldar shouted. "I didn't know I could do that. I'm liking these Hevon Gems better all the time."

Eldar turned around to have a look at the source of the bellowed shout that saved his life.

He was rewarded with the sight of one of the beast-men flying through the air, mount and all. It landed with a water-drowned scream as it went into Sabu's wall of water. The six-foot seven-inch source of both the shout and the flying horse came running across the field, large sword out in front of him.

"Bronto!" Eldar shouted out, as he raised his greeting.

Another figure came leaping down beside Bronto. Landing in the midst of several of the mounted fiends, he whirled his sword about with a speed and accuracy that most mortal men would never learn. He landed on the back of one of the mounts, quickly beheading its rider with his sharp sword, and jumped up again as another nearby rider slashed down at him.

The creature slashed down through empty air, instead hitting down upon the spine of the riderless mount, for Shong was now on the back of another rider. Its spine severed by the blow, the riderless mount collapsed to the ground in an unearthly scream of agony.

A high-pitched battle cry caused one of the mounted creatures to turn towards the source, just in time to have a long curved knife plunge straight into his forehead. As the rider fell wide-eyed onto the ground, Kilgar ran over to retrieve his knife.

"It's about time you guys came and joined the fun!" Eldar shouted as he slashed about with his own sword.

Another blond-haired figure came slicing down into the midst of the creatures, curses for the foe upon his lips, his sword singing out in front of him. From up on the hilltop, Sabu and Sindar watched while Lindel let loose with another arrow.

"Lorel looks to be brave enough," Sabu commented, "but foolish."

"He doesn't know those creatures as do we," Sindar agreed calmly, "he could get himself killed."

A bolt of blue flame shot down in front of Eldar. The elf leaped aside, looking up a bit angrily at the rider, several yards away, that had sourced it.

"Hey, cut that out!" he shouted, then brightened with an idea. "Okay, two can play at that game."

He pointed his flaming sword at the rider and briefly concentrated. A long tongue of red flame leapt out of the sword and towards the rider. Both rider and mount exploded into a screaming flaming mass, charging off through the battle.

"Ha! That'll show ya'!" Eldar exclaimed.

Lorel bravely chopped his way through the battle, as if trying to face off the entire small army by himself. He fought by the sides of the city's troops, his sword in front, as a rider's blue steel sword met with his own. Blue steel cleaved through normal steel, shattering Lorel's sword upon impact. Lorel took a few steps back, his eyes searching about for a new weapon.

"I shall smite thee with my bare hands, if need be," he shouted out.

One of the city's troops slammed back against him, the body sagging limply to the ground, a large hole through his chest. Without a thought, Lorel quickly grabbed up the dead man's sword, brandishing defiance with it, as another body flung itself at his feet, dead. Lorel looked around himself.

The six or so city troops that he was fighting with were now all dead. Surrounding him were the grinning beast faces of the riders, all looking ready to sharpen their swords upon his bones. Lorel, not a frightened thought in him, continued to hold onto his sword defiantly.

"Okay," he said, ready in his battle crouch, "let's see how many of you want to come down with me."

At that moment, the mount and rider that Eldar had turned into a living campfire came riding by at breakneck speed, past the backs of two of the riders encircling him, and straight towards the wall of water. Lorel looked at the flaming hand of death ride by, his eyes widening, his jaw quivering.

"Fire," he said softly, "why'd it have to be fire…"

His voice trailed off as his sword dropped from his hands, eyes widening with the pure fear that only the truly fearful can have. The riders watched in puzzlement as Lorel dropped down to his knees and began to whimper.

"I hate fire," he said quietly, as the flaming rider and mount finally hit the wall of water in an explosion of fire and steam, "fire,…"

He curled down into a crumpled heap, twitching spasmodically.

"I was afraid he would get himself killed," Sabu said as they watched Lorel from atop the hill.

"He and your other friends who just charged onto the field, weren't protected by my spell," Bathow said. "I had no warning."

"Well, Bronto and the others probably don't need it anyway," Sabu smiled, and then frowned, "but Lorel,…"

The riders closed around Lorel, ready for some brief fun before they went back to the rest of the battle. Lorel began to twitch violently before he was closed off from sight.

"Too late now," Sindar pointed, "they've got him."

"Now's when the fun starts," Mauklo said to himself as he looked on.

Suddenly, one of the riders exploded from off of his saddle, knocked from his saddle by some sudden force. It landed on the ground, clutching at his crotch and rolling around screaming. A small figure leaped up on top of its mount, blood dripping from its mouth as it looked at the screaming creature, chewing something. It swallowed and grinned out at the others around it devilishly.

It was short, little more than four feet tall and ninety pounds; green hair hanging down in scraggly lengths to its shoulders, dark green eyes looking out from a face dimpled with warts. Its tough-looking skin was green and leathery, with what could be either warts or old feather stumps, all encasing its shriveled looking body. Clawed nails tore off the last vestiges of once-clean armor and smooth cape, flinging them to the ground as it gnashed its fanged teeth in anticipation. Its eyes held the looks of an insanity far beyond even what the riders seemed to want to put up with.

It lunged at the nearest rider.

The rider brought his sword to bear a bit too late, as the small creature went clawing and tearing for the rider's throat. The rider's sword arm flung from side to side trying to ward the creature off. But the small one didn't seem to want to kill its prey, instead slashing at it, ripping the skin away in ragged lengths and spitting acid saliva into the wounds. The blue sword flashed brilliant with bolts of blue flame behind its back as the rider struggled vainly to stay conscious. The other riders nearby hurried out of the way of the randomly flying bolts of blue flame. Finally, the small one stood up on the mount, looking down at his handiwork, as the now dead rider started to slip off of the mount. It spotted the blue sword and bent to pick it up by the hilt, then slashed with the sword a few times in the air while the mount under his feet bucked, sending him to the ground.

"Ow!" it said in a voice like unto gravel with a sore throat. "Pain! Schanter not like pain! Schanter love pain!"

It stood up, carrying its new found sword. It pointed the sword in the direction of the fleeing mount.

"Schanter no like shaggy horse," it said.

A bolt of blue flame leaped out, hitting and engulfing the fleeing horse, as it exploded into bits of hot hairy charcoal landing upon the ground.

"Ow! Schanter don't like fire," it said, leaping up and down in both fear and delight. "Fire! Fire pain; love pain!"

It started to aim the sword at other points in the battle, the look of madness in its eyes perhaps even more scary than the attacking beast riders.

"Our friend Lorel appears to have been keeping a secret," Sabu observed casually from atop the hill, as the small creature began chasing one of the mounted riders with bolts of blue flame.

"Yes, a rather serious case of insanity coupled with subconscious lycanthropic abilities," Sindar responded, "and I can see in its rather twisted mind that, while Schanter appears to know of Lorel, Lorel isn't aware of the existence of Schanter. He appears completely ignorant of his condition."

"Well, let's not tell him," Sabu advised, "I think it better that way. We'll have to warn the others about him too."

"It *is* kind of funny," Mauklo said, smiling pleasantly.

"Funny?" said Quickfoot, coming up to the others. "He's *seriously* insane; that guy's wacko!"

"The humor, my little friend, comes in when you realize that Po-Adar saw this within him when we encountered them both. That was his joke upon us all; waiting for it to come forth unexpectedly. That was why he let Lorel live. Old Po must be somewhere laughing at us all by now."

"Well, joke or not," Lindel interjected, "we have a battle to fight, and there's still too many of those creatures out there."

Sure enough, more of the creatures kept leaping out through the wall of water, and others had even found their way around the long crack in the ground. As great a help as the strength of Bronto, the sword skill of Shong, Kilgar's knife, and Eldar's attitude were, there were still more and more of the creatures. The city's troops were slowly backing up against the hillside, standing against the inevitable weight of sheer numbers.

"He's right," Sabu said, "there's too many of them, and there's too many of the city guard down there for me to try any large scale magic without hurting them too."

"I may be of help," Bathow walked over, his purple robes flapping in the wind. "I have within me a spell, the likes of which no dark force may suspect that I have. I can erect a shield around this entire city, protecting it from these raids for good."

"Then just don't stand there," Candol said as he too joined them, "in the name of Indra do it!"

"You appear to have been hiding a lot from your people," Sabu remarked.

"Hiding I have been doing for far too long," Bathow replied. "This spell shall take a lot out of me, but I shall try. I will need to concentrate for a while."

Bathow closed his eyes in concentration, raising his arms heavenward. They could feel the energy crackle around him as the winds picked up in force.

"Sindar, call the others back," Sabu said, "we don't want anybody getting caught on the wrong side of this shield."

Sindar nodded and sent out his mental message as power rose around Bathow. The old mystic lifted his eyes towards the sky.

"I do for this town what I couldn't do for my own family, so long ago," he shouted out into the winds. "To protect!"

Thunder crackled as a shell of air seemed to harden itself over the city. Everyone watched the mystic as he concentrated on the most powerful magic in his long life.

Sound of thunder clashing down upon one's soul. Red streamers, as life's fluid goes streaming out from outstretched hands. Old body shivering as purple robe stains red with the blood flying out from every pour. Thunder crackle quickly dispersed as a dying mystic loses hold of his spell, to collapse upon the ground.

"Bathow!" Sabu and Sindar both shouted as they leapt over to the fallen mystic's body.

Bathow coughed up blood as Sabu bent over him, young learned eyes searching for a reason. From up off the field, Eldar came running to join them.

"Hey guys," Eldar said cheerfully, "I heard Sindar. What's——"

He stopped short as he saw Bathow lying there upon the ground, blood from head to toe, his skin as raw meat. The silver-haired elf quickly knelt down at his side, cheerfulness suddenly turned to concern.

"What happened?" he asked.

"We don't know," Sabu answered, "one moment he was casting this spell, and then——"

A loud dry cackle interrupted them. From atop a nearby roof stood a robed figure, clawed hands peering out from its sleeves. The wind flung back its hood, revealing a face that could only be called female in the loosest sense of the word. Black hair hung down like dry rags about her deformed features, her eyes dark with hate. She glared down at them with dark intent.

"Loma," Bathow choked out, "I might have known you were behind the raids."

"You reveal yourself too soon old fool," came Loma's dry cackle of a voice. "You should have stayed in hiding and let it all pass you by."

"Who is this hag?" Eldar asked.

"A witch," Bathow wheezed out weakly, "the dark forces she serves are best left alone, but she——"

A spat of coughing up blood cut off what he was saying, while Loma just cackled joyfully. Candol came over to Bathow's side.

"I can help him," Candol said as he knelt down, "it isn't too late."

"Touch him and die priest!" Loma yelled, as she pointed a clawed finger at them.

A red-colored bolt of lightning leaped out from her pointing hand. It sailed through the air, arrowing straight towards Bathow, the force of its passage knocking them all aside. Bathow's weak eyes just had time to see the rapidly approaching moment of his death before it struck. In a scream of agony, the red bolt hit, sending reddened chunks of flesh flying everywhere. The remains of the old mystic that weren't splattered all over everyone, were left as a withered husk of old meat, too beat up as to be recognizable as anything but a slaughterhouse leftover.

To say that Bathow was dead, would be putting it mildly.

"Now for all the other would-be heroes," Loma's cracked voice called out.

"As if this brave man hadn't had a hard enough life, you have to have him end it this way," Sabu said getting up. "I'm getting real tired of seeing this sort of thing happen all the time."

"Then you can die as did he," she cackled, "that you won't see it anymore. Feel the wrath reserved for all those who cross the mighty Vold and his allies."

Suddenly the distant roar of Sabu's wall of water changed pitched as it collapsed back down into the crack from whence it came with a loud splash. Both armies looked on in puzzlement at the sudden change, as an entire army of riders was revealed, stretching out beyond the deep crevice into the fields beyond. Then the ground began to shake as a central portion of the deep crack began to close, the armies on the other side looking on in anticipation.

"Hey, who canceled my spell?!" Sabu said indignantly, as the others rushed to their feet.

Bronto, Shong, and Kilgar came rushing up over the hill to them, as they looked around for the source of the interference. Even Loma looked up.

Mauklo stood, facing out towards the crack, hands raised as he controlled the forces that were now closing the crack. Lindel angrily notched an arrow and aimed it in Mauklo's direction.

"Traitor!" he shouted as the arrow was sent flying.

As the crack closed and Mauklo turned around, lowering his arms, Lindel's arrow coming straight towards him. At the last instant, though, the arrow seemed to loose its momentum and skittered to one side, to land harmlessly upon the ground. Mauklo smiled pleasantly as he fingered the amulet he wore around his neck.

"I knew this amulet of Torai's would come in handy," he said, as he started to float up off the ground, facing towards Loma. "I've decided to join up."

Loma smiled, a wicked crack crossing her wrinkled face. She pointed in his direction. Behind them all, the riders on the far side of the now-closed portion of Sabu's ravine started to spur their mounts into a gallop across. The riders already in battle began to rally, as what was left of the city's troops began to run back towards the city, reaching their legs towards the imagined safety of its, mostly wooden, walls.

"You betray your friends," Loma cackled. "Do you find such betrayal so easy?"

"I imagine if I really thought of them as my friends I might," Mauklo shrugged as he floated over to her rooftop, "I suggest that you kill the one with the staff first; he's the bright one."

Sabu glared up at Mauklo, clasping his hand tighter around his staff.

"If you're so eager to join with me," she said, "why don't *you* do it? This could be some sort of trick."

Mauklo looked honestly shocked as he landed on the roof next to her. Below them, Sabu had his staff ready, while Lindel notched another arrow. Bronto, Shong, and Kilgar, weapons ready, were looking up at the yellow-skinned human. Beyond them the riders tore across the field, cleaving all in their path.

Except, that is, for a small area around a short leathery-skinned figure firing out random bolts of blue fire from a sword; firing, jumping up and down in glee as a rider is roasted, and then firing again.

"A trick?" he said with honest hurt in his voice. "Would I risk an entire *city* on some trick?"

He gestured to the battle field beyond. Riders poured across the ravine by the hundreds, a number of them now flooding into the city, fighting the city's troops in the streets.

"I guess not," Loma smiled, "nobody's *that* rotten."

"But, if you must have proof," Mauklo said, holding out his right hand, "then why don't we kill them together?"

"Don't do it Mauklo," Sindar shouted up at the two of them, "she'll just betray you in the end!"

"It sounds like a delightful way to start a partnership," Loma cackled agreement, as she put her hand in Mauklo's. "Let's fry them together."

"I so admire a woman of power," Mauklo said, as Loma looked down at the rest, her eyes glowing a bright red, "especially one who can so organize such an offense against the rather lackluster defense of this town."

"Oh, well it helps when you have the local Mayor to assign them on the opposite side of town," she smiled, as she pointed a glowing finger at Sabu.

Sabu raised up his staff up defensively, Lindel aiming his bow.

"How deceptive of you," Mauklo smiled evilly, "to have the Mayor on your side. But, to business."

"The Mayor is a cultist of Vold," Loma commented, as she clasped tightly onto Mauklo's hand. "But now it's time for them to die. On the count of three. One."

Mauklo concentrated his energies, as Loma powered up her spell. The others below clutched helplessly at their various weapons, readied spells they may not have a chance to utter.

"Two."

Beyond them, the riders flooded across the field and on into the edges of the city. Mauklo readied to channel his own magic through Loma. Lindel carefully aimed his bow up at them.

"Three!"

Mauklo let loose his concentration, channeling it through Loma's tightly clasped hand. But, it wasn't assisting magic that came through. His hand glowed red hot, heat like unto fire. Fire shot swiftly up the inside of Loma's arm, turning her entire left arm a brightly glowing cheery red.

Loma screamed out in pain, but Mauklo held on tightly, smiling at her. Lindel let loose with his arrow.

"What's the matter," he asked, as Loma started to double over, "don't care for my assistance?"

Her entire arm exploded in a blast of fire, disintegrating her arm and part of her shoulder. At the same time, Lindel's arrow impacted solidly into her right chest. She screamed as she was thrown over the edge of the building, Mauklo left holding the burned remains of her hand in his own.

"I guess not," he shrugged, as he casually tossed the hand over his shoulder.

Loma's body never hit the ground. Sabu's raised staff sent out a wave of pure force, hitting the very target that he'd been aiming at all along.

The witch Loma disintegrated into a fine spray of dust.

"It's a good thing that we know you well," Lindel shouted up, as he lowered his bow, "but one of these times that act isn't going to work."

"Maybe one of these times, I won't be acting," Mauklo grinned back down. "But you actually shot that arrow at me. I might have been hurt."

"I'd noticed your little amulet several rises ago," Lindel said, as Mauklo started to float back down to the ground, "so I played along. But right now, your little act may have still cost us the city."

"This was the only way," Sindar said, "she would have killed us otherwise and enslaved the entire city. But we *do* have a difficult battle on our hands now."

"And a traitorous Mayor," Eldar added, "what about him?"

"Consider him...taken care of," Mauklo said as he landed on the ground, "there are those that will know what to do about him."

"Good," Bronto said, swinging out his sword, "then we can do something about saving this city."

"What about Wacko out there?" Quickfoot pointed out towards Schanter, still gleefully chasing riders with his new found toy, leaving bits and pieces of limbs behind him.

"Put him on the end of a stick and set him loose against the rest of the riders," Sabu shrugged. "I think he can handle himself."

"Come," Shong said, starting down the street with his sword, "the battle's gone past us."

They raced down the streets, not knowing how or if they were going to save the town, but only knowing that they had to try.

The riders were everywhere, spreading throughout the city like a large swelling. Everywhere they went, they slashed with their blue swords and fired out their bolts of bright flame, cleaving down not only the city's troops but anyone else they saw as well. Sindar came running out of an alley with the others just in time to see a group of the riders slice down a shopkeeper, his patrons dead and burned around him, his store fast becoming a pile of burning embers behind him. In front of a neighboring building a young girl, perhaps no more than about nine, was screaming, trying to run down the street away from another rider chasing her. The rider caught up with her, his claw-hoofed mount galloping at full speed as it tore right through her, shredding her into several pieces with its hooves, flinging parts of her body in random directions as it galloped rapidly over her. The rider grinned with delight as he left mangled chunks of meat behind him. From elsewhere, the severed head of someone's mother came rolling to Sindar's feet, dead eyes gazing skyward in frozen wide-eyed terror.

Bronto and Shong went running into the fray, the big man's deafening battle cry of *ka'ru* giving momentary pause to the riders' destruction. Shong went diving in, rolling low in front of one of the shaggy mounts, sword slicing at its forelegs as he did so; when the mount fell onto its two severed legs, Shong rolled to his feet and sliced skillfully at the unseated rider. Eldar even went into the battle, chasing a few of the riders down the street with bolts of red flame from his sword. Sabu stood beside Sindar, watching the carnage.

"There are too many of them," Sindar said, shaking his head in sad disbelief. "We can't get them all; at least not without harming innocents."

"Maybe I should start working on a way to get my spells to affect just select individuals," Sabu pondered. "It sure would come in handy for a situation like this."

"That won't help these people now," Sindar responded. "There's got to be something else we can do."

"It may be the will of Indra that we cannot be the heroes of every situation," Candol said as he came up next to them. "We can't salvage every situation any more than we can be everywhere at once."

"We've got to try," Sindar said quietly.

Two riders went sailing off into the distance as Bronto began tossing riders in random directions, sometimes flinging them across the city.

"How's Schanter doing?" Sabu asked Candol. "He still chasing down riders with his new sword?"

"Yes," Candol replied, "although he's not too discriminate about it; he burned one or two of the city's troops as well. That creature is quite a contradiction; he seems to really hate fire, but he loves the pain it gives him."

"I wonder how we're going to turn him off when the time comes," Sabu pondered.

"Put him to sleep?" Candol offered.

"That'll work," Sabu replied, "but as for this battle right now…"

"They move towards the center of town," Sindar said, "my mind sees their progress down the streets."

"Then the center of town it is," Sabu replied, as he tapped his staff once on the ground.

Immediately they were in the town square, standing beside the old fountain. People were fleeing everywhere, most running west away from the invaders, but some not sure which way to go. The sound of distant fighting was closing. They saw Lindel on a nearby rooftop, readying his bow, waiting for the fight to come to him.

"Maybe we can at least stop them from going any further now," Sabu said, "to save what we can."

"I wonder," Sindar said as Sabu thought of what spell to use first. "If the witch Loma lead them, and she's now dead, what general do they now follow? Why do they still fight in so organized a fashion?"

"They have another leader with them then," Sabu agreed, "and if we can find and kill him——"

"Then that might turn back the army," Sindar finished with just a trace of enthusiasm.

"How in the name of Indra do we find such a person though?" Candol asked. "I know you can seek out minds, Sindar, but among so many?"

"True," Sindar admitted, "the battle might well be lost before I've found their leader. But I've got to try."

Their musings were interrupted by the thunderous sound of hoofbeats coming down one of the streets. They looked up and saw twenty riders stream out from one of the streets, plowing down townspeople as they went. From atop his rooftop perch, Lindel let loose with his arrow. Before it had struck a rider at the base of its neck, he'd already notched his next arrow. Candol turned to face them when he saw them coming out.

"We've got more immediate problems right now," Sabu said as he raised his staff.

Before Sabu had his staff fully raised, there was a rupturing in the ground. A thin crack appeared in a straight line in front of the riders. Out of that crack grew a row of thin thorny branches. They grew all along the crack with an unnatural rapidity, until they were eight feet tall and half as thick. Thorns the size of people's fingers were what the riders suddenly ran into, as both rider and mount were suddenly caught up in the unforeseen bramble. The riders behind the first few, unable to stop their fast gallop in time, plowed straight into the one's stuck in the thorns, making it even worse for all concerned. Thus the pile of riders and mounts in front of the large bush grew.

"Now where'd *that* come from?" Sabu asked.

"I suggest that you make use of my little distraction," came a calm and unassuming voice behind them, "while you have the time."

They all turned around to see from whence came the voice. Several feet behind them approached a man, tall and thin of limb, like unto a tall stick figure in travelling clothes, his dark sandy hair partially hanging down over his hazel eyes. He wasn't thin to the point of emaciation, but more like an average build that had simply been stretched out a bit. His white, somewhat pasty skin, spoke of one who's trade was *not* in the more physical arts. He wore a simple green cape overtop of his shirt and loose pants, and had a look of intellectual reserve about him.

"Who are you?" Sabu asked, getting to the point. "And how do we know who's side you're on?"

"If names be important, then mine is Sheil-Bor(h)," the stranger replied, pronouncing the guttural 'h' at the end of his name, "and we have something in common."

He held up his left hand, palm outward. In the center of the palm were two small crystals, one dancing red with internal flame, the other a watery blue. He put down his hand.

"We have the same quest," Sheil-Bor(h) said, his soft-spoken voice denoting just a trace of humility, "if not the same reason."

"Good enough for me," Sabu replied quickly. "Sindar?"

"He's okay," Sindar nodded, trusting to what his mental senses told him.

"Good. Welcome to the group," Sabu said, as he quickly faced back around to the battle at hand, "we'll talk later."

The riders were trying to hack their way through the thick thorny bush, Lindel using the opportunity to try and take a few out. Then from down one of the other streets, they heard the shouts of someone yelling 'fire' and 'pain' several times.

They looked over as Schanter came running out of the street, still brandishing his blue sword. He stopped when he saw the large thorny bush, riders piling high in back of it. He looked at the bush.

He looked at his sword.

He grinned dementedly.

"I think the little one's about to buy us some time," Sabu smiled.

There was a *whoosh* of blue flame as Schanter pointed his sword at the large bush. Several sets of rider eyes looked at what was coming at them, as they struggled in the bush. They started to push each other aside when the flame hit.

Large screaming bonfire of flesh, bone, and bush, lighting up like some large cairn to the gods, engulfing all within it in a flaming cage of death. Burning clawed hands reaching out from the burning bush, trying to reach safety, but finally going limp with the burning death. Bones rapidly crackling under the heat as flesh cooked.

Schanter jumped up and down in glee at the sight, fear showing across his face at the sight of the hated fire, but also pleasure at his love for the pain it caused both himself and the others.

"Quickfoot was right," Sindar observed, "he *is* wacko."

"We need to find their leader now," Sabu said. "Any suggestions?"

"I may be of some assistance," Sheil-Bor(h) volunteered, his quiet voice and calm countenance rising softly above the surrounding din of battle. "My humble arts help me in my quest after knowledge for its own sake, my talent that of finding such. My magic may be more specifically tailored, than your own, for such a search."

"Very well," Sabu said. "Find him and then we'll get him."

Sheil-Bor(h) closed his eyes in concentration and clasped his palms together as if in prayer. As their new companion was concentrating, several of the others came running up to join them: Bronto, Shong, Kilgar, Eldar, and Quickfoot. Lindel stayed at his rooftop perch, plugging out arrows as fast as he could.

"They're all gone," Kilgar summarized almost casually, wiping his bloodied knife onto a pant-leg.

"The entire east section of town is dead," Shong elaborated, sweat from the intense fighting covering his brow and arms, as he caught his breath, "they've killed everybody."

"It was a slaughter," Bronto added, a trace of anger in his voice, big sword in his hand, "there's not so much as an infant left alive back there. We did what we could, but those riders are everywhere."

"There's no more town guard left," Shong said, his grip tightening around his sword. "If we don't hold them here, there won't *be* a west side to this city!"

"We're working on something now," Sabu said, and then pointed at Sheil-Bor(h). "This is Sheil-Bor(h); he's with us now, and he holds two Hevon Gems of his own."

"The more the merrier," Eldar said, "but what's he doing?"

Sheil-Bor(h) looked up at the elf, and calmly answered him.

"I have found their leader," he said, spreading his palms apart, "and he comes from that road."

Sheil-Bor(h) pointed down one of the roads. Everyone arrayed themselves out facing towards the indicated road, while Eldar signaled up to Lindel, who then went to the other side of his building to line up his own shot down that street. They waited in anticipation, adrenaline surging, muscles tensed.

Thunderous hoofbeats, like lightning from the sky, roaring down the bloodied street. Pounding louder and louder. Muscles tense as thirty shaggy mounts come into view, each bearing its animal-faced rider. Blue steel swords slashing out in front of them, as they come out into the central courtyard, empty now of the city's normal residents. A circle of wicked flesh they make round the courtyard, finally stopping when but shoulder to shoulder. Wary human eyes looking around at the grinning beast eyes that glare at them mockingly.

"They're not attacking," Shong said from his battle crouch. "Why?"

"It's not like we can *go* anywhere," Quickfoot observed impatiently, "they're all around us."

"It just makes it easier to know what you're hitting," Kilgar said calmly.

"Fortune may hold our answer," Sheil-Bor(h) said, pointing down the street from whence the riders had come. "Their leader comes."

Walking down the street was a humanoid figure, walking with a tread that suggested it was the best there and knew it. It was seven feet tall, with smooth plastic-like skin, and small scales from wrists to elbows. Both its fingers and bare toes grew three-inch long razor-sharp thick claws, also green in color. Four fangs sprouted from the mouth, one set growing down, the other facing up from its jaw. It was hairless everywhere, but for the sickly green scraggle of hair atop its head, and sexless, having no sign of genitalia on an unclothed body. Its eyes looked as if they held the source of all fear within their terrifying orbs.

As it walked out into the courtyard, they could see that it held two swords, one in each hand, each one fully as long as Bronto's large six-foot sword, but carrying them as if their weight meant nothing. Each of the swords glowed with a pale amber light. It opened up its frightening mouth, gnashing its fangs at them.

Quickfoot crumpled into a shuddering heap, shaking with a fear he'd never known. Kilgar, brave young Destir though he was, just stood there, paralyzed with a fright he never knew he was capable of. Even the mighty priest of Indra was wide-eyed with fear. Shong's body shook as he sought to control his own rising fear, sword still at the ready. Eldar swallowed nervously.

"What *is* that?" Eldar asked.

"I don't know of it," Sabu answered. "I've been studying magic more than nightmares that walk."

"I know of it," Sheil-Bor(h) answered, concern on his calm face. "It is called a *tezar*. They are said to serve Miro, as his police-force as it were. That creature is perhaps more dangerous than its small army of riders."

"Hey, maybe if we can get Schanter to play with it," Eldar suggested.

"That must have been some rough fight I was in," came a voice from behind them, "it was all just a blur."

They looked to see Lorel walking up to them, tattered remnants of clothing flung around him, steel blue sword in his hand, tousled blond hair drifting with the wind.

"I don't even remember how I got this new sword," he said, looking at his blue sword. "I *assume* it was in some battle against those fiends."

"Well, so much for *that* idea," Eldar sighed, "we got Lorel back now."

"It looks like those vile scum have surrounded us," Lorel said. "Well, no matter. We shall vanquish them nonetheless. Hey, what's that green thing over there?"

Lorel walked up to them and looked past them at the tezar. At his first sight of the creature, he just started shaking, quivering with fear, as he slowly collapsed down to the ground.

"Okay, you can rule out Lorel as well," Eldar sighed, as he faced back towards the tezar.

A whizzing was heard going swiftly through the air, as Lindel's arrow lanced straight for the tezar's throat. They watched as the dark-metal shaft landed dead center to its throat.

And splintered. The arrow shattered upon impact, leaving the creature unconcerned. It looked up over at Lindel, long tongue going over its fangs in anticipation of a victim.

"Get it!" Eldar shouted.

Several fiery Hevon Gems glowed as bolts of flame shot out from everyone that had them. Bronto brought out a spare shortsword from his belt and tossed it like a dagger. The area around the tezar exploded in a wash of fire, enough to melt the flagstones beneath the tezar's feet.

But not enough, apparently, to melt the tezar, who stood unharmed. In a single swift move, it brought up one of its swords to block Bronto's thrown shortsword, shattering the small sword into several pieces upon impact. It growled its fangs at them and then leapt straight up into the air.

Thirty feet straight up it leapt, to come down sword-first on Lindel's roof. With a backhanded swipe from the flat of its sword, the tezar sent Lindel flying off the roof, to land with a sharp cry of pain in the center of the square, a leg and arm badly twisted. Before the rest could react, however, it leapt again, to land in their very midst. It worked its swords like a human-sized blender, cleaving a huge spine-snapping gash across Shong's back as the young fighter fell into a paralyzed heap upon the ground, bowling Bronto over on top of Candol, and nearly decapitating Eldar before the elf ducked almost too late.

Sabu sent a bolt of lightning at it, but to no avail. Sindar used his magic to try and encase it in a web of steel, but it just ripped its way out of it as easily as if through paper.

"Nothing hurts it!" Sabu exclaimed as he backed up with his staff.

"I think Shong's back is broken," Sindar shouted back, "and Lindel's about as bad."

"We can't even escape," Eldar said, looking at the surrounding riders.

"The Fountain of Knowledge may hold our answer," Sheil-Bor(h) offered, his features ever placid as he pointed his left hand at it.

His palm glowed with the watery blue of his Hevon Gem, but no water came out from it. Instead, the ground rumbled under their feet while the tezar readied to launch himself at Sabu. Suddenly, the ground under the tezar's feet exploded into a geyser of water, towering forty feet up and three feet wide, as it swiftly carried the tezar up with it, tumbling it about as it fought to gain some sort of footing on its watery pedestal.

"That's different," Eldar smiled.

"Well," Sabu shrugged, "it *is* a fountain."

"One cannot jump if one cannot stand," Sheil-Bor(h) explained, "but it still holds onto its weapons."

"I can handle that," Sindar answered.

Sindar looked up at the tower of water. The tezar was fighting for some sort of control, its arms flailing around helplessly. Sindar aimed his mind up at the swords and the clawed hands gripping them. Suddenly an unseen force seemed to jerk at the tezar's hands. The tezar held on with a grip of steel, but the force pulled steadily. The water tossed the creature around, preventing it from getting any balance, or of properly holding onto the swords. One final jerk tugged at the swords in the loosening grip.

The swords tugged free, flying across the square to land imbedded hilt-deep in the chest of a rider, each sword to a different rider. The other riders nearest those two backed away from their fallen comrades a bit worriedly.

"Consider it disarmed," Sindar said calmly.

"It is still dangerous," Sheil-Bor(h) warned quietly, "even without its sting."

"Not on the way down," Bronto said as he got to his feet, picking up his sword. "Just turn off the water works when I tell you."

Bronto walked over by the base of the pillar of water, readying his sword as water splashed down everywhere. He held his sword in both hands, arced its blade low over his shoulder, and looked up at the tezar.

"Come to mama, it's time for a spanking," Bronto grinned.

With a motion of his hand, Sheil-Bor(h) turned off his fountain, the pillar splashing down all over the ground as its force suddenly left it. For a brief moment, the tezar hung suspended there, forty feet up in the air. Then it fell down, claws out, fanged mouth open, throat screaming out its hate. Bronto waited, and swung.

As seen from just outside of town, one would spy a seven-foot tall green humanoid hurtling up through the sky, high above the treetops. Then one would see its upper half slowly separate from the rest of its body as it started to arc downward, aiming its long plunge for a rather hard landing on top of one of the few stone buildings that a local farmer could boast of, a puddle of green goo being all that would remain left of him for anyone to see.

"I think you scored with that one," Eldar said, looking up as the tezar arced away.

The riders too were looking up, their eyes following their leader through the sky. Sheil-Bor(h) then calmly walked out a bit from the others, facing himself in the general direction of the bulk of the riders. He raised up his hands, and as he did so, he seemed to grow in size, his features contorting into frightening ways. He looked down at the assembled riders and growled out a long and loud growl that could be heard all across the city. The riders reacted.

As fast as the riders had swept through this city, faster still did they leave. No leader, be it witch or tezar, to command them, and the appearance of a large giant in their midst, their morale broke. Their panicked retreat lead them back through the streets as fast as they could, tumbling and riding over each other in the process. Fully a third of them were killed in their frightened retreat, their screams fainting with distance.

Sheil-Bor(h) walked back to them, now of normal size and features, as Kilgar and Candol started to come out of their frightened reverie, and even Quickfoot started to whimper less.

"Nice illusion," Sabu observed. "Cheap but effective, given the circumstances."

"Fawïr'mo," Sheil-Bor(h) replied, giving a short bow with his shoulders and head, "I figured such an impetus would suffice."

Eldar started to giggle as Candol came to his feet.

"What's so funny?" Sindar asked.

"He just shouted 'Boo'," Eldar giggled.

"What vile creature...," Lorel began as he started to come around.

"It's okay," Bronto smiled tiredly, "you saved the day."

"I did?"

"Yeah, fought it off single handedly. Too bad you don't remember," Bronto gave a weak smile, as he then thought about the death that had been wrought this day.

"Oh, well, glad I could help," Lorel said, very much puzzled.

Sabu grinned at little Bronto's joke as Candol came over to him, having just had a look at Lindel and Shong.

"I can fix them both up," the priest said, "but it will take most of the night before they can move on their own."

"Good," Sabu replied, "then we can leave by mid morn."

"I'll have to cure the worst of it here before either one of them can be moved," Candol said as he went over to Shong first.

"At least we saved *half* of the town," Eldar said.

"In the long run, it will not change the fate of this wounded city," Sheil-Bor(h) corrected, "those beasts will just come back when we have gone."

"We know," Sindar said, looking sad and downcast. "There's nothing we can do to stop it."

"We can stay and fight!" Lorel protested.

"And what about the innumerable other towns that we *aren't* there to help?" Sabu asked Lorel. "What about the regions already under the rule of misfortune and evil?"

Lorel had no answer.

"No," Sabu continued, "as hard as it may seem, we've got to move on and hope that our quest may solve some much larger problem."

A loud clang interrupted Sabu, one that almost shook the ground around them. All eyes turned to see Bronto, standing straight and tall, holding onto the hilt of his large six-foot sword as its tip was plunged a full foot into the hard stone of the city's open square. The grip of his strong hands was tight, the expression on his face hard, as he looked off into the distance of the now-quiet city.

"Are you okay?" Sabu said gently.

The big man just stood there for a few moments, neither breathing nor moving, as he gazed sternly into the distance, his hands closing vise-like around his sword. Finally, he sighed and relaxed his grip.

"Yes, I'm fine," he turned his head to answer his friend, the sternness relaxing into a sad smile, "it just frustrates me that for all our vaunted abilities and foretold destinies, that there's absolutely nothing we can do for this city but leave and go on about our travels, knowing that what's left of this city may not even exist a motab from now."

"We all feel the same way," Sabu answered, "but it's just one of the hard choices that Fate thrusts upon one."

"Yeah," Bronto said, as he yanked his large sword free of the stone with his right hand, "I guess so."

"For good or ill," Sabu finished, "we leave at sunrise."

"Maybe then, Mauklo and those two assassins will decide to rejoin us," Kilgar said. "They've been no help at all in this battle."

"So, what is this offer you would make?"

The man sat down at the tavern table, his straight reddish-brown hair coming down to his ears, his skin a light dirty tan, his dark blue eyes piercing. The almost five-foot-ten man didn't look too much the physical type, his medium build showing just a trace of a paunch. A long cloak with a decorative clasp hung over his old pants and nondescript shirt, his leather boots completing his outfit. He briefly scratched the unshaven stubble on his chin as he sat down with his drink, looking at the two seated figures across the table from him.

The room was dingy with dark smoke, the bulk of its patrons looking even dingier and less appealing. The tavern was one in a seedier section of the west side of town, the old wood of the table having several old blood stains and sword cuts on them. The two figures across the table were each dressed in identical dark robes, the hoods drawn partially over their faces, with just a bit of chin showing to suggest which be male and which female, the black robes obscuring all other physical details, black leather gloves covering their hands.

"You come to the point," Kor-Lebear responded, the hubbub of the tavern covering their conversation, "that shows more intelligence than the last few we've interviewed."

"So, I've heard," Bedor said, "although I don't plan on disappearing like the last three wizards you've talked to."

"They failed the interview," Kor-Lebear shrugged.

"And one must keep one's little secrets," Kilinir added in a pleasant voice.

"I can sympathize," Bedor said, taking a sip from his drink, "I've had to keep a few secrets myself. But what is it that you need one of my talents for?"

"You are versed in the arts of alchemy and mysticism?" Kor-Lebear asked.

"As well as in conjuring up the occasional piece of supernatural help every now and then," Bedor answered a bit impatiently. "I take it this is for long-term employment or you wouldn't be wasting your time and mine being so thorough."

"Oooh, and he's intelligent too," Kilinir mocked.

"It is not for mere employment that we seek one such as yourself," Kor-Lebear explained, "but for a long-term partnership."

"Ha!" Bedor snorted. "That's just another way of saying that you're broke and can't pay. Well, my services don't come cheap; when it comes to conjurations I'm among the best around here."

Bedor started to impatiently get up, as if to leave, but a lightly-restraining hand from Kor-Lebear pushed him back down into his seat as he spoke.

"If you were truly the best, you would have long ago swept the land with demonic hordes and carved yourself out a nice little kingdom," Kor-Lebear observed.

"That is no test of ability but of folly," Bedor shot back. "Such obvious conquests are a perfect way of making oneself a target; a practice I have no desire to perform."

"Come now, if you were already that good," Kilinir added, "you wouldn't need us and your price would be too expensive."

"No, while not the best," Kor-Lebear continued, "you *do* have the potential to some rise be so, and it is this potential that we seek."

"You are both rather observant for ones whose face I cannot see," Bedor said, taking another sip.

"Consider it part of the mystique," Kilinir smiled from beneath her hood.

"You have a reputation for being rather unforgiving with those who cross you," Kor-Lebear went on in an emotionless voice.

"One must be ruthless in one's pursuits," Bedor said. "But, okay; I may be open to a *profitable* partnership. Of what, then, would this partnership be for? And why don't you just use one of those other wizards that I've seen you with?"

"I told you he would be the right one when we saw him following us," Kilinir remarked.

"You knew then," Bedor said. "Well, not all of my observations were physical; I always use my own arts to check prospective employers."

"We know," Kor-Lebear said simply.

Their conversation paused briefly as the tavern's serving girl came by and refreshed their drinks. After she walked away, Kor-Lebear came straight to the point.

"We would form a team," Kor-Lebear said. "Our own skills are enough to handle the bulk of what we do. But, it is in magical support that we lack."

"And our associate Mauklo journeys to his own destination for now," Kilinir continued. "A quest that we find doesn't suit our present needs. So, we need one whose destiny is not yet written."

"One whose reputation may grow with our own; one that may go where we go," Kor-Lebear said flatly, and then a slim smile began to cross his lips. "We may not yet be the best, but we *will* be."

"Sounds intriguing," Bedor gave an evil grin. "And in what would our little group become the best in?"

"Liquidations," Kor-Lebear said. "The perfect combination of skills for the removal of the unwanted."

"Assassins?" Bedor asked. "That's it?"

"Not just assassins," Kilinir elaborated, "but the *best*; that to be feared by it's very name."

"Consider it a dream of ours; we even have our first contract," Kor-Lebear added. "We have everything covered except for the magic."

"Even the best assassin's plans can be foiled by a street-wizard with the right spell," Kilinir observed.

"And that's where *I* come in," Bedor finished. "You need some help with magic, but you don't want it to be someone that could use *you*. You yourselves have no skill in magic."

"Yet," Kilinir said very softly under her breath.

"An even cut on profit?" Bedor asked.

"Of course," Kor-Lebear said evenly. "But with a few ground rules."

"Like what?" Bedor asked.

"Nothing too unreasonable," Kilinir said with mild pleasantness. "Just that Kor-Lebear decides on which contracts we take and we never go back once an agreement is reached."

"Ethics?" Bedor sneered.

"More like practicality," Kor-Lebear clarified. "An assassin that isn't known to keep to his contract and his word, will soon be a dead one."

"That part was my idea," Kilinir said. "But, that isn't to say that we won't be rather direct and brutal to those that break their word with *us*. And we've heard that you're just *so* good at being brutal."

Bedor gave a short snort of laughter as he sipped from his drink. The dark smoke drifted between them as Bedor silently thought over the offer. Kilinir's robes hid the movements that her hand was making under the table; hid the dagger that she was so carefully unsheathing just in case. Finally, Bedor answered.

"I like it," Bedor smiled, "getting paid for doing what I like."

Kilinir's hand discretely eased her dagger back into her robes as a smile escaped from beneath her hood.

"But we shall need a symbol," Bedor pointed out, "something to inspire fear when seen. A symbol around which to build a reputation."

"We've already got that covered," Kor-Lebear said. "Our method of elimination shall be our symbol as well as our name."

"It's agreed then," Kilinir said as she put a single gloved hand out on the center of the table.

Kor-Lebear's hand joined hers, followed by Bedor's; three hands clasping their agreement there on an old table of a nameless tavern in an unimportant town. An agreement perhaps born in the pits of Hades, but one whose effects would ever-after be felt.

They were assembled, with their fresh horses, at what was left of the east end of town, everyone ready for travel except for the absent Mauklo, Kor-Lebear, and Kilinir. In back of them empty and burned buildings stretched, evidence of the previous day's raid. Several mangled bodies still lay in the street, their dead eyes staring open at the ghost town around them. Char marks were scattered along the streets, the still-smoldering remains of both people and buildings littering everywhere, burned dreams smoking in the gutter. Everything east of the town square lay in silence and death, the townspeople still yet afraid to cross over into it, as if it were some feared line of death.

Ahead of them lay open farms for perhaps halfway to the horizon, and beyond that the ever-encircling forests of Catho. Several of the fertile fields lay burned and scorched; again testament to the deadly raid, the occasional farm house still smoldering, the occasional cow still mooing piteously to be milked by its now-dead master. Then, far beyond all this, rose the majestic mountains of Catho, their snow-capped peaks soaring far up into the clouds, over two hundred miles away. Lindel gazed wistfully out towards the mountains, while Lorel looked back at the desolate section of town behind them.

"I wish there were something we could do for them," Lorel sighed from atop his horse.

"It is Indra's way," Candol consoled. "Would you rather stay and die with them, or live long enough to stop the threat forever?"

"I would wish for a third solution," Lorel answered. "I but wish that I could have fought more fiercely than I did."

"Oh trust me," Eldar smiled from atop his horse, "you tore through them pretty good."

"We'll be riding through rough country after we leave the farms," Bronto interjected, "that means we'll probably have to abandon our horses when we reach the mountains."

"Not entirely, we won't," Sabu said. "When the time comes, I can just pull them through my little portal to our island."

"Will they fit through it?" Shong asked.

"They can be made to," Sabu answered, "and with no harm to themselves."

"They'll be massacred when the raids start up again," Sindar said, while gazing at the not-so-distant body of an eviscerated child lying dead in the streets behind them. "Within a *kev* the population here will be halved once again."

"Prophesizing again, Sindar?" Eldar asked.

"I hope not," Sindar answered, "but if that Mayor continues to stay in power, then their fortune is told; otherwise, they might have a chance."

"Is there anything we can do?" Lorel asked forlornly.

"We can look forward to what is before us, instead of worrying of what already passed," Lindel advised. "You Humans are always so concerned about what is past and unchangeable. Look instead towards those magnificent mountains ahead of us. They just seam to radiate possibilities."

"I guess so," Lorel said half-heartedly.

"I'll have to agree with Lindel here," Bronto said from atop his larger horse. "Let's let the past take care of itself, and work for the time when we can prevent such death and misery from happening again."

"I agree with the elf also."

That last voice came from down the dead street. All eyes turned to see from whom the familiar voice came. The lone figure walked up to them, towards an empty horse.

"Mauklo," Sabu called out, "It's about time that you joined us. We've been waiting here almost a *nev*."

"Yeah," Kilgar said angrily, "where were you during that fight?! We could have used the extra firepower that you and your two cowardly friends would have given."

"My dear young one," Mauklo said as he mounted his horse, "I was out preventing any future raids from doing as much harm; surely something more important than fighting a battle that would have been lost regardless?"

"How could *you* stop them?" Quickfoot questioned, from on back of Candol's horse.

"I said I would take care of their Mayor," Mauklo answered calmly, "and I have. Without his traitorous leadership, this town may live out the motab."

"You killed him?" Kilgar asked.

"Me? Of course not," Mauklo said innocently. "A mere killing would not have prevented the other members of his greedy little administration from taking over and again using the citizenry as pawns for their power. No, I made sure that a more meaningful message was left."

"Sounds fun," Eldar commented. "How'd you do it?"

"I did nothing," Mauklo said, the ring of truth in his voice, "but I *did* hire ones who are rather proficient at what they do. Beyond that, I will say no more."

"Then we'd better leave," Sabu said. "We waited long enough for you to arrive."

"Wait, where's Kor-Lebear and Kilinir?" Shong asked. "They aren't here yet."

"Oh, they've decided to stay on here for a bit," Mauklo said. "They have their own little...business, that they wish to start up. Besides, the mountains aren't their preferred surroundings, cities are. But I gave them the means with which to communicate with me, should the need arise, as well as gain remote access to our island. So, we needn't wait for them."

"We know," Sabu answered. "Sindar foresaw that they wouldn't be coming, so we prepared for it."

That's when several other pairs of eyes noticed that, while there had been a spare horse for Mauklo, there were none available for Kor-Lebear and Kilinir.

"I see," Shong said. "I just wish that someone would tell me these things ahead of time."

"We leave then," Bronto said, aiming his horse out towards the mountains. "We have a long ride ahead of us."

The others spurred their horses on behind Bronto, forming a double column of horses behind the big man, Shong bringing up the rear. Lorel gave one last look at the death they left behind and then faced towards the distant mountains, rising high into the deep purple sky, as they set a steady pace out across the fields.

"Mr. Mayor, sir," the functionary came into the richly-decorated office, walking across the many rugs strewn overtop the floor, "the strangers have left."

"Good," the rather rotund Mayor said, getting up from his chair. "They nearly wrecked my plans! As it is, I'll have to make due without Loma. Now I'll have to find another way to spirit people away."

"If I may sir," the nameless functionary interjected, "perhaps the erecting of public shelters against the raids?"

"Then, when people go hiding in them from the raids, we get them then," the Mayor finished. "Good man, Tylok. We'll have to schedule a few smaller raids as soon as we can then. We need to replace the one's that the strangers cost us as soon as we can."

"Sir," Tylok asked, "think the Master will be displeased with our performance?"

"Not if we're fast enough with transforming more of the townspeople," the Mayor answered. "He needs as many from these out-of-the-way cities as he can get. Don't worry, we'll earn our way through the ranks yet."

"Good to hear, sir," Tylok said with almost visible relief. "Oh, this package was left for you."

He brought up a small package that he'd been holding and placed it on the Mayor's desk. It was wrapped in plain brown paper and tied with a simple knotted string. The Mayor looked down at it.

"Who left it?" the Mayor asked.

"I've no idea, sir," Tylok answered, "we just found it in the front room; we aren't even sure how anyone was able to get in to leave it there. But your personal magis says it holds no danger, be it from magic or trap.

"Very well," the Mayor said, "you're dismissed then. See to those shelters."

The functionary clicked his heals together, turned on one toe, and left the room. After the door shut behind him, the Mayor looked down at his package and picked it up in one hand.

"So," he said to himself, "from an admirer, perhaps? Or maybe the Master chooses a new way to communicate? Well, there's only one way to find out."

The Mayor tore off the string and ripped open the wrapping. He then opened up the simple wooden box that was revealed and reached in for its contents.

"A present maybe," he mused.

He pulled out a dagger with a note tied to it. As he untied the note, he saw that this dagger was not of ordinary make. It was made from a single cut of black obsidian, flawlessly shaped, its edges keen and sharp to the touch. In the center of its hilt a tiny red gleam seemed to shine forth from unseen depths, reflecting balefully from no light source that the Mayor could discern.

"Hmm, I guess it *is* a present," he said as he opened up and read from the plain block text of the note. "'With this very knife, shall your death be wrought; let this symbol be my name.' Is this some kind of joke?!"

The Mayor looked angrily at the note and dagger. He angrily crumpled up the note and tossed it across the room. Then, holding the dagger, he went behind his desk.

"This is outrageous," he fumed. "The idea that someone could ever get into here, much less have the audacity to *give* me the very weapon they plan to use! Well, there'll be no getting it in here."

He opened up a drawer, tossed in the black dagger, closed the drawer, then took out a key and locked it. He smiled satisfaction down at the drawer.

"Let's just see that joker use it against me now!"

He looked up, smile on his face, happy with himself. But his smile suddenly froze as he looked on his desk. He frowned as he reached out and grabbed what he saw on his desk.

It was the black dagger.

He picked it up, looking at it in puzzlement. He then grabbed his key and quickly unlocked the drawer.

It was empty.

"By what...?" he sputtered. "That magis said it was harmless. Of what cruel joke be this?!"

He then put the dagger back in the drawer again, locked it, and held tightly onto the key. He looked up with grim satisfaction.

And stopped.

He walked around his desk and out into the center of the room. He looked down at the object on the floor.

It was the black dagger.

"How?" he was confused. "All the protections and guards posted, not to mention the magis; I pay *him* well enough for his magic. There's no way anyone——"

He stopped and stared at the dagger as he suddenly had an idea.

"That's it."

He bent down and picked up the dagger.

"I'll just have the magis have a look at this. And if *he's* responsible, then he knows what punishment the Master will bring."

He walked over to the door and reached to turn the knob.

It was locked. He tried it again, but the door still wouldn't open.

"That's impossible," he said, fear starting to creep into his voice, "this door doesn't lock from the other side."

He kicked at the door a couple of times, but the solid wood wouldn't budge. He then cupped his hands and began to call out loudly.

"Tylok! Tylok! Where are you? Get me out of here or it's your hide!"

But he heard no response. As a matter of fact, he couldn't hear any outside noises whatsoever. He stopped his screaming and angrily tossed the dagger across the room.

He saw it drop down behind his desk, but heard it land a lot closer. He looked down at his feet.

It was the black dagger.

He screamed and jumped back a foot, one simultaneous motion of shock. Sweat now began to bead upon his brow, his breathing to become more rapid. He looked around himself quickly, nervousness now obvious.

"How? Who?" he shouted into the empty room around him. "What do you want? Why me? I'll pay you to leave me alone; twice what you've been paid!"

He spotted the window in back of his desk; facing out to the street, it was curtained off. He practically leapt across the room, over his desk, and ripped the curtains down, thinking now he could escape. Perhaps ten feet above the ground, but at least he'd make it out of here alive. He looked down at the window.

And screamed.

The window's brown wooden shutters closed the room off from outside view, but there, on its inside ledge, it lay.

It was the black dagger.

He backed into his desk, practically falling back over it. He then raised a foot and tried to kick the shutters open.

"Someone get me out of here!" his shout had more than an edge of hysteria to it. "Get it out of here! The black dagger, it's after me! Help!"

Repeated kicks had failed to open the window, its frail wood somehow easily holding against his two hundred and fifty pound frame. In frantic panic, he picked up the dagger, holding it as if he would stab someone, a mad fear in his eyes. He ran back across the room, black dagger in hand.

"If this knife's so indestructible," he said, "then let *it* bring down the door!"

He stood in front of the door, grinning inanely, and raised his hand up high, black dagger gleaming over his head. He then came stabbing down hard on the door, the dagger biting hard into the wood.

He screamed, in pain and fear. He raised up the dagger again, and once again stabbed down with the blade. It bit into the door's wood and once again he screamed and cried out. Again he stabbed, and again he screamed, crying out for anyone that would listen. Again and again. Several times he stabbed at the door, each time screaming out his pain and fear, and each time no one answered his frantic calls. With each stab he seemed to get weaker, his scream fading a bit more, his breath coming harder and more ragged.

Finally, after stabbing at the door for the tenth time, he leaned heavily against the door, holding himself up with the dagger imbedded in the door. He was weak and could barely breath. He looked up at the black dagger that he now held himself up with, imbedded into the door.

"Why?" he gasped weakly. "I've obeyed the Master. I can *pay* you."

His grip weakened, as he started to slide down to the floor. He held onto the black dagger for perhaps a moment or two more, and then finally released his grip, sliding down against the door to land face-down on the floor.

He was dead.

They found him with a black dagger stuck through his back, the last of ten vicious stab wounds, delivered perhaps by someone of around two hundred and fifty pounds. There was no dagger in the door, nor was there any sign that its wood had even been chipped, much less stabbed at ten times. The shutters to the window were found fluttering open and the door unlocked. Beside the dagger was a note, formerly crumpled up, but now smoothed out for everyone to read, the only clue that the Mayor had been killed by the work of assassins.

Except for the one puzzling bit to this scene that the magis had found. Like any good mystic, he'd used his magic to determine who the killer was. By so doing, he'd determined the identity of the only person to have held and used the black dagger.

It was the Mayor himself.

How the Mayor could stab himself in the back ten times was even more of a mystery than *why* he would. But, mysteries they would remain, as the former Mayor's administrating aides gazed nervously at the scene of death and the note found on him. Few words were said, each afraid of what to say.

Later that same day, despite all precautions, the mysterious black dagger disappeared, no trace of it left, nor of where it went. Only the note was left for them to gaze at, and after a few rises, it too disappeared, dissolving into a pile of dust.

The next day, the magis, the functionary Tylok, and three others of the administration, left town, never to return.

It wasn't too long before rumors of The Black Dagger started to circulate on the street, of who or what it was, and of how one may hire it. No one ever found out anything about The Black Dagger.

Only the now-dead Mayor ever heard any clue to the identity of his assassin. In his last dying breath, as he slid down towards the ground, he'd heard it, faintly behind him, fading as his life gave up its last, its only witness.

The faint laughter of two people, one male and one female, as a gloved olive-skinned hand placed the un-crumpled note upon his back.

CHAPTER TWENTY
The Dragon Mountains

R.K.: 9,990, 29 Arüdwo:

The country has been rough-going the last two hundred miles since leaving Sydelburg, what with an almost complete lack of usable roads around here. Occasionally we'll find the broken remnants of some ancient stone road, but we're usually lucky if we find a horse path through these woods. The few paths that we have found are always going to and from some small town that we'd be passing.

Or rather, the remains of a small town.

So far we've passed through three towns, all of them deserted, with half of their buildings burned to the ground. All of them had obvious signs of heavy fighting, and char marks that were probably left by the swords that those animal-faced creatures carry. We've seen the slaughtered remains of both livestock and horses, pets and trained beasts, but there's one thing that we haven't seen.

Of people's bodies, there are none. Not child, adult, nor ancient; not human, elf, nor dwarf. Not one single body in any of the towns or the woods around them. Yet, the smell of death lingers strongly. Sindar says he's picked up several strong psychic impressions of many people being killed and dying in the streets, yet of physical evidence none can be found. What did the invaders do with the bodies? And why?

We have no answers to these mysteries.

The forest we travel through is quiet. Lindel tells me that the birds don't chirp as often as they should. Maybe even the birds know of all the death around here and mourn for it. The only other sign of life we've encountered as we travel are some distant sounds of thunderous hoofbeats. Faint hoofbeats, always distant, never closing. Sometimes we even hear them in our sleep. Perhaps the raiders are busy with some other unfortunate village.

It is a small comfort that they don't get nearer.

R.K.: 9,990, 30 Arüdwo:

The mountains are getting closer; we should reach the foothills in a few rises. The hoofbeats get closer now. Perhaps they are raiding some small town nearer to us, or perhaps they lair in the very mountains that we now travel to. Sheil-Bor(h) says he can use his arts to divine their destination, so that we may avoid the needless difficulty of an accidental encounter.

Sheil-Bor(h) is a rather quiet individual; he tends to meditate a lot as we travel, although I didn't know you could meditate and ride a horse at the same time. We have exchanged stories of our travels and asked about his own encounters. He has been somewhat vague and unconcerned about his own feats, saying merely that the guardians for his own Hevon Gems that he encountered were as nothing to what we have gone through. He says that his own search for more knowledge about them had lead him to us. Eldar wants to know if that makes us famous. Mauklo doesn't trust him, which, by Eldar's reasoning, means that he's okay.

R.K.: 9,990, 31 Arüdwo:

We are on the run. Both Sheil-Bor(h)'s arts and Sindar's psychic sensings have confirmed of where the raiders travel. They travel in our direction and hunt for us! Perhaps they seek revenge over what we did to them at Sydelburg, or perhaps they are just hunting down every living thing in these woods and we qualify. Whatever the reason, we are now their targets. As such, we have quickened our pace, hoping to reach the mountains within a rise and gain some safety there. We even travel at night whenever our mounts are up to it. Sheil-Bor(h) says that about a hundred of those mounted creatures follow us. Maybe we can outrun them.

R.K.: 9,990, 32 Arüdwo:

The raiders have apparently realized that we know of their pursuit, for their thunderous sound now increases much faster than it did before. They no longer trail us, hoping to catch us at whatever opportunity of their own, but travel straight to us. Sheil-Bor(h) says they have doubled their pace, while Sindar says he can see visions of their mounts being pushed to the point of dropping. We travel as fast as we dare through this tightly woven forest, hoping to get to the mountains before the raiders get to us.

R.K.: 9,990, 32 Arüdwo, degrise:

The foothills are in sight; we may be able to make it. Unfortunately, the sound of their hoofbeats is near deafening as they close; they must indeed be numerous to be so loud but not yet in sight. We must hurry if we are to live.

"Hurry!"

Bronto's shout carried above the nearing thunder coming unseen through the thick woods behind them. Ahead of them loomed the foothills of the mountains of Catho; with snow-capped peaks that might reach close to sixty thousand feet high, it was the only thing they could discern through the thick woods cloaking about them. The ground trembled with the beat of the approaching menace, as they spurred their horses to their limits. Lindel whispered in the ear of his own mount, as if to coax it on in its own tongue, while Mauklo's own horse just galloped on with glazed-over eyes, as if only the dark wizard's own will controlled it, his desires overriding the horse's own need to stop and rest.

"I see a pass over there," Shong said above the rumble, "let's try that one."

"No!" Sheil-Bor(h) shouted back. "That way lies death; a dead end in which shall we be trapped. I think that ravine over *there* holds a way out."

"The ravine it is then," Eldar shouted out for all to hear.

They headed for the crack in the mountains, looming no more than a mile away. Safety within reach.

Crack of thunder, blue-hot flame shooting through warm afternoon air. Sound of exploding kindling as a nearby tree rips asunder.

"I think they've caught up with us," Lindel shouted as he glanced back over his shoulder.

Perhaps a hundred feet behind them, he saw the first few of the animal-faced riders coming up fast through the forest, their mounts frothing, a sheen of sweat on both mount and rider, determined to catch up with their quarry at all costs. They dodged through the trees nimbly, slowly gaining ground.

"Sabu!" Eldar shouted over to his friend. "A spell right about now would be nice."

Sabu had both his arms wrapped around the neck of his own horse, as if clinging to it for dear life, his rear end bobbing up and down with the pace of the horse.

"I don't think I can manage a spell and the act of staying on this creature at the same time!" he shouted back, his voice seeming to shake up and down with the beat of the horse.

"My hero," Eldar grinned to himself. "Well, let's see if I've got a few tricks left."

As his horse carried him along, he reached a hand into a pouch, pulling out a few small round red pebbles. He then dropped his horse back towards the rear of their charging group, back behind Shong, and tossed the pebbles out behind himself, high over his head. They landed in the path of the riders as Eldar brought his mount up towards the middle of the group again.

The ground started to slope upwards. Eldar pulled up alongside Sabu as they entered the ravine.

"What was that you threw?" Sabu asked, from the crouched position on his horse.

As if in answer, behind them they heard several sudden explosions, interlaced with animal-like screams and the inhuman sounds that clawed mounts can make when suddenly flash-fried.

"Oh, just a little something for them to play with," Eldar said offhandedly. "Now, how do we get up into those hills?"

I can discern a passage up ahead, Sindar's mind spoke to both of theirs, *and Sheil-Bor(h) says that his divinatory powers tell him it leads up into the mountains and safety. The passage is up over to the left of the ravine, up near that clearing in the trees by the fall of rocks.*

"Then that's where we're heading," Eldar agreed, and then shouted out, "Bronto!"

When the big man turned to look, Eldar pointed out towards the direction that Sheil-Bor(h) had indicated. Bronto, in the lead of the group, nodded and spurred his horse in that direction. The rest followed as the sound of thunder once again started to draw near.

They galloped over the rough terrain, the horses having to slow down as the ground became rockier. Soon, their gallop had reduced enough for Sabu to sit upright in his saddle and look around.

"I fear our reduced speed may mean our doom," Lorel said as he road up alongside. "Those vile creatures will surely catch us before we reach safety."

"Well, before you start telling me how many of them we can take with us when they kill us," Sabu said, steadying himself on his horse as he reached his right hand up into the air, "maybe now that we *are* a bit slower, I can do something about it. Although, it may end up making targets out of us."

While Lorel gave a somewhat puzzle look, Sabu flexed his right hand. Instantly his staff appeared in his grip, his hand holding it about the middle. Sabu began shouting some mystical words into the air as his staff began to glow.

"Beefrey tygor oomfra, klidor!"

Suddenly Lorel noticed that the ground seemed smoother, as he bounced less on his mount than before. Eldar looked around as he too noticed how suddenly smooth the ride seemed to be. It also seemed to Lorel that the trees were getting shorter.

Then he looked down.

Lorel's eyes bugged out as he saw that his horse was now galloping through the air some twenty feet above the ground and climbing. His hands tightened around the reigns as he started to realize that he may just be afraid of heights.

Eldar looked down at the distancing ground beneath him and then up at Sabu with a big smile and a raised fist over his head.

"The *ooonly* way to fly," he shouted over to his friend.

They could hear the thunder below them as they flew through the air, soaring high above treetop height, a dozen horses galloping through the air as if it were just but natural. They flew towards the far left corner of the ravine, Sabu holding his glowing staff over his head. With their new vantage point, they could now see the riders, swarming swiftly through the woods like a hundred disturbed ants, their mounts pounding through the tall trees as they each waved their blue steel swords over their heads. A hundred riders with a hundred swords of flaming death. Candol looked down and swallowed hard as his mount carried him aloft.

"Indra help us if they spot us," the priest said quietly.

"What's that supposed to mean?" Quickfoot asked from behind him where he clung to the priest, arms tight around his waist.

"Nothing, small one," Candol said as he looked up ahead again. "I hope."

"That doesn't sound too good," Quickfoot complained as he looked down fearfully, "why doesn't it sound too good?"

The thunder pounded down below them as they flew on, the horde of riders now having caught up to where they would have been had Sabu not sent them flying.

"We're almost there," Eldar shouted out. "*Ka'ru!*"

Eldar's victory cry carried out over the hills, rebounding for all to hear, even above the thunderous hoofbeats below.

Below, several animal-faced heads turned to look up.

"Okay small one," Candol said to Quickfoot, "*now* it's not good."

"Who told that *rik* to shout?!" Mauklo said angrily.

"Eldar never needs a reason to make life interesting," Bronto shouted back to Mauklo. "He'd get too bored otherwise."

Several blue-steel swords aimed upwards. Perhaps a dozen bolts of hot blue flame sliced up through the sky towards them.

"Now we're in for it!" Shong shouted.

"Sheil-Bor(h)," Sindar shouted over to him, "Sabu's busy with the flying; assist me."

"Right," Sheil-Bor(h) said simply.

The two wizards concentrated as their mounts, a hundred feet in the air and climbing, soared closer to the edge of the ravine, now but moments away. Two Hevon gems glowed as they concentrated. Below them a thin sheet of water appeared, stretching beneath them like a net, held in place by force of will alone. A dozen blue bolts hit it, their deadly fire getting lost within its thin watery extent. A dozen more then sliced up, turning parts of the strange wall to steam. Fifty more and the wall was no more, with blue flame soaring through the air all around them like mad fireworks, as sky riders sought to swerve their mounts aside.

"Well, that didn't last very long," Sindar commented. "There's just too many of them to handle. Let's hope we're getting out of their range."

From atop his mount Lorel cringed in fear as he watched blue fire turn the entire sky ablaze. All he could do was mutter the word 'fire' over and over again to himself as his eyes glazed over.

"I fear your friend is in trouble," Sheil-Bor(h) observed to Sindar.

"Indeed," Sindar responded. "He seems to have this thing about fire. Maybe if it——"

But before Sindar could offer any help, a bolt of blue flame hit the bottom of the horse straight on. In a flash of fire, the horse was reduced to flaming bits of charcoal shot through the air. The sudden ball of flame obscured what happened to Lorel.

"He is gone," Sheil-Bor(h) observed as he urged his mount on faster.

"No," Sindar said, "his mind, such as it is, still lives."

Then a body was seen flying clear of the diminishing flame, up through the air. But, wear Lorel's clothes though it might, it was far too small to be him.

"Uh oh," Quickfoot moaned, "it's Wacko again."

A screech was heard coming from Schanter as he soared through the air, looking for a place to land. Wicked glee crossed his face as the small leathery creature saw that there were a hundred possibilities below him.

"May Indra help us and send us aide in our time of need," Candol prayed to himself.

Several more bolts of flame hit as Schanter made his downward descent. Shong was suddenly horseless, with heavy scorch marks throughout his entire lower body, while Kilgar had jumped off from his own horse just before it was vaporized. Eldar found himself screaming out his victory cry of *ka'ru* as he was suddenly plummeting down towards the trees below, while Candol looked down to see three bolts of flame shoot up towards him. Quickfoot clung tightly to the priest's waist, hiding his small face in his robes, as Candol looked at the approaching flame, hoping his mount could out-fly it.

Suddenly, Candol felt himself being lifted up by his shoulders, strong taloned feet swiftly flying him and Quickfoot up off his horse just as it exploded into charred bits beneath them. Quickfoot gave a high-pitched scream just as they were borne aloft, the flame biting at their toes below them. Candol looked up to see what creature he was now at the mercy of.

Humanoid in basic shape though it was, it bore no trace of having evolved from anything near human. Two legs with taloned feet, now wrapped around the priest's shoulders, and two arms ending in sharp claws. Great feathered wings grew from its back, now flapping rapidly as they sought to gain height quickly. The entire body was feathered, and had more the proportions and angles of a bird made to walk upright then just that of a man with wings and feathers. Feathers and a great plumage adorned its head, while much smaller downy-like feathers wove their way around its hawk-like eyes and beaked mouth. Candol guessed that it looked to be male, but only the creature itself could be certain.

Getting over his initial shock at still being alive, he looked around. Taloned feet came and plucked the falling Shong out of the air, as well as the elven figure of Eldar, now a bit disappointed that he wouldn't be able to die in so glorious a fashion as to fall onto one's enemies from a hundred feet in the air. Another one grabbed onto young Kilgar, while two more of the flying figures carried the struggling form of Schanter, who seemed almost angry at not having gotten hurt. Dozens of others of these flying creatures now swarmed the skies, dodging bolts of flame to soar down upon the beast riders, raining spears and rocks down upon them.

"Almighty Indra has saved us," Candol smiled. "This servant thanks you, oh Great One."

The remaining flying horses now landed upon firm ground, as they finally reached a large ledge, high above the ravine, its trail leading back and up into the mountains.

"They are Hawkmen," Sheil-Bor(h) said to Sabu above the now more distant thunder of hooves below. "I do not know the specific tribe or species, but they are known to be friendly."

"Hawkmen," Sabu said. "I've heard of them, but I've never seen any. Offhand I'd say you're right about their being friendly, though."

Several of the Hawkmen landed, each depositing a carried passenger. Soon, between those still with a horse and those carried in by the sudden aid, all were up on the high ledge, Quickfoot still clinging to Candol, whimpering quietly. When Schanter was dropped down onto the ledge, he looked around desperately for something to hurt; seeing nothing, he picked up a small rock and began beating his own foot with it, crying in both pain and pleasure as he did so. Below, the thunderous hoofbeats quieted as the riders became occupied with attacks from above, in the form of fifty or so of the flying Hawkmen. Meanwhile, up on the ledge, a total of five of them had landed, folding in their wings behind them, regarding them with their unsmiling beaked faces, as the horses suddenly realized they could go no further and dropped.

"I wonder if they speak Selgish," Sabu pondered as they regarded each other, "or maybe even Tradespeak."

"My friend," said Bronto jovially, "there's one language everyone always understands."

And before anyone could stop him, Bronto walked up to one of the Hawkmen. He produced a large right forearm, and clasped it to the opposing arm of the stern-looking creature. Bronto gave a chuckle as they clasped elbow to elbow, pumping his arm up and down, looking at a strange creature as tall as himself like he was some long-lost brother. For long moments, his was the only voice that sounded forth from that ledge.

Then, the fine downy feathers around the corners of the hawkman's beak began to curved upwards into some resemblance of a smile around the expressionless beak. The creature then began to let out a shrill whistle from its beak, perhaps the sound a bird might make if it could laugh. This was soon followed by similar sounds from the other assembled hawkmen and, soon after that, by smiles and sighs of relief by the others on the ledge.

"Your large friend does seem to have a certain talent for social interaction," Sheil-Bor(h) observed quietly to Sabu, "a most commendable trait."

"I don't think that there's too many people that he really hates," Sabu agreed.

"We do speak Selgish," finally came from the hawkman's beak when he'd finished shaking Bronto's arm, in a high-pitched voice with a few musical bird notes whistled here and there as it spoke, "from back since the time of the old human Kingdoms."

"Ah, you know of the Kingdoms and Thïr Tÿorca then," Sabu said eagerly, stepping forward. "Perhaps you could——"

"Not here," it half-whistled, half-spoke, "the Orkai below are still a danger."

"Well," Eldar brightened, "at least now we have a name for those animal-faced pieces of—"

"You will go down the path," the hawkman interrupted, "while we keep the Orkai busy. We will meet you where this path dips over the next ridge."

With that the five hawkmen flew off, leaving the others to gather themselves up and walk their tired horses down the path, while below them spears rained down on creatures that shot back with hawkman-roasting flame.

"Not much for speeches," Eldar observed.

"It's action that counts," said Kilgar, as he started to walked down the path, "and they've already proven their worth in that."

"The horses will have to rest for a few rises," Lindel said as he examined their mounts, "we've pushed them too hard."

They were up on a forested ridge, Schanter having since changed back to Lorel. All around them were tree-covered mountains, far beyond them the snow-capped richness of Catho's inner mountains. They looked down at the small trail as it wove on through the mountains, and listened to the natural quietness, the sound of thunderous hoofbeats having been left behind.

"We'll have to leave them behind anyhow," Sindar said. "They'll be useless for the trails and passes ahead."

"What do we do with them then?" Lindel asked.

Sabu smiled, got out a cloth sack, and laid it open upon the ground. A few quick gestures and the opening had elongated enough for a horse to step down through.

"Perhaps you could take them back to the island and see that they're tended to while we wait for our winged friends," Sabu suggested.

Lindel took up the reins and began leading the horses down the makeshift portal. Soon after Lindel had left with the last horse down through the portal, a score of hawkmen came gliding into view, drifting out upon the thermals and air currents of the mountains, slowly spiraling down toward their ridge. The twenty soon landed around them, one walking up to Bronto, its blue and red feathers standing our from the others' green and yellow.

"Not that we're complaining," Quickfoot asked, "but why did you help us?"

"I am flight-master of my nest," the blue and red one said. "The bulk of my name is unpronounceable with your language, so you may call me Masouda."

"Our small friend has a point, Masouda," Bronto said. "Our problem was not your own, yet you made it so."

"My people lived in these mountains when the Humans had their great kingdoms," Masouda explained in his chirping voice. "We lived next to each other in peace; we patrolled the mountains and the skies for them while they gave us trade from far lands and protected our nests. It was a golden time for both races."

"Yeah, but——" Quickfoot tried to interrupt.

"Though that time is now long past," Masouda went on, ignoring Quickfoot while he spoke to Bronto, "there is in you some of the blood of those people that my ancestors called friends. We never forget a friendship or a debt; those orkai have been getting dangerous the last few rels and you were in need."

"Well," Bronto said, "you'll discover that I never forget a favor or a friendship either. Consider myself in debt to you for saving my friends."

Masouda nodded and chirped an acknowledgment. Eldar then took the opportunity to walk up and interject his own request.

"Perhaps you could help us in something else then," Eldar said, silver hair blowing in the slight mountain breeze. "We seek one of the cities of those old kingdoms. Thïr Tÿorca."

The hawkman looked up at the elf and then around at the others, as if considering something. From one face to the next its sharp eyes went, before finally answering.

"Except for that dark one there," Masouda said, pointing a clawed hand at Mauklo, "your motives would seem forthright."

Lindel, then came back up through the makeshift portal, lugging several small backpacks of additional supplies, while Masouda spoke. When Lindel was clear of it, Sabu folded up the sack and put it away.

"We know of the once great city of Thïr Tÿorca," Masouda said. "From where we now stand, it lies straight North and East of here. But be warned, for the route lies directly through the tallest of the peaks and past the lairs of several very dangerous dragons."

"Dragons haven't worried us too much lately," Bronto replied with a grin, "and what's a little cold."

"You do seem as brave as were your ancestors," Masouda observed, "this is good. When you get close to the valley, there will be more tribes of my people; seek out their nests and they will guide you the rest of the way to the valley. From there, you will be on your own to find what is left of Thïr Tÿorca. But be warned: there are dark forces that move about the valley."

"We thank-you, Masouda," Bronto said, with a polite nod, "and may a new age of gold soon arise; one in which both our peoples may once again live as friends."

"That would be a time I would wish to live to see," Masouda said, with a slight grin at the edge of his beak.

Masouda spread out his wings, as then did the other hawkmen around them. Bronto backed off as, with a few flaps of his great wings, the blue and red hawkman lifted up into the air. Up he rose, until he was hovering ten feet above the big man, while the other hawkmen flew out into the deep purple sky.

"A good journey to you," Masouda shouted down, "and may the winds be with you!"

They watched as the hawkmen flew off, over the mountains, out beyond a ridge, and out of sight. Lindel distributed the new packs of supplies he'd brought with him as they made ready to continue their journey, this time on foot. Eldar came up next to Bronto as the big man watched the last green wingtip disappear over the mountains.

"Bronto, you big lump," Eldar said as he slapped the man on the back, "you never told us you had such a prestigious bloodline."

"I never knew," he shrugged. "Anyway, we've got to get going."

The sky deepened to a light shade of purple as, in single file, they started on along the trail, winding their way further into the mountains, with only three white hawks circling high in the sky overhead to be of any witness to their departure.

It was slow-going through the rugged mountains, as they crept along narrow ledges through forest-lined passes, and over one cresting ridge after another. They went single file most of the time, in pairs the rest of the time. Bronto was at the lead, Shong the rear, with Lindel up front with Bronto to read the trails that they would travel down. The weather was pleasant, if a bit brisk with the fullness of mid-Fall. During the day, the *orain*-colored sky loomed brightly overhead, a slight *trüb*-colored haze around the bright-blue of the sun. Around them trees, bushes, and other plants abounded, their colors ranging the spectrum from the green-blues of the tall trees, to their *orain* and *tairu* colored needles and leaves, to the occasional *narlu* and green colorings of sage and berry bushes. Around them, birds warbled their high-pitched songs, while the occasional squirrel or rodent scampered along the tree limbs. The air carried with it the fresh scent of pine and sage, with a slight hint of the innumerable herbs growing wild upon the hillsides.

"We've been on the run so much," Sabu was saying to Sheil-Bor(h) as he walked alongside of the other's taller frame, "that we haven't had much time to talk. For instance, you never said what specific field of magic that you study."

They were walking around a not too narrow ledge, tall mountainside to their left, steep fall into the bowels of a ravine to their right. Sheil-Bor(h)'s dark sandy hair tossed in the breeze as his green cape fluttered lightly. He seemed to be lightly meditating as they walked along the ledge, his eyes only partly noticing the terrain on which he walked. He blinked his eyes and breathed in deep of the mountain air, as he came out of his reverie. Sheil-Bor(h) looked first up at the sky, a thoughtful look upon his face, before he answered the wizard.

"In my quest for knowledge," he answered, in his ever quiet voice, "I try to never limit my studies. Thus do I study any field of the magical arts that I come upon."

"That would make you rather versatile," Sabu acknowledged.

"Ah, but with the time and effort that such extreme studiousness takes," Sheil-Bor(h) pointed out, "you are no doubt much more versed in the more specific fields that you study than I am in any of the several endeavors in which I now involve myself."

"The quest for knowledge hath its price," Sabu smiled.

"Tell me," Sindar said, coming up behind them, "how much have you encountered in your studies concerning that of Hevon?"

"Somewhat less than what you tell me you have found in that dimensio-book, I am afraid," Sheil-Bor(h) sighed, "It is a mystery of which I still seek the answers."

"We've got enough intellectuals around here to start our own sage school," Eldar's voice was heard to say from somewhere towards the rear of their marching line.

"I'll remember that when——" Sindar started to say.

Sindar suddenly stopped what he was saying as he stopped walking and just stood there, looking up into the sky, eyes distant. Sabu stopped and turned around to look at his friend.

"What is it?" he asked.

"Danger," Sindar answered, his gaze still far off. "A winged threat comes upon us. They come from…"

He tilted his head upwards a bit, facing the mountainside soaring high above them, and then shot his arm straight out pointing.

"There!" he shouted, eyes suddenly no longer distant, body tense with adrenaline.

Everyone stopped walking, all looking up expectantly in the direction Sindar indicated, hands slowly drawing out weapons as they looked to see of what their companion warned. At first they could see nothing. The sky seemed to shimmer several feet overhead, as if from heat waves meeting. Then the shimmering coalesced.

Six figures materialized in the middle of the air, appearing seemingly out of nothing, flying down at them. They had thick rubbery skin stretched tightly over their unnaturally thin bodies. Whip-like tails sliced back and forth behind them, while large taloned feet reached out for targets. Their gaunt faces screeched malice at them from fang-covered mouths, as their large leathery wings carried them down on top of them.

Immediately, an arrow went bulleting through the sky, sent from Lindel's bow, straight towards the heart of one of the creatures. The thing deftly avoided it in a spiraling dodge as it arced straight for the golden-haired elf. Another one dived for Bronto, as the rest seemed to come straight for Sabu, Eldar, and Sindar.

Their screech pierced through the air like knives to the skull. Everyone grabbed at their ears, several of them collapsing to the ground in pain. A few small rocks came tumbling down from above, loosed by the high-pitched screeches. Shong collapsed to the ground, hands over his ears, as he thought his skull might split. Candol folded up into a heap upon the ground, while Quickfoot's eyes rolled up in back of his head as he too collapsed. Even Mauklo seemed overcome by the skull-splitting sound. Only Bronto stood tall as he swung his sword at the one swooping down upon him.

Lindel reached in his quiver for another arrow, this time taking out a gold-tipped one. He notched his bow just as one of the creatures came down upon him.

A whip-like tail snapped out at Lindel's bow, slicing it in two and sending its pieces flying through the air. A clawed hand then swiped at the elf, leaving a ragged claw mark ripping across his green tunic, blood dripping red, as the elf was sprawled across the ground on top of the huddled form of Shong.

"He broke my bow!" Lindel remarked angrily and then glanced up at the flying menace. "You owe me a bow! *Turen!*"

Meanwhile, the one up front power-dived at Bronto, just as the large man swung his big sword. Sword hit creature, just as the full weight of the creature charged straight into Bronto's chest. The creature exploded from the impact of Bronto's sword, but the momentum from its charge sent the big man flying back over the edge of the trail, out over its cliff-like drop and hurtling back and out into the deep ravine below, still holding onto his large sword. Like a slow backwards dive, he disappeared down out of sight.

The remaining four creatures swooped down upon the cluster of huddling mages at the center of the group. One dove straight at Eldar, sending him sprawling out towards the edge of the trail; only by his fingertips did Eldar stop his plunge out over the edge. One slashed at Sabu, ripping a deep gash across the young wizard's chest, while another picked Sindar up by his shoulders, as if to lift him high into the sky. Sheil-Bor(h) dived to the ground, with greater agility than one might think of him, as another tried to lash its whip-like tail out to where his head used to be.

"Ever get the feeling someone wants us *real* bad?" Eldar quipped from his precarious hold.

Lorel came charging up to the cluster of creatures, sword slashing out, as he grimaced from the pain of their screeching. He sliced out with his sword at the creature clawing away at Sabu, as it defended by slicing out with its sharp tail.

Tail met sword with a sharp *crack*, as half of the sword was sent flying off, severed off from the rest of it as tail sliced through steel like it was butter. The thing then turned it head full on towards Lorel and screeched at the top of its lungs. Lorel's eyes rolled up in back of his head as he dropped to the ground like a wet sack. It then turned its attentions back on Sabu.

And was immediately greeted by a sudden bright flash of light to its eyes. It screeched in sudden blind pain, as Sabu rolled aside, his quick spell having gained him a few moments more.

Sindar was five feet above the ground, in the talons of one of the creatures, when he suddenly stopped struggling and just calmly looked up at the creature holding him. The creature made ready to screech down at his victim, when suddenly its eyes rolled in back of its head, its body shook, and it fell to the ground, releasing Sindar en-route. Sindar managed to land without breaking any bones, but the creature just plopped down like a dead rag. Sindar looked over at the thing as he got to his feet. There was a thin grey liquid oozing out from inside of its triangular ears.

"That'll teach you to mess with a psychic," he smiled satisfactorily.

Lindel finally got up off of Shong. He tried to get the fighter up also, but the high-pitched screeching seemed too much for him. Giving up on that, he looked over at his broken bow and grimaced. He thought a bit, and then started to glance quickly around him.

"There's got to be something," he muttered to himself, "that I… Ah!"

He ran over to a tree growing out of the hillside and bent down to pick up a long branch that he'd spotted. This he held in his right hand, holding it about its middle. He then closed his eyes and concentrated, trying to ignore the noisy battle around him.

As he concentrated, the dead branch slowly began to reshape itself, growing straight and smooth, and then curving itself back into an arc. When Lindel opened his eyes, he was holding a new bow.

"Now all I need is something to be the bowstring," he said looking around again.

The creature dived down at Sheil-Bor(h) again, feet talons forward, mouth open to screech once more. Sheil-Bor(h) lay upon his back, one hand covering an ear, the other propping himself up.

"I tire of your screeching prattle," he said softly but firmly, as he pointed a hand up at the creature.

There was a series of snapping sounds, and then the mystified creature suddenly found itself with a thick rope tying its mouth shut, another one about legs and tail, and a third binding its clawed hands together. It fluttered around uselessly, hovering in the air.

"That should give you pause for thought," Sheil-Bor(h) said as he started to get to his feet.

A pea-sized pellet of flame went shooting out from Sabu's hand, weak though he was from the blood oozing from the wound to his chest. It shot out and bathed the blind creature in a body-encompassing halo of fire. The thing screeched out angrily at the new pain, but otherwise appeared unharmed.

"Hmm," Sabu said to himself, "the hide appears too thick for my flame to penetrate. Maybe if...I know!"

Staff appearing in hand, Sabu concentrated, the red Hevon Gem on the top of his staff glowing brightly. Then another, brighter, perhaps harder looking, fiery pea went flying out. Just as the creature shook its head with recovering sight, with a *pfft* it penetrated the thick rubbery hide and sank deep inside the creature's lean frame, leaving but a pea-sized hole to mark its entrance.

The creature looked down puzzledly at the minor wound, apparently no worse for its making. It then looked up at where the young wizard crouched as he slowly got to his feet. Sabu just smiled.

"Say good-bye," he waved almost amiably.

The creature looked puzzled for a brief moment, then opened his mouth to screech one more time. He never made it.

From deep within the thing's belly, the pea detonated, exploding suddenly outward from within the confines of its body. Fire gushed out of the creature's mouth, flame leapt out of now-melted eyes and streamed out of its ears. Flame boiled up within it as, with a final death screech, it gave its all.

It exploded.

A tattered sheet of torn rubbery skin lay drifting upon the ground in front of Sabu, barely enough to make a proper coat out of, all that was left of the creature, steam still rising up from its cooked inner lining.

Sabu leaned upon his staff, looking at the others about him, as he strove to overcome the pain leaking from his chest.

The one over Sheil-Bor(h), meanwhile, was flapping about, trying to free itself of its bindings. Its hands were almost free when something came flying through the air, straight towards it.

It was small, it weighed ninety pounds, and it had a warty complexion that not even a mother could love. Schanter landed upon its back, biting and clawing at its wings, taking delight at the chance to torture such a bound and almost-helpless creature. The creature screeched out its anger, sending waves of pain through Schanter's skull as the small one grabbed for an ear with his hand.

"Ow! Schanter in pain. Schanter not like!" he howled, and then began to get a wicked smile on his face that only the truly deranged can manage. "Schanter *love* pain! Want more! More!"

He then plunged both of his clawed hands deep into the creature's back, straight to its spinal cord. Its wings quivered and went suddenly limp as, with a screech of pain and puzzlement, it went plummeting down to the ground, straight towards Sheil-Bor(h).

Sheil-Bor(h) nimbly leapt aside as the pair came crashing hard into the ground. The creature landed head-first, its skull twisting back at an unhealthy angle upon its neck, as it lay there very still. Schanter jumped up and down on its back, kicking it as he did so.

"Again! Again! Schanter want again!"

The screeching reduced, some of the others were starting to recover. Mauklo was looking up, as the creature that had smashed Lindel's bow was now bearing down on him. It screeched anger and malice at Mauklo as it swooped down upon him. Mauklo, anger forming upon his face, raised up a hand to cast a spell with which to defend himself.

But the spell was never needed. A golden point suddenly protruded from inside of its skull, sticking out of its forehead like some metallic growth. Its eyes stayed fixed as its flight arced limply to the ground. As it turned down, Mauklo could see the rest of the arrow's shaft sticking out from the back of its skull. He turned to see Lindel standing perhaps fifty feet down the path.

"He broke my bow!" Lindel said, stern expression on his face, as he held a new bow, tightly strung, its wood looking polished.

One more of the creatures was left, harrying around Eldar, after he'd finally climbed up from the ledge. He swatted at it with his sword, as it fluttered around him, deftly avoiding his attacks.

"Come down here you overgrown chicken!" he shouted at it.

It screeched at him again, as Eldar swung once more, ignoring the thing's cry.

"Haven't you caught on by now?" he mocked. "Your cry doesn't affect elves."

He slashed at it again, and again missed. It came diving down at him, all claws out, determined that this one elf at least shall die. Swiftly it closed.

Then it stopped, struck by a long curved knife sticking out from its chest, buried hilt deep. It doubtfully fluttered around from the shock.

"Bad bird," Kilgar said from where he stood, readying a spare knife, "you'll pay for Bronto."

It looked angrily at the young boy, then screeched again. It turned and looked down at Eldar, regarding him, and then started to resume his plunge at the elf.

But he was stopped by another knife, this one not curved as was the first, but also buried hilt-deep in his chest. It screeched in pain, this time Quickfoot standing forward to claim the credit.

"You gave me such a headache," the small hair-footed one said. "I hate that!"

It fluttered more weakly now, but was still determined to get to Eldar. It tried once again to fly down, claws out, to the elf.

And this time was toppled through the air by an unexpected jet of water, catching it full on in the face. Candol stood up, watery gem upon his forehead aglow, hand pointing towards it. It toppled down over the side of the path, down into the ravine.

"Those things take a lot of killing," Sabu remarked as he used his staff to hobble over to Candol.

But the thing came fluttering back up, having recovered its flight. It slowly rose up level with the cliff edge, the two knives still sticking out of its chest, oozing green blood. But then it stopped. It screeched and flapped it wings as if to try again, but still it couldn't fly up any higher.

"I think it's stuck on something," Eldar observed.

"I wonder what it's stuck on?" Quickfoot asked as the thing tried once again to rise up.

"I don't think it's a 'what'," Shong said as he got to his feet.

Shong, sword out, ran over to the cliff edge where the creature was flailing around. Eldar and Kilgar followed him, as, avoiding the thing's flailing claws, they all looked over the edge to see what held it down.

"We'll, I'll be," Eldar smiled.

There, hanging onto the hillside, was Bronto. His right hand held a firm grip onto his large sword, which was now plunged three feet into the solid stone of the cliff several feet below them, while his left hand was holding onto the creature's whip-like tail as it tried to free itself from his grip.

"I don't even want to *know* how you managed that one," Eldar chuckled.

"If one of you could manage a spare hand," Bronto called up, "all this hanging around is getting a bit tiresome."

A smile crossed Kilgar's face as he saw that his friend was indeed safe and not lying a mile down on the rocks below. Shong looked over at the creature that Bronto had by the tail, regarding it casually.

"Well have to take care of that thing first," he said.

"No problem," Bronto shouted up.

The big man gave a strong tug on the thing's tail, jerking his arm swiftly down. The creature gave a yelp of shock as it suddenly found itself drawn straight down with enough force to send it plummeting quickly towards the ground far below. Bronto snapped it down, like one would a whip, letting go when the creature's torso had passed below his waist. They watched as it went spiraling helplessly down, screeching its way out of sight, to crash hard upon the rocks a thousand feet below.

"Now, if someone's got a rope?" he asked, almost casually.

They were assembled on a fair-sized ledge, just down the trail from where they were when the creatures attacked them. Candol was tending the wounded, with Lindel helping him out with his own herbal medicines. Sabu had a freshly healed scar across his bared chest, courtesy of Candol's tendings, while Quickfoot was nursing his still-tender ears. They were discussing their recent encounter.

"They were headed straight for me, Sabu, and Sindar," Eldar was saying. "I think they were after our Hevon Gems."

"They were definitely sent," Sindar agreed, as he sat down with the others, "I don't believe them to be among the normal denizens of these mountains."

"They were demons," Mauklo said as he paced by them, "of a type given to surprising their victims and rendering them near helpless with their screech. Faerie Folk are immune to the effects of their voice, but they can still be rather annoying if you don't see them coming."

"Conjured resistance," Sabu nodded. "Something either wants our Hevon Gems, or doesn't want us to reach Thïr Tÿorca."

"It would not be the Gems," Sheil-Bor(h) shook his head, "if someone knows enough to know that we have them, then he would also know that they are more a part of our souls now, and not something that can be merely taken away."

"Then it's the valley that they don't want us to find," Eldar said, leaning back upon a convenient boulder.

"Then it's the valley that we *must* find," Bronto said, walking over. "This sounds like more reason for us to quicken our pace on towards our goal and find whatever secrets that valley has to offer."

"Agreed," Sabu said. "We'll rest here for half a *nev* and then move on."

"We should be able to make that next ridge before nightfall," Lindel pointed out from where he stood looking out across the mountains.

"Good," Sindar nodded, "but we've got to be more alert for such ambushes in the future. I don't think they'll give up so quickly."

"Then that gives me some time for a quick nap," Quickfoot said from across the other side of the ledge.

As the others went about the job of resting and repairing themselves, Mauklo sat and thought to himself, his devious mind at work trying to out-guess an unseen opponent.

As he watched the others ready themselves for an even faster push towards Thïr Tÿorca, he couldn't help but think how that attack was responsible for all this; that the sudden and almost deadly attack was the one thing that could hasten them along their journey.

The perfect thing…if someone *wanted* them to find Thïr Tÿorca.

The trail got narrower the farther up they went. Soon, the thin trail gave out altogether, forcing them to hike across the rough terrain. Up along hillside slopes they climbed, the air getting colder as they saw the snow-line getting closer. Through the thick trees they weaved their way, as they tried to push their pace to the limit. But trees and *sÿlva'* slowed them down nonetheless. Steep ravines blocked their paths; some they would use a rope and climb across, others Sabu or Sindar would use their magic and fly them over. But always ever onward, climbing up steep inclines and over rough terrain as they strove northeastward.

Occasionally they could hear thunder echoing off the tall mountainsides, never certain if it were the orkai beast riders, come to hunt them again, or just normal thunder echoing from some distant storm. Not even Sindar's mental powers or Sheil-Bor(h)'s foretellings could be certain. Whichever it was, just that doubt was usually enough to spur them on for at least a few more miles before resting.

Bronto was their strength. His never-tiring frame was always at the front, never slowing, always happily whistling some old bar tune as he strode along as if he were going off to some picnic. The few times that young Kilgar would admit to being tired, Bronto just heaved him up on his shoulders, as if he were but nothing, and carried him on along until the next ridge.

"I think we've been marching for *kevs*," Quickfoot said one afternoon, as his smaller feet scurried along to keep up with the others, "don't these mountains ever end?"

"Actually," Sindar responded, "it's only been about four and a half rises. The illusion of expanded time is just due to your rash impatience and small stride."

"Hey," Quickfoot said turning to Candol and tugging at his robe, "was I just insulted?"

Candol just smiled down at Quickfoot and kept on walking.

Lindel was towards the front, near Bronto, when he looked up in the sky and pointed.

"What's that over there?" he said. "I see something flying over by that peak."

Bronto looked in the direction indicated, squinting his eyes that he could see better. He could just make out a large winged form flying up around a snowy peak.

"Your elven eyes are probably better than mine," Bronto answered, "but it does look kind of large. I can't quite make it out though."

"I wonder what it is?" Lindel asked.

"Well," Bronto smiled, "they *do* call these the Dragon Mountains."

"That's *all* we need, is to meet another one of *those* things," Quickfoot said from the middle of their marching group. "I don't like being dragon-kibble."

"I wonder what it would be like to *ride* one of those things," Bronto mused as he looked out at the distant form.

"*Ride?!*" Quickfoot shook his head. "You're crazy."

"Don't worry," Eldar said, "I'm sure that you're *much* too small a morsel for their large appetites."

Before Quickfoot could think up a good response, they heard a rumble of thunder echo off in the distance, trailing long and slow through the air. Several of them paused to look up into the sky.

"So, which was that then?" Shong asked cautiously.

"It sounded like normal thunder," Lindel answered, "I don't think it was those creatures. Besides, these trails are too steep for their mounts."

"So it may be," Sindar put in, "but I still feel that we are hunted nonetheless. If not by them, then by others."

"Maybe once we get up to the snow that'll slow down our pursuers," Eldar suggested.

"If we don't then die of cold first," Quickfoot complained. "It's getting chilly up here!"

"We near the snow-line," Sheil-Bor(h) explained patiently. "Perhaps in a rise or two more we will reach the edge of the snow. Even now, the trees aren't quite as thick as they used to be."

"Oh, *that's* encouraging," Quickfoot rolled his eyes.

"It could be worse," Eldar suggested with a smile, "it *could* be winter."

Quickfoot just shook his head as they walked on.

"Actually, if I figure right…," Sabu began.

"Which you usually do," Eldar interrupted.

"…then we should reach the valley of Thïr Tÿorca before winter comes," Sabu finished.

"What about making it back *out* of there before winter comes?" Lorel asked.

Sabu just shrugged.

Lorel was about to ask Sabu to expand upon his shrug, but was interrupted. A swift hissing sound went flying through the air, just missing his ear, and landed buried in a tree. When the others turned to look, there buried hilt-deep in the tree was a long dagger, aflame with fire, even now still sizzling inside the wood of the tree. They turned around to see the source of the weapon.

"I am afraid that our pursuers have renewed themselves," Sheil-Bor(h) said calmly, as he raised a hand and pointed.

Over through the trees, perhaps a few hundred feet along the slope in back of them, were two small figures, each ablaze with fire, wearing it as one would clothes, jumping up and down as if in victory at having found their quarry.

"Uh, Lorel," said Eldar, suddenly putting an arm around the fighter and turning him away from the flaming sight, "why don't you check with Bronto and make sure that nothing's going to surprise us from up front."

"Uh, sure," said the puzzled warrior as Eldar steered him away from the fiery sight.

"That's all we need," said Quickfoot, "is him turning into Schanter right now."

"Hey," Shong said as he pulled the knife out of the tree, "this blade may be red-hot, but the handle's cool to the touch. I think I'll keep it; if I can find a sheath that won't burn, that is."

As Shong found a place on himself for the burning knife, Mauklo turned to the others.

"They're minor fire demons," he explained quickly, "they only appear if someone's summoned them."

"I guess they got tired of sending beast-faced riders and screeching birds after us," Shong commented, as he finally found a fire-proof sheath for his new knife. "These must be our latest pursuers."

"If they get back to whoever sent them——" Mauklo began.

"Then they'll find us even in all *these* mountains," Sabu finished. "We've got to get them."

Another flaming knife went whizzing through the air, just clearing the top of Candol's head as it went plunging off into the hills beyond.

"Their aim's getting better," Eldar said offhandedly.

"Allow me," Candol offered, miffed at the flaming weapon having come so close to his head, as he rolled back his sleeves. "*Fire* demons you say?"

A watery gem started to glow upon his forehead as he stretched out a pointed hand. From his finger there shot out a thin lance of water. Soaring through the air like a swift missile, it went straight between the trees and directly at the two small demons. It hit with an explosion of water and steam, the sudden cries of the creatures soon fading as faint echoes upon the mountains.

"I think I'm getting pretty good with this Hevon thing," Candol commented as he brought down his arm.

"There'll be more," Mauklo said grim-faced.

"And we probably don't want to see what will be sent against us once they find us," Sindar pointed out.

"Then let's move it," Bronto said in a commanding voice. "We can be over to the next mountain in about a nev."

"Right," Lindel said, as they all went, once more, quickly on their way.

Through the forest they went, over more ravines and around tall mountain peaks. Closer they came to mountains so high their peaks were lost up amongst the clouds. When evening came, and they had to rest, they could hear the cries of unnatural creatures roaming the night. From the mountain from which they'd come these cries came, perhaps sourced from strange creatures native to these hills, or perhaps from that which still hunted them. No one slept easy, on this, or the next several nights.

Dawn found them already on the move again, trekking higher still through the mountains. Early morning light filtered down over the peaks and through the tall covering of trees. The woods were filled with the sounds of birds nesting and small animals scurrying about. Occasionally, they would see another of the distant large flying shapes that Bronto had identified as dragons, a fact that didn't make Quickfoot any less nervous. By noon, Lindel's bow had brought down a deer for lunch, with enough left over to serve as trail rations as they moved along.

The air got colder the farther up they traveled, as they aimed themselves for those high snowy peaks. Chill winds buffeted them more frequently, making it seem even colder than it actually was. Of somewhat greater worry was what they saw along their trek. Two more sightings of dragons they saw over the next few rises, always distant and always in flight. Then of their pursuers, once did they hear distantly from behind them a rolling thunder they knew definitely not to be natural. To escape those that would find them, they then took to the narrower steeper trails, figuring that at least this would thwart the orkai and their clawed mounts.

A few more rises of determined travel brought them close to the snow-line, as even now they passed by the occasional small puddle of snow clinging to the branches of a tall pine tree. Trees too got fewer as they traveled upwards, the mountainsides now given more towards bushes clinging low to the ground. They traveled single-file all the time now, going along what few narrow trails that could be found, but having to make their own trails more and more often. Their heads would turn at the infrequent high-pitched screeches echoing throughout the mountains, unsure as to if the echoes were near or very far away.

"I'm not made for this kind of weather," Quickfoot said as he shivered his way up along the cliffside.

"I think for once the small one's right," Lindel observed, "we aren't dressed for this type of cold, much less the snow coming up ahead."

"What do you mean *for once*?" Quickfoot asked angrily.

"Perhaps there *is* a need for more wintery clothing," Sabu admitted, ignoring Quickfoot's outburst. "I could open the portal back to our island and find some—"

"No need," Eldar interrupted, as he got out a small vial from inside of his backpack. "I have this potion I've been wanting to try out..."

"Not another one of his potions," Quickfoot said in exasperation, "my stomach will *surely* rebel."

"I don't know," Bronto mused, "the last one he gave me tasted kind of like cloves."

"I'm not sure that I have enough for everyone though," Eldar said doubtfully.

"Thank the gods," Quickfoot said, eyes gazing skyward, hands clasped together.

"Then give my portion to someone else," Bronto offered, "I'll just tough it out with a few more furs wrapped around me."

"There shall be no need for anyone to go without," Candol said as their trail started around a bend. "The power of the mighty Indra shall clothe you all in warmth if need be."

"Actually," Sheil-Bor(h) interjected in his quiet voice, "if I remember the exact temperature that those mountain heights are said to reach, perhaps a combination of both potion and spell might be in order."

"It sounds like we can handle the cold then," Sindar said, "although when we get up to fifty thousand feet——"

"I think," Bronto interrupted from his lead point around the bend in the trail, "that we have a more immediate problem."

"What's that?" Eldar asked.

"I think you'd all better come and see," Lindel said seriously as he rounded the bend from behind Bronto.

One by one they caught up with Bronto, each one rounding the corner, each one in turn showing concern at what they saw. Perhaps thirty feet or so in front of them, the trail gave out...along with half of the hillside. The trail ended at a sudden drop going down hundreds of feet below them. The rift went on for perhaps two hundred feet along the mountainside, the trail picking up again at the far side.

"It looks like this place saw quite a landslide," Lorel said.

"Yes," Sabu began, "I would estimate——"

"*Please* don't," Eldar said with mild pain in his voice.

"A bit too far for a rope," Shong observed.

"I'm not climbing across *that!*" Quickfoot quickly put in.

"We can always fly across," Sabu shrugged.

"You could do that fly spell of yours on *all* of us?" Shong asked.

"I've been practicing," Sabu answered, "and with Sindar's help..."

"I too might be able to assist you in such an endeavor," Sheil-Bor(h) offered. "Among the many fields of magic of which I study, is that of the air."

Quickfoot started to open his mouth to once again complain about flight as a mode of transportation, but was interrupted. There was a loud rumble overhead.

Several pairs of eyes looked up.

"I'm almost afraid to ask," Lindel began, "but does anyone——"

"*Sylva'* appears to be unquiet within this ridge," Sheil-Bor(h) observed.

"And I do not see that rumble as boding us anything but ill news," Sindar finished.

The rumble sounded again, louder this time.

"I would say 'run'," Eldar offered, "but I wouldn't know where *to*."

Some dust, small rocks, and bits of snow began to drift down on them from above.

"Wait," Lindel quickly pointed with his right hand, "I saw movement up there."

"Sindar?" Sabu turned to his companion behind him.

Sindar concentrated only briefly before answering.

"I sense several minds," he answered. "Beast-like and primitive, but they are the minds of orkai."

"Not *them* again!" Quickfoot whined.

"I thought their mounts couldn't follow us?" Kilgar asked.

"I don't think they are the same ones," Sindar shook his head. "Perhaps a more primitive tribe that——"

Sindar's theorizing was interrupted by a loud rumble overhead, followed quickly by the sight of several huge boulders come pounding down towards them from the tall peak high overhead.

"Tell us later!" Bronto shouted. "Sabu, if you've a way out of here..."

"Uh, right," Sabu raised up his staff. "Now, a good flight spell and——No, we couldn't fly out from under those rocks. Perhaps——"

"Sabu," Eldar encouraged, "speed please?"

"Accounting for wind speed and rate of descent..."

The boulders, but a pounce or two away, came falling down straight at them.

"Sabu!!!" Eldar screamed above the deafening roar of the quickly approaching landslide.

Sabu looked up to see a particularly large rock falling straight for him. He quickly clasped his free hand to Sindar's shoulder, drawing additional magical energy from his friend, and simultaneously pointed his staff out towards a far mountain peak.

"That way!" was all he shouted in the way of magical incantations.

Not only did the staff glow but Sabu's eyes as well, so much did he flood himself with magical energy. Sindar gave a brief gasp at the sudden quantity of magical energy drawn by his friend but, considering the circumstances, let him have all he needed. There was a very quick flash of light encompassing the entire length of their trail, then a flash and a loud 'pop' that was drowned out by the roar of the landslide as it not only buried their trail but carried part of the mountainside down into a ravine a thousand feet deep. Rocks, boulders, dust, and large drifts of snow roared down with the sound of a hundred battles and the force of a thousand swords.

Meanwhile, on a snow-covered peak, many miles away and of significantly higher elevation, in a loud 'pop' and bright flash of light, they all appeared. Standing on a snow-covered field, feet sinking into the deep white cold, they appeared, standing exactly as they'd stood down on the trail. Quickfoot reeled with dizziness as several of the others also waited for their sense of balance to return.

"Sorry about the vertigo," Sabu apologized, "but we *were* in a hurry."

"It's okay," Bronto said, being the first to recover, "although I think we could all use something to keep us warm now."

"Aerg! It's really c-c-c-cold up here," Quickfoot stuttered with freezing concern.

Frost began forming on their faces as Eldar quickly uncorked his potion, and Candol, touching each person in turn, bestowed the warmth of Indra on them. A quick trip through Sabu's portable portal also produced several furs and winter clothing. Soon they were all bundled up and ready for the cold winds that constantly whipped about their peak.

"Those primitive orkai probably caused that avalanche," Sindar said after he'd finished bundling up. "Apparently the dark hand of Miro reaches even here."

"Well, that little trick of Sabu's probably saved us a rise or two of travel," Lindel finally observed once he was warmer. "How high up are we?"

"About twenty thousand feet or so," Sheil-Bor(h) answered, "and it will soon be cold enough to freeze alcohol."

"The bad news," Bronto said as he came walking up in his three layers of fur, "is what's ahead of us."

They looked in the direction in which Bronto nodded. Ahead of them, beyond this tall peak on which they stood, loomed a large mass of snow-covered mountains, rising higher even than that on which they now stood. Frozen winds whipped around these peaks, peaks that dared to touch the sky. And, rising higher than them all, straight in the path to which they would travel, rose a peak that was twice as high above their own peak as their peak was above the distant sea. A snow-capped glory, it rose majestically in the distance, its top forever lost in the clouds.

"Shakoo; that's got to be the tallest mountain around," Kilgar said with a bit of awe in his voice.

"Just look at it as another frontier to be conquered," Bronto put a hand on Kilgar's shoulder, "a *haik!* to be crossed."

"Actually," Sabu said as he closed up and put away his little portable portal,

"I estimate that peak to be around fifty or sixty thousand feet high; the mountains on Frecaloth are said to reach over a hundred thousand feet high."

"Well, this one's plenty high for me," Shong said. "How are we going to get around that thing?"

"With the grace of Indra," came Candol's immediate reply.

"By perseverance, shall we prevail," was Lorel's reply.

"Oh shut up, the both of you," Mauklo sneered, "and try thinking up something useful instead of religious euphemisms."

"How about another one of those teleports of yours, Sabu?" Quickfoot asked, "A queasy stomach is much better than being frozen food for the dragons around here."

"I would prefer to rest a bit before doing something like that again," Sabu answered. "We were in such a hurry that I didn't have time to use my energy too conservatively, and you guys *do* weigh a bit much, you know."

"But perhaps a simpler spell," Sindar suggested, "maybe one of flight?"

"Not with those winds up there," Sheil-Bor(h) shook his head. "The winds of such high peaks can be fast enough to smash even a Roc upon the mountainside; and cold enough to freeze it solid within a *diidlo*."

"Well then," Lindel said, pointing up, "someone tell *that* thing."

He pointed to what looked to be a tiny dust mote flying around the high peak. Sheil-Bor(h) waved a hand in the air in front of him, and immediately a much closer view of the peak appeared hovering in the air in front of him. They looked at the white-scaled form that they saw flying with ease through the frosty winds; winds that would have torn any other creature up there apart and dashed its bits upon the ice-covered rocks.

"It is a snow dragon," Sheil-Bor(h) answered their unspoken inquiries, "even extreme cold does not bother it."

"Maybe we can go around it, over some other peak," Shong suggested. "It'd add a few more rises to our trip, but Sabu's teleport just saved us a couple of rises anyhow."

"That would sound reasonable," Sabu said thoughtfully, "and there's no reason for us to intrude upon a snow dragon's lair should we not have to."

"Yeah, I guess that would be safer," Eldar said, with mild disappointment.

It was then that Mauklo noticed a far away look upon Sindar's face, as if his mind was letting him see that which normal eyes could not.

"Oh no, I know that look," Mauklo said testily. "He's going to tell us that we *need* to go; for Fate or some such!"

"Now, don't go thinking it's bad news before he's spoken," Eldar admonished. "So what is it Sindar?"

"We have to go up there," Sindar said, as he came out of his trance.

"See, I told you it wouldn't be bad news," Eldar smiled. "I've never climbed up that high before."

"That peak holds something that we need," Sindar continued, "something that *one* of us needs. I can not see anything else."

"Hmm," Sabu pondered, "rather vague. Sheil-Bor(h); how good are your own divinatory abilities?"

Sheil-Bor(h) looked out towards the distant peak, icy wind blowing about his covered head, palms clasping together, as he cast forth his magic into the winds. He started to answer, voice coming out in a monotone, his gaze fixed on that distant peak.

"An item of power, long lost to man but made by his hand," he intoned, "to be used by one of great strength, it must be; power over creatures of great power and nobility. A steady hand does its use await, as against evil does it rate."

He looked away from the peak, down at the others around him.

"That is all I know," he finished, dropping his hands to his sides.

"He *must* be a soothsayer," Bronto chuckled, "because I didn't understand a *word* he said."

"I do not interpret the meaning of what I divine," Sheil-Bor(h) explained with calm patience, "I just tell of what I see that needs be done."

"The mountain peak it is, then," Sabu sighed, "but we still have to plan how best to get up there."

"If you crazies are so *insistent* about getting up there," Mauklo said, raising up a hand as he began an incantation, "then maybe I should do *something*."

He muttered a few magical words under his breath, moving his hand in a few swift but intricate motions. Suddenly, the frosty wind about them dropped down to nothing. Within thirty feet it refused to blow, though outside of the small circle of safety they could see the winds still blowing, taking the snow with it in wispy snowy hands. Mauklo looked up at them with vague smugness on his face.

"Well, I suppose that's part of our problem," Shong observed, and then thumbed in the direction of the tall mountain peak, "but what about climbing that hill over there?"

"I shall invoke the hand of the mighty Indra to catch us should anyone fall," Candol offered, "for if He would have that as our goal, then we must go."

"Let's get going then," Bronto said as he started walking away towards the distant peak.

"I protest," Quickfoot said, pounding his foot on the hard-packed snow. "There's dragons and cold up there, and I hate them both. I refuse to go on!"

"Objection noted," Bronto said, as he came over and casually picked up the small hair-footed one by the back of his neck. "Now come on."

He carried Quickfoot, kicking and screaming, by the back of his neck as they started on along their long icy trek. Across the snow they went, holding close to each other, staying within range of Mauklo's protection from the icy winds. Up the mountain and through the snowy blizzards they traveled, holding on against the cold. But though they had Eldar's potion, Indra's warmth, and several layers of furs wrapped around them, still the cold bit through them like icy needles. Slowly they trudged the deep snowy drifts, going higher and higher still, until they came to where the ice was packed so deep for so long, that it was more like walking on hard dirty ice than on snow.

Treacherous their trail truly was, Bronto's solid frame up front lead them through blinding white blizzards and across icy footholds. Sabu used his staff to maintain his footing, digging it into the ice with each step. Others used their swords or just heavy boots to make it across the slippery surface, while Quickfoot ended up riding atop Bronto's back, and Kilgar tried to prove that he could travel on his own. While the winds did steer around them, leaving them with nary a breeze to blow in their faces, the ground was still icy and the air cold. All it would take is for but one person to slip, sliding out of range of Mauklo's windy protection, to be at the mercy of the frozen winds, now blowing like a constant low-grade hurricane.

A seemingly endless amount of up and down travel finally brought them to the base of that immense peak, soaring fully thirty thousand feet or more above their heads, its wide base now being farther around then one could travel in an entire *kev* were it *not* snowing. They looked up at the mountain that they must climb.

"By the beard of Indra, that peak just keeps getting taller."

"And c-c-c-colder too," Quickfoot shivered from atop Bronto.

"Naw," Eldar said dismissively, "Indra probably doesn't even *have* a beard."

"We'll need ropes and climbing sticks," Shong said, getting down to the practical aspects of the matter. "If we tie ourselves to each other in a line then we should be able to make it."

"Do we *have* to climb that thing?" Quickfoot moaned.

"Why don't we just leave the little one behind in that little portable portal of yours?" Lorel asked.

"Yes!" Quickfoot jumped at the idea. "Then I can see how Blag-ak is doing with his eggs. He probably has the whole island messed up."

"Now, that's not a bad idea," Eldar said, an idea dawning on his face, "the weaker among us could just sit it out back at the island, letting the rest do the climbing for them. Then, just open up Sabu's portal when we get up there."

"And you would be among the one's staying on the island?" Mauklo said almost pleasantly.

"Are you kidding?" Eldar said in shock. "I wouldn't *miss* climbing something like this!"

"It would seem a practical solution," Lorel said, "Quickfoot, the boy, and our priest could wait back on the island with half of our mages, while the rest of us climb on up with our greater strength and courage. Definitely a plan to ensure the survival of our weaker members."

"Are you saying," Kilgar said, suddenly holding a curved knife to Lorel's groin area, as he tried not to shiver, "that I'm weak and scared? I'm nine; I'm not a little boy anymore."

Lorel looked down at the knife threatening to spill out his manhood all over the ground, unsure of what to do.

"I merely seek to protect the lives of women and children," Lorel tried rephrasing.

The knife got closer.

"It's a good thing that Kilinir isn't here," Mauklo grinned, "or she'd have thrown you over the mountainside with that 'women' remark."

"You haven't been with us too long," Bronto smiled. "Kilgar can handle himself as well as anyone. We've learned not to underestimate him. That's something you don't do with *any* Destir."

"I see," Lorel looked at the serious expression on the young boy's face, and then at that of those around him. "Then just the small one, the priest, and——"

"You *don't* want to get into that," Candol interrupted.

"Actually," Sabu stopped the exchange, "the only one who's bound to want to stay on the island is Quickfoot. But, if he wants to, I can slip him through the portal before we go on."

Eagerness was on Quickfoot's face as he looked around at the faces of those around him. Disappointment registered on every face his eyes met. Disappointment and condensation.

"But that mountain's fifty thousand feet high," he protested, "and with dragons!"

"It's okay," Candol patted him on the head, "we understand if you don't have faith in either Indra or your companions. It is only the very few that can make such a journey."

"But-," Quickfoot began doubtfully. "Can any of you bright mages here guarantee a little safety? Otherwise, this is insane!"

"There would be an awful lot of opportunity for one to slide down a four-mile slope," Lindel pointed out, "We must prepare for this climb, or Quickfoot's fears could turn out to be prophetic."

"Perhaps I can be of assistance," Sheil-Bor(h) suggested humbly. "I know of a spell that can make one nearly weightless. Then, if everyone is tied together, should the worst happen, the lead person may still support our combined weight."

"We would still need enough traction against all that ice up there," Sabu pondered.

"Wait a *tid*," Eldar said, a thoughtful look on his face. "Isn't ice and snow just frozen water?"

"Of course," Sabu answered, "Why?"

Eldar grinned, then held out his sword. He waved it about in front of him in a grand sweeping motion. As he did so, a watery-colored gem on its hilt glowed brightly, causing the sword to glow a dim watery blue. The blue glow seemed to fall lightly to the ground, like raindrops of light, absorbing into the snow as they plopped down upon it. With each such drop of light, the snow and ice under Eldar's feet seemed to get a rougher look to it, looking kind of like frozen sandpaper.

"Consider our traction problem solved," Eldar smiled.

"Of course," Sabu slapped himself in the forehead, "the Water Gems. We've more than enough of those to cover us for the entire slope. All we need now is the rope."

"Allow me," Sindar said, raising up a hand to invoke a spell.

He gave a few quick snaps of his wrist and a couple of quick words. Moments later, there was a brief flash of light around everyone's waist. When they looked down, they saw that they were all connected at the waist by bands of light wrapping around them. All in a single line, Bronto at one end, Shong at the other, Quickfoot in the very middle.

"A variation on my light-bridge spell," Sindar explained, "but I can rearrange our order if you like."

"Let's start climbing then," Bronto said.

"You may have need of these first," Sheil-Bor(h) interrupted.

He gestured to the ground and concentrated. Bronto watched as a rock outcropping reshaped itself into a number of short thick metal spikes, a pick-headed hammer, and some lengths of rope.

"Good enough," the big man said as he picked up the gear, sticking it in various places around his belt, "let's go."

They started climbing up the mountain, occasional blue glows lighting the path beneath their feet as someone would use one of the Water Gems to put more traction beneath them. At first they walked steadily on up the icy slope, Bronto using his large sword as a staff to dig into the ground. But then the slope got steeper, forcing them to climb, Bronto using the pick-hammer and metal spikes that Sheil-Bor(h) had produced for him. Up they climbed, the frozen winds parting around Mauklo's shield, the snow and ice rough beneath their feet. Cold, such as no one there had felt before, started to creep through their furs, potions, and spells. Ice formed about their gloves and faces as they climbed single-file up the slope. But, always Bronto's strength kept pulling them up, while Shong was the physical and emotion anchor at their rear. Over ice-covered boulders the size of a small house, around cliff-like ledges, and through blinding snow flurries.

Then a third of the way up the mountain is when the tough climb really started.

A continual icy blizzard blew straight down from the top of the mountain, riding along the edge of the slope, carrying with it great gusts of snow and sleet. As well, the angle of their climb then steepened; they often found themselves climbing up a sixty-degree slope, sometimes almost straight up, Bronto climbing one slow handhold and iron spike at a time, the others dangling by Sindar's light-chain in midair below him. The wind blew down with a force that would have ripped loose their grips were it not for Mauklo's shield.

Quickfoot whimpered through most of the long climb, while Kilgar tried his best to push his half-grown body to the task. Time, though, soon found them with Kilgar clinging to the back of Bronto, while Quickfoot clung atop Lorel. The mages amongst them also found it hard, unused to such extreme physical exertion as they were, the edges of their robes sticking out from under all their thick layers of fur as they tried their best to keep up.

On more than a few occasions did someone slip, sometimes taking others with him, to go dangling out over a drop that was now lost in the clouds below. But always did Bronto's strength keep him pinned to the mountainside like he was part of it, allowing the others to regain their footing. Up they went, the winds forming an almost solid icy shell around the outside of Mauklo's barrier.

Climb, rest, and then climb some more; that was their life, sometimes just resting as they hung there in mid-climb, strung out along down the slope, passing rations down to one another as needed. At night would they rest, huddled upon a frozen ledge that neither plant nor animal would ever think of calling home. The break of dawn would see them climbing once again. Up through air so cold they each thought they might break if someone would just but hit them.

On occasion the constant blizzard might clear, allowing them a look at the icy world below them. All around this tall peak lay a ring of other peaks, far below them now. But this outer ring of peaks was tall in itself; thirty thousand feet in height worth of icy gloom, but dwarfed now by the climb they were still making.

They concentrated just on climbing upwards, always up; the slope was their world. Even thoughts of snow dragons left their minds as they just put their combined concentrations in each successive step. Sometimes it would take them an entire *nev* just to climb a few short feet. Rise after rise passed, the snowy winds even howling past them in their dreams, like icy hands come out to pluck at them. Time seemed to stretch to infinity.

Soon they could look down and see nothing but arctic clouds, not even the other tall peaks surrounding them being visible. The world was made of ice and slow white winds.

So it went. So involved were they with scaling such an impossible mountain, that not even Sindar's mind-sense warned them of the sudden danger that flew down upon them. A blast of sudden frosty cold cut through Mauklo's shield, almost freezing Quickfoot, Kilgar, and Candol solid. The blast completely collapsed Mauklo's shield, sending a sudden burst of arctic gale winds rushing down through their line. Wind with enough force to send most of them sailing out into the open air, fluttering like the tail of a kite as their chain of light held onto Bronto.

Bronto anchored himself to the ground, as the others fluttered behind him, the wind whipping them about like some dangling toy. Quickfoot's scream was lost to the blizzard, while Kilgar clung desperately to Bronto's back. Obscuring snow surrounded them.

"What was that?!" Kilgar shouted into Bronto's ear.

"I'm not sure!" he shouted back against the wind. "But it may have had something to do with that!"

He nodded in a direction off into the white air around over them. Kilgar looked into the wind, squinting his eyes against the glare of the frigid wind. In the midst of the flying ice and snow, he could just make out a large winged shape, its white coloring being almost one with the whiteness around it as it winged its way up and around.

"A snow dragon?" Kilgar shouted back.

"Yes!" Bronto shouted back. "And it's coming for us!"

Sabu watched the distant ground sail back and forth beneath him, as he fluttered helplessly in the wind. He found it rather difficult to concentrate on a spell while the wind froze off his eyebrows and tossed him around so violently. Twice he was almost dashed upon the mountainside, only to be sailed back out in time by the frigid winds. The others were just as helpless, as the winds tossed them about like leaves.

Sindar tried to concentrate, closing his eyes against the violent turbulence about him. He opened his mind to the others, now their only communication against the angry winds.

We shall be either dashed against the rocks, he thought out to everyone as he rocked through the air, *or frozen within moments by this blizzard. We must do something.*

We've got another problem, he picked out from Bronto's mind, *that was a snow dragon that blasted Mauklo's shield, and it's still here.*

Mauklo, Sindar thought out, *how soon can you put your shield back up?*

If the wind would just stop moving, Mauklo answered, *then but a few moments. But that dragon will just blow it down again.*

It's coming, came Kilgar's own thoughts, *it's heading straight for me and Bronto.*

They watched a large white shape fly effortlessly through the hurricane-force winds, angling in for the large man that was their only anchor against a fast drop of several miles.

I have an idea, Bronto thought out suddenly, *Mauklo, form your barrier as a cushion of air around everyone but me; so none of you will get smashed into the rocks.*

Fine by me, Mauklo thought back.

Mauklo's words of incantation were lost in the fierce winds, but their power still took hold, as wind seemed to circled around them like large cottony hands, bracing against impact.

Sindar, Bronto continued, *extend my light rope by several feet. I want a lasso with at least an extra twenty-five feet of length.*

Oh, this *sounds fun,* came Eldar's merry thought.

AAAAAAAAAAAAAAAAAAAA, was all that came through from Quickfoot's mind.

Someone shut that hairy-toed pest up! came Mauklo's mind-shout as he finished his spell.

Bronto's chain of light suddenly lengthened itself, the extra length lying coiled in front of him, its end in a wide loop. He plunged his right hand into solid rock, smashing through it like paper, as an anchor against the winds, and grabbed up the extra length of light-rope with his other hand.

"Hang on kid," he shouted back to Kilgar.

Kilgar ducked his head down behind Bronto as he clung onto his waist, his own light-band tethering him securely around the big man. Bronto began to swing the light lasso around over his head, its length seeming to be unaffected by the snowy gale blowing through it. The snow was blinding, the wind whipping around from all directions.

Suddenly, a large white reptilian face came right out of the blizzard, appearing as by magic. The snow dragon barreled down on them, large toothy maw open as it breathed out a second gust of frozen air. The white bolt pierced through the whiteness like a lit beacon through the night. Bronto braced himself for the impact, his one hand still held aloft while it swung the light lasso around.

The bolt hit with the force of a large frozen hammer, hitting him full in the face, as he used his own body to try and shield Kilgar from its effects. The blast crystallized the bulk of Bronto's furry coverings into icy bits blown into the winds, while the rocks around him were pounded into icy sand. The force threw him from the mountainside, as the rock in which he'd imbedded his hand was blasted into frozen bits by the cold force of the dragon's breath. Just as Bronto was sent sailing out into the air, he threw his lasso of light.

The wind tossed him far out into the air, the chain of light taking the others with him. Like a whip they cracked through the air, Shong and Lindel at its tail being cracked up against the mountainside. But, just as they saw the icy rocks get nearer, hurtling towards it with more than enough force to reduce them to a bloody mass, they bounced back, cushioned by Mauklo's cushion of air. Thus were the others braced against their wild ride, Mauklo's air cushions protecting them against the worst of their tumbling, but not from any nausea that it may have caused.

As Quickfoot proved, by heaving up quickly-frozen bits of his last lunch out into the air and all over Lorel.

Bronto was the only one not cushioned, as he went plummeting swiftly downward. He screamed defiance into the wind as he plummeted on towards the frozen depths far below.

But suddenly, his descent stopped with a jerk. The line of light on which he held grew taught, as he put both hands to holding it.

"Ha!" he shouted into the wind. "Got you!"

He started to slowly climb up the rope, hand over hand. The rope changed directions in sudden movements, but Bronto would not be deterred. He climbed up through the wind, dangling miles above any ground, climbing through the air. Kilgar looked up to see by what magic this strange rope hung in the air.

The whiteness cleared as they climbed up, at least enough for the boy to see what they climbed towards.

The lasso end of the light rope was looped firmly around the snow dragon's mouth. The weight of Bronto and the others kept it tightly closed, as it tried to claw at the ephemeral length, but light doesn't give way easily to that born of mere matter, even that of a dragon. The beast glared down at Bronto, flexing its claws as if it would go after him instead.

Bronto stopped his assent when he was just out of reach of the dragon's claws. Then, he started to swing, back and forth, at the end of the light rope.

Hang on, he thought along Sindar's still-open mental channel, *this is going to be the difficult part.*

Did he say this *is the difficult part?* Quickfoot's mind wailed.

Like a pendulum, he swung back and forth, his arc getting wider and wider, the dragon trying vainly to claw at him. The winds whipped around him, threatening to freeze him solid, now that the bulk of his furs were gone. The dragon started to dive towards one of the peak's cliffs, aiming itself so as to catch Bronto hard up against the rocky surface. Bronto arced high, back towards the creature's tail, and then came back down and around towards its head. Just as he got near the top of his arc, in a sudden lurch, he swung his legs forward with the full force of his great strength. The dragon swooped on down towards the cliff.

Bronto's mighty form slowly swung up, the force of his sudden push taking his trail of friends with him. He arced slowly up over the dragon's head, the others behind him following along like a long slow whip cracking out behind him. He might not have quite made it over, were it not for the dragon's own swift flight; its rapid forward motion succeeded in suddenly whipping Bronto back over its back, carrying the others along with him just as the dragon swooped down a few scant feet above the rocks.

The dragon soared upwards, a light trail of people dangling from behind it like an extra tail. Shong cracked down, like the end of the whip, coming down fast towards the rocks. But again, Mauklo's windy cushion held, as he bounced harmlessly off its surface.

The dragon felt a lurch on the back of its neck, like a weight suddenly landing there. It tossed its head back and forth.

From where he rode, atop the dragon's neck, Bronto pulled tight on the loop of light encircling the dragon's mouth. Like some large mount, he reigned it upward. Kilgar clung to the big man's back, as the rope of light trailed behind them. He held onto the rope with one hand, his strong legs squeezing tight against the scaled neck. With his free hand, he patted the beast's long neck.

"Okay there fella," he shouted, "you be nice and give us a ride to the top of this mountain, and I'll give you a reward afterwards. What do dragons like?"

Several shouts came from behind them, as fists were raised in triumph, with several shouts of *ka'ru* piercing through the noisy gale. With a motion of his fingers, Sindar shortened the length on his line of light, bringing each person in turn within reach of climbing onto the dragon's long white back.

"I *knew* this was going to be a fun ride!" Eldar exclaimed as he climbed on board, "Lassoing a dragon in flight. Yes!"

Quickfoot just whimpered.

"I don't suppose that anyone can speak with dragons?" Sindar asked, as he sat down upon its back.

"It's okay," Bronto said, "I think me and him understand each other pretty good. It's a magnificent creature, really."

He patted it on the neck, as if to show there were no hard feelings. The dragon responded with a toss of its head.

"Now," Bronto ordered, "to the top of this mountain!"

Up they flew, soaring through frozen heights that would have taken them another *kev* to scale, assuming no mishaps. They clung to the dragon's back as Bronto guided it up through frozen gales, into icy clouds, and past a long and treacherous rock climb that they now would not have to make. Eldar shouted into the wind, his silver hair blowing back, as their winged mount carried them aloft.

"This is what I call a ride!" Eldar shouted out.

"A finer mount have I've never ridden," Bronto shouted jovially. "But Lindel, you appear to be the expert with such creatures, of what would a snow dragon need that I could repay it with?"

"You would *reward* this creature?" Mauklo asked, disbelievingly. "It tried to kill us! If you have mastered it, then keep it enslaved and dispose of it when it's no longer useful."

"I would expect you to say something like that," Candol said to Mauklo. "Dragons are still intelligent creatures in the eyes of Indra."

"Your point?" Mauklo asked with honest puzzlement.

"I know of dragons that dwell in the forest," Lindel answered Bronto, "but of those of the frozen heights, I know naught."

"I know a little of such beasts," Sheil-Bor(h) volunteered. "It is said that they eat crystalline forms: gems, and the like; especially snow-tear diamonds. They consider them a delicacy."

"They *eat* gems," Quickfoot responded in horror, "how can they eat money?"

"To them it is food," Sheil-Bor(h) answered.

"Well, gems it is then," Bronto said as he held tight onto the light-reigns, "and a royal feast shall he have!"

"Not out of *my* share he won't!" Quickfoot exclaimed.

"Don't worry, small one," Bronto reassured, "mine shall be the only pocket that it comes out of. It's only right. After all, we *did* invade its territory, and I *did* force us upon it. I would gladly repay such a noble creature!"

"Creatures of great power and nobility," Sabu muttered to himself, "and one of great strength. Hmm."

The snow dragon finally rose to the very top of the fifty-thousand-foot peak, landing on a wide frozen ledge near its large top. Bronto held tight onto the reigns while the others slid off, holding the dragon steady as it tried to toss its head back and forth and snap its jaws.

"I never want to play crack-the-whip with a dragon again," Quickfoot moaned as he staggered down off the dragon, almost collapsing to the ground when he was several feet away from the head of the beast.

"And I never want to get vomited on in such cold," Lorel commented as he brushed the last few frozen bits of Quickfoot's puke off his furs. "It's somewhat akin to shrapnel."

Bronto was the last to get off, taking a large pouch out from his belt as he slid off. The pouch he tossed down in front of the snow dragon, large gems spilling out at the creature's feet.

"There my fine scaled friend," he said, patting it on the neck, as icy winds whipped around him. "I'd give you more if I had it. I hope it makes up for our intrusion through your domain. Sindar, unleash it."

"Are you crazy?!" Quickfoot exclaimed, ducking back behind Candol.

Sindar snapped his fingers, the rope of light disappearing in a flash. Everyone stepped back, ready for an attack from the large creature, except for Bronto. He just stood there, hands on hips, grinning up at it. The dragon looked down at the gems, sniffing at them the way a dog would his food. Its long tongue licked in and out, tasting the valuable crystals. Then, it finally reach out with its mouth, and in a single bite, scooped up both the gems and some of the rock underneath them. Quickfoot cringed as it crunched down on the gems, reducing a fortune to crushed bits within moments. It swallowed and then looked up at Bronto, regarding him.

"You're free to go, my white-scaled friend," Bronto said as he backed up to join the others, "no obligation for the gems."

It looked at Bronto a bit more, staring at him eye to eye. Then, with a single flap of its large wings, it leapt off the immense ledge and flew out of sight.

"I guess you have a way with dragons," Eldar slapped him on the back. "Who needs the Dragon Lord for dealing with dragons!"

"Well, where to now?" Kilgar asked.

"How's about that cave over there?"

Lindel was pointing towards the very rear of the ledge they were standing on. Sure enough, there where the ledge met the mountain, was a large cave mouth, opening out onto the icy ledge, snow all but covering the front of it. Gale-force winds whipped around the ledge as they regarded the cave.

"Any port in a storm," Bronto shouted above the wind, "come on!"

They trudged their way to the cave, hanging on to each other so as not to get blown off the large ledge. Eldar used his Water Gem to once again roughen up the ice beneath their feet, lest anyone slide off. Then, one by one, they made their way into the cave.

The walls were frozen eddies of color: blues, greens, reds, and some ultraviolets, swirling out along the walls, ceiling, and floor of the cave, their source lying frozen beneath the smooth covering of ice that permeated the entire cavern. Ten-foot long icicles hung from the top of the fifty-foot high ceiling, as frozen rock outcroppings littered the large floor. A dim light reflected throughout the cavern, reflected and colored by the painted walls, like several different colored mirrors flickering their message along.

"Shakoo," Eldar exclaimed quietly, as Lindel readied his bow.

The curved entrance to the cave completely sheltered the inside from the freezing gale outside. All they could hear was a distant, almost melodic, echo of the freezing death. The air was even warmer in here, as several of the companions found themselves thawing out.

"Someone lives here," Sindar said as they carefully walked along, "I can feel it."

They rounded a bend in the cavern, as it opened up to the main bulk of its size. It was there that they could see how truly large it was. The cavern sloped down to a floor ten feet below them, its length stretching on for hundreds of feet. Ledges of rock and ice adorned the upper sides of the walls, like natural catwalks. Large multicolored icicles caught the light, acting like strange icy lanterns hanging from the ceiling. A large rocky mound lay to one side of the far end of the cavern, while beside it lay a glittering pile of gems and shiny weapons.

It was from a few of these weapons, one large sword in particular, that the cavern's light emanated.

"Money!" Quickfoot happily exclaimed, as he tried climbing down the ten-foot drop to the main floor.

"We came all the way up here, just for a bunch of old gems?" Mauklo asked, exasperated.

"Those weapons must be left over from the armories of the old Kingdoms," Sheil-Bor(h) pondered, "but what are they doing up here?"

"Some of the weapons look to be in pretty good repair," Shong noticed, "perhaps we can find some better swords among them."

"I see one I like," Bronto pointed.

Sticking up in the center of the pile, emitting the brightest light of all the others, was a single large sword, point imbedded into the pile of gems, hilt pointed towards the ceiling. Even from this distance, they could see that its gleaming hilt was carved in the shape of an ornate dragon's head. The gems around it reflected and magnified its glow, turning it into a large beacon with which to light up the whole cavern. Shong gave a long low whistle in appreciation.

"That's one *nice* sword," he agreed.

Quickfoot finally plopped down to the ground, and started to scamper across the main floor towards the large glittering pile.

"Wait!" Sindar shouted out to the small one. "The rocky mound—it's alive!"

Quickfoot stopped, halfway across the cavern. He turned around, putting his hands on his hips, his face looking mildly angry, as if he were about to scold a small child.

"Oh come on," he said, "rocks aren't alive. You're just trying to get first pick at this treasure. Just trying to trick poor old Quickfoot."

It was then that he noticed the others were staring beyond him, drawing swords, with Sindar calmly pointing behind him. Doubt suddenly washed over him, along with an unexplained fear. He swallowed a lump in his throat and slowly turned around.

The large rocky mound had grown a pair of rather large eyes, and was staring straight at him.

Quickfoot's legs shook in their fur-covered wrappings, followed quickly by the rest of his body. The power of speech seemed to leave him, as he stuttered and stammered in a vain attempt to speak.

The rocky mound raised up its large triangular-shaped head, small rocky wings unfolding out from along its sides. A long tail uncurled from around its body as it stretched out its four large legs.

"D-D-D-D—" Quickfoot started to say, "D-D-D-D—"

"It's probably been here for a long time," Sabu said calmly to Sindar, pointing, "look at those wings."

"Yes," Sindar agreed, just as calm, "much too atrophied to use in flight anymore."

"Dragon!" Quickfoot finally finished.

The dragon heaved in a large lung-full of breath, as it reared up its stone-like neck, pointing its large toothy mouth down at Quickfoot. Quickfoot stood paralyzed with fear, unable to move his feet, unable to do anything but stammer as the dragon's will locked him into place.

The dragon breathed out a large gout of flame. Quickfoot watched it come straight at him.

Suddenly, the small one found himself flying back through the air, watching as the cavern and the ball of fire quickly receded from in front of him. The ball of flame exploded on the ground that he'd been standing on, sending out great globs of flaming liquid, sticking on the ground and surrounding rocks as it continued to burn.

Quickfoot found himself landing beside Sindar, the latter's psychic powers plopping the small one down gently by his side. Quickfoot looked on at the flaming floor as he slowly began to come out of his initial shock.

"Next time," Sindar admonished, "you'll wait."

The dragon turned its large stone-like head in their direction. When it opened its mouth to speak, a voice sounding like small boulders grinding together came out.

"Why do you intrude upon the lair of Saknoth The Invulnerable?"

The cavern shook with the rumble of its voice, the repeated echoes adding to its deep reverberation. Its look wasn't so much that of anger as it was annoyance; the same way a man might be annoyed by an ant crawling up his leg. Bronto came a step forward on their ledge to speak.

Lorel was staring at the flames.

"Friend dragon," the big man rumbled, "we are merely passing through these mountains, searching for the lost city of Thïr Tÿorca. We would wish no harm upon the noble breed of dragons along our way."

"No one just passes through at *this* height!" it roared. "You come for my treasure!"

"I assure you that—" Bronto began.

"You said yourself," Saknoth continued, anger now in its voice, "you seek Thïr Tÿorca. *This* horde is from that place! And it's mine!"

"That's fine by me," Quickfoot said quickly, as he scampered around behind Sindar.

"We appear to have a rather possessive dragon," Eldar observed.

"If that stuff is from Thïr Tÿorca…," Sabu pondered to himself.

"We'll leave if you want," Shong suggested with a shrug.

"You have hungered me now," Saknoth rumbled as it stretched, "you will be my supper."

"And if we object?" Eldar asked, his sword in his hand.

"There is no way down from here, except by flying," Saknoth answered, "and the other dragons will not cross my will. Now, who's first?"

"Uh oh," Lindel said with a bit of a groan, "it looks like we'll have to kill this one."

"But, I'm beginning to *like* dragons," Bronto sighed.

"Not this kind," Lindel assured him. "If a dragon is strong enough of will, it will sometimes dominate other lesser dragons, forcing them to perform its needs."

"Kind of like a king," Shong suggested.

"Yes, but this one's also old and bitter," Lindel went on quickly. "It happens sometimes when it's enough of a recluse; a sort of a dragon insanity."

"Then we'll just leave it, right?" Quickfoot asked hopefully.

"I am afraid not," Sheil-Bor(h) shook his head. "Remember, these are called the *Dragon* Mountains. If that creature is dominating the others, then we will never make it out of these mountains alive."

"A dragon enslaving other dragons," Bronto said a bit angrily as he drew out his big sword.

A sudden fiery explosion interrupted their little discussion. They looked up to see the whole area of the ground in front of them pasted with small mounds of sticky flaming liquid, the bulk of it having splashed back away from them. A fiery shield stood between themselves and Saknoth, the apparent source of their protection from the dragon's breath. Mauklo was standing in the middle of the large fiery shield, flame roaring up around him, his Fire Hevon Gem glowing a bright red.

"If you are all finished with your intellectual discourse," he said testily, "I *think* it wants to kill us!"

"Right!"

Bronto was already jumping down to the main floor before he'd finished that one word. Waving his large sword overhead, he charged up towards the dragon. A bolt of white flame shot out as Candol pointed a hand out at the creature, combining his priestly magic with that of the Fire Gem. Sheil-Bor(h) raised up both his hands, muttering quick magic phrases to himself, as he sent down a rain of large heavy metal spikes upon the dragon. Sabu and Sindar both linked their powers together, sending a bolt of electricity towards it, instantly ionizing the air as it went swiftly along. Seeing the bolt of lightning, Eldar gleefully sent out a bolt of water from his sword, aiming it to hit the dragon just when the lightning did.

The bolt of white flame hit, blasting rock around it, reducing some of the gems to charred bits. A rain of a hundred heavy sharp spikes landed down upon its hide, hitting with the sound of a thousand steel bolts cutting through rock. The bolt of lightning hit with the thunder of a Funnel Storm, just as the stream of water struck it full in the face, sending electricity arcing over that entire side of the cavern. Bronto ran up to hit, swung back his sword, and hit it with the full might of his great strength, hitting with enough force to cleave through granite.

Saknoth just stood there and blinked at them, not even scratched save for a small bruise on its nose. It then swiped a rock-hard claw at Bronto, tossing him back across the cavern, smashing him into the icy colored walls behind them. Shong dove aside as his friend passed within inches of his head. Several large cracks exploded through the ice around Bronto, radiating out from him like a fan. Saknoth laughed.

"Well, now we know why he calls himself Saknoth The *Invulnerable*," Eldar stated the obvious.

Shong and Kilgar ran over to the imbedded form of Bronto, as the creature glared down at them.

"So much for your strong man," Saknoth said, "now for the rest of you."

Saknoth heaved out a wall of liquid flame, filling the cavern as it raced towards them. It blasted through Mauklo's shield of fire, sending liquid fire down upon them all.

Quickfoot rolled along the ground screaming, as he tried to douse the flames on his body, while Lindel turned his back to the flames, trying to shield his precious bow. Candol, Sabu, and Sindar dived aside, taking refuge behind a large rock, as the fiery liquid sprayed everywhere. Mauklo was flung to the ground, flaming from head to toe, but it was his own flame that still burned about him, protecting him from the flaming liquid as it passed over. Sheil-Bor(h) dived quickly to the ground, flattening himself face-down, as the fire passed by overhead. Using his sword, Eldar poked at a bit of flaming goo on the outside of their rock.

"Hey, this stuff's some kind of thick liquid," he said, a bit surprised.

"Yes, not your ordinary dragon's breath," Sabu nodded. "This stuff will stick to you and keep on burning. A rather ingenious adaptation."

"But it *is* liquid," Eldar said, as he stood up.

As he held his sword, the watery-colored gem on its hilt began to glow. As it did so, a slick watery film seemed to ooze out from it and cover his body.

"And what's made of liquid," he continued, "can *slide off!*"

"He does seem to get flashes of genuine intelligence at times," Sindar commented.

"Apparently," Sabu agreed.

"What do you mean 'at times'," Eldar said, somewhat miffed.

"Now all we need is a distraction," Sabu said, as he, Sindar, and Candol repeated Eldar's act with their own Water Gems.

It was then that they heard an insane scream, as a small flaming figure came leaping over them, blue steel sword in hand, out towards Saknoth. It screamed its battle cry of pain and pleasure as it sailed towards the beast.

"I do believe that Schanter is developing a certain amount of timing," Sindar commented as he watched the small wrinkled form shoot by overhead like a flaming comet, fiery goo sticking to his warty leathery hide.

Lindel came rolling towards them along the ground, trying to douse the flames on his back as he made his way towards them. In the distance, Quickfoot was still screaming as the hair on his feet caught fire.

"Allow me," Candol said, rising up, "the rest of you figure out a way to take care of Saknoth."

Candol walked out from behind the rocks, while Eldar tried to help Lindel with the flames. The priest walked out into the open, burning bits all around him, Quickfoot on fire, Mauklo battling his own flames, Kilgar and Shong near the bend at the cave's entrance as they tried to help Bronto. Candol raised up both his arms and looked ceiling-ward, just as Schanter landed on Saknoth's head and began stabbing frantically at its nose and stone-like head ridge.

"By the Power of Indra!"

A small watery form glowed upon his forehead as an aura of light covered his body...

"By the power of Schanter, by the power of Schanter," a demented voice rapidly echoed, as the insane-one continued to stab down at the huge nose, "by the power of Schanter!"

...Suddenly, a wall of water exploded out from Candol's body, filling the whole upper part of the cavern. Flames were doused as everyone and everything was soaked from head to toe. He then pushed his wall of water outward, until it formed a barrier between them and the main floor of the cavern.

"A bit drippy, but effective," Eldar said to Lindel, his silvery hair now coming down in wet strands. "Are you all right?"

Lindel sputtered out a lungfull of water as he grabbed his still-intact bow and sat up.

"Yeah," he said, "I'll be fine. But, I noticed something about that dragon."

"What?" Sabu asked, as he and Sindar gathered around the elf.

A scream, like unto the sound an avalanche makes, filled the cavern as Saknoth tossed back his head. They looked up and saw, through Candol's wall of water, Schanter atop Saknoth's head, painful flames still dancing on his body, as he stabbed at the dragon's large nose. A large bruise was forming where Schanter stabbed.

"That confirms it," Lindel said, as he checked out his bow. "I noticed that after all we threw at him, only his nose got so much as bruised; the rest was like solid rock."

"A weak spot," Sindar nodded.

"Wacko over there just verified it," Lindel continued, "but Schanter's still just an annoyance to him."

"It's like stabbing rock," Sabu said, "a softer rock, but rock nonetheless. We need something harder."

"So, what do we do?" Lindel asked.

"We punch him in the nose, of course," Eldar smiled. "Give me your best arrow."

Schanter came flying back through the air, tossed back by a swipe of Saknoth's large paw. He bounced off a rock and landed upon the ground with a soft thud, flames finally going out as he passed through Candol's large wall of water. Saknoth looked up at the wall of water, anger and contempt on his stony wedge-shaped face.

"Looks like we've run out of time," Sindar said, looking up.

"FOR THAT INSULT, YOU ALL SHALL PAY!!!"

The roar from Saknoth was loud and deafening, sending a few of the ten-foot long icicles plunging down towards the ground. Quickfoot sat up just in time to see a large one coming down straight for him. He rolled aside as it came crashing down, heading for cover behind Candol's robes.

"I wish there was a way to enslave that fine beast," Mauklo said as, flames now gone from about his body, he came up next to Candol, "but I'm afraid that's just not possible now."

"Come to help?" Candol asked, arms still raised to keep up the wall of water.

"Something like that," Mauklo said, as he thrust out a hand in the direction of the dragon, focusing his magical energy through that hand.

Saknoth gave another roar and breathed out another belch. This one impacted against the wall of water, turning it instantly to steam. It looked up through the superheated steam and rose fully upon all four legs.

It started walking toward them, each step a rumble.

Mauklo's beam passed on by it, missing it completely, as it landed behind it.

"I'm afraid that you missed it," Candol observed.

"That depends on what I was aiming for," Mauklo smiled.

Saknoth reared up, opening wide its toothy maw, as if ready to pounce upon them all.

A large icy boulder came plunging through the air, landing full in its mouth, hitting with force enough to send Saknoth reeling backwards with an earth-shaking crash. It crunched the boulder to bits between its teeth, as it tried to right itself on its feet.

"WHO DARES!"

"I dare!"

At the back of the cavern, standing in front of a cracked wall with a man-shaped imprint in its ice, stood the large form of Bronto, Shong standing to his right, Kilgar to his left. No sword did he hold, just his hands did he have as weapons.

"YOU SHOULD BE DEAD! I CRUSHED YOU!!"

"Okay, we got some time," Sabu said, "Quickly now."

"This is my best arrow," Lindel said, pulling out a long steel shaft, "made by an ancestor of mine. I was saving it for something really tough."

Lindel handed the arrow to Eldar, as Bronto walked across the open part of the upper cavern.

"No little love-tap like that is going to keep me down," Bronto laughed, "I faced a Lesser Son of Traugh. You'll have to do a lot better than that!"

Mauklo left the open area between Bronto and the dragon, taking Candol with him, as he guided him over to where Sabu and the others were hiding. Quickfoot scampered in behind them.

They arrived to see Sabu, Eldar, and Sindar, each concentrating their magic over the single arrow, weaving complex spells, to store them about the very point of the arrow head.

"Just in time," Eldar said, looking up. "Put what spells that you can upon this arrow. We're going to punch it in the nose."

"I hope you mean that figuratively and not just literally," Mauklo sneered.

"Both," Eldar answered simply.

Mauklo sighed as they went swiftly about their work.

Another rock went sailing through the air, but this time Saknoth batted it out of the way like a toy ball, sending its rubble flying out in all directions.

"Kilgar," Bronto shouted out behind him, "you and Shong get over with the others; if I know Sabu and Sindar, they've got something planned by now, and they're going to need someone to guard their rear while they do it."

Kilgar just nodded acknowledgment as both he and Shong ran over to the others. Bronto faced back towards Saknoth, advancing towards the edge of the ledge as trickles of water sluiced over its edge like a small waterfall and steam fogged the air.

"I bestow the blessing of Indra upon this arrow," Candol was saying when Kilgar and Shong arrived, "may it aim straight and true."

"Schanter bless too...," a weak voice mumbled from one corner of the cavern before passing out.

"Bronto says you might have something planned," Shong said as he squatted down beside the rest.

"*I'll* say we've got something," Eldar said enthusiastically.

"That man sure has a lot of faith in us," Sabu commented as he finished his own spell.

"Well, I hope it's justified," Kilgar said, fingering his own dagger, "'cause he's out there facing off that beast, and he knows he can't win."

"There," Mauklo said, finishing up his own spell, "I've put in what I could."

The arrow was now glowing a bright blue light; bright enough to light up their entire corner of the cavern.

"There is now," Sindar said, carefully handing the arrow back to Lindel, "enough magical firepower in that single arrow to level half of this peak. It will detonate upon impact, but you only get the one shot."

"That'll be enough," Lindel said confidently, "that spot on his nose is only as small as my fist; I can hit that from a hundred yards away."

"Well, you're going to get a whole lot closer than that," Sabu said, as Lindel stood up. "Mauklo, ready one of your shields around us."

A few gestures from Mauklo produced a shimmering field of light about them. Beyond them Bronto was busy, now dodging swipes at him by Saknoth's large stone claws.

"What about Bronto?" Kilgar asked.

"We'll get him out at the same time as we move Lindel out from in front of it," Eldar said.

"What do you mean 'in front of it'?" Lindel asked, the arrow half notched.

"Oh, didn't we tell you?" Eldar grinned. "You'll be shooting that thing from point blank range."

"Great," Lindel said slowly, as he rolled his eyes, "I just love this silent communication thing that you three have going."

Bronto dodged another swipe from Saknoth just as Lorel came stumbling up to the outer edge of Mauklo's shield, his clothing and armor in torn bits around his shoulders and waist, blue steel sword still clutched in his hand. Mauklo gestured as he let Lorel walk through his shield.

"That must be some tough dragon," he said, staggering on his feet. "You wouldn't believe the headache I've got."

"Just in time; now sit down," Sabu ordered, and then turned to Lindel. "Okay, get ready."

As Lorel shrugged and sat down, Lindel posed himself as if he were taking aim: bringing up his bow, glowing arrow notched in it, bowstring drawn back, eyeing along the length of the arrow.

"Ready," he said.

With a wave of his hand, Sabu made the elf vanish from sight.

Bronto leapt aside another of Saknoth's claws, pounding his fist straight into it as he did so. The dragon yowled with pain, but appeared otherwise untouched. It was now at the edge of the ten-foot ledge, looking down over at Bronto's large running form.

"THERE IS NOWHERE TO GO," Saknoth rumbled. "I WILL GET YOU EVENTUALLY!"

There was a sudden 'pop' on the other side of the ledge, away from where the dragon was facing.

"Hey! Luggage Face!"

Saknoth turned to see an elf, wet hair the color of spun gold hanging down to his shoulders, stance steady as he drew tight on a bow and a long steel arrow, its bright blue glow lighting up the elf, not ten feet from the edge of Saknoth's long rocky snout.

Before the dragon had time to even acknowledge the elf's presence Lindel released his arrow. The moment the arrow had left his bow, Lindel vanished from sight, along with Bronto. Swifter than the wind, perhaps as swift as lightning, the arrow sliced through the air, straight at Saknoth.

Lindel and Bronto appeared with the others, Lindel still in his stance, Bronto in mid run as he bumped into Shong.

The arrow sailed up one large nostril, its hardened steel slicing through the softer rock like it was foam. Through the large sinus cavity, it made straight for the brain. It pierced straight through the inner skull and impacted inside of the soft grey matter. Saknoth howled with pain.

Then the arrow detonated.

As seen from inside the cave, Saknoth's head was rearing back and up, howling out the pain in his head, when his skull exploded. A sudden fiery flash, vaporizing even the bits of grey matter that went flying outwards. Fire, electricity, and ice; it was all there in the maelstrom that expanded from its head, filling the whole of the cave.

As seen from the cold snowy height outside the cave, one half of the very peak of that fifty-thousand foot tall mountain exploded, as if a volcano was suddenly going off. A white-scaled snow dragon drifted high upon the winds as it watched rock turn into exploding plasma, then half of that peak start to slide off from the rest of the mountain. Large flaming boulders tumbled down into the frozen abyss, followed by a large dragon-like form. Carved from stone, this dragon looked to be, its head a ruined mess of burned fragments, as it first teetered on the edge of the precipice, looking down into the frozen clouds far below, and then finally slid over the side, tumbling down with the rest of the rocks.

The snow dragon watched as the dead dragon's body plunged down to a drop tens of thousands of feet deep, carrying the weight of half of the mountain peak with him; a flaming shower of meteors, soon lost in the cradling clouds far below.

The snow dragon descended in long slow circles to the shattered peak below.

Inside the ruined cave, Mauklo's shield had dimmed to solid black, shielding them from not only the flame and power that they'd unleashed, but also from being blinded by what they'd unleashed. They looked around, surprised at still being there.

"It held!" Eldar said in shock.

"Of course it did," Mauklo said, a bit indignantly, "you aren't the only ones who've been practicing."

"Is it dead?" Quickfoot asked timidly, as the blackness of the shield began to fade.

"Dead?" Bronto chuckled as he rose to his feet. "It couldn't be any more dead, my small friend. Look!"

As the shield cleared, they could see out beyond them the open sky. The cave entrance with the ledge and the entire half of the cavern opposite them was completely missing, reduced now to a steep slope of molten rock than was even now cooling in the freezing temperatures. Fierce winds started to blow cold wind in about them as Mauklo dispelled his shield.

"Oh," Quickfoot moaned, "all that treasure; gone! What a waste!"

"He's right," Sindar agreed, "I would have liked to have seen what those relics of Thïr Tÿorca might have told us."

"I would have loved to see that dragon-hilted sword, myself," Bronto shook his head.

"Oh, I don't think that *all* is lost," Mauklo smiled as he and the others stood up, and then faced Candol. "Like I said, it all depends on what I was aiming for."

The blackened shield now completely gone, they looked about at the back of the once-cavern; the only other intact part of this tall peak. There they saw a blackened globe of light, covering where the very rear of the cavern would have been. As Mauklo snapped his fingers, the shield faded away, revealing what lay under its protection.

A glittering pile of gems and sharp weapons, topped by a dragon-headed sword.

Smiles crossed several faces as they looked on at the intact find. Quickfoot jumped up and down with a loud shout of joy, and then huddled himself up as he realized that it was once again freezing. Eldar grinned over at Mauklo.

"This is great!" he exclaimed. "But you could have told us."

"I thought I just did," Mauklo responded nonchalantly.

They carefully stepped along the thin ledge that led to the remainder of the cavern, climbing down the ten-foot drop to the lower floor, and then across the remaining half of the main floor. Quickfoot ran across to the large pile, diving into the gems, squealing with pleasure, while the others examined some of the other weapons that lay there. Bronto went straight for the dragon-headed sword standing at the center of the pile.

"Some of these weapons are in excellent condition," Shong remarked as he examined one of the blades, "good enough to outfit a few of the King's troops with them. If there's anymore of these at Thïr Tÿorca, then we might be able to help just by supplying these for use against the orkai."

"Or to give to our *own* troops," Mauklo added.

"But, we don't have any troops," Candol corrected.

"We could," Mauklo responded, "or hasn't it occurred to you that, to fight Miro, it will take a lot more than the troops that even the King has. We'll probably have to raise our own just to survive."

"But," Candol began, "to raise and lead an army——"

"This sounds like a discussion for another time," Sabu said, "just pack them away through my portal and we'll sort out where they go later."

Bronto, meanwhile, carefully pulled out the sword from where it rested. It was made of a dark black metal, the blade fully four feet long, its hilt yet another foot. The hilt was indeed carved into the shape of a dragon's head, while the long dark blade was imbedded with carvings of long sinewy dragons. Its sharp edges gleamed in the cold light as he turned it over slowly in his hands, gazing wistfully at its workmanship. Sheil-Bor(h) came walking up beside him.

"A beautiful sword," Sheil-Bor(h) said softly, as he walked up to his side, "one worthy of your talented grip. But, its intricate design and style of workmanship seem somehow familiar."

"It has perfect balance," Bronto said, holding it by the hilt in his right hand, giving it a test swing, "feels light as air; looks like it could cut through solid stone. It's a beauty."

Bronto looked at the sword with almost loving eyes, as Kilgar and Sabu came up to also have a look at his find.

"The one who made that sword was definitely a master," Sheil-Bor(h) went on, "one upon whom the gods would smile. But to what purpose? With such designs and workmanship, it must have been made for some specific reason."

"Agreed," Bronto said as he held the sword aloft, gazing at it. "Just what are you, my lovely sword."

As if in response, the sword glowed brightly; bright enough to shine as a beacon from atop their cold peak. Then a low voice came out from its blade, ringing out loud and steady for all to hear.

"*I am the Dragon Sword. For thousands of rels have I awaited a new master to wield me. Now, have I found that master.*"

Everyone stopped what they were doing and looked over in unexpected shock at the voice from the sword. Bronto gazed warily up at the sword he held aloft, and then spread a slow grin across his face.

"Now I know why that sword seems familiar," Sheil-Bor(h) exclaimed, his quiet tone rising just a bit. "The Dragon Sword; I have heard of it. Long ago when the first of the old human Kingdoms first started to expand, they met with several flights of dragons roaming throughout the land. The sword was then made to combat those dragon hordes and protect the land, but with the fall of the last of the Great Human Kingdoms, it disappeared."

"This must be how Thïr Tÿorca was able to survive for so long in the middle of the Dragon Mountains," Sabu said, brightening. "They must have used this sword to turn them all back."

"And when the Kingdoms fell," Sindar finished for his friend, "the dragons must have found and hid it, so that it wouldn't be used against them again."

"Or rather, *someone* put it up here," Mauklo whispered quietly to himself.

"It has great power over dragons," Sheil-Bor(h) agreed, nodding his head a little, "although I am not sure if even *this* will hold off for long against one such as Traugh."

"All I know, is that I've found a friend," Bronto said, waving the sword about, as its light dimmed back down to a low glow.

"And to think," Eldar put in, as he came over, "Saknoth was using it as a nightlight!"

"Well," Shong interrupted, "you may have a chance to test it, because here comes your friend again."

Looping down through the air, was the same snow dragon that they'd ridden up there on. It fluttered its large bulk down onto the new already-cooled slope, folding its wings back behind it. It looked up, regarding the crowd with its icy-blue eyes.

"Well," Bronto said, walking over to the edge of the new cliff, "now's the time to find out."

Everyone watched as he stopped at the cliff's edge, looking down at the dragon on the lower slope. The creature stared eye to eye with the big man. Bronto then brought out the sword, holding it out towards the dragon in his right hand. The snow dragon stared at him for a moment longer.

The snow dragon bowed its head down to the ground, wings swept in back of it in supplication.

"That's okay there fella," Bronto grinned down at it, dropping the sword to his side, "I don't plan on abusing this."

The dragon lifted up its head, and shouted forth its cry; a sharp roar that echoed over the peak. Bronto nodded his head at it, as if signaling understanding, and then turned back towards the others, sheathing his new sword through his belt.

"Hurry up and get all that stuff packed away," Bronto said, waving a hand in the direction of the gems and weapons. "Soakoth here says that he'll give us a lift over the next range of peaks and down to the field of ice."

"You understood him?" Candol exclaimed. "By the beard of Indra, we may make it through these mountains yet."

"It looks like the Dragon Lord has some competition," Eldar smiled, slapping Bronto on the back.

As they started to go about the chore of gathering the treasure back through the portal, and bringing back a new selection of warm furs while they were there, Sabu gazed on at Bronto and his new sword.

"'Creatures of great power and nobility, and one of great strength'," he quoted once again to himself. "It looks like Sindar, Eldar, and myself aren't the only ones here with a destiny."

CHAPTER TWENTY-ONE
Mountain Hazards

An ice-covered vista, soaring far below their feet as they flew through the death-cold air. Winds whipping at their fur-covered faces like large icy fists. The empty feeling one gets in one's stomach at a sudden thousand-foot plunge; adrenaline and exhilaration as one rides the scattered downdrafts and updrafts. Banking around high peeks, soaring over frozen valleys and through miles of frozen clouds of ice. Riding the winds of Life as it courses through your veins.

"This is great!" Eldar shouted, face into the wind, as the snow dragon carried them over ridge after ridge of snow and ice covered mountains.

"At least it beats walking," Quickfoot agreed cautiously, as he tried not to look down.

They were all bundled in multiple layers of fur, an invisible barrier of Mauklo's blocking out the worst of the fierce winds around them. Below them endless snowy drifts caressed their way over the peaks and through the ravines, as winds the color of snow majestically wafted their way through the mountains. Bronto rode up at the front of their large mount, near the creature's long scaly neck as he talked to and caressed it. Kilgar sat just behind the big man, tied, as were the others, to each other and to the body of the dragon, so no one would slip off in mid-flight to a messy and frozen death below.

The flight seemed long and endless, but still much preferable to the climb that had awaited them on the ground. They had little option but to sit and talk; Sabu and Sindar often spending the time to practice some new spells, Quickfoot quickly growing board, Eldar just enjoying the ride, while Sheil-Bor(h) spent the whole time meditating. Occasionally, food supplies would be passed along as the need arose. Waste removal was another problem however, especially since there was no safe place to land even if their mount had wanted to. They finally settled upon a scheme of Sabu or Sindar using their powers to conjure the needy ones back and forth to their faraway island. They flew on like this for a couple of rises, sleeping as they sat upon the dragon's back as it glided on along. They were flying through the tallest of the mountains of the entire range.

Perhaps a hundred miles they flew on thusly.

Suddenly the tall peaks ended, dropping away like an immense cliff edge, with naught but an ocean of frozen clouds and mist expanding on below. Down to half the height of that one fifty-thousand-foot peak they suddenly swooped, a fast accelerating drop at a steep angle that threatened to peel Quickfoot off of the dragon's back.

Eldar just whooped in delight.

"AAAAAAAAAAAAAAAYYYYYYYYYYYYYYYY!" the elf screamed on their way down the four-mile plunge. "Someone should charge *admission* for a ride like this!"

"Some of us have *different* ideas of amusement," Mauklo shouted above the rushing wind.

"Speak for yourself," Candol said, as he held onto his robes, "the elf is right; such unrestrained flight makes one feel closer to Indra!"

"Soakoth says that the field of ice is below us," Bronto shouted back to the others, voice rising above the rushing wind. "He'll take us to its edge, but after that he has to return to his territory. He says it gets too warm for him around here."

"Too warm?!" Lindel exclaimed. "It's almost cold enough to freeze one solid!"

As they dropped below the layer of clouds, plunging through the barrier of cold, the land below them started to come into view. Through the mist they could see an immense sheet of ice, stretching on for miles, away towards distant frozen mountains on its other side. Like a large flat frozen ocean it was, as they dropped rapidly down towards it.

"It's a glacier," Sabu observed, "and it seems to stretch on for quite a distance."

"Indeed," Sindar nodded, "we should make better time on such a more horizontal stretch than on our previous vertical travels."

"One of these rises," Quickfoot commented, "those two are going to learn to speak a language that *everyone* knows."

As they came down to the ice sheet, the dragon changed his flight into a more gradual glide, skimming down to but a few scant feet about the surface of ice. They watched as the ice raced by but a dozen feet below them, watched as clouds of frozen vapor seemed to rise up from the ice itself as they passed over. Finally, when it had slowed enough, the dragon swooped in a sudden upwards climb for several feet, rounded out his flight at the top of his arc, and then dropped straight down to the ground, large clawed feet first. It landed upon the ground with nary a jolt.

"Now *that's* a graceful creature," Bronto said, patting Soakoth's neck as it lowered itself close enough to the ground for its passengers to dismount.

"Maybe not all dragons are like Traugh's brood," Shong admitted. "Some, at least, appear friendly enough."

Sheil-Bor(h) came out of his meditative trance as the others started to untie themselves from the dragon's back; collecting up their rope and supplies as they jumped down to the ground.

"Dragons are indeed like most sentient peoples," Sheil-Bor(h) observed as he slid down off of the large scaled back, "they vary as much in personality and tendency as they do in numbers."

"Ah, but that would also imply," Mauklo countered, with a crafty smirk on his face, "that even the good among them can be corrupted, making them no better than people and no less able to be enslaved; even by one as untalented as my humble self. Would this then not make them no more graceful and stately then the lowliest street bum?"

"I will not see this noble race insulted while I am about," Bronto said sternly, as he stood upon the ground collecting up the supplies.

"I am indeed sorry," Mauklo bowed his head with almost mock humility. "I did but seek to make an observation."

"Enough of this," Eldar said, "let's not ruin such an exhilarating trip with quibbling."

"And besides," Kilgar pointed out, "we still have this ice field to cross."

"That may be a bit harder than we thought," Quickfoot said, as he strove to keep his balance on the slippery surface.

Bronto was caressing the large dragon's head as he said farewell to his large friend in their own silent way. The others had by now gathered themselves up and were some small distance away from the large beast making ready for their journey. The snow dragon finally shook its large head as Bronto nodded to it in return. He backed away from it as it started to spread out its large wings.

"He says farewell," Bronto said, as he came up to the others, "and says thank-you for freeing himself and the others from the domination of Saknoth."

"Noooo problem," Eldar said as he hefted his own travel-pack up onto his shoulders, "just tell him he's welcome."

"I did," Bronto said, as Soakoth started to slowly flap his large wings. "He says that he hopes we find what we're looking for at Thïr Tÿorca, but to be careful if we do."

"An astute observation," Sheil-Bor(h) nodded.

"If somewhat vague," Lorel commented, "but then, since traveling with you all, I should be used to that by now."

A sudden gust arose as the dragon lifted itself off the ground. It rose up several feet before it started to climb forward, soaring out over the icy plane and then veering upwards. It arced upwards, climbing high as it circled back towards them; looping around overhead of them, each time climbing higher. Three times did it thus loop, at the end of which, distantly high up above them, it bent its head down towards them and let out with an icy roar that echoed throughout the large icy field. It then faced away and bulleted upwards, quickly disappearing into the thick ever-present white clouds.

"That creature *does* have a sort of grandeur about it," Shong admitted as he watched it depart.

"It's time that we started off," Candol suggested, "for even a humble servant of Indra tires of so much ice and snow."

"Agreed," Bronto said, as he took the lead.

"Waaa—"

They looked back towards the source of the scream, and saw Quickfoot on his back on the ground.

"This ground is slippery," he said.

"Maybe you should learn how to walk better," Eldar grinned.

"No, the small one is right," Sindar agreed. "It could pose a problem for more than a few of us, born, as we are, to the need for traction."

"Suggestions?" Eldar asked around, as Quickfoot got to his feet.

"If I may," Sheil-Bor(h) stepped forward. "A simple solution for a simple problem."

He then closed his eyes and concentrated. Moments later, there were several soft popping sounds. When he opened up his eyes, everyone had on tall boots with several metal spikes affixed to their bottoms.

"An ingenious solution," Sabu nodded.

"A solution often used by the inhabitants of Norlan," Sheil-Bor(h) explained.

"Good enough," Bronto said as he started onwards.

In single file they trudged along, striking off along the frozen sea. High winds greeted their journey with large icy fingers striking through their furs. Wide white gusts continually drove at them, almost blinding them in their efforts to keep to a straight line of travel. The continual white of snow, ice, and wind was their world. Only the divinatory powers of Sheil-Bor(h) kept them on course, moving as straight as they could across the icy wastes.

The wind howled about them, at times almost seeming like the thunder of hundreds of clawed hoofbeats, and other times seeming to be the screech of winged demons. Never could they be certain, although Sindar tried to assure them all as to the impossibility of having been followed on such a journey as they have had.

But, always there was that doubt.

They were traveling across the middle of the immense sheet of ice, the only view through the icy mists being that of distantly high mountains on all sides of their far flat horizons. At nights they stopped, sleeping in what makeshift structures that magic could conjure up out of the surrounding ice. But always there was the white. They were traveling through a world of white.

"Will this glacier never end?" Kilgar asked through the cold.

"Don't worry kid," Bronto answered, "just think of how much better that nice hot sun will feel when we get to it."

"I'm not good with cold," the boy said, "I was born to a much hotter place than this."

"You and me both," Bronto chuckled.

They heard another distant wail upon the winds, this one nearer than most.

"Will those sounds never stop?" Shong said, walking up to them, "it weighs upon the soul to hear them so."

"I think that's the idea," Bronto acknowledged.

"Then we *are* being chased?" Kilgar asked.

"Only by sounds, I think," Bronto answered. "Perhaps by some magic designed to darken our souls and test our resolve, but not by any creature."

"Fake sounds to make us afraid," Kilgar nodded, his boyish features appearing stern and resolved, "then I shall ignore them."

"That's the spirit," Bronto grinned.

The wail came again, louder this time.

"Sorry," Kilgar said above the noisy winds, "it won't work now."

"Right," Shong agreed, talking into the winds, "so go bother somebody else."

The wail came again, this time almost forming words that got swept away by the winds.

"Boy, whichever spell was sent after us sure is persistent," Shong shook his head.

"Agreed," Bronto said.

The wail came yet one more time, this time forming words screaming upon the wind.

"IIIIII sssaaaaiiidddd...geeeeet mmmeee dddooowwn frrrrom heeeere!!!"

The three looked a question at each other, then looked straight up above them.

There, tossing about in the snowy gusts, perhaps fifty feet above their heads, was Quickfoot. He was being tossed around in the white gusts like some large ball. Bronto stopped his march and turned swiftly around to the others.

"Sabu," he shouted, "we've got a problem!"

The others looked up to where Bronto was pointing.

"I see it," Sabu answered as his staff materialized into his right hand.

"Well I'll be," Eldar chuckled, "now *that's* what I call an updraft."

"No problem," Sabu said, raising his staff, "although one wonders at the physical parameters needed for such lift."

"SSSSSSSaaaaabbbbbuuuuuuuu..."

"Okay," Sabu replied, "I'll just let you down gently."

Sabu raised up his staff. A windy hand grew out from its tip, reaching out towards the small one, to gently wrap itself around him.

A sudden gust of wind jerked Quickfoot away from the reach of Sabu's help, tossing him even higher up into the air.

"Hmm," Sabu muttered, "let's try that again."

Once again he thrust out his staff, this time a more solid palm of wind leapt out to quickly seize the small Quickfoot. But the wind responded again, this time putting up a hard wall of wind between Quickfoot and Sabu's own conjured wind.

"That *can't* be natural," Lindel frowned puzzlement.

The wind tossed Quickfoot around, wrapping him up in silvery and white bands of snow and wind, spinning around him like some maddened maelstrom, with Quickfoot suspended safely at its center. The maelstrom then seemed to grow a face; vague and windy of features, it hung there in the air, regarding those below it.

"It *isn't* natural," Sabu said, face brightening as he realized the answer, "it's some sort of elemental. A small one from the looks of it."

Quickfoot continued to scream through his windy prison.

"It likes him," Sindar said, "I sense feelings of fondness coming from it."

"Oh, he'll be glad to hear that!" Eldar said mischievously, and then turned to shout up at the small one. "Hey Quickfoot, I think it wants you as a pet!"

"GGGGrrrreeeaaaatt."

Came back the windy reply.

"It's only a small elemental," Sabu said, "I can handle it."

He once again raised up his staff, but this time a windy hand came swiftly down from the almost-face in the maelstrom. It wrapped itself around the staff and quickly yanked it out of Sabu's grasp, juggling it high up overhead.

"Hey, that's my staff!"

"You said something about having no problem," Mauklo calmly cocked an eyebrow.

They watched as the wind playfully tossed both Quickfoot and Sabu's staff up around in the air. The face then seemed to once again form in the wind, this time grinning down at them.

"Well," Eldar said, "anymore ideas?"

"Yes," Sabu said after he paused, thinking, for a bit, "it's still *my* staff."

As Eldar puzzled over his friend's answer, Sabu reached up a hand into the air, clenching his fist as he muttered a few quick magical words into the air.

"Intonautey Electris Vairus!"

Suddenly, streaks of lightning leapt out from the head of his staff, arcing out in several directions as the long electrical fingers licked out to several points in the strange wind, neatly missing the frantic form of Quickfoot. The windy maelstrom glowed with electric life as the windy face howled in pain. The wind then just dropped Quickfoot and the staff, hurtling down towards the ground.

"AAAAAAAAAAAAAAAAAAA...," Quickfoot screamed on his way down.

Sindar's mind reached out and gently cushioned the small one's fall, gently depositing him upon the ground, while Sabu just snapped his wrist and his staff disappeared and reappeared back in his hand. Overhead, the elemental made angry swirls as it worked out its pain.

"Good, now we can get rid of it," Mauklo nodded.

"Hey, I don't want to hurt it," Sabu said. "It's just playful, is all."

The silvery wind whipped around angrily, as if deciding what to do. Then it blew down at them, seeking to pick up another victim as it aimed for Kilgar.

114

Kilgar dived aside as Bronto tried to take a punch at it, but hit only air. It swerved around and started for another pass.

"I think this is getting annoying," Mauklo grimaced as the elemental's wind tossed his robe and furs about his legs. "You get one chance at getting rid of it or I blow it to the far corners of Maldene."

The elemental made another windy pass, this time lifting up Kilgar and Lindel. Kilgar slashed about with his curved knife as they both dangled there in the air helplessly. The windy form seemed to laugh once again, like some weird child at play.

"Kinda looks like fun," Eldar shrugged, "but if Mister Personality here is so impatient, I guess something *should* be done."

Eldar reached a hand into a hidden pouch as Bronto was trying to pull Kilgar down out of the sky. Windy laughter could actually be heard coming from the elemental as it dropped Kilgar and next went for Candol. Soon, the priest's dignity was abused by being tossed around, about thirty feet above the ground.

"This should slow it down a bit," Eldar said, pulling something out of his pouch, "at least until we can get off of this glacier."

Eldar held a small red ball in his palm, gripping it tight with his warm hand. Then, with a grin, he tossed it high up into the air. When it hit the icy chill of the elemental's wind, it exploded into several fast-moving fiery sparks, whirling around like hundreds of annoying fireflies. The windy voice seemed to giggle, as if tickled by the small trickles of flame dashing throughout its airy mass, while Candol and Lindel each batted at the small fires as they came near. The wind dropped its unwilling passengers as it swirled around to chase the numerous small sparks. Sindar's mind gently deposited Lindel and Candol upon the ground as they fell.

"A little cold-activated toy I came up with in my alchemy research," Eldar explained. "Now, let's get going while it's having fun."

Indeed, the windy creature seemed to be having fun chasing the hundreds of flying little sparks about. Sindar looked through the thick white mists at the still far away peaks and then over at Sabu.

"Sabu," he said, "think you're rested up enough from the last time?"

"I think so," Sabu responded, "that flight on the dragon gave me a chance to rest up a lot. Do you think that you can get me a good enough fix?"

"It's far away, and the mists are thick, but I think I can manage," Sindar nodded.

As the windy creature chased around the now-fading dancing sparks, Sindar clasped his hand to Sabu's shoulder as Sabu raised up his staff. Sindar fixed his gaze upon their intended destination, as the tip of the staff then glowed, spreading its incandescence to every member in their group. Everyone briefly glowed as if with foxfire and then vanished. When they reappeared, the far mountains were but a few feet in front of them and the glacier was behind them.

"Hey, *warn* us next time you do that," Quickfoot said, as he stumbled into an icy boulder that hadn't been there a moment before.

"Now, why didn't you do that earlier?" Lorel asked.

"*You* try climbing a hundred miles of frozen mountain and see how much energy *you* have left over for spell casting," Sabu said as he lowered his staff. "Besides, I'd never been on a glacier before, so I thought I'd catalog any indigenous life that we came across. Disappointing really."

"You were *what?!*" Quickfoot asked, more than rather miffed, as he picked himself up.

"What'd you expect from a flat ice ball?" Eldar said to Sabu as he started up towards the mountain. "Now, come on."

They once again found themselves climbing up a mountain. This one, though, wasn't nearly as high as the tall peaks behind them. They trudged on up it for a while before finding a ravine going through it. Then through snowy passes and down ravines littered with icy rubble, through cold blizzards and over steep climbs. For an entire rise they climbed, finally making their way around to the other side by nightfall. When morning came, they looked down at the vista spread out before them.

The early morning dawn brought with it a view of more tall snowy mountains, but of gradually decreasing height. In the far distance they could even see lower altitude mountains with no snow upon their green peaks.

"Ah, hope!" Quickfoot exclaimed happily as they all eyed the distant green.

"Yes, but it will still take us several more rises before we get down there," Lorel observed, "unless there be some way of shortening our journey."

"All this snow *does* get depressing after a while," Lindel sighed. "I long for the vibrant colors of a good forest."

"I begin to wonder if maybe Kor-Lebear and Kilinir were right in not coming along," Shong commented.

"Well, you *can* see that green peak over there pretty clearly from here," Eldar cocked an eyebrow in Sabu's direction. "An almost perfect view for one to fix his gaze upon."

"Who *cares* about the view," Quickfoot complained, stomping his foot, "I just want *out* of these mountains."

"Quickfoot," Sabu grinned, winking at Eldar as he raised up his staff, "consider yourself warned."

"What?" the small one turned around.

The scenery around them seemed to blur with colored lights, the glow of foxfire, and then it suddenly changed. No longer were they on a snow and ice covered mountainside, but on top of a chilly, although definitely much warmer, snow-free mountain peak, the snow-covered peaks of their journey being tall and distant behind them. Before and below them ranged more mountains, but these were tall and with the colors of life. It was cold and brisk, but a paradise compared to where they'd just come from.

"Ow!" Quickfoot said as he stumbled against a rock. "No fair!"

The small one began sneezing at the sudden shift in temperature, while the others began to divest themselves of some of their furs. Bronto looked around at their warmer surroundings.

"Ah, a *definite* improvement," he said as he breathed in deep of the brisk air.

"There's still more mountains through which we must travel," Sabu said, bringing down his staff, "but I think we can walk it from here."

"So, how come you don't just hop us across the mountains with those teleports of yours?" Lorel asked.

"Well, first," Sabu answered, as the others dressed down a bit, "I need to either know where I'm going or I need to have a line of sight. Second, it's getting really tiring teleporting all of us around repeatedly. Besides, the walk will do you good."

They gathered their extra furs through Sabu's portal and then started on their way. On through the rough terrain they traveled, through trees free of snow, and over ground warmed by sunlight, a slight cool breeze blowing in their faces. Bronto once again found reason to pick up his singing of old bar tunes, while Quickfoot soon found himself scampering over the cool pine-needle strewn ground, happy at not having the hair on his feet frozen off anymore. Lindel breathed in deep of the fresh mountain air, delighted at once again being surrounded by such an abundance of life.

Several rises they spent traveling down the mountain slope, around treacherous cliff-sides and along steep ravines. Their journey gradually leveled out, the crisp air at eight thousand feet of elevation sweeping against their faces. Their journey was relatively smooth and uneventful.

Except, that is, for the nagging suspicion in the back of Lindel's mind that they were being followed.

On one of their usual mid-rise rest stops, Kilgar came over to Lindel to find the elf kneeling down beside a tree, sifting through the soil with his hands.

"Something wrong?" Kilgar asked as he stood beside the elf.

Lindel looked up at the boy, the noontime sun haloing the young Destir's sandy-colored hair. The boy always looked so stern and serious and acted so adult, that it was easy to forget he was still a young boy, with many rels until his manhood. Lindel tossed back his long golden locks as he answered.

"The moss behind this tree has been crushed in two places," Lindel explained.

"We're being followed then?" Kilgar asked.

"Bright boy," Lindel answered. "Yes, someone was standing behind this tree before we stopped here; someone standing on two legs——which leaves out any animals."

"In the desert I can track as good as you can here in the woods," Kilgar boasted.

"Well, then maybe I can teach you a little about tracking outside of your desert home," Lindel said, as he turned back, pointing, to the moss. "Look here; the footprints seem to be clawed, perhaps meaning that our spy here could be either some sort of mutant or one of those demons we encountered a while back. So, which one would you guess it to be?"

Kilgar glanced around at the ground surrounding the moss, then bent down for a closer look at the ground.

"It didn't have wings," he finally said. "If it did, the leaves and ground near it would have been blown around."

"Good boy," Lindel smiled, "That leaves a mutant of some kind. Now, what types of mutants do we know of that would want to have followed us for the past several rises?"

"The orkai," Kilgar answered immediately.

"Right," Lindel nodded, "and I confirmed that with a *seeing*."

"A seeing?"

"I may not have the magical abilities of some of our friends here," Lindel explained, "but, I still have my own minor magic: spells to help along the trail, spells for plants, even a few minor spells to ask the winds of what they will bring us. And, of course, spells to tell me a bit more about the tracks I find."

"Minor or not," Kilgar said, getting up, "such magic can be as good as Sabu's spells if used right."

"Perhaps," Lindel responded as he also stood up, "but only if we tell them what we've found. Come on."

Lindel put an arm on Kilgar's shoulder as they walked over to where the others rested. They walked over to where Sabu and Sindar sat, engaged in a conversation that no one else could seem to follow, then quietly sat down next to the two intellects.

"We're being followed," Lindel interrupted them quietly. "It's the orkai again."

"That confirms what I've been seeing," Sindar nodded. "I've been having a feeling of impending danger the last few rises."

"You can make that sense of danger a bit more immediate," Eldar said, as he too came over and sat down, speaking quietly. "I *sense* more than several dozen of those orkai around and under us."

"Gentlemen," Sabu said, trying to stay casual, "it looks like we're about to be ambushed. Sindar, you'd better tell the others."

Sindar sent out his tightly-focused mental call. As his message was received, swords were discretely drawn and spells quietly readied, as everyone tried to make ready for a battle without allowing their unseen pursuers to notice. Casually though they talked and seemed to still relax, tension filled the air as they waited for the attackers to pounce.

They would not wait long. Dozens of cries, sounding like a cross between a baby crying and a rabid monkey in heat, sounded out from all around them. Leaping out from the trees overhead, out from behind the rocks around their camp, and up from the very ground underneath their feet, they poured out. Perhaps a hundred of them, coming in from all directions. They were indeed the animal-faced orkai that they'd come to know so well, but this time no blue flaming swords did they wield, but wooden swords, long sticks, slings, and primitive bows. As well, several of them held shields, primitively wrought, each with a rough carving of what appeared to be a large skull with a bolt of lightning slashed through it. They swarmed in on the travelers.

A skillful slice by Shong and two of them were pierced through the heart; a strong heave by Bronto, and one went flying out towards several more of his companions. Lindel got off a couple of deadly bow shots but was soon overwhelmed with orkai and had to resort to his little-used sword. Kilgar knifed one in the groin, dived under its legs, and came up behind it to stab at another. Eldar gleefully sliced around with his own sharp sword, hacking off limbs wherever he struck. Lorel cleaved all around him with his steel-blue sword, slicing through limbs all around him, while Quickfoot stayed behind a rock, waiting for one of them to pass close enough for him to stab it in the back.

Sheil-Bor(h), though, appeared to remain undisturbed. He sat upon the ground, legs crossed, eyes closed in meditation. One of the creatures came running screaming up to him, shouting forth its battle cry. It stopped just in front of Sheil-Bor(h), waving his wooden sword at the unconcerned man. But still Sheil-Bor(h) remained unmoving. The creature stopped his screaming, puzzled. It then bent down to look at the man, using his sword to poke at the still form a couple of times.

There was a sudden crack, as if of lightning hitting stone. The orkai's eyes were wide and still, its sword broken in two pieces, dropping from its fingers as blood trickled from the multiple fractures emanating from where Sheil-Bor(h)'s open palm had impacted against its forehead. Sheil-Bor(h) gave it a gentle backwards shove as he removed his hand, the dark imprint of his hand still showing upon the cracked skull of the creature as it collapsed to the ground.

Candol was having some difficulty. Every time he tried to invoke the name of Indra, several of the creatures would pounce on him, dragging him to the ground. He would then use his Hevon Gem to immolate himself in fire, thus solving the problem, but only to have this repeated after he'd gotten up once again. Sabu and Sindar, meanwhile, were fending off the creatures by shooting off little bolts of lightning at any that came near them. Mauklo, refusing to have his dignity impaired when a few came running up to him, calmly looked them in the eyes, wicked look upon his face as he muttered a few silent words under his breath; they stopped…

…then ran in complete terror. Of what they saw in Mauklo's face may never be known, except by the dark wizard himself.

Still more of the creatures poured out. Always would they surround someone, trying to pile in on him as if to weight one down by sheer numbers. Thus was Kilgar captured, for as fast and quick as the boy was, he could not dodge his small form from so many; he soon found himself struggling, being held down by five or six of the creatures. Quickfoot was also soon rooted out, the small one screaming as they carried him aloft. Lorel got tackled by a dozen of them, while Shong was finding it increasingly difficult to fend so many off. Sindar and Sabu soon found themselves surrounded by a ring of the creatures, all aiming their swords and shields inward at them, keeping a small distance from the two mages.

"Observe their shields," Sindar said, pointing to the skull with the lightning bolt crossed through it, "another symbol of Miro, if I'm not mistaken."

"Yes," Sabu agreed, as he zapped another one that got too near. "Carved by their own hand no doubt, but definitely the same mark. They are obviously too primitive to be of the same tribes recruited to work for Miro…"

"Which makes one wonder from where they copied the design from," Sindar finished for him, as he too calmly zapped another of the creatures, reducing it to a char mark upon the ground. "Something worth investigating. It also appears that they wish to capture us."

"I had noticed that they haven't killed Kilgar or Quickfoot yet," Sabu pondered calmly, "nor have they really tried to harm us. Perhaps we should allow ourselves to be captured?"

"And then investigate the mystery behind the symbol on their shield," Sindar nodded agreement. "Yes, I believe that to be the best course. I'll inform the others."

As Sabu caused his staff to vanish from sight, Sindar's wordless call went out to the others. Puzzled looks crossed several faces as they reluctantly put away their weapons. Eldar looked especially disappointed at having to give up on such fun. But give up they did. Sabu and Sindar put their empty hands up into the air, urging the others to follow suit. As the fighting stopped, the orkai looked on in puzzlement. Then evil grins crossed their faces as they saw their foe helpless before them. They ran in to tackle and surround the others, carrying them off at sword point, tying them up in thin homespun ropes, urging them forward. Several of them went up to the wizards, roughly kicking them in the direction they wanted them to go as they talked and laughed in their guttural language.

The ones that approached Mauklo, however, stopped, looking doubtfully at the tall yellow-skinned wizard. Mauklo scowled back. They ended up keeping a distance of a few feet clear around him, surrounding him in a ring of bodies as they guided him along, but not going nearer than a few feet. Mauklo smiled to himself as he walked along.

Around a cliff-side they guided them and up into a wide cave carved into the mountainside. The cave lead them into the mountain, through dark tunnels and along twisted passages. Little, if any, light shown down here, reducing vision to a haphazard stumble in the dark. Only the two elves and the many orkai seemed able to navigate properly.

"I wish I could see in all this," Sabu complained mildly. "At least you have your mind sight, Sindar."

"It does allow me to sense shapes and outlines," Sindar admitted, "but its use is limited."

"Perhaps I can be of some help," Sheil-Bor(h) said, as he tried to come up next to them from between the orkai. "I know a minor spell for such occasions."

"Well then," Sabu said towards the blackness from whence came the other's voice, "by all means proceed."

Sheil-Bor(h) muttered a few syllables under his breath and then brought a palm up to lightly touch Sabu across his eyes. When the palm was taken away,

Sabu found that he could see perfectly well in the total darkness. He then saw Sheil-Bor(h) repeat the feat for Sindar.

"Hey, this is great," Sabu said as he looked around, "can you do this to the others?"

"It is indeed an improvement," Sindar agreed when he too could see. "It would prove advantageous for everyone to be able to see thusly."

"If I can but reach them," Sheil-Bor(h) nodded assent, "then I will try."

Sheil-Bor(h) then backed away into the crowd of orkai, as they were ushered along deeper into the mountain. Sabu looked around at the tunnels through which they were ushered. Nothing remarkable about them, he thought, they looked to be natural tunnels of which these creatures had made long use. He decided to walk along and keep silent, waiting to see where the orkai would lead them.

As others began to see, courtesy of Sheil-Bor(h)'s quiet spell, they too decided to not let their captors know of their new vision, and stumbled along in the dark as they had before.

The tunnel eventually opened up into a large cavern. It had high ceilings covered with wet drippy projections of rock, and several large boulders and twists and turns hiding its true size. There were long ramps of rock leading up to second and third levels of the large cavern and several other tunnels leading off in different directions and perhaps other caves. In the cave were innumerably more numbers of the creatures, scattered around the caves as they went about their work. Some were hammering out more weapons and shields, others carving the skull and lightning bolt symbol on them, while others fought each other in sometimes fatal mock battles. The group was ushered roughly forward.

"Well," Sindar began, "so far nothing too unexpected."

"Except for where they copy those symbols from," Sabu added, "I guess we'll have to wait and see."

They were guided through the cavern, past animal-faced creatures scowling menace at them, around twisted rocky columns, and under stony overhangs that threatened to kiss the ground. They rounded a bend and came upon a sight of several of the creatures fighting each other, as if in some sort of competition, with many others of the orkai watching. They watched as a fight was ending, its winner being pulled off to one side by an overseer, and left to stand with other past winners. They also saw of what the overseer was.

A tezar.

"Now we *know* the hand of Miro is about in these mountains," Lindel exclaimed quietly as they were shoved along. "I think it's time we *did* something about this now."

"One should look more carefully at just what such a hand would hold," Sheil-Bor(h) said, as he nodded in the direction of the tezar. "Perhaps we should observe."

"I think he's right," Sindar said, "we still don't know enough about what they're up to."

They watched as the tezar ushered the winners over to another section of the open cavern. Then a second tezar came out of the shadows, holding in his hand a large steel-blue sword. The orkai guiding them stopped pushing the group as if they too wished to watch the proceedings. The tezar with the sword took it up before him, saliva dripping from his long fangs as it held the sword at shoulder height. The first tezar then shoved one of the winners forward. The chosen one stood up, tall and proud, as the second tezar touched him on the shoulder with the sword. There was a blinding flash of blue light around the orkai as he screamed in pain. When the light faded, the orkai had changed.

It now had a steel-blue sword of its own and rode atop a claw-hoofed mount, looking significantly less primitive.

A cheer rose up from the other orkai as this new rider guided his mount off into the darkness of the far end of the cavern. The tezar still had his own steel-blue sword as the first tezar shoved the next orkai up.

"This place is a training ground!" Eldar exclaimed. "They use this primitive tribe of mutants, train them, then take the best among them."

"And transform them into the fierce creatures that Indra has chosen us time and again to thwart," Candol finished for the elf.

Their own guards then pushed them along, as they once again were guided through the cavern.

"That sword the tezar has must be a special one," Sabu theorized, "allowing it to so transform these creatures. If it is destroyed, then that might prevent any new ones from being made."

"Or at least slow them down a bit," Sindar agreed.

"This might mean that these tortured creatures are being used by the tezars," Sheil-Bor(h) suggested. "Perhaps they are not normally as bad as we might think."

"Are you feeling *sorry* for these vile creatures?" Lorel said aghast. "After all the cities and lives they've destroyed?"

"If one is not under one's own will, can one really be at fault?" Sheil-Bor(h) answered calmly. "We do not know what these creatures were like before the taint of Miro reached them."

Before Lorel could think of any answer, they were ushered through another tunnel, this one not too long, as it soon emptied them into an adjoining cavern. This cavern was fairly well lit, allowing them to see what lay on its floor below them.

Dozens of people, very much human, lay in the dimness before them. Dressed in rags they were, or what was left of such. From young children to adults to the old and infirm, they lay there, groping about for what scraps of bread that their guards would toss them. Several of the primitive orkai, and a few of the riders, stood guard over them, as the group's own guards shoved them roughly in with the rest.

"These are from the towns they've raided," Sindar observed quietly, "no wonder we never found any bodies."

"But what do they use them for?" Lindel asked.

"It matters not," Lorel said, "we must save them from their vile captors!"

"Slow down Lorel, and act not in haste," Sindar said, "for I have a bad feeling about all of this."

"Uh oh," Eldar said, "his bad feelings are never good."

"Then let us act," Lorel protested.

"And what about those other dozen guys with the blue swords; the one's we *can't* see?" Eldar asked, "I can sense the energy from more of those things than you want to know about."

Lorel had no answer as one of the primitive orkai came trudging through the refugees, poking at the people as he would pass by, squeezing their arms or looking at their teeth and then moving on. He came to an old and feeble man, poked at him, then grimaced. He spat on the old man and then knocked him hard to the face, sending the old man sprawling to the ground, never to move again, skull cracked and bleeding. Next he came upon a child, a small and frightened boy. The orkai smiled and licked his teeth, as he lifted the young child up by one frail arm, dangling the small struggling form in the air for a bit, the orkai grunting merrily in its own tongue as it watched. It then walked with the boy back over to a group of other orkai, grunting something out at them just before it casually tossed the boy the remaining five feet towards them. The boy landed with a short cry, at the foot of the five other orkai. The creatures looked down at him. They ripped off what few rags remained on the child and reached down towards him…

And then proceeded to tear him apart. The boy's screams rolled through the cavern as a young arm was casually snapped off, followed by a lower leg and then part of a thigh. The orkai that had tossed over the boy came over to rip a large chunk of the boy's midsection out, taking a big bite out of the mess down in his hand as the others proceeded to feed on the tender meat now at their disposal. Misshapen teeth stripped flesh from arms and legs, clawed hands reached messily into soft organ tissue for more food, and bones were cracked open so that their sweet juices could be sucked out. The other refugees looked on as the orkai held their grizzly repast, silent now from the child's cries.

The boy couldn't have been any older than Kilgar.

"I *think* we have our answer," Eldar said, as he swallowed a hard lump in his throat.

"I *will* kill these vile ones," Lorel proclaimed, "I don't care *what* you say."

"You won't have to," Bronto said slowly as he watched the creatures feeding, "I'll do it *for* you."

As they watched, a contingent of the creatures, perhaps twenty of the primitive ones and three of the ones with the steel-blue swords, came through the cowering crowds. They picked several of the refugees out of the crowd, choosing only the full grown young adults. They came slowly towards the group.

"Kilgar," Bronto turned to the boy, "I'd rather they not separate us when they mistake you for lunch."

"Right," the boy responded, as he reached for his throat.

Kilgar turned the clasp to his cloak, the cloak he'd picked up, now so long ago it seemed, back on the island where they'd first joined up with Shong and the others. As he turned it, he faded from sight, rendered invisible by the cloak's magic. Just as he vanished, the creatures came up to them, motioning all of them forward, towards the other end of the cavern.

"Just tell me when I can kill these despicable creatures," Lorel said, tension in his voice.

"Not just yet," Sindar said, "I sense that we may yet meet the one who leads them."

"I got that one," Bronto nodded as they were lead across the cavern along with the refugees.

Through the dim light they went, to the far wall of the cavern. Here they were stopped before a large door, fifty feet tall and twenty feet wide, made of steel and bound by stone. On either side stood a guard of four tezars. On the front of the large door, inlaid in gold, was carved a large skull with a single bolt of lightning slashing through it. Candol hid a very nervous Quickfoot beneath his robes as they came up to the sight.

"Well, now at least we know from where they copy the symbol on their shields," Eldar offered.

At a signal from one of their guards to the tezars, the large gates slowly began to open. When they were open wide enough, they were shoved through behind the refugees.

"Get ready everyone," Bronto cautioned, "it looks like we're finally going to see what's behind this."

As they were being guided in, Sabu stopped by the door, running a hand along its surface, studying its make.

"Hmm, the make of this door appears to date back to the time of the Kingdoms," he muttered. "Perhaps this is an old outpost, a remnant from the times when—"

"Sabu," Eldar said as he shoved his friend forward, "now is *not* the time."

They entered into a large cavern, rocks along the walls aglow with warmth, a large pool of black liquid in the center. All around them were the primitive orkai, lining everywhere except for one wall. The gates closed slowly behind them, sealing shut with a crash of finality. One of the guards then went over to the first of the refugees and started shoving them into the dark pool.

Five refugees, men and women, fell into the pool, hitting the thick black liquid like it was tar. They immediately started screaming as the thick goo started crawling swiftly up their bodies, covering them and pulling them down as they struggled against it.

"Fascinating," Mauklo uttered as he watched the struggling forms dragged deeper into the goo.

"I think that it's time to stop being fascinated and start doing something," Lorel said, as he reached for his sword.

"I think we may find this educational," Mauklo nodded. "Look carefully; that liquid isn't feeding on them, it's transforming them."

They watched as, sure enough, the wriggling forms started to contort. Bony projections grew out of them, skin roughened up into tough hide, fangs protruded, and faces contorted into hideous animalistic shapes. Their screaming went to a level only the insane can reach and then stopped, silenced as their minds finally broke.

The five forms then stilled, the tar washing down off of them as they started walking calmly up out of the black pool. But, what came out of that pool wasn't human.

It was orkai.

As the newly born creatures left the pool, the next few of the refugees were pushed in.

"*Very* fascinating," Mauklo smiled, as he turned to Lorel. "So, the very same 'vial creatures' that you would have erased from the world, were originally the very same townspeople that you would save from them. What dichotomy! What say you now to killing them?"

Lorel was in shock, torn between two conflicting morales, not now knowing if the creatures were the enemy or merely its tools. Lorel's mouth worked silently several times before he found the power of speech.

"This can't be," he said, staring at the changing forms. "What vile *kai*…"

While Lorel's voice trailed off, the others held a quick conference as the next batch of orkai came walking out of the pool.

"That's an interesting twist," Eldar admitted. "The more towns they conquer the more troops they get."

"And with the fear aura that those tezars seem to emit," Lindel pointed out, "they could just walk into some small towns and capture them whole; more victims to transform into the hideous creatures. This is an affront against *sylva'!*"

"Well, *I* know enough," Bronto said, drawing out the Dragon Sword. "Come on boy, it's about time I tested you out."

A loud scream leapt out from Bronto's lips as the big man whirled around, cleaving one of their guards in two before it had time to react. Lorel joined in as his own blue-steel sword leapt to his hand, a bolt of angry blue flame searing its way through the air towards one of the other sword-wielding orkai. Another one of their guards gave a scream as something invisible stabbed it in the groin, while Shong somersaulted out into the fray, drawing his sword in mid leap and coming down with it on top of two more sword-wielding orkai. The remaining refugees were shoved into the black liquid as the orkai poured in around them.

"We're into it now!" Eldar said, then screamed out a battle cry and went slashing against the nearest guard.

But the battle was cut short. Suddenly, erupting from the ground, came several large stony fists. As large around as an ogre, one grabbed at Bronto, closing a large stony fist around him and pinning his hands to his sides as easily as one might hold back a very small child. Another one erupted underneath Candol, grabbing at the priest and holding him firm. Several more formed out of the very stone around them, one grabbing Lorel, another lunging at Shong, and yet another nearly crushing Lindel as he, too, was caught. Quickfoot tried to use his small size and quick speed to evade them, but a large stone hand suddenly shot up underneath him, enclosing him entirely. Eldar and Sheil-Bor(h) were among the last to be restrained, but soon only orkai lay free. Everyone tried to struggle against the immovable stone, but to no avail. Sabu, Sindar, and Mauklo tried to evade them, as they floated themselves high up towards the ceiling, escaping the grasping hands. They looked at their imprisoned friends below.

"By who's magic-," Sabu wondered, as he watched Sheil-Bor(h) try to struggle free.

He didn't have time to wonder. A loud scream came down from overtop of him. He looked up just in time to see two large swords come down to either side of him, a fanged face of fear screeching down between them. The tezar impacted hard against him, taking him down with it to a thirty-foot fall upon the hard stone. Just as it landed, the tezar jumped up into a leaping roll, landing safely on its feet ten feet away.

Sabu was left on the ground with a broken leg, numb from his shoulders to his hands, and had trouble breathing. Pain shot through his body as he turned his head just enough to see Sindar and Mauklo also upon the ground, each with another tezar a short distance away from them. Sindar bled from a long bloody gash to his leg, while Mauklo lay bruised and battered. Sindar didn't move.

"No one mentioned that those things can *jump* like that," Sabu said weakly.

From where he lay, he could see the one wall upon which no orkai stood guard. He then saw this wall of rock start to shift and roll, as if changing its form. He saw boulders slide around each other, gradually forming a large face, complete with stony eyes looking down upon them, regarding them. When its voice came, it was like the rumble of rocks, the slide of stone, the grating of sand.

"*IT IS BY MY POWER THAT YOU ARE TRAPPED, AND BY MY MERCY THAT YOU LIVE,*" it said. "*I AM GREENOK.*"

"An elemental," Sabu said, as he spat up some blood, grimacing with pain as he tried to sit up.

"*NOT JUST ANY ELEMENTAL, I AM A* LORD!" it rumbled.

"An elemental lord that sides with the likes of Miro," Candol said, from within his stony restraint, "which makes you nothing more than his slave."

"*DO NOT TRICK ME WITH YOUR WORDS, PRIEST,*" Greenok said, as the hand of rock around Candol squeezed a bit tighter, "*LEST I CRUSH YOU LIKE A WORM THAT WOULD BURROW THROUGH THE GROUND.*"

The others struggled in vain attempts to free themselves from their rocky prison. Sheil-Bor(h), though, had stopped struggling, having now closed his eyes in a deep state of meditation.

"What does Miro give you in exchange for supplying him with his troops?" Eldar asked, as he vainly struggled within his own rock.

"HA! YOU THINK THESE THE ONLY TROOPS HE HAS?" the large mountain of rock rumbled back. *"WHAT I SUPPLY ARE AS BUT THE ONES TO PAVE THE WAY FOR THE FIRST WAVE. THE MASTER'S FORCES ARE MORE NUMEROUS THAN YOU CAN KNOW, AND MIGHTIER THAN YOU CAN COMPREHEND. I PROUDLY SERVE SUCH A ONE WHO WOULD CONQUER THE WORLD! AND NOW, YOU SHALL SERVE HIM ALSO. YOU SHALL MAKE GOOD ORKAI."*

"Not if I can help it!"

Bronto strained against the rock holding him pinned. Muscles bulged as he strained against the rock. Sweat poured down his face as he tried to force his arms away from his sides. Greenok just let out a loud rumble of a laugh as he watched him struggle.

"Not even Bronto can free himself from solid stone!" Shong said as he tried to slip through his own stony hand.

Sabu watched as Greenock continued to laugh. Sindar still hadn't moved, and Sabu still had trouble from the numbness of his own arms; he couldn't even make a fist much less hold onto his staff. Mauklo he saw seating his own battered form up on the ground. The tezars watched their every move with military precision. Sabu tried to think fast while the elemental's attention was focused on Bronto.

That's when he noticed the small pouch discretely sliding across the ground towards his feet. Sabu watched it slide up to him as he tried vainly to move his arms over to it. The pouch opened itself and then produced a few small pieces of ground root and herbs. These floated up as a small bundle towards Sabu's mouth.

"They're from Lindel's pouch of herbs," came Kilgar's quiet unseen voice in his ear. "He says it'll relieve some of the numbness in your arms."

"Good boy," Sabu whispered back, as he chewed and swallowed the offered curative, "now you've got to help Sindar; he hasn't moved since those tezars jumped us."

"Okay," Kilgar whispered back.

As Sabu tried to listen for the silent pad of Kilgar's invisible feet walking away, he could even now start to feel Lindel's herbs working, as feeling started to come back into his shoulders and arms. He tried to think of what to do next while waiting for more feeling to return. He looked over at Sindar, still unmoving.

That's funny, he thought, he could have sworn that Sindar's leg gash was a lot worse than it is now. His bleeding had also stopped. Hmm.

As Bronto strained against the immovable stone, the elemental lord's laughter finally quieted down.

"*ENOUGH OF THIS,*" it finally said, "*YOU SHALL BE THE FIRST.*"

The hand holding Bronto started moving through the ground, carrying the big man towards the black pool. Bronto struggled, unable to get his arms out from his sides.

A low hum began to fill the cavern, like unto one humming a mantra. All eyes turned to see Sheil-Bor(h), still imprisoned within as the rest, but now humming a note low in his throat. The single note carried softly throughout the entire cavern.

"*WHAT TRICKERY BE THIS! STOP YOUR HUMMING AT ONCE! NO ONE CAN HEAR IT TO HELP YOU ANYWAY.*"

Sheil-Bor(h)'s humming increased, slowly growing in intensity as its volume filled the cavern. Dust and small rocks began to shake loose from the ceiling. Greenok got a pained look on his face as the tone increased.

"STOP THIS," he cried, minor cracks beginning to form in the hand holding Sheil-Bor(h). "*I SHALL CRUSH YOU!*"

Greenok tried to tighten his stony grip around Sheil-Bor(h), to crush the breath out of him and stop the monotonous humming, but all he succeeded in doing was fissuring the large hand even more.

"It's starting to weaken!" Bronto cried out, as he strained even harder.

"I'll have to ask him to teach me that ultrasonics spell," Sabu said to himself.

He flexed his fingers, once again feeling the blood flow through them. His leg still hurt at its unnaturally twisted angle, but at least he could cast a spell now. He pointed a hand towards Bronto.

"Big man within the stone," he intoned, "I hereby grant you greater strength and stronger bone."

There was a brief flash of green light around Bronto as his muscles seemed to suddenly bulge out a bit more. Bronto growled defiance out into the high cavern as the orkai started readying their swords. With a mighty heave and a scream he thrust out his arms with all his might.

Sheil-Bor(h)'s mantra to weaken it, Sabu's spell to strengthen him, Bronto shattered the rocky fist out from around himself, dropping to the ground, Dragon Sword in hand as he did so. He then leaped over to the humming Sheil-Bor(h), spun around with his sword, and struck straight through the stone holding him.

The Dragon Sword cleaved straight through the rock. Greenok gave a ground-shaking yowl as Sheil-Bor(h) dropped to the ground.

"Keep up your humming," Bronto said as he faced towards the next nearest stony hand, "I'll free the others."

"NOT IN MY DOMAIN YOU WON'T!"

A new hand suddenly grew out from the rocky wall from where Greenok's face shown. The large stone hand, large enough to grab a horse rather easily, lunged for the dodging form of Bronto.

Bolt of light crisping through the air, charged light impacting through stone. The sound of hundreds of stone fragments as they violently splinter apart, a stone hand no longer.

Sabu turned to see Mauklo standing upon his feet, hand still pointed towards where Greenok's hand of rock had been chasing Bronto. The yellow-skinned one had an angry grimace on his face, his robes almost shredded in places from the tezar's attack. He glanced over at Sabu.

Unable to do more than half-kneel upon the ground, Sabu righted himself as best he could. His staff snapped to his reaching hand as he looked back over towards the silent unmoving form of Sindar. Using his staff as a crutch to get to his feet, he shouted out in Sindar's direction. The other wizard's leg wound was almost healed now.

"Sindar!" he shouted. "The elemental; he's stone! Be with me."

I am here, came the thought into Sabu's head.

Sindar rolled over and sprang to his feet, the wound on his leg now just but a small cut, quickly healing over. He pointed out his hand in Sabu's direction just as Sabu raised up his staff, pointing it straight towards Greenok. A bolt of *orain*-colored magical energy leapt out from Sindar's hand, hitting Sabu's staff just as it started to glow brightly. Behind them, Bronto could be heard slashing at more stone hands, the tezars and orkai now surrounding the large man as he cleaved at them like a madman. Sabu aimed his staff at Greenok.

"Greenok!" Sabu shouted out, trying to both lean on his staff and aim it at the same time. "Why don't you soften up a little!"

Just as Greenok shifted its face towards the young wizard, a cone of brown light leapt out from the tip of Sabu's staff. The light sprayed out upon the elemental, and where it struck the rock softened, slowly flowing down upon the large face.

"NO! I WILL NOT HAVE THIS!"

Greenok's large stone nose suddenly exploded out into a shower of mud, as the elemental's screams rocked the cavern.

"You're looking better already," Sabu smiled weakly.

Another beam of magic hit upon Sabu's staff, as now Mauklo too added in his own magic to the spell. Sheil-Bor(h) mantra was still filling the cavern, but now it caused fragments of rock and mud to fly off from around them as large chunks of the elemental lord exploded out from the walls that were its body. The elemental lord's face was dripping down into loose mud, his words lost in a burble of wet earth. The remaining stone hands started to crack and fall apart as the others struggled free of them. Greenok reached out with another stone hand he formed out of the wall, lunging it towards Sabu. A few scant feet before it reach him though, the large hand disintegrated into gurgling blobs of mud and ooze. The caverns of the orkai shook with Greenok's screams as his once stony face rapidly transformed into rivers of mud sluicing down the walls.

The orkai, several bodies of which now lay around Bronto and Shong, looked at their master melting into a large pool of rock, and ran back towards the large gate, struggling to open it faster. The tezars looked from the orkai to the ones now menacing Greenok; two of them ran back, barking orders at the retreating orkai, while the others leapt up into the air, swords out, one of them coming down next to Sabu.

What it didn't see was the blue bolt of flame launched straight at it from a grinning Schanter, nor the sharp sword come slicing up for it from Eldar's hands. It may not have been killed, but the combined impact at least sent the creature hurtling away from Sabu.

There was a final blast of brown light and a final burble from what was left of Greenok, before the elemental was just a large puddle of mud and a memory. As Sabu turned off his light, Quickfoot's voice came shouting excitedly from across the crumbling cavern.

"Look! Gems!"

As the elemental's face melted away, behind it was revealed a small nook, inside of which were indeed a small pile of earthen-brown crystals.

"Are you all right?" Eldar asked as he supported his friend around the shoulder. "It looks like we found some more Hevon gems; I can feel their presence from here."

There was a crash at one end of the cavern as a large chunk of rock and mud came crashing down upon one of the tezars.

"Except for a broken leg I'm okay," Sabu answered as he raised up his staff, "and as for those gems…"

Sabu raised his staff up high, its tip shining bright. The distant pile of crystals seemed to shudder for a moment and then went flying out across the room. One impacted straight into Sabu's staff, melting away into its tip as it did so, while another went into Eldar's outstretched sword. Sindar and Mauklo also got theirs, Sindar upon his brow, and Mauklo by catching it and watching it melt away into his palm. Another landed upon the calm form of Sheil-Bor(h), now no longer humming his mantra, while the last one was caught by the servant of Indra, just as a tezar was leaping straight towards him.

Candol caught the gem in one hand just as he was pointing the other hand at the tezar coming down at him from midair.

"By the power of Indra——" his voice rose.

Immediately a large rocky column seemed to erupt from Candol straight towards the leaping tezar. The rock caught the tezar full in the chest, carrying it back across the cavern and smashing it through the far wall.

"We've got to get out of here, fast!" Bronto shouted out as he battled two tezars and their whirling wall of four large swords. "Any ideas?"

"Yes," Mauklo said quietly to himself, "two can play at this game."

The dark wizard gestured, Earth Gem showing forth on his palm. As he did so, several earthen hands came up out of the ground, grabbing at the tezars, pinning their arms and sword to their sides.

"Good job," Lindel called out, "but how do we get out of here; I think we've got about half of the orkai nation just on the other side of that conspicuously open gate."

"I'll take care of the gate," said Bronto as he ran over to heave the large gate closed with one free hand.

"As regards our liberation," Sheil-Bor(h) suggested calmly, "these newest Hevon gems *do* concern that substance of which we are presently under."

"Of course," Sabu exclaimed, "all I have to do is——"

"Allow me," Sindar finished for him, "you've got a broken leg to tend to. Candol! See what you can do about his leg while I get us out of here."

Candol finished admiring his handiwork with the tezar and came over to Sabu. Sabu winced as Candol placed his hands upon the broken leg, while Sindar turned towards the muddy wall that used to be where Greenok had been. He pointed up a hand and concentrated, his new earthen gem now glowing brightly. Sheil-Bor(h) stepped in next to him, lending assistance in Sabu's stead.

The earth and rock seemed to part before them, tunneling through the mountain as it formed an upward-slanting ramp to the surface. The rumble of the moving earth echoed, not only throughout their own cavern, but throughout all the caverns of the orkai. They heard hundreds of running pairs of feet just as the large gate closed with a resounding crash. They listened to the growing sounds of their enemy marshaling under the cruel leadership of the remaining tezars. But, like a large rent leading them from the pits of the underworld the new tunnel opened, the ground shaking with the movement. When it stopped, the new tunnel rose up and out, on towards a distant point of light.

"Okay, I think you can walk now," Candol said as he finished with Sabu's leg, "but I'll have to look over it more thoroughly later."

"We're ready to leave now," Sindar called out to the others.

"Not quite," Mauklo said as he looked at all the mud strewn before them.

As Mauklo looked at the mud, a glow came over it, changing it back into a more solid form. When the brief glow stopped, there was but a rocky surface, with steps carved into it like a staircase.

"*Now* we're ready," Mauklo stated.

"Come on then," Bronto motioned.

They ran up the tunnel, Sabu able to jog with the help of Eldar as they heard the sounds of a large gate opening up behind them. As they ran, Schanter slowly began gaining in height and weight, loosing his misbegotten features as he loped along. Kilgar appeared beside them as he twisted the clasp that deactivated his invisibility. They ran in a mad dash for the surface.

"You did good, kid," Bronto nodded to the boy as they ran alongside.

"I take it you're mental powers now include those of healing yourself," Eldar commented to Sindar, "because I could have sworn that you were badly injured."

"I was," Sindar said as he huffed alongside them, "but I put myself into a deep state of healing before it got any worse."

"Maybe you can teach me that sometime," Sabu said as he hobbled along.

They ran up the tunnel, the distant light growing steadily brighter. Behind them they could hear the shouts of tezars and the growls of more than several orkai as their pursuit was begun. Hundreds of orkai could now be heard running up behind them, quickly gaining. Eldar pointed his sword behind them, his Earth Gem glowing.

"Maybe this will slow them a bit," he said as he ran.

A small pea-sized pebble shot out from his sword, bouncing along down the tunnel. But with each bounce it grew bigger, until behind them could be seen a large boulder rolling down the tunnel. Eldar grinned when he heard the surprised animal-like cries as the boulder found several targets.

Eldar smiled and turned back to the task of running.

It was a long tunnel, perhaps made longer by Sabu's limping pace or by their need for speedy escape. When they finally exited, afternoon light shown down on their faces as a panoramic mountain view lay before and beneath them.

They were on the edge of a cliff, the tall walls of the mountain rising up at their backs. Before them lay a steep drop and behind them were the orkai.

"Sotüva! You *sure* know how to pick exits," Quickfoot complained. "Nnnext time why don't we just jump into the black pit and get it over with!"

"That can quite easily be arranged," Mauklo scowled at the small one, "if you don't let us solve this next problem."

Quickfoot cowered behind Candol as the others quickly pondered their problem. Schanter, meanwhile, was looking more like Lorel with each passing moment.

"Close the tunnel," Lindel suggested, "or at least enough of it to seal off those creatures."

"I'm afraid that won't do any good," Shong pointed up above them.

High up on the cliff above them were several more of the orkai, climbing out from innumerable holes and caves, coming slowly down towards them.

"That doesn't make it much easier," Lindel admitted.

"They *do* appear to know this mountainside better than we do," Sindar observed.

"A word if I may?" Bronto asked, face alight with sudden inspiration.

"We're open to any suggestions," Sabu said, "what is it?"

As the orkai got nearer, Bronto faced out towards the wide openness before them. He heaved in a great breath and shouted out a single name.

"Masouda!"

The shout echoed and re-echoed throughout the mountains before them. Nothing answered his call.

Lorel turned to the big man, head shaking.

"Nice try, but I am afraid that we are a bit too far away for that noble bird to help us," Lorel said, "but I'm sure the thought is appreciated."

"That's not who I was calling," Bronto grinned, "Look."

From over the hills and mountain peaks, through the air like they were born to it, flew hawkmen. More than a score of them.

"This is the *other* tribe that Masouda spoke of," Bronto grinned, and then turned to shout up at their swiftly arriving assistance. "We are friends of Masouda and enemies of the orkai, who now chase us!"

The hawkmen looked to see orkai crawling around the cliff-side like a swarm of ants, with the small group upon the ledge as the sugar. With nary a word, they came swooping down, each passing hawkman picking up someone by the shoulders. By the time the orkai came pouring through the tunnel and over the cliff, they were all airborne, flying high upon the twisting winds of the mountains. The one holding Bronto looked down at him, as it half-whistled half-spoke out its greeting.

"You are friend of Masouda and of the old blood," it said, "the rest we shall sort out later."

"I would give one last gift to the orkai," Sabu said as they looked down upon the distancing mountain.

As the small ledge swarmed with angry orkai shouting curses and two dour-faced tezars waving their large swords, Sabu pointed down his staff. His own Earth Gem glowed, giving forth its energy at his will. The mountain began to rumble, rocks to fall, as the orkai lost their footing. Several went plummeting to the ground far below, screaming out their fierce animal cries of defiance as several tons of rock and dirt soon followed them down. The tezars were dextrous enough to avoid the deep plunge, but even they weren't nimble enough to save themselves when the entire ground beneath their feet gave way. Before they flew out of sight, the ones rescued by the hawkmen had the satisfaction of watching the entire cliff-side fall into a ravine far below, several tons of mountain crashing down out of sight as half of the peak slid away, burying orkai, tezars, and the black pool with it.

Sabu gave a satisfied smirk as the hawkmen flew them away. Lorel, though, once again himself, couldn't help but think of all those innocents changed into the horrible orkai, their lives twisted to vile designs.

In the end, he hoped that the landslide put an end to their unnatural existence.

"So, then I just took a chance that we were far enough through the mountains to be near the other tribe of hawkmen that Masouda spoke of," Bronto was saying, as he took another sip from the golden chalice. "I figured we didn't have anything to loose."

The hawkmen's nest was in the side of a mountain; a series of open caves, their sheer cliff sides facing out towards the open mountain air, each cave a home. The mouth of each cave looked almost suggestively like the open beak of some large bird, rocky overhangs shaped somewhat beak-like, vague stone eyes peering out over the mountainous domain, no two cave mouths carved in quite the same way. Like balconies overlooking some scenic view, these caves littered the top of the mountain. Cool air flowed lazily in through the wide cave mouths, ruffling feathers and hair alike as it made its passage. Many of the winged birdfolk fluttered around outside the caves, coming and going as they wafted their way down over the mountains. Colorful patterns of feathers coursed through the air, landed upon their cliff-like landings, and strutted around their caves. Musical twitterings and distant calls sounded through the hills, such was their language; bird-like in origin but with almost human-like overtones.

They sat upon short rocky seats, near where their own cave's edge poked outside, overlooking the panoramic view before them, while their beak-faced hosts sat upon their own peculiar seats. Several short stone pillars, each no more than about three feet tall and but wide enough for a single person to stand on, stood around the ledge and just inside the large cave, making a circle of themselves around the perimeter of the cave's mouth. Each pillar was ornately carved with varied images of flight upon their sides: large feathered birds in suspended flight, dragons taking wing, and aerial swirls of clouds lacing around the pillar's surface. The top of each pillar lengthened out to a large carved bird's head, stone feathers swept back, beak pointing towards their common center. Upon each of these short pillars rested a hawkman, squatting down upon its flat top, taloned feet curling around the stone's edge, wings folded neatly around behind them. Atop one of the pillars squatted Eldar, trying to mimic the way their new friends perched on their stone seats. The hawkmen were silent and attentive as they listened to Bronto's telling of their journeys.

"Your chance was well chosen," one of their hosts sang back, "for Masouda had told us of your coming."

"But, how?" Shong said, puzzled and somewhat shocked. "Surely a journey over those ice-covered mountains must be long and hazardous, even for ones with your power of flight. No messenger could have——"

"No messenger was sent," a hawkman with blue streaks through his wings explained. "There are sometimes those born among us with the power to speak one mind to another; every nest has such a Sender. Masouda had his Sender send a message on ahead of you."

"We had been waiting for your arrival for the last few rises," another one continued, "we are glad that you have made it through."

"So are we," Bronto chuckled.

"Your race," Sindar asked with interest, "psychic powers are inherent within you then?"

"Perhaps more so than with humans," the blue-streaked one answered, "but still not frequent enough to be considered as commonplace among our kind."

"Hmm," Sindar wondered, "it should be possible to enhance both the frequency and potency of such powers. Mental powers would be of a great benefit to *any* race."

"These chalices," Sabu broke in, turning his own chalice around in his hand, "do they date from the old Kingdoms?"

"Yes," the blue-streaked hawkman nodded, "they are from the very few remnants of a time when Thïr Tÿorca was once a great power. Perhaps all that is left."

"Our people were more wide spread back in those times," another of the hawkmen stated, "trading with the Humans and traveling about in their cities. Now, we are thought of as strange beasts, to be avoided or attacked. Thus, do we make our homes far from those of the ground-dwellers."

"If you were so numerous and well liked," Sabu pondered, "I wonder what caused people to so change their minds about you. Surely not just the fall of the Kingdoms?"

"It is said," the blue-streaked one said in his half-whistle of a voice, "that it was with the consort of demons that the old Kingdoms fell. When Beltor marched with his armies of undead and demons, before the final fall, that was taken as final proof of a demonic accord. Such demons were often described as being large feathered creatures that roamed the skies; it was then only a matter of time before they accused us of being such creatures."

"Wait a tid," Eldar interrupted, squatting forward as he turned to face Sabu, "you didn't say anything about that Beltor guy having hordes of undead and demons under his control."

"I didn't want to worry you," Sabu shrugged. "Besides, would it have made any difference?"

"Not really," Eldar tossed back his silver hair after a moment of thought, and then squatted back down upon his rocky seat. "Continue."

The blue-streaked hawkman sat up straighter, ruffling out his wings a bit, smoothing back his multicolored feathers against the high mountain breeze, as it continued in its almost-whistle of a voice.

"When the humans turned on us so suddenly," it continued, "they attacked us almost as much as they did the minions of Beltor. We lost many of our kind in those dark times. We were forced to retreat back from our friends, never to mix with human-kind again. It's a pity, really. For we would have assisted our friends of Thïr Tÿorca; perhaps it would never have fallen if we had been allowed to help."

"Fate didn't seem to be with you," Sindar nodded sadly, "if not for a random turn of events, the great city may not have been lost."

"Fate can take but many forms," Sheil-Bor(h) said, as he walked over to them from across the cave, "not all of them need be the frailties of Man."

"Anyone want to translate that?" Eldar asked around.

From the opposite end of their ledge, Mauklo, who'd been silent up until now, began laughing quietly, but audibly, to himself. Heads turned in curiosity at the dark one's mild outburst as it echoed about the cave.

"Okay giggles," Eldar asked, somewhat unamused, "what's so funny?"

Mauklo looked over at them, reducing his mild laughter to an amused smile, as he leaned back and answered them.

"I laugh in appreciation of such a masterful job of manipulation," he answered. "Sheil-Bor(h) is right; his words have the sound of *kleum* to them. Do you not recognize his hand?"

Puzzled looks were his answer.

"All he had to do," Mauklo continued, "was to but whisper a few words and point a finger or two and Thïr Tÿorca was robbed of its greatest ally. To but use their own fears and faults against them, make enemies of their allies, and then sit back and watch their society and *thïrear* disintegrate in one of the great calamities of history—*that* is truly worthy of admiration."

"You're saying then," Sabu said, eyes looking up as he caught on to what Mauklo was saying, "that Miro's hand *did* reach even the old Kingdoms?"

Mauklo just smiled.

"I thought you said that Miro didn't have anything to do with their fall," Eldar put in, "that it was the one place that fell of its own accord and that's why we came here?"

Silence reigned momentary supremacy as the implications of Mauklo's words sank upon them all. Finally, Sindar sighed and rose to his feet, pacing his way over to the edge of the ledge and then stopped.

"I can see now that Miro is indeed trickier than we'd figured," Sindar said, as he gazed out over the mountain view, "and subtler than we might fear."

"But, why then did he cause Thïr Tÿorca's downfall in the first place," Sabu wondered.

"Perhaps," Mauklo smiled, his grin hiding much, "he did it for *our* benefit."

Something about Mauklo's smile, or perhaps about just the way he said it, made everyone pause in thought. The group's reverie, though, was interrupted by a high-pitched voice come walking in from the interior of the cave.

"It smells like a chicken coop in here," Quickfoot said wrinkling his nose. "It stinks!"

The others looked at the small one and then up at their unperturbed hosts. Several faces looked at him as if he'd just committed some social faux pas.

"What'd I say?" Quickfoot whined. "I'm just telling you it stinks in here."

"Forgive our small companion," Bronto said, standing up, "the sensitivity of his nose is matched only by the size of his mouth."

"Actually," the blue-streaked one said, twitching its beak, "he's right. This cave should have been cleaned out a motab ago, but we never seem to get around to it. Forgive *us* for presenting our guests with such unclean surroundings."

"See," Quickfoot shot back, "I was right."

"Truth is appreciated," the hawkman said, turning its beak down towards Quickfoot, "but not discourtesy."

The small one looked down at his feet, kicking at a small pebble, downcast at the sudden reprimand. Bronto grinned and tousled the hair on the top of Quickfoot's head with his large hand.

"It's okay, little one," he chuckled.

As Quickfoot looked up, feeling a little better, Kilgar came walking out from the shadowed interior of the cave, his skinny boy-frame striding confidently out.

"All our supplies are checked out," he said, coming up to the others, "we can leave anytime."

"I am afraid the boy is right," Bronto sighed as he turned to the blue-streaked hawkman, "it is time for us to go and see of what the lost city holds for us."

The big man put out a large arm, his host taking it in a feathered forearm grip of farewell. The hawkman, at least as tall as was Bronto, looked him in the eye, pointed beak whistling out his reply.

"As my name is Narudwa, so shall you have an ally," the blue-streaked one said while it shook hands. "Nobility flows through the veins of both you and your companions. In the times of the Old Kingdoms, our Human friends had named us *Kÿecian*; those times may be long trilenium past, but I sense a new type of Kingdom rising from this small group, and it is to that new hope that I now pledge my people."

"Gladly accepted my friend," Bronto shook arms with Narudwa, "for you and all Kÿecian."

"We shall fly you all as far as the next range of mountains," Narudwa said, nodding its beak out in the direction of a distant hill. "From there just travel straight North and East and you shall find the valley within a short span of rises."

"Good enough," Bronto smiled.

"Our friend *definitely* seems to have a way with people," Eldar whispered over to Sabu, as he leapt down from his stone perch. "I begin to wonder if there is anywhere that he cannot find friends."

"Maybe you should take lessons," Sabu quipped back.

The cool wind blew over their faces as they were gently carried over the living greens, blues, and *orains* of the mountains. Mountain streams and tall pine trees swept away below them. When they were finally deposited upon the next mountain, it was with mixed feelings that they waved good-bye to their hosts. As sad as they were to see their winged hosts go, also were they excited by the nearness of their destination, so close at hand.

For three more rises did they travel over the mountains, in a gradual downward plunge in elevation. Through mountain passes and over hills grown thick with the vegetation of life; down tall grassy hills and over large streams; across rocky ravines and along animal trails older than most countries. As fast as they could travel did the terrain and flora seem to change. The weather too seemed to be changing more rapidly, the winds to grow warmer, the sun to get hotter upon their skin.

Towards the end of their third rise of travel, they walked down through a final ravine and came out on a final tall hill, to see what lay before them.

R.K.: 9,990, 54 Arüdwo:

We have made it at last! The Valley Of Many Lights lies spread out before us in all its beauty. Tomorrow we go down.

We have arrived just in time for the celebration of the three rises of Kilio.

The rising sun greeted the ones walking down into the lost valley, kissing its rays of light upon the first outsiders to enter there in thousands of rels. Three large white hawks circled around three times overhead, watching with interest at those that walked down into the valley, on this, the first rise of Kilio.

The three white hawks dove, the bright morning sun reflecting off their feathered backs, as they flew down towards the travelers.

Chapter Twenty-Two
Interludes

Horses and people went back and forth along the wide cobbled streets, the blue sun shining down through an *orain*-colored sky onto a warm mid-Spring afternoon. The town was some miles out from Sydelburg, back along Threegan Road towards the coastal direction rather than more inland towards the mountains. Street performers were everywhere, from fire-swallowers to strongmen, acrobats to street-magicians, with even a traveling carnival wagon parked alongside the wide road. It was a holiday and the performers were trying their best to please the audiences, while the local merchants were doing *their* best to take advantage of it.

In front of the traveling carnival wagon two masked acrobats amused the audiences with their jumps and twists, somersaults and leaps, bouncing off of each other with a lithe grace rarely seen. Their skin-tight black body stockings flowed with every supple movement of their tightly-woven muscles. If one looked carefully enough through the creative padding of their simple costumes though, one might even discern the more slender curves of a female anatomy about one of the acrobats, an observation lost to the applauding crowds before them. Their painted green and black face masks presented just but a gay face to the oblivious onlookers as they tossed their coins at the dancing feet of the two performers.

To one side of the wagon, a street-magician leaned up against the wooden side, resting until the time for his own act. His robes were brightly colored for the benefit of the audience, but beneath he still wore his old pants, his leather boots sticking out from under the long flowing robes. His face he hid in the shadows, his piercing dark blue eyes and unshaven chin-stubble being all that showed from under his ear-length mop of straight brown-red hair. He gazed out at the audience with a cold calculation, as he fingered the freshly made amulet just under his robes around his neck; an amulet made by his own hand.

Walking up to this cold figure was a man in traveling clothes and a dingy hood. Dressed too warmly for this weather, he looked more like a man trying to not be seen, but by his very attempt at doing so, failing miserably. He approached the street-magician with a quiet and nervous voice.

"I'd heard that I should speak with you about hiring someone for certain services," the nervous stranger asked.

"We are merely a carnival troop," the magician answered coolly. "What kind of *services* did you have in mind?"

The stranger leaned closely to the magician, almost whispering directly in his ear.

"There is someone I would like killed," he said quickly, as the acrobats cartwheeled beyond him.

The stranger suddenly found himself unable to move his mouth, try as he might. The magician's eyes glowed a bright red as he looked at the stranger with a stare as cold as the Southern Wastelands.

"Don't ever use the word *kill* or *murder,*" the magician said, staring directly into the stranger's eyes as the latter tried unsuccessfully to open his mouth or even move his eyes away from that cold stare, "we deal in *services*. Got it?"

The stranger nodded.

"Good. Now, who would you like serviced?"

The stranger gasped for air as he found himself suddenly able to open his mouth, breath again, move his eyes, and speak. After a couple of gasps, he took out a quietly jingling pouch and placed it in the magician's hands.

"Jason Wis," the stranger explained, "that greedy merchant has stood in the way of my business, and my father's before me, for too long. I want him gone."

"So you can expand your *own* greedy business," the magician smiled from beneath the shadows. "How nice."

"Can you do it?" the stranger asked. "He's got all the best bodyguards in town protecting him."

The street around them erupted in applause at the latest acrobatic feat of the two performers as the street-magician gave his answer.

"Of course. But, why have you not tried seeking such help earlier?'

"I have," the stranger lowered his head, "but he's so rich he just buys out the contract and the person ends up *working* for him instead of kill——uh——*servicing* him. This is all the gold I can spare; I'm told that you don't renege on a contract."

"My associates have one rule to which they hold rigidly: once a contract is agreed to, they follow through with it. No amount of money can then buy out or cancel the contract. It matters not how much this merchant of yours has, your contract is safe."

"Good," the stranger almost breathed a sigh of relief.

"But remember then, that the same holds if someone ever takes out a contract against *you*."

"I understand," the stranger nodded. "You will do it then?"

"The weapon which will service him will be delivered to his door by tonight; by morning he will be…removed."

"You *give* him the weapon?" the stranger said perplexed.

"A little trademark of my associates," the magician smiled again. "They believe in *giving* their victims the very weapon with which they will be…serviced."

"But, why?"

The magician leaned very close to the stranger, his cold stare directed straight into the eyes of the stranger.

"Wouldn't *you* be afraid of someone that could get you even if you were holding the *very weapon* that would be used against you?"

The stranger swallowed hard and finally backed away, giving a last glance at the magician before he disappeared back into the crowds. The magician smiled at the stranger's discomfiture as he turned his attention over to the two performing acrobats.

He watched as they flipped over each other, garnering applause from the audience standing around in the street. He gave a slight nod of his head in their direction. This was returned by an even slighter nod from the slimmer of the two figures as they finally finished their performance and bowed to the much-earned applause, still not taking off their painted masks.

Bedor smiled to himself as he watched them take their bows, his own act being up next. Street-magician indeed, he thought, although this traveling carnival bit is proving to be a very lucrative idea.

Who would expect the rising fame of the Black Dagger to be cloaked within the gaiety and innocence of a small band of traveling performers.

Jason Wis, richest merchanteer in the entire city, employer of fifty stout warriors he could call his own private bodyguards, walked down the hallway of his mansion home. He walked past two guard checkpoints and rounded the corner to the pair of double doors that entered upon his bedroom. He nodded to the two guards to either side of the doors as they opened it up for him. Jason Wis walked into his bedroom as the doors closed behind him, confident in the knowledge that the two guards would be but a moment away if he but sneezed.

His room was lavishly decorated in silk; silk draperies hanging in front of all the walls, silk hanging in front of his bed, large silk pillows thrown about his room, even silk woven into the fabric of the plush carpet upon which he now walked. He liked the lavish life-style and he had the money with which to indulge it. Even the aged grey of his shoulder-length hair sort of resembled a dull smooth silk.

He shook off his fine leather shoes, his now bare feet leaving deep tracks in the long plush fur of the carpet. He shrugged out of his vest and climbed out of his pants, soon fitting himself into a finely made night-shirt, made, of course, of silk. He walked over to his four-poster bed and drew back the silk curtain, to ease himself down for a good night's sleep.

He stopped. There, laying on the exact center of his silk pillow, was a very curious object: a single-cut black dagger, a slight red point of light gleaming brightly from the center of its hilt, blade-tip pointed down towards the foot of the bed. He reached down and carefully picked up the sharp-edged object.

What foolery be this, he thought, someone has the audacity to threaten me with this small slip of a weapon! How'd it get in here past the guards anyway? I'm going to have to speak to someone about security being lax.

He turned the dagger over in his hand. Nothing remarkable about it, except for that continual gleam in its hilt. Nice workmanship though. Maybe it'll make a good souvenir.

He grasped it by the hilt with his right hand as he turned to walked back towards the door. He would have a word or two to the guards about *this!*

He stopped in mid-step. His right hand had tightened convulsively about the dagger, grasping hard enough so that his hands bled as the sharp edges of the obsidian cut through. He reached over with his other hand to try and pry it loose.

But his other hand wouldn't move. His whole body was slowing down, his walk turning into a slow-motion parody of normal movement. First his whole right arm tightened, every muscle going suddenly tense with unknown effort, then spreading swiftly to his right side, then throughout his entire body. He opened up his mouth to scream, but nothing came out.

His vocal cords had tightened beyond use. He was without movement, without voice. In pain from his sudden rigidity but unable to scream, or even whisper a call for help to the guards, so close just beyond the door.

A dark silent figure came up behind him, its soft-leather bound feet leaving not even a mark in the long plush of the carpet, nary a trace of its passage. It came up behind Jason with nary a sound. The merchant heard naught, but sensed it more as a presence or portent. He strained to turn around and look, but his tense body was immobile. Only his eyes would move.

Leather-gloved hands reached around from behind him, gently grabbing him by the right hand and moving it upwards. A soft male voice sounded in his right ear, fear rising in Jason as not even a face could he put to this unknown.

"The convulsions will be starting in a few moments," the soft voice said, as he brought Jason's right hand, still clasped about the dagger, up against his own throat, "rather violent convulsions at that. If you aren't careful, you just might slit your own throat."

The leather-gloved hands carefully positioned the right hand so that the sharp tip of the dagger lay resting directly upon the merchant's Adam's Apple. Only the fear in Jason's eyes could give any sign to the thoughts in his head.

That, and the fact that his bladder was apparently still functioning.

"The poison on the dagger is rather unstable," came a different, more female voice, from behind his left ear. "It breaks down and evaporates so very quickly in air, it's a pity that there won't be a trace of it for anyone to find. They won't know how you really died; except, maybe, by your own hand."

Some of the merchant's facial muscles finally found a small amount of movement as the terror he felt began to show upon his face.

"The convulsions continue for sometime after your actual death," came the male voice from behind his right ear. "By the time they've stopped, you'll have probably sawed off your own head. A rather slow process at that."

Jason's eyes bulged wide with fright as his hands began to shake.

"There we go," came the female voice, distancing slightly as if it were backing up, "they're starting already."

Convulsions began to rip through his body as every muscle tried to violently shake loose its tension. His hand shook back and forth, carrying the sharp black knife with it. Blood spurted out and the obsidian edge sawed through his soft throat. No scream of pain, fright, or anguish could the merchant cry forth as he convulsively sawed at his own neck. No willful act save the showing of his fear and pain in his eyes, the slow stretching of facial muscles as they sought to give slow expression to terror. Blood gushed down his silk nightshirt and across his bed as he cut his own vocal cords. Life slipped out of him as he severed his own windpipe, but still he convulsed.

Two dark figures, hiding behind the silk draperies covering the walls, watched as Jason Wis, rich and greedy merchanteer, sawed through his own spine. They watched as the convulsions prevented the now-dead body from even falling to the ground, but just teeter back and forth on stiff legs.

"You were right," came the soft female voice, as the body finally toppled noiselessly onto the soft silk bed, "this *was* an easy one."

"Fools usually are," replied the quiet male voice, as the soft impact of the body on the bed drove the dagger through the remainder of the neck's spine, "and the fear on his face should help our reputation as well."

"I told you it would be a nice little touch," replied the female, as the severed head rolled over towards the other side of the bloodied silk bed. "A little well-placed public relations never hurt anyone."

The male gently clasped the female's gloved hand in his own, enclosing it like a prized treasure.

"Business is over with," he said, "and the night's still young."

"I thought you'd *never* ask, Kor," she replied, gaiety creeping into her soft voice. "There's this place I saw earlier; nice food, clean—Rich people stuff. I think we can afford it now."

"As you wish, my love," smiled the dark male figure, "a night out on the town it is."

The two guards outside never saw Kor-Lebear and Kilinir leave. Later, when the decapitated body would be found, they would swear that they never heard a sound from within the closed bedroom. Similarly, the rest of the fifty guards spread all around the dead merchant's mansion swore that it was impossible for anyone to get past them, nor could anyone climb in through the barred windows. Impossible, yet it happened.

All anyone ever saw was the fear on the severed head. A head severed, apparently, by the merchant's own hand, using a single-cut black obsidian knife. A knife that all who saw the body had time to see and examine; a knife that they were learning to connect with the fear on Jason's dead face.

Despite all precautions, the strange knife disappeared the next morning.

"Captain Starke," came the deep bellow, "your report."

Starke walked into the round brightly lit room. His long thin black mustache trailed down to either side of his mouth, neatly combed as it trailed a short distance past his chin. His yellow-brown skin shown muscular through the short-sleeved leather jerkin he wore beneath his chain mail vest. Light metal plates of armor covered his torso while leather armor studded with small round knobs of metal adorned his legs. His vortex sword was sheathed at his side, in the same special sheath that Sabu had made for it, as he walked in with strict military precision.

The large round room had a single tall window carved into the stone walls, permitting light to enter from the bright afternoon and affording a tall view of the Castle's main practice-yard outside. The mahogany-paneled stone walls were adorned with several maps depicting different areas, continents, and kingdoms from all over Maldene. As Starke entered through the single archway that was the room's only entrance, he saw General Baldegron standing to one side of the room's circular table, his seven feet of black muscular frame sporting his usual assortment of skins and leather with occasional bits of scale armor thrown in, his own mysterious sword held tightly to his side in its rune-covered sheath. The room also held two other Captains with whom Starke had gained a passing familiarity; one of them elvish, the other human. Starke stopped directly in front of Baldegron and gave a smart salute.

"Sir," Starke began, "scouts have confirmed the reports from the mountains to the north and have also made contact with representatives of the Dwarven Kingdoms there."

"How many?" Baldegron asked, standing somewhat more casual than was Starke. "And try and relax a bit."

Starke relaxed his stance imperceptibly as he continued with his report.

"A confirmed count of at least one tribe of thousands of orkai, two tribes of goblins, and some unconfirmed sightings of tezars and bucknaids. Their general movements would put them in a position for a strike against either us, the dwarves to the north, or the Elven Woodlands to our northwest."

"In your professional judgement," Baldegron said, as he slowly walked around the circular table towards one of the wall maps, "would they be ready for an invasion of any such of these regions?"

"From what I've seen of the way the Dwarves have dug themselves in up at the mountains, the creatures would have to at least triple their numbers to be a threat. Nor could they have a chance against the elves. But sir, reports are that they can achieve this in about two rels."

"Hmm, yes," Baldegron said, stopping in front of a map of a particularly large continent. "That goes along with the other two reports."

He gestured to the map he'd stopped in front of.

"Captain Fis here," motioning to the other human Captain in the room, "has found similar movements in the mountains and forests of My-Thov, although much more numerous."

"Likewise, Captain Dale," nodding to the elven Captain present, "had similar findings in the interior mountains of Cenivar."

Baldegron looked at the maps thoughtfully, before looking back to Starke and the other two Captains. He sighed before he finally gave his own summary.

"Every dark place and hidden crevice on the planet seems to be acrawl with dark servants, just waiting for when they can attack."

"It sounds like they're preparing for attacks on all fronts," Captain Fis interjected, "a world-wide war."

"It does indeed, Fis," Baldegron agreed.

"Sir," Starke interrupted, "should the public be alerted to the danger?"

Baldegron looked around at the maps, as if deciding, then back at the assembled Captains before responding.

"No," he said, "we have no real proof yet. The King's right; we don't want to worry the populous needlessly, the danger is still several rels off. Besides, this soon, several of the other local kingdoms out there wouldn't go along with us. They would just see it as a grab for power on our part."

"We need to do something though," came the mild tones of the elven Captain. "My long elven life-span gives me more of an appreciation of how short ten rels really is. We could find ourselves caught off guard by an enemy that thinks hundreds of rels in advance."

"You're right there," Baldegron said thoughtfully. "Very well. Increase your patrols and vigilance. Also, I want increased scouting reports; *I* want to know what they have for *breakfast* every rise. Dismissed."

Starke whirled around on foot as the other two Captains started to file out. Starke, ever the precise and strict military figure, started to march out after the other two Captains.

"Starke," Starke stopped as Baldegron called after him.

"Sir?" he answered.

Baldegron's voice took on a more mild and friendly tone as Starke turned around.

"From what I hear, your friends are okay," the large man said.

Starke paused, thinking about Sabu, Eldar, and the rest, pitting themselves against unknown dangers for a destiny that no one was certain of. His chin held high in the air, he looked up at his large General.

"Thank-you sir," he finally replied.

Starke then turned smartly back to the door and left the room.

Baldegron paced around the table, working his way over to the single window. Behind him, one of the walls suddenly produced a doorway, the empty arch appearing in the middle of the wall out of nowhere, just as the only other exit to the room was suddenly filled up with a mahogany-paneled wall. Through the new doorway walked Filmar.

The Crown Prince, as tall as Baldegron and perhaps as well built, strode in wearing simple blue-and-gold pants and shirt. Clean-shaven, sword at his side, he walked quietly into the room as Baldegron gazed out the window, down at the troops fighting in the practice-yard below. Baldegron, without turning around to look, spoke as his Prince came in.

"Both the Elves in the Woodlands and the Dwarves up north will back us, Sire," he said. "I haven't heard back from the Elven Islands yet, and reports back from the mountain people on My-Thov and Cenivar look good."

"Very good, Baldegron," Filmar said, as he walked over to the General, "my father will be pleased. And remember, it's only *sire* if there's others around."

"Yes, Filmar," Baldegron gave a light chuckle.

Filmar came up and stood beside the large General. They both looked out through the window at the practice-field, watching the soldiers as they played at the arts of war, practicing their attacks, thrusts, and counter-thrusts.

"Starke's a good man," Baldegron finally said, "I hope his friends make it back; that Shong will soon be able to teach *me* a thing or two about sword-play, and Bronto owes me a wrestling match."

"I'm afraid that Mystigir says he's lost all contact with them," Filmar sighed. "His magic has been unable to divine either their status or location. Something blocks their presence; something that wants them in that valley—alone."

The clink of swords sounded below them, an almost melodic sound to the ears of Baldegron.

"It is as the gold-skinned one foretold," the bald warrior said, "'they shall be on their own, and only their own abilities shall tell the outcome'. You traveled with them; do you think they'll make it?"

Filmar leaned his arms down against the bottom of the window, gazing out with the General.

"If they don't," the Prince said, "then what comes may not be won."

An endless expanse of sea, dotted by thousands of islands. From large islands to the size of small rocks, they all soared swiftly by underneath. Waves lapped about the rough waters, as low lying clouds rapidly passed by below.

The creature was searching, a job for which it was well suited. Its colorful small two-foot-long dragon-like body belied the fierceness of which this small creature was known. The dragon runner flew swiftly over the Sea Of A Thousand Islands, malignancy in its heart, its sharp eyes searching carefully for any sign of its master's desires.

Far beneath it another island slipped by as it flew overhead. A large ogre stood at the edge of a cave, taking no note of the small speck that sped swiftly away. Behind him the dragon eggs still lay, silent as ever while Blag-ak watched over them. The large ogre's slow brain was thinking, wondering, which for Blag-ak was the same as talking out loud.

"Blag-ak wonder how friends do," he rumbled as he looked out at the forest beyond. "Blag-ak hope friends come back."

He listened to the sound of the waves breaking upon the island's distant shore, listened to the quiet of the green forests, and looked up at the simple beauty of the castle they'd built upon the top of the cliff.

"Blag-ak miss them."

A slight noise sounded behind him as one of the eggs in the cave stirred lightly. The ogre let out a rumble of a sigh and then turned back to rejoin his charges. With a single-minded loyalty that only the simple of heart and mind can truly muster, Blag-ak went back into the cave, determined to keep to his promise of watching the eggs through to their hatching, eggs that he considered his own.

Far overhead, the searching dragon runner flew on, searching for the very island that it unknowingly passed over; the island upon which Blag-ak now stood sentry.

The mountains of My-Thov were dark and moody, as if a continual pale of darkness hung over the very soul of its ridges and forests. Within its dark recesses, even darker creatures moved. Large tribes of them moving about their secret unseen paths, slowly gathering their forces.

Further south in these very same mountains, tribes of mountain men went about their daily lives. Consciously were they unaware of what gathered to their north but, so attuned to their treasured mountains were they, that they were almost subliminally aware of the evil disease that threatened their natural domain.

One figure watched from atop a tall mountain peak. The figure watched with sharp eyes, seeing the secret trails of the creatures as they traveled along them. The figure quietly watched as they slowly gathered their numbers. The figure bent down to count the tracks left by their movements, listened to the sounds the forest made as they spoke to him of the dark stain treading through its growth, and listened to what the wind carried with it of distant cries chanting in the distance.

An earthen-colored traveling cloak covering his shiny plate mail from other watching eyes, Lo looked down at what he saw in the forest below him. He looked at the trees that seemed to scream in pain, and listened as the sounds of birds and *sÿlva'* lessened almost imperceptibly, as if they were slowly fleeing their own homes, trying to escape the black disease that slowly crept along the mountains. He felt the soul of darkness creep almost unnoticeably across the mountain chain.

Lo shifted his stance as he looked south along the long mountain chain, in the direction of the mountain people. Being to the mountains what the Destir are to the deserts, they would be the first to defend their mountains against the dark forces that moved, be the first to stand up against the plots and manipulations of Miro, be the first to raise arms against the orkai and other unnamed creatures of darkness, be the first to recognize their threat.

And, deep in his heart, as he stepped down off the ridge to follow the long trail out, Lo knew that they would also be the first to die.

"I will show the world!" the craggy voice echoed strongly through the caverns. "After my transformation, they will know better than to use *me* as their scape-goat! No longer will the world abuse Po-Adar!"

Torch-light flickered throughout the carved stone halls as twisted-faced goblins patrolled them with their jagged-edged polearms. Of the several branching caverns, the voice came from one in particular. Pale yellow light flickered from that particular cavern as the goblins nervously stood guard outside. As hard and cruel as the goblins tended to be, even *they* were made nervous by the source of the voice within that cavern.

Skipping calmly down the stone hall, knife in one clawed hand small pouch in the other, a diminutive figure skipped down the hall, his thick ear-length green hair bouncing from side to side, his demented goblin-like features puckered into a crocked smile as he happily whistled some nameless tune. The small figure skipped up to the cavern that the goblins were guarding, giving a happy flip of his head as he passed them on by. The goblins shook their heads as the small figure entered the feared cave; they could never figure out how Jumpit could be so willingly devoted to Po-Adar.

Jumpit skipped into the dimly-lit cavern. The place he entered looked like some demented alchemy lab had exploded in there. Large bottles of strange ingredients littered several stone tables strewn all about the large cave. Ceramic beakers bubbled forth unknown multicolored liquids, while open plates held what looked to be bits and pieces of strange plants and even stranger creatures. Cages, barely a foot across, were scattered about these tables, and sometimes about the floor at random, each small cage holding creatures that looked to be made from some kid's jigsaw of animal body parts, thrown together with no concern for appearance or function yet somehow kept alive. At one end of the cave was a large pool carved into the stone floor, frothing forth with bubbling oddly-colored liquid that almost bordered on some new state of matter other than liquid, solid, or gas. One wall held a shelf of scattered books, some so potent with magic one could almost see them glow, others having no more magic than a child's story book. Mechanisms of all indefinable sorts lay scattered along the walls, some still working at their unknown functions, others long since non-functioning. A smell pervaded the room, the odor being someplace between the stench of sulphur and the enticing smell of roast pig.

A tall figure stood in front of the bubbling pool, long dark robes covering his over seven feet of hideous features. It was towards this figure that Jumpit skipped merrily along.

"Master," the small one said, "I brought it."

The tall figure turned around, looking down at the small pouch that Jumpit held out to him. A smile crossed the figure's demented features as he reached down to take the offered pouch.

"Very good, Jumpit," he said, patting the small one on the head with his other hand, "the last ingredient I need."

Jumpit smiled happily as the tall figure opened the pouch and turned to face the pool. The pouch was turned over as its contents were emptied into the pool. A trail of grey powdery material floated down from the pouch to land upon the bubbling pool. As the powder so landed, the pool's contents seemed to shift color, from one nauseating version of orange to an even more nauseating variation on green and yellow. The tall figure chuckled to himself as he tossed the pouch over his shoulder.

"Now, will I transform myself, and you, my only friend, Jumpit, shall be my witness."

"Jumpit like, Jumpit like," rejoiced the small one as he jumped up and down in place.

"Every race and creed of being has abused me," the tall figure continued, "even my own Human species has offended me time and again. But, no longer."

He turned around to the rest of the cavern, as if facing some large audience for which he must give a speech. Po-Adar's hideous face shown forth from under his hood as he raised up his arms as if to address such an imaginary crowd. Sleeves rolled back over withered and spotted arms as he gave his oratory.

"No longer will I be used by Humans or any other species on this blighted world. No longer will I even be Human! I will be my *own* race! Then we shall see the fear with which creatures will utter the name of Po-Adar!"

Outside the cavern, the goblins nervously stood guard, shifting from foot to foot with more than a trace of fear. Inside, Po-Adar turned around, back to the strange pool. With a wave of his hand, his robes flew off as if with a life of their own, landing across the cavern. Po-Adar stood before the bubbling pool, his horrible features now exposed fully bare to the world. Jumpit watched as his master muttered several mystical syllables under his breath, adding his magic into the alchemical nightmare bubbling forth in the pool.

The pool began to bubble and churn violently now as the magic seeped into the mixture. Tall pillars of the mixture leaped up head-high before falling back down into the pool, yet never did nary a drop of it splash outside of the pool. The pool almost seemed to have a life of its own as the incantation was finally finished. Po-Adar looked at his handiwork, chuckling loudly. Jumpit continued to smile and jump with glee at his master's delight.

"Now, shall I truly make my own way in this world. I disinherit myself from the race of Man, nor do I henceforth lay claim to any species, known or unknown. I am my own!"

He set first one misshaped foot then the other into the frothing pool. His hideously naked body walked forth towards the center of the pool, pillars of the putrid muck leaping all about him. He laughed as it surrounded him, screamed in insane pleasure as it forced its way into every pour of his body, and chuckled loudly as his entire gruesome form was cut off from view by the leaping pool.

Jumpit watched as the stuff of the pool enveloped his Master, smiled in hideous pleasure as the roar of the pool thundered throughout the cavern and beyond, out along the long stone hallways of the mountain in which they lived. He stopped his jumping, watching in anticipation as the pool leapt and crashed around his unseen master. Then, with a final crash, the liquid leaped up into the air, splashing against the rocky ceiling thirty feet overhead, to then deposit itself back down into the pool with a final splash.

The pool lay calm and smooth, nary a ripple crossing the smooth complexion of the now orange liquid-like muck. Jumpit strained his eyes, but no sign of his master could he see.

Outside the corridor, the goblins stood guard. The sudden silence made them almost as nervous as what went before. After several moments of silence, curiosity got the better of the evil creatures. Slowly, carefully, they peeked around the edge of the entrance, looking into the cavern to see what had happened.

At first they saw only the smooth calm of the pool, Jumpit faithfully waiting at its edge. The goblins looked at each other in puzzlement.

Then the pool began to move, as something began to stand up. In basic shape it looked humanoid, or so the goblins thought as the orange liquid washed down off its rising form. It rose up fifteen feet tall, the liquid now washing clear of its naked form, as it slowly stepped forth from the pool. The goblins had their first good look at the new body of Po-Adar.

One of the goblins screamed in terror, the other's eyes growing wide as his strong goblin heart failed to keep pace with the sudden frightful sight that his eyes showed him. The screaming goblin ran out of the cavern and down the stone hallway as fast as his feet would let him. Other goblins, zombies, and ghouls watched as the terror-stricken creature ran out of the mountain, screaming insanely, as he lost himself in the surrounding forest. They later found him, gibbering insanely to himself, forever-after incoherent. His companion was also found, still slumped in the entrance to the cavern, eyes wide with the fright that killed him.

In the cavern, Jumpit smiled with pleasure, as he watched his master step up out of the pool. A pale demented hand patted Jumpit on the head as a low chuckle arose from the thing that was now Po-Adar.

A slithering tentacle curled out from his form as Po-Adar reached out for his discarded robe.

The morning rays greeted them as they walked down the hillside into the lost valley. Bronto hummed merrily as Eldar practically skipped childlike down the grassy hill. Lindel breathed in deeply of the fresh air as Quickfoot ran boldly about. After their long travels through the hard and snowy mountains, such a valley was almost like a holiday. Overhead, three large white hawks circled down towards them.

"I think we should stop here for a bit," Sabu said, stopping. "We've got a good view of the whole valley from here to better decide where to go."

"Oh, come on," Eldar said, as he stopped skipping, "who needs to plan a route? How hard can it be to find a lost city in *one* little valley?"

"By my estimate," Sabu answered him, "this valley appears to be approximately four hundred and fifty miles long by about half that wide."

"Oh," Eldar said simply, suddenly a bit more seriously. "Okay then, where to?"

"I see a large lake over there," Kilgar said, as he stood atop a large rock, pointing off into the distance, "and I think there's a few rivers going to it."

"That boy's eyes are sharper than a hawk's," Bronto chuckled as he stopped his humming.

"It could wisely be said," Sheil-Bor(h) interjected, "that a great city is often established near to a large waterway, where trade might travel a bit easier."

"He's right," Sindar said, "the lake's our best bet. Probably next to one of the rivers."

"It also appears to be somewhat centrally located," Lindel said, his superior elven vision also picking up what the boy had spotted.

"The lake it is then," Bronto said, as he turned to continue on down the hillside.

He was stopped, though, by three large white hawks, landing directly in his path. The three birds, each at least two feet tall, looked up, regarding him and the others with expressionless bird features.

"Well, it looks like you've found some friends," Eldar commented as he came up next to the big man.

"It is more than that," Sheil-Bor(h) observed, walking up to also look at the hawks, "it is an omen."

"Three lousy white birds an omen?" Quickfoot almost snorted. "I think you've been sniffing too much of your incense."

"*He is right.*"

They all looked as the source of the voice seemed to come from one of the white birds. A startled Quickfoot took his usual place behind Candol's robes.

"Enchanted creatures indeed," Sabu said, as he came up with the others to form a circle around the birds.

"*We are not birds,*" the central bird spoke, its beak moving as it spoke.

"It's a trick, right?" Eldar asked.

"It must be sourced from some vile magic," Lorel said, reaching for his sword.

"*We are no trick, nor are we borne of evil magics.*"

"What are you then?" Sabu asked, his intellectual curiosity now fully aroused.

"*We are those that cannot be named,*" all three sang in unison. "*We are the Nameless Ones that cannot be freed by mortal means. We are the watchdogs of your destiny.*"

"The Nameless Ones, eh?" Mauklo questioned. "That doesn't tell us just who or what you are."

"*A better question,*" another one of them said, "*might be to ask yourselves who you are.*"

156

"Nice and vague," Eldar quipped. "They're beginning to sound like Sheil-Bor(h) here."

"I thank you for the complementary comparison," Sheil-Bor(h) nodded in response, "to what are obviously the three servants of Fate."

"*We are no servants of Fate,*" the third one answered, "*but of something far greater.*"

As they puzzled that, a white light encompassed the three hawks. The others drew back as both the light and the hawks expanded, growing and changing, until there stood amongst them three white-haired men in brightly glowing robes, the morning light shining through them so that all could see them as transparent images floating upon the wind.

"Angels!" Lorel exclaimed. "Truly our quest is blessed."

Mauklo just made an indecipherable sound in his throat.

"*No, Lorel, angels we are not,*" the central one said, "*though this transparency be the only way you can see our true forms.*"

"*What we are isn't as important as what you are,*" the one on the right said, "*or what you might be.*"

"You said that before," Shong asked, "what does it mean?"

"I also noticed that you said something about 'cannot be freed'," Sindar interjected.

"*It is true,*" the one on the left said. "*The simple form of animals is the only corporeal form we can take when away from our imprisonment.*"

"*An imprisonment induced by forces that would see you all fail,*" said the one on the right.

"That doesn't sound too encouraging," Lindel commented.

"This is indeed a sign from the all-mighty Indra," Candol said boldly, "and this humble servant of His would see the enemy of our enemy freed. How may we help?"

"There he goes volunteering us again," Mauklo muttered.

"*We have been watching you since 'ere you left the Harbor Of The World,*" the central one said, "*we show ourselves now to warn you of the path you choose.*"

"It's a bit late for that," Eldar said, "we're already committed."

"Or we *should* be," Mauklo commented.

"*We speak not of 'if' but of 'how', my young Elf,*" the central one spoke. "*Our imprisonment shall last until the stones of Hevon wouldst meet with our prison.*"

"*When your quest is near complete, then shall you find us,*" said the one on the left, "*and then shall you have an ally for that which is to come.*"

"*The cosmos is in imbalance,*" said the one on the right, "*and in your souls lies the key.*"

"You mention Hevon," Sindar said, "of what can you tell us about the Gems of Hevon?"

"And what manner of creatures are you?" Sabu asked.

But the questions went unanswered. The three grew fainter as the light rose towards mid rise, the frail substance of their forms fading upon the winds. Soon, no trace of the visitation was left. The ones gathered about looked at each other in puzzlement and curiosity.

"Such a strange and unexpected happening," Sindar commented. "I wonder of what is their nature, what is their interest in our travels."

"And our Hevon Gems would appear to be more than one would at first think," Sheil-Bor(h) pondered thoughtfully. "I wonder of what is their true nature."

"Too many questions," Sabu agreed.

"I thought it was great," Eldar commented gaily. "Just the type of mysterious encounter to make this outing really fun! Now we *gotta* finish this!"

"Maybe that's what they *wanted* us to do," Mauklo quietly observed, "it could be a ploy with which to trap us."

"What do we do?" Candol asked, one hand searching his robes for a convenient coin to flip. "A visitation by such spirits could mean good or ill for us."

"And how do we find out what they want of us?" Lindel added. "And if we should follow such a course?"

Sheil-Bor(h) held up a hand to signal for silence. They all quieted as they looked over at the calm face, wondering what new piece of wisdom he would give as advice this time. When he had their attention, he said but two words.

"We walk."

Sheil-Bor(h) turned and started walking down the hill to the valley, walking off in the general direction of the large lake that Kilgar had first spotted. The others looked at him as he walked away, and then at each other. Eldar made ready to ask something and then stopped and thought. Finally he just shrugged.

"What the hey," the silver-haired elf said as he turned to follow.

"That's the spirit," Bronto chuckled, slapping Eldar on the back as he too started walking.

Smiles quickly spread as the simple wisdom of Sheil-Bor(h)'s action did more to sum up what they should do than any amount of discussion.

They all walked down the hillside to the Valley Of Many Lights.

CHAPTER TWENTY-THREE
The Valley of Many Lights

The *orain*-colored sky shown down brightly upon the *narlu* and yellow colorings of the tall grass, waving waist-high to the horizon. The foothills were still in back of them, the surrounding snow-capped mountains now a distant memory. The day was bright, the air clean with the fresh smell of mid-Spring flowers in full bloom and grass waving in the breeze, the horizon clear of immediate dangers. Coming out of the hills they'd found a small stream which they were now following, Bronto in the lead as usual, the ever-vigilant Shong bringing up the rear. They were walking as carefree as they dared, for by now they had learned vigilance as an instinct, being wary even in their sleep.

"Now *this* is the type of country that I prefer to travel through," Lindel said as he happily breathed in deeply of the fresh air.

The small stream, barely more than a dozen feet across, babbled alongside them in agreement, as it wound its way through fields broken only by the occasional lonely tree.

"I'm with you there," Eldar agreed. "Nothing could go wrong in a place such as this."

"That's what worries me," Mauklo interjected, as he kept to himself, a few feet away.

"Oh, always the one to play a dim note in any concert Life and *spirma* has to offer," Candol offered. "By the will of Indra, we have escaped all the hazards that have been thrown against us and now find us delivered into this safe haven.

We are just where we have wanted to be; of what problem could there be in that?"

"You just summed it up for me," Mauklo said.

Candol shook his head is mild exasperation as they continued on.

As they walked alongside the stream, they began to see evidence that the valley was not entirely deserted of life, but was indeed teeming with it. Lost to the outside world for several millennia it may have been, but of its own world there was no lack. They looked off into the distance as a pack of wild dogs went chasing after something that looked vaguely like deer, while overhead a large Roc soared distantly by, hunting for something large enough for it to call a meal. Their hike through the hilly countryside brought them through fields roamed by packs of wolves the size of small ponies, a couple of large furry beasts looking vaguely like a cross between a large bear and a dog, and the occasional large bird soaring by overhead. They took in the many sights around them as they traveled through this new land.

"Well," Shong was saying, "this place certainly doesn't *look* like it's suffered much since the fall of the Kingdoms."

"As are indeed the way with all appearances," Sheil-Bor(h) nodded, "they can hide the reality that is around you."

"Finally," Mauklo snorted, half to himself, as they walked through the tall grass, "someone agrees with me."

"Is that large Roc going to come over here?" Quickfoot asked nervously, looking up at the distant Mastodon-sized bird.

"Don't worry little one," Lindel smiled, "you would make much too small a snack for such a large creature."

"Oh, that's a relief," the small one sighed, wiping his brow with the back of his hand.

"No, you just have to worry about that creature over there," Eldar said pointing.

Quickfoot looked to where Eldar pointed. Flying up through the air, perhaps a few miles away, was what looked to be a large tiger-like beast, with a pair of large wings and a coating of feathers mixed in with its striped fur. It soared through the air, looking about for prey, its large clawed paws ready.

Quickfoot gave a yelp and was immediately behind Candol's robes.

Eldar and Lindel laughed as Candol pulled the small one out from behind him. The priest shook his head at Quickfoot.

"After all we have faced, have you no faith in the abilities and protection of your friends?" the priest admonished.

Quickfoot looked around sheepishly as Candol sighed.

"Perhaps I should finally cure your fear-ridden tendencies before they bring you to harm," Candol suggested.

"Or get *us* into trouble," Mauklo added.

Before Quickfoot could wonder and think to escape, Candol placed a hand firmly on his forehead and began reciting a quick incantation.

"May your fears be gone," Candol intoned, "and may the courage of the mighty Indra be your guide."

The small one began to shake and quiver, eyes rolling up in back of his head as a power seemed to come from Candol's hand directly into Quickfoot's small body. The priest released his hand as Quickfoot dropped to the ground from the convulsive shaking.

"What'd you do to him?" Lorel ran over as he asked, one hand flying to the sword at his side. "Even the small one is deserving of better than just killing him like this!"

"Have no fear," Candol reassured, "for now *he* has none. He is okay and shall awaken with no more fear within him."

"*That* should be an improvement," Mauklo put in.

"Let us *hope*," Sheil-Bor(h) added.

The shaking stopped and Quickfoot began to stir. Lorel was kneeling over him as the small one began to awaken.

"Are you okay?" Lorel asked, as he offered him a hand.

Quickfoot's eyes opened as Lorel helped him to his feet. Quickfoot shook his head clear and looked around, before focusing on Lorel.

"I'm fine," he said. "In fact, probably better."

"If you need——" Lorel began.

"Naw, don't worry," Quickfoot waved him off, "if there's anything I need I'll just steal it from you later. In the meantime, someone should help to scout ahead and, since I'm rather good at that sort of thing, it might as well be me."

Quickfoot took out a knife from one of his many pockets and started to walked on ahead past Bronto. The others just stood and looked at him as he went.

"Someone's also got to teach that young pup Kilgar about how to properly throw a knife," they heard the small one say as he faded away into the tall grass.

Several sets of eyes looked over at Candol.

"Me thinks," Sabu was the first to speak, "that you may have overdid it."

In the distance they heard Quickfoot's voice tell Bronto to move aside.

"*That's* an understatement," Eldar amended Sabu's statement.

A crack of thunder from overhead interrupted their brief state of shock.

"We'd better find shelter before that storm hits," Shong said as they started walking again.

"What storm?" Lindel said, looking up. "There's no clouds in the sky, nor rain in the air."

"Then where'd that thunder come from?" Sindar asked.

"It's the wrong conditions for a Heesur storm," Lindel pondered.

Eldar's eyes began to de-focus momentarily as they walked on wondering. The elf stopped in his tracks as his eyes refocused. Another peel of thunder sounded in the distance.

"Guys," he said, looking up at the others, seriousness on his usual jovial face, "if my special sense is right, then there's magic in that storm."

"Someone sent it after us?" Lorel asked. "Even in this remote valley?"

"I think it's a natural occurrence," Eldar shook his head.

"Hmm, a natural magical phenomena," Sabu pondered as he looked up at the sky. "Most interesting."

They watched, as with another much louder thunderous crack, the sky turned a dark purple with fiery red streaks flashing though it.

"I think we can save 'interesting' for the grove of trees I found for us to shelter under," Bronto said as he walked up to them, Kilgar at his side, "and what the heck got into Quickfoot?"

"Yeah," Kilgar added, "he got too pushy so I had to knock him out."

Lorel turned to Shong in mild shock.

"That scrawny *solron* punched out Quickfoot?"

Shong just shrugged as he answered.

"If he wasn't a friend, Kilgar probably would have killed him."

Green streaks flashed across the sky as a high-pitched whine seemed to come from high above.

"Come on," Bronto motioned, "this way."

Sabu just stood and looked up at the display while the others quickly ran in the direction Bronto indicated. He looked up as several different colors flashed through the deep purple sky, wondering at the source of such displays, while his mind tried to calculate the amount of magical energy contained within such a display. His musings, however, were interrupted by a slender arm pulling him aside.

"Come *on!*" Eldar said as he pulled his friend along with him. "This is no time to get distracted; you can analyze it just as well from under shelter."

Sabu looked momentarily distracted as his friend pulled him along, but a flash of green lightning soon cured that. They ran up a grassy hill and over the top. They looked down to see the others already under a grove of perhaps six large leafy trees. They ran down to join them, getting there just as Quickfoot was waking up, a round black circle around his left eye.

"Now remember," Kilgar was telling Quickfoot, as Eldar and Sabu came under shelter of the trees, "brave does *not* mean foolish."

"Hey I'm sorry already," Quickfoot's high-pitched voice whined out, "I'm just not used to being brave is all. It's a new thing for me."

Sindar was looking up as the sky began to display colorful auroras, its colors ranging the entire spectrum from a bright *trüb* to a deep red. The colors swirled in around themselves, seeming to almost take on definite shapes before being dispersed by a flash of yellow or green lightning. He stared up in wonder at the display.

"*Semdo;* the magic that must be trapped within this valley," he said in slow wonder, "to create such a display."

"I just think it looks pretty," Lindel sighed as he gazed up at the colorful display.

"Now we know why it's called the Valley Of Many Lights," Candol said, as he too watched the ever-changing display. "Truly one of Indra's most beautiful works."

"Of all the gods in this world, why do you always have to pick Indra," Mauklo said derisively.

"I am his humble servant," Candol replied, "it's part of the job."

"The isolation of this *bodaln*, within a range of such tall mountains, must be what traps such magical energy within it," Sabu speculated, as the brightly-colored auroras grew ever brighter. "There must be a natural magical focal point within this valley, feeding magical energy into the land, but the mountains stop it from getting any further. Such energy! If one could just but tap into such a display of magic, the things one could do with it."

"Like, for instance, using it as a lens to find things with?" Mauklo suggested, as colored lights flashed around them.

"That would be one possible use," Sabu agreed.

"That's what I thought," Mauklo sighed.

Mauklo nodded up towards one section of the sky, as he and the others looked up at what he'd indicated.

One of the auroras was taking on another of the almost-shapes, except this time the shape wasn't dispersing. Rather, it was forming into a most definite shape.

A face.

Hundreds of small fiery streaks began to fall down through the sky, landing as burning-hot hail to smolder in the thick green grass. The face, sour of expression and grim of feature, seemed to look down upon the grassy plains. Star-speckled eyes slowly glanced back and forth.

"It searches," Sheil-Bor(h) concluded. "I suggest we not find out if we are the object of its designs."

"Why would it look for us here?" Lorel asked. "We are strangers to this valley. We are not known to any within this land."

"Take a clue!" the usually ever-calm Mauklo spat out in Lorel's direction. "We've been lead by the nose to this place all along!"

Thunder cracked from the sky, seeming to form words; words that came upon the wind and the display of magic overhead, words that seemed to speak for the large searching face.

"*I know you are out there*," the words said, deep and rumbling, "*you have entered my land.*"

"But, we came upon this land of our own decision," Sabu corrected. "We read about the place in one of the dimensio-books and came of our own free will. Why, even Lo, servant to the King, seemed to find nothing wrong with our decision."

"Ones such as Lo have no crooked twists and turns to the contours of their thoughts," Mauklo countered, "he cannot think in terms of deception and cunning. Ask yourself: where did we *find* the dimensio-books?"

"Why, in the domain of the Dragon Lord," Sabu answered.

Sparkly lights flashed in the large face overhead as it surveyed the plains around them.

"And the Dragon Lord is friends with *whom?*" Mauklo persisted, as the storm of magic now raged loud and bright all about them.

No one said a word for several moments, not until Sindar first broke their silence.

"Miro," Sindar nodded.

"But, we almost died on several occasions getting those things," Eldar protested.

"Not to mention that we ended up there by *accident,*" Quickfoot added, "courtesy of a certain too-large whirlpool."

"Accidents?" Mauklo asked scornfully. "Coincidences? We *are* talking about the same Miro, aren't we?!"

"He's right," Sindar agreed, "we've been lead to this valley all along."

"But, to arrange and plan for so much," Sabu wondered, "our getting to Devoon, knowing that we'd get past his ally's forces and find the books, harassing us into this valley…"

Outside their small shelter of trees, small tufts of the long grass started to catch on fire from the raging storm of magic.

"The manipulations of a true master of the art are subtle indeed," Sheil-Bor(h) acknowledged, as he sat down cross-legged upon the ground, "and would make one wonder just how far back he *did* plan."

Green and *orain* flashes of light punctuated their verbal silence, while colorful three-dimensional auroras swam by overhead. The large star-speckled face looked down omnipotently.

"I would suggest some more cover," Lindel said, "I'm feeling pretty exposed right now."

"It would be my pleasure," Sheil-Bor(h) was the first to respond.

Sheil-Bor(h) lifted up a hand and gestured to the trees overhead. Suddenly, between one bright flash of the storm and the next, the leaves and branches of their small grove of trees seemed to thicken and grow together, forming a thick canopy of green between them and the observing sky overhead.

"That should do for a while," Bronto looked up, examining Sheil-Bor(h)'s handiwork.

"But, what I still don't get," Shong said, "is *why* Miro wants us in this valley."

"An easy answer," Lorel offered, "he seeks to trap us. All around us are mountains to block our path out, while within this valley there is one of his minions to hunt us down."

"He probably wants revenge for that dragon of his that we killed," Kilgar suggested.

"But, that wouldn't trap us," Sindar said, confused. "We have the capability to either teleport out of here by magic, or to exit by way of Sabu's portable portal."

Thunder crash, green lightning strike; auroras rolling into deadly shapes.

"Try it," Mauklo suggested.

Sindar tried a simple teleport spell, concentrating on the lines of magic that would shift him out of this valley.

Nothing happened.

Sabu got out his special sack, to lay it down and open up his portable portal to the island.

It was just a sack, no portal.

Hot hail raining, burning through trees, face looking down, peering intently as it waited for the canopy to burn away.

"We *are* trapped," Sabu admitted, "and that face up there is going to find us as soon as those leaves burn away."

Multiple peels of thunder sounded out, running their quick rumbles together as they were punctuated by almost musical whines singing their way through the winds.

"Uh," Eldar said, suddenly looking concerned as he held his sword out in his hand, looking intently at its hilt, "a rather unsettling thought just occurred to me."

"I'm almost afraid to hear this one," Sabu sighed.

"But, uh, I was just wondering," Eldar went on, as the leaves began to smolder overhead, "just who or what really *did* arrange for us to find our Hevon gems. And why."

Pyrotechnic displays chewed through the dark purple sky as Eldar's pondering went unanswered. Colorful lightning strikes raged all about them, low rumbling thunder and high-pitched whines screaming through the air. An emotion akin to hopelessness swept through the group. Bronto was the first to bring them back to more immediate problems.

"That large face is about to spot us," the big man said, "and I personally don't like playing the role of a sitting duck."

"He's right," Kilgar spoke up, "survive now, wonder later."

Sindar looked around at the display of magic, thinking quickly, as the others began to come out of their reverie. He looked up at the large face and got an idea.

"Sabu," he said, "if another can make use of this prevailing magic field, why couldn't you; at least for something simple?"

Sabu's face brightened as he thought.

"I've got just the thing," he said, "the most simple of magics."

As the rest waited, tense, for whatever might happen, Sabu held up his rune-covered staff. Not even muttering any words of magical incantation, he pointed the staff at the sky.

A bolt of light shot up from the tip of his staff, soaring straight up to the center of the magical auroras. The immense starry face watched as its large eyes followed the path of the simple bolt of light. The bolt curved around, like some missile of light, and impacted straight into a waving *tairu*-colored aurora.

The effect was spectacular. Sabu's bolt blossomed into a large magical torch of light, just like one of the many normal ones he had often used to light their way. But, fed on by the wild magic of the storm, it quickly grew, rapidly expanding, like some swelling plague of light, across the deep purple sky. The different swirling auroras connected into a single bright throbbing pulse of light.

"Shield your eyes!" Bronto shouted.

The light flashed across the entire storm of magic, setting the sky ablaze with a single flash of light. A thunderous scream was heard as the large face-like aurora grimaced in pain, its starry eyes shutting closed from the sudden light. The light flashed through the face, encompassing it entirely as the distant thunder-voice screamed in unexpected pain. For several long moments, the light burned up in the sky, feeding off the magic of the storm. It shone brightly through the trees while those under it closed their eyes against its brightness. Long moments later, the light began to fade, leaving in its wake, not a dark purple sky filled with the magic of the storm, but the normal-looking sky of a bright afternoon.

Several sets of eyes blinked as their sight was recovered. Eldar, grinning ear to ear, was the first to speak.

"Spectacular!" he almost jumped up as he shouted with joy. "How'd you do *that* one?!"

Sabu shrugged.

"I cast a normal light spell," Sabu answered simply, "but I just sort of open-ended it; I allowed the magic of the storm to feed it. The storm did the rest."

"It must have also spent the magic of the storm," Sindar observed. "We need not worry over being found by the lord of this valley."

"Not to mention about that peeper *seeing* for a while," Eldar grinned madly. "I'd love to see his reaction to all his great magic being stopped by a large *torch* shoved in his face!"

"All well and good, but where do we go from here?" Lorel asked.

"We decided *that* when we killed Miro's pet dragon," Bronto said, as he started to walk out from under the trees, "we go onward."

"Any objections?" Sabu asked.

All eyes looked at Mauklo.

"I, for one, don't like being used," Mauklo said calmly as he started after Bronto, "and I intend on finding the *source* of that face and sticking something long and pointed down its throat."

No objections were heard, not even by the now-somewhat-braver Quickfoot. With nary another word being said amongst them, they picked up their course, walking back to the stream and continuing on up its length as if nothing had happened.

As the afternoon waned into early evening, the stream widened and emptied into a small lake. Maybe a mile or two across, it lay flat and glistening in the midst of the tall field of grass, its still surface calmly reflecting the orange setting of Gamro and the simultaneous rising of the blue-green orb of Gamri. A few trees and small shrubs dotted along the lake's shore, the sun settling down for a long evening's rest as they approached the still waters.

"This looks like a good place to camp," Bronto said as he looked around. "Camp out close together and remember to ration the supplies; we don't have Sabu's portal for emergencies anymore."

"I'll scout out around the lake and see what I can find," Quickfoot volunteered.

And, before anyone could stop him, Quickfoot had disappeared into the brush. Shong and Lorel both dropped their backpacks down on the ground while Mauklo sat down and brought out a small palm-sized chest. When he opened up the chest there was a brief flash of light; when the light cleared, Mauklo was surrounded by blankets, pillows, and a small cooking fire complete with cooking utensils and lit fire. Eldar, dropping his own small backpack to the ground, looked at the wizard relaxing back on his pillows.

"I gotta get me one of those," the silver-haired elf shook his head.

"Naw, you wouldn't like it," Bronto answered Eldar with a smile. "It eats too much and would just leave left over necromancy stuff all over your floor; hard to train too."

Eldar grinned at Bronto's response, his grin quickly turning into a laugh as several of the others also began snickering. Mauklo looked around him with calm regard about the joke.

"I think," Lindel said laughing a bit himself, "he meant the *box*."

"Oh," Bronto said with mock realization, "that *would* be better; especially around feeding time."

"If you are *quite* finished," Mauklo said as the giggling and grinning died down, "I will attribute the jocularity at my expense to the long trip we have been through."

"As good a reason as any other," Lindel said, bringing out his bow. "I'll go see about getting us some dinner."

As the elf went out beyond the surrounding bushes, Sindar got a momentary vague look on his face. The young wizard shot a meaningful glance over to Sabu, who discretely began to finger his staff. Eldar, noticing the quick exchange, casually sat down and brought out his sword as if to clean it. Kilgar was nowhere to be seen.

It was then that Lindel came backing out of the brush, looking at something still out of sight to the others. His unnotched bow was in one hand as his face held more than a trace of concern on it.

"Uh, guys," the elf said, "there will be a slight delay in getting that dinner."

Following Lindel out of the brush, came a tall figure. Over six feet tall, with brown fur from head to toe, clawed fingers grasping around a longsword, cat-like facial features giving no doubt as to its ancestry. On two legs it walked, like any normal man, but with a slender tail curled behind it and a feline grace of movement, this figure looked like one of the family of large cats given bipedal form. Around its torso and legs it wore a stiff leather vest, laced about with several scattered scales of leather. A belt-pouch was tied tightly around its middle as it held its sword aimed at Lindel's throat. If one could tell from its facial features, then this specimen was a male.

It was joined by six more, coming out of the grass and bushes around their camp, each holding a sword, walking in a half-crouch as if ready to either fight or jump. Lindel quickly backed up to the others, the creatures now forming a half-circle around them, the lake that they were camped up against forming the other half of the circle.

One of the creatures held the struggling form of Quickfoot, one large paw cupped over the small one's mouth.

"They're felinians," Sabu explained, "I don't know the exact species."

"Do you speak Selgish?" Sindar called out to them. "Or Tradespeak?"

"We mean you no harm," Lorel said, standing boldly forth, "we mean only to seek out and vanquish evil in all its forms. To boldly stand against—Umph."

Lorel found himself suddenly bound head to foot with thick rope, his mouth having about three layers of thick white cloth gagging over it. He fell to the ground with a *thump* as Mauklo brought down the hand that he'd just pointed to Lorel with.

"Uh," Mauklo said, smiling pleasantly as Lorel wriggled around on the ground, "he doesn't speak for *any* of us."

The felinians growled amongst themselves in their own harsh tongue before one of them stepped forward.

"We speak your Selgish," he growled, holding his sword out in front of himself. "You travel through our territory."

"We didn't know it was yours," Sabu said.

"Everyone knows of our territory," the felinian growled back, "you come to invade."

"We *didn't* know," Sabu insisted, "we're from outside of your valley."

Several deep chuckles began to arise from the felinians. Their leader once again spoke up as he laughed.

"No one comes from outside this valley," he grinned. "The mountains cannot be passed; they are too high and the dragons within them too hungry. Your lie traps you."

"We did *so* come from outside," Quickfoot said, getting his mouth free as he was struggling against his captor. "We got by the dragons, met with the hawkmen, and everything."

"Hawkmen!"

The one holding Quickfoot growled out that statement as he tossed the small one across the camp. Quickfoot landed hard against a tree as his former captor glared at him, crouching down as if making ready to jump.

"They are friends of those cowardly winged pests," he said. "Spies!"

"You ally yourselves with our racial enemy," the leader growled angrily. "By your own words, you call yourselves enemies!"

The one that had held Quickfoot suddenly jumped from his crouch, leaping out towards him. Quickfoot, still lying on his back from being tossed there, tried to quickly scramble aside.

Thump!

Just as the felinian was in mid leap, a long curved knife buried itself deep in his forehead. The felinian's eyes bulged wide as his body fell unmoving to Quickfoot's side. He was dead.

Kilgar stepped out from behind the very tree that Quickfoot was laying up against. The other felinians watched, teeth bared and muscles tense, as he calmly walked over and pulled his knife out of the dead cat's skull.

"You know," the boy said, yanking out his knife, "you're braver than before, but you *still* get into trouble."

The other felinians quickly growled amongst themselves, astonishment showing on their faces, as a couple of birds flew off from behind some bushes behind them.

"The *boy* killed him?!" one of them finally said in Selgish.

"Yes!" Bronto said, stepping forward. "To save one of our own, as I'm sure you would do for your own kind."

"Umph mmph—" came the muffled interjection of the still tied up form of Lorel.

Bronto reached over his back and drew out the Dragon Sword as he continued.

"And yes we made friends of the Hawkmen," he went on, "but that doesn't mean we wish to make enemies of you. We'll stand by their side in battle against any who would do them harm, but we won't seek after everyone that bears them a grudge; that is your own affair!"

He took the Sword up in both hands and plunged it down into the ground in front of him, as if to punctuate what he said next.

"But," he said as the sword came plunging down into the ground in front of him, "march you against any whom we hold as friend and then we shall stand firm! Be you then our friend?"

The leader looked first at Bronto, then over at Kilgar standing over the body of their dead comrade, then back at Bronto again. An almost menacing grin spread across his cat-like face.

"You are bold and firm in your views," he said. "That, at least, we respect. But, there is still no proof to the rest of your words. How can anyone come from the outside? The hidden passes have been closed ever since the fall of the Kingdom long ago."

"You mean, there was an *easier* way we could have gotten through those mountains?" Quickfoot said with some exasperation as he got to his feet. "Where were you guys earlier with this revelation!"

A sudden fluttering of several birds drew Lindel's attention as he looked around and saw hundreds of birds suddenly taking to the air for some distance around them. A worried look crossed his face as he looked up into the sky.

"While you two are trying to decide whose testosterone level is higher," Lindel said in the direction of Bronto and the leader felinian, "I think we *both* have some company."

The leader felinian looked up to where Lindel was gazing. He growled deep in his throat as the rest followed his gaze.

High in the sky above them, covering them like a large feathered blanket, was an army of birds, hovering over them, waiting. Birds of all types, from the very small sparrow, to the large twenty-foot wingspan of something looking like a large black eagle. In the center of them all, squawking out to the rest like generals giving orders, hovered perhaps a dozen strange birds. Eight feet long and perhaps some six feet tall they were, not counting their large wingspan. Their darkly-feathered bodies were speckled with occasional splashes of green and yellow feathers, their beaked faces seeming to emanate a mean disposition. They were gazing down with malevolent intent at those arrayed below them, and not at the felinians was the murderous intent in their eyes aimed.

"Geedlors!" the leader felinian exclaimed as he advanced towards Bronto, sword in hand. "You bring them to us!"

"I fear they are not after you," Sheil-Bor(h) said looking up at the feathered sky.

"What are Geedlors?" Shong asked, as his sword suddenly appeared at his side, so fast did he draw it out.

"Masters of the air," Lindel explained, notching a black arrow to his bow, "they can control anything that flies. It's said that they are an artificial race."

There was a loud cat-like growl as the felinian leaped at Bronto, claws out, sword slashing forward. Bronto left the Dragon Sword standing where he'd planted it in the ground as he caught the felinian in the middle of his leap, blocking the swipe of his sword with a single strong slap of his own massive arm. He threw the felinian up and over him just as the Geedlors overhead gave a loud screech. When the leader landed, the hundreds of birds overhead started to swoop down upon the area.

The air was quickly blanketed by wave upon wave of flapping feathers, screeching beaks, and sharp claws. Feathers blinded everywhere as claws raked and tore. Candol, ready to once again invoke the power of Indra, found himself blinded by a wall of claws. Shong's sword danced swiftly about him, but even he found it hard to aim for anything when all he could see were feathers, sometimes hitting Eldar instead. A dark shaft from Lindel's bow pierced through the air, its aim true to its target, its flight fouled by the beating of hundreds of wings about in the air. Sindar tried to conjure up a quick spell as he watched one of the larger birds start to carry Kilgar up into the air. Sabu fought as several of the birds sought to wrestle his staff away from him. Quickfoot, knife slashing behind him, tried to run behind a bush for cover, only to come face to face with one of the Geedlors.

A quick slash of an iron-hard beak and Quickfoot was sent hurling back against the same tree which the felinian had hurled him against earlier, only this time his right arm had been nearly bitten off as the small one slumped unconscious by the tree, blood from his wound pooling at his side.

The felinians fought the wall of feathers and claws with their own whirling walls of fur, claws, and swords, slashing and stabbing away at anything with feathers that came near them. They fought with an intense ferocity and great nimbleness, but to little avail. There were just too many birds, their many flapping wings blinding all within them, their claws and beaks seemingly everywhere. It was like being inside of a living wall of thorns.

One of the felinians, sword slashing about him, was felled upon by several of the birds. He screamed defiance at them and then screamed in pain and terror as one of the Geedlor came diving in on him, slashing out with its large claws, stabbing out with its strong beak. Blood and fur flew everywhere as the felinian's scream was soon silenced. Dismembered limbs and disemboweled guts lay strewn about where he'd been before.

Even Mauklo was harried by several of the larger birds, fighting to concentrate as they clawed at his face. Eldar, though, sword in hand, set it alight with fire, screaming out his joy of battle as he went slashing his flaming dance amongst the feathered wall.

Of course, the sight of fire had the expected reaction upon Lorel, as the stout warrior stretched against his bonds while his body quivered and shrunk into the warty form of Schanter.

Wind rising round. Feathered menace swirling away as a whirlwind of feathers and claws grows larger, expanding out through the grassy field. Wind rising tall overhead, parting the feathered plague like a priest the waters of despair. Like the eye of a storm, calmness at its center, did the winds form around them.

At the center of the storm was Sheil-Bor(h), sitting cross-legged upon the ground, forming his windy shell of protection around their small camp, sheltering too the felinians.

There was a light thump as Kilgar came falling down from the sky, the sudden winds having released the birds' grip upon him. The small boy landed nimbly upon his feet, weapon already in hand. The felinians paused in their fighting, as with the others, they all looked around at the wall of birds, kept at bay by Sheil-Bor(h)'s winds.

The Geedlors, unfortunately, seemed unaffected by it, hovering directly above them as if untouched.

"Nothing of the air can touch them," Lindel said, his face bleeding from more than a few scratches, his bow almost as torn and ragged as was he.

A sudden insane scream distracted them. Several ropes lying around him, Schanter stood grinning insane malevolence. With a leap high even for him, Schanter leapt to the top of Quickfoot's tree, quickly scrambled up to the very top and thence leaping onto the back of the nearest Geedlor, clawing fiercely at its feathered back.

"Okay, so we don't try air," Sabu said as he lifted up his staff.

Sabu, however, was beaten to the punch by Mauklo. Robes lying torn and battered about him, Mauklo was standing, blood on his face, as he pointed up at one of the foul creatures. A glowing spinning wire mesh went tumbling quickly through the air towards the nearest Geedlor. It flew quickly aside to dodge the strange menace, only to see the spinning mesh veer its course to overtake it. The creature screeched loudly as it was enveloped in a tight cage of wire, the tightly-woven mesh permitting nary a claw to poke through. It struggled for flight as the mesh pinned down its wings, tumbling towards the ground as the metal net bound tightly to its flesh.

Then, the net began to *shrink*.

The creature, lord of the air, screamed in pain as it plummeted quickly to the ground, but just as quickly did the metal net shrink down about it, cutting easily through flesh, feathers, and bone, sending great gouts of blood gushing out after it. By the time it landed upon the ground, all that was left was a ruined pile of feathers and flesh, looking like it was fresh out of a large meat grinder, the metal net now folding in upon itself to a small disappearing ball of wire.

"Messy, yet effective," Eldar commented, as he turned and raised his sword up towards the sky.

Sabu's staff went next, a stream of sand streaking out as if through a high-pressure hose, the sand-blaster cutting through another of the feathered forms as the high speed of the beam of sand simultaneously de-feathered and ground it to a fine meaty mist, a sudden explosion of feathers being the only sign that there had once been a large bird there.

Several of the other birds beyond the wall of air seemed to get uneasy. Lindel watched as some of them began to flutter away and others to get restless.

"Their control is slipping," Lindel shouted above the noise of the surrounding winds, "the other birds are starting to leave."

"Then one less should help out even more," Bronto said, pulling his Dragon Sword up out of the ground.

A loud cat-like cry from behind him got the big man's attention. Bronto turned in time to see the leader felinian charging at him. The cat leaped at Bronto as Bronto made to draw back his sword. But the leap was a bit high. Instead of hitting Bronto, the felinian's feet landed on his shoulders, the cat spending no time to rest as it fluidly launched itself off of Bronto's shoulders and up into the air, claws stretched out.

The felinian went full-on straight into the face of a screeching Geedlor, his claws slashing at the large bird's face. His claws caught it in the eyes, gouging out one of them on its way to the creature's brain. Both cat and bird came tumbling down to the ground in a jumbled pile of fur and feathers.

Which made it the first of two Geedlors more to come tumbling down. The one upon which Schanter rode now came flying down, trying to dislodge the insane menace from its back. It flew up against a tree, finally sending Schanter flying from its back to land crouching upon the ground. But just as it tried to fly away, Schanter made another grab for it, grinning with a toothy smile, as he pulled at its tail. The Geedlor squawked in fright as the small creature at its tail tried to pull it back to itself.

"You no go," he said, "Schanter still want to play!"

Lightning then lanced through the air, several small fingers of it dancing amongst the remaining Geedlors. The creatures all screamed in pain as they saw the single source below them. Sindar was holding up his right hand, a spinning maelstrom of perhaps a dozen fingers of lightning reaching up into the air, burning feathers and singeing skin in their wild dance.

The creatures had had enough. The remaining Geedlors turned around and went winging away, flying away from them as fast as their remaining feathers would allow them. Schanter found himself with a handful of tail feathers as the one he'd had hold of also flew out of there. Their control broken, the other gathered birds quickly went on about what normal birds tend to do, the large flock soon dispersing.

When all was calm, Sheil-Bor(h) released his wall of wind, the air settling back down to normal. Bronto helped the leader felinian out from under the Geedlor body, while Candol went over to tend to Quickfoot. The remaining felinians gathered around behind their leader after Bronto helped him to his feet.

"You fought with us," the leader said, "that at least proves you are not enemies."

"As we were trying to tell you," Shong said, wiping the blood from his sword.

"If you *did* come from outside this valley," the leader continued, "then those of the old Kingdom have returned to reclaim what they once lost."

"Of that, we can make no promises," Bronto spoke, "just that we will do what we can."

"Our destiny leads us to where it will," Sheil-Bor(h) said as he stood up, "and we but try to read the road signs that it posts along the way."

"Spoken like those of old," the leader said, and then paused for several moments, as if deciding, before continuing. "You may pass through our territory, but beware the master of the valley."

The felinians then backed off into the brush and were gone.

"What do you make of that?" Eldar asked.

"Well," Sabu began, "I'd say that they're descendants of some felinians that worked for Thïr Tÿorca when it fell. They then got trapped or just decided to stay and——"

"No, not *that*," Eldar sighed, "everything else."

"The Geedlors were obviously sent after us by whichever force seems to rule this valley," Sindar offered, "hunting after us. The felinians seem friendly enough once you get their trust."

"They probably learned distrust from that master of the valley they mentioned," Bronto said.

"Which means," Shong summarized, "that we're going to have to be careful with whomever else we meet; it may be that no one trusts anyone around here."

"Ow," came Quickfoot's voice from beside the bent form of Candol. "Okay, it's better already."

Quickfoot stood up, rubbing his arm, as Candol also got to his feet. The small one walked in towards the others as he spoke.

"I never used to get this battered up when I was a coward," he said. "Bravery is dangerous!"

"It has its price," Kilgar said as he bent down by the lakeside to wash his hands and face.

"I don't suppose I could be a coward again?" Quickfoot asked the priest.

"Tell you what," Candol offered, "I'll tone it down a bit. You won't be as brave as you are now, but neither will you be the coward you once were."

"Good enough," Quickfoot said happily. "Now, when do we eat?"

"Some things never change," Eldar said, as he sat down on the ground to open up his backpack. "Now let's get this camp ready for nightfall."

"I would suggest some extra precautions," Sheil-Bor(h) quietly put in.

"Any particular reason why?" Shong asked as he helped make their small camp ready.

"It begins the season of *Kilio*," Sheil-Bor(h) answered simply.

"A child's holiday," Shong shrugged, "a time for them to play at hunting goblins, spirits, and witches without actually meeting the real thing. There is no danger in it."

"Maybe where *you* come from," Eldar quipped, "but from where *I'm* from, it's three rises worth of excuses for the supernatural to have at the mortal world."

"Ah, but you're forgetting," Shong said, laying out a blanket, "for such creatures to gain power from the time of *Kilo*, they have to be somewhere around you. Now, where in this whole hidden valley are we going to find a couple of undead to make trouble for us on Kilio?"

Shong's casual observation seemed to end the discussion. As night fell, they erected their camp by the lakeside, Lindel hunting down one of the deer-like creatures for their dinner. They relaxed as they ate under the blue-green glow of

Gamri, the moon's half-phase shining peacefully down. The lake lay still and calm under the evening sky.

"You know," Bronto said as he sat back and tore at the warm piece of meat he held, "you're not too bad a cook."

"Thanks," Lindel answered, "although I usually go for more of a vegetarian diet, but these plains are rather sparse on that point."

"Yeah," Bronto continued with a smile, "some rise you'll make someone a great wife."

Snickering and scattered smiles came out from those gathered around the fire as they responded to Bronto's jest. Lindel, though, seemed to take it in good stride.

"Funny," he said sarcastically, and then broke into a slow smile.

The stars overhead shown out as distant pinpricks of light, three shooting stars gracing their way down across the sky. Eldar started to sing an elvish tune, his soft melodic voice carrying lightly upon the evening breeze, the elven words of his song drifting like musical droplets upon the air. Kilgar was sitting next to Bronto, cutting off another piece of meat with his long curved knife as the big man gave a hearty belch in appreciation of his own repast.

"Bronto," Kilgar said as he sliced off a piece of meat, "what do you think will be at Thïr Tÿorca once we get there?"

Bronto leaned back against a tree as he answered, gazing up at the sky as two more shooting stars raced their way across the sky.

"I gave up worrying about the future a long time ago," the big man answered. "I'll leave all this stuff of Fates to the intellects and sages. Me, my needs are simple: a good life. The rest will come in its own time."

"But," Kilgar continued, "don't you ever wonder about where we're going?"

"It's been a grand adventure so far," Bronto smiled, "no doubt the lost city will hold more of the same."

"I sometimes wonder if there isn't something waiting for us," Kilgar said, as he bit into his meat. "Mauklo may be right; this could all be a trap, and we may not be ready for it."

"Kid," Bronto placed a large hand on the boy's shoulder, "Sabu and Sindar are more intelligent than anyone I've ever known. They'll be able to figure something out."

"One of the elders in the desert used to say, that if you're going to walk into a trap, you should always have your own trap ready."

Bronto chuckled and shook his head.

"One of these rises I'm going to have to visit that desert of yours," Bronto said.

Several shooting stars streaked across the sky as Sabu and Sindar sat together, talking quietly. Eldar came out of the bushes, having just relieved himself of Nature's call, and sat down next to them.

"So," he asked, "what's the topic of conversation?"

"The shooting stars we've been seeing," Sabu answered.

"Yeah," Eldar said, looking up at the sky, "they *are* kind of beautiful."

"They also *aren't* shooting stars," Sindar corrected.

Eldar cocked an eyebrow as he waited for Sindar to continue.

"Shooting stars," he went on, "don't change course and backtrack."

"Now *this* sounds interesting," Eldar smiled. "What are they then?"

"That's just what we were discussing," Sabu explained. "They appear to be flying in some sort of search pattern."

"And we don't have to guess what they're searching for," Eldar finished for him.

Overhead, one of the shooting stars seemed to be arcing straight down towards them. A faint whistle of wind seemed to come from it, a whistle that was quickly increasing to a high-pitched wail. Immediately weapons leapt to their owners' hands as they looked around for what approached them.

"I guess we'll see what they are *now*," Eldar said, his own sword springing to his hand.

Soul draining scream, intense cry of despair, fear soaking to the bone. Ghost-like feminine fright, drawing weakness through muscle and sinew, terror through the soul. High-pitched wail echoing out over the lake, cry of death piercing through the veil of Life like a knife.

Bronto leapt to his feet, sword in his hand, as the shooting star came down, now appearing as a brightly glowing ball of pale white light. Its high-pitched wail screamed out as it landed in their midst, forming into the vague outline of a translucent woman, long ghost-like hair flying around her, her cry sending shivers through the soul and fear to the bone. Lorel immediately stood up, ready to do battle, but felt the strength leave his legs as the wail seemed to drain him of energy. Complexion turning pale, legs buckling, Lorel fell to the ground in a weak faint.

Similarly, Quickfoot too was felled by the unnatural scream, while Shong felt his own limbs growing weaker. Sheil-Bor(h), face turning pale as well, merely sat down cross-legged and meditated, concentrating on countering the effects of the deadly scream. Kilgar, boy though he was, proved once again the durability of his people as, knife in hand, he leapt straight towards the transparent creature. Bronto lunged with his own large sword, slicing down at the creature.

But both Bronto's large sword and Kilgar's well-placed knife went straight through the creature. The feminine nightmare glared malevolently at them, screaming out its horrid disposition as it reached out a ghostly claw towards Bronto. He tried to parry the strike with his large sword, but you can't parry something that passes straight through metal.

The creature raked a ragged line down Bronto's forearm. Blood spurted out in a quick gush as Bronto gritted his teeth in pain. He leapt back, the eight-inch gash on his large arm already stopping its bleeding and healing; perhaps another contribution from one of Eldar's potions, or perhaps just a result of his indominable constitution.

While Bronto was dodging the baleful creature, Lindel leapt up, determined to help, but soon found he had problems of his own. Something leaped at him from behind, digging dirty claws deep into his back, biting furiously at his neck. Lindel flailed around, trying to poke the thing on his back with his sword, but while trying not to also stab himself. Eldar looked over at his friend and saw the thing on Lindel's back. Like a small demented man it was, but leathery of skin with long sharp claws and equally sharp teeth, looking like a small vicious caricature of a man, a corpse-like stench emanating from both its body and breath. Eldar started to run over to help the other elf.

But was stopped. Several more of the creatures suddenly leapt out of the bushes. Like mad dogs, three of them piled on top of Eldar, while six more tackled Sabu and Sindar. Shong found himself surrounded by two more of the growling clawing beasts, his swift sword keeping them at bay, while another one lunged at the still-meditating Sheil-Bor(h). Three more charged at Mauklo as the dark wizard got to his feet.

"It's a banshee," Mauklo shouted above the wailing, its cry seeming to leave him unaffected, "and it's brought ghouls with it."

One of the ghouls leapt up at Mauklo, aiming for his throat, just as the wizard pointed a finger at it, sending out a darkly-colored bolt that reduced the creature to dark ash. The other two ghouls then approached a bit more warily.

Then another shooting star swooped down upon the group, this one forming its essence around Bronto as it shaped itself into another Banshee. It screamed out its pain as its ghostly form enveloped the large man. Bronto, face starting to turn pale from the enveloping creature, growled defiance, while Kilgar turned his knife to another ghoul that was determined to turn the young boy into an easy meal.

"*Fairmseja!* This place must be lousy with undead!" Shong shouted out as he sliced off the head of one of the ghouls. "I see at least a dozen more of those shooting stars gathering overhead."

"And *you* said we wouldn't have any trouble with undead on *Kilio!*" came Eldar's shout, as he fought to free himself from underneath the pile of ghouls.

"I appear to have underestimated the *spirit* of the holiday," Shong shouted back, as he parried at another charging ghoul.

"That ain't all," Kilgar said as he stabbed his ghoul in the neck. "Look!"

Shong turned to see, coming across the fields straight towards them, score upon score of the ghouls, as well as other demented creatures of the night. To his other side, across the lake's surface, he also saw floating towards them, above the surface of the water, the black starry forms of wraiths gliding silently nearer.

"We're surrounded," Shong summarized, as he saw Bronto try to fight off the immaterial form holding him within it, "and how do you fight something if your sword goes straight through it?!"

"*With the power of a god!*"

Candol's voice came booming out as he walked boldly and slowly out to the center of their small camp. He raised up a single hand as four more ghouls came running up behind him.

"By the power of Indra," he began, as a dozen more banshees came flying down at them and more than three times that in ghouls come charging into their camp, "I do dispel thee! I send thee all back to thy dark rest!"

A bright flash of light came out from Candol's up-stretched hand, released with a thunderous clap of power. Shong watched as the flash of light blew apart the two banshees in their midst as if they were but lit matches in a fierce wind. He watched as the other dozen approaching banshees dissolved in the bright flash, like melted candle wax drifting upon the wind. As the light passed, Shong saw more than a few ghouls reduced to charred and smoking corpses, baked into the positions that they'd held but moments before. The ghouls charging across the field stopped their charge, as if the light had suddenly drained their courage from them. He watched as the ghouls retreated quickly back across the fields.

He also noticed that Candol had missed the wraiths still floating across the lake. Wraiths, that he remembered, were of the same type that had killed Tinweril, oh so long ago it seemed to him now.

A slight wind began to pick up, just but a breeze it seemed to Shong as he readied his sword for whatever good it would do against the wraiths. But the breeze had a different effect on the wraiths. To them, it seemed to be as if a hurricane, tearing at their dark smoke-like forms. They screamed as their black forms were torn apart, shredded and sent hurling back across the lake in multiple directions, drifting remnants upon the wind.

Kilgar turned and saw the source of the strange breeze. Mauklo, hands still pointed at the dispelling wraiths, had sourced the immaterial wind. He lowered his hands as the lake was once again clear of any movement.

"There'll be more coming," Candol pronounced, as the others got themselves up from under the charred ghoul remains. "Darkness is the domain of the undead; especially during *Kilio.*"

"Easily cured," Sabu said, drawing his torn robes around him as he picked up his staff.

A brief gesture from the young wizard saw the camp alight as if with the light of day. In the distance, ghouls stopped and watched as their intended prey lay protected from within the deadly light.

"That should keep them away for a while," Sabu said, as Candol went over to tend to Quickfoot and Lorel.

"When you're finished with them, priest," Lindel said, wincing in pain as he walked over to where Candol bent over Quickfoot, "one of those things tore up my neck pretty good."

Blood dripped down the side and back of Lindel's green leather tunic. Bronto, pale skin starting to return to its normal color, long gash on his arm already completely healed, walked over to Sabu and Sindar, breathing deeply as he tried to regain the energy he'd lost to the Banshee.

"We'd better set sentries," he said, "they've got all night to try again."

"How'd you hold out against that thing?" Sindar asked, mild wonder on his face. "That Banshee should have drained the very life out of you!"

Bronto just shrugged as he answered.

"Maybe I'm just tougher to feed on then it figured," he answered.

As they picked themselves up, off in the dimness of the night a few of the ghouls could be seen, prowling around the perimeter of light, testing its boundaries and scurrying back into the night again.

"You *do* realize that those creatures were *sent?*" Mauklo asked quietly, walking over to Sindar and Sabu.

"Yes," Sindar agreed, "even for during the time of *Kilio,* those were far too many undead creatures to have singled us out at random."

"Sent by the mysterious master of this valley then," Sabu added, "the same one that used that magical storm to try and find us."

"We had best be more careful then," Sindar said quietly, "he seems to grow increasingly dangerous the farther on we go."

"I can sense the presence of those creatures now," Eldar said as he walked over to them.

"Your special sense has attuned to them, then?" Sabu asked.

"Yes," Eldar nodded, "and I can tell you that this place is full of all sorts of creatures as they that attacked us. I can sense them for as far out as I am able to sense."

"And *we* were lucky enough to hit this place at the start of *Kilio*," Quickfoot snorted, as Candol's ministrations began to bring him around.

"It looks like it's going to be a long night then," Shong said, coming over. "I'll take first watch with Bronto. The rest of you get some rest."

"Wake me up in a few *nevs* to renew my light spell," Sabu said as he slumped down to the ground.

Off in the distant night, they heard the eerie cry of an unseen creature of the night. This was answered by another creature, also not borne of Nature. They looked around at the distant sets of eyes, waiting for the protective bright light to go away.

They ended up resting in a tight circle, several swords pointing outwards like a giant human pincushion, ready against any intrusion of the night.

No one slept that night.

Early morn saw them doubling their usual pace. Both Eldar's own unique sense and the mystical prowess of Sheil-Bor(h) had confirmed one thing: that the valley they were in was almost literally crawling with undead creatures of the night, the presence of which was made even more deadly during the havar of *Kilio*. Neither Sabu nor any of the other wizards in their midst said of just how much they'd found; they just told the others that it was indeed urgent that they travel quickly.

So move quickly they did. Across the open fields they traveled, no way to retrieve their horses from Sabu's portal now, they traveled quickly along on foot. A quick pace did they set, one that would have left little Quickfoot far behind had not Bronto volunteered the strength of his shoulders upon which to carry him. Shong suggested that Sabu or Sindar could use their magic to try and fly them all across the valley, but they just shook their heads. Magic, they said, must be conserved against what awaits them come the fall of night.

Past small scattered groves of trees, past animals grazing and hunting in the tall grass, far beneath large birds with wingspans the size of a small ship, did they travel. Even Eldar sensed the urgency of their flight.

"Eldar," Lorel said, coming up to the elf as they walked across the fields, "you're usually the carefree one around here; why so serious?"

Eldar forced a glum smile upon his face, but Lorel could tell that the elf, for once, did indeed have serious thoughts on his mind. And anything Eldar took that seriously *had* to be bad.

"Something worries me," was his answer.

"Maybe I should record the date," Lindel commented with a smile, as he came up next to the other two, "for this would appear to be a first: Eldar worried."

Eldar just looked up at them and gave another worried smile. Lindel too then saw the seriousness in his face and grew more concerned over the state of his friend.

"What then worries you?" Lindel asked, this time sincerity in his voice.

"During the past dozen nevs since we started traveling early this morning," Eldar said, looking back at them, "Sabu hasn't stopped to comment on *anything*. Not one bird or animal species, mating habits, or feeding preferences has he stopped to take into question. Not *once* have I had to force him along to get him notice the *real* world. He hasn't even stopped to calculate weather patterns; he's actually *paying attention* to what's going on around him."

"Uh oh," Lindel grasped immediately, "if Sabu's not stopping for any of his usual intellectual comments, this *is* serious."

"Well then," Lorel began, "if danger is afoot, then we shall confront it."

But Eldar and Lindel had already quickened their pace and were far ahead of him, leaving a slightly puzzled Lorel walking behind the group.

They stopped for little rest, trying to make it as far as they could before nightfall. They pushed themselves to the limits trying to make it to somewhere far less open then that through which they now traveled. As they tired, only Bronto's indominable constitution seemed immune to the effects of the rapid journey; more than once did Candol wonder about taking one of the potions that Eldar gave the big man, hoping for some relief from his fatigue. But, while Quickfoot stayed on Bronto's shoulders, the young boy Kilgar, determined to hold his own, carried himself, moving quickly through grass almost as tall as was himself as he tried to keep up with the rest.

But they were never really alone in their travels. The tall grasses through which they walked hid large fanged cats, small packs of wolves whose howling seemed almost to speak to them, and the occasional distant large creature that seemed to look like a cross between a small elephant and a large furred cat. But most of the creatures seemed to stay away from them, even the ones that might have seen them as prey, thanks to Lindel's unnatural rapport with that of Nature and *sÿlva'*. Before the others might try to defend themselves against those that threatened, he would talk to the animals that came near, asking them he said, if they would leave them pass in peace and seek prey elsewhere. Much to Lorel's amazement, they did so.

But the grass itself also held its dangers. Once Kilgar stopped them as they came near to a patch of blood-red grass, its stalks waving in a breeze that wasn't there. A batch of blood-grass like unto that which they'd encountered by the Dragon Lord's manor, they passed around the innocent-looking grass, now familiar with its deadly reality.

As night came nearer, no shelter was there in sight. They agreed to travel as far as they could until a somewhat defensible position could be found. But, as night fell, no small grove of trees was there in sight, nor the protective coolness of a nearby pond or small lake. Night saw them still walking, bright bulb of daylight emanating from the tip of Sabu's staff as they traveled by night. This night at least saw no aerial displays; for that at least, they were grateful, for another night of such displays could only worsen their open position. They walked somewhat slower at night, but still they walked.

Distant howling, the sound of mournful loss or soulful hunger. Cry of a lost soul, drifting upon the breeze, calling to the heart of one's fear to join in with its never ending flight.

Gamri was full overhead, shining down blue upon the lonely plains.

"It sounds like they're getting ready for another long night," Shong said, listening to the distant howling sounds, steadily getting as loud as the crickets chirping happily away in the nearby grass, "I hope it's not as bad as last night."

"The power of Indra shall be ready to hold off the night creatures, no matter how large a legion they may make."

Sometime, Mauklo thought to himself, *I'd like to see that priest's enthusiastic bubble get popped. Just once.*

"Even Indra would be hard pressed to fight off an entire *valley* of these creatures," Sindar offered.

"It seems like quite a few of such creatures for just one valley," Eldar pondered, as they carefully stepped through the night.

"That's what worries me," Sabu said, "if indeed an ally of Miro rules this valley, then we may have stumbled upon a storehouse of his troops. A gathering place."

"Like for an invasion maybe?" Eldar asked rhetorically.

"Depending on how many such creatures arc hidden in this *bodaln*," Sabu continued, "someone could be planning for a pretty big invasion."

"Perhaps one should ask, not how many are in this *one* valley," Sheil-Bor(h) put in, "but how many *valleys* there are."

"I like *that* idea even less," Lindel said slowly.

A lonely howl was heard off in the distance, answered by several more, somewhat nearer, howls.

"Perhaps we should make camp," Bronto said as he stopped and turned around to them, "some of the others are getting kind of tired, and we should have something ready for the ghouls and their friends when they find us."

"He's right," Lindel said, putting down his backpack, "if we keep going until we drop, it'll make it that much easier for the creatures to pick our bones."

"Very well," Sabu said, stopping to lean on his staff from his own exhaustion. "Candol, see if you can get Indra to set up a perimeter around us that the creatures can't penetrate."

"It shall be the pleasure of this humble servant of his to do so," Candol answered as he gave a short bow of his shoulders and left to be about his work.

"The rest of you should——" Sabu began tiredly.

"The rest of us *fighters* will worry about our defense," Bronto interrupted, "we need you *wizards* rested and ready, not falling-down-tired. Now, go to sleep."

"I hear and obey," Sindar smiled at Bronto's order, as he turned to look for a nice spot in the grass.

"I so love an underling that knows how to handle his position in life," was Mauklo's answer as he sat down for a rest. "Leave the guarding to the *guards*."

Bronto, having by now learned to ignore most of what Mauklo said, went about making their camp secure, working with Candol, Shong, and Lorel about the duty of securing their location. Kilgar even tried to help, but one look at the boy told Bronto how tired the boy must be, though he held it back as best he could. Bronto told the boy to go sleep with the others, that they needed an alert guardian nearby to them. This Kilgar did, with all his usual adult seriousness, as Bronto shook his head in mild amazement at the boy's tenacity. Kilgar was asleep a few moments later.

Candol's protections laid, a ring of traps quickly made by Lindel, and their camp, such as it was, was ready. They started their vigil against the long dark night.

Kilgar was the first to fall asleep; tough though he tried to be, he was still yet a boy of nine. The others fell asleep in turn, soon leaving only Bronto, Shong, Lorel, and the two elves to keep watch. The night passed with fearsome noise pervading the darkness. Howlings that struck at the soul, inhuman screams that seemed to come from just over their very shoulder, distant scampering sounds of unnatural creatures weaving quickly through the tall grass. More than once Lorel found himself startled by a noise he thought to be just over his shoulder, only to find nothing there. Eldar and Lindel rested back in the tall grass as their sharp elven eyes followed bright baleful points of light dancing in the distance. The night seemed alive with creatures drawn out of the pit of one's fears, danced with unseen nightmares peering out from the dark, driven to a frenzy by the draw of *Kilio*. More than a few times Eldar thought he'd seen, out of the corner of his eye, something watching him from some nearby spot, but no sooner had he quickly turned around to look and the ephemeral image was gone, shrunk back into the shadows of the night. Even Lindel was uptight, on alert against surroundings that seemed born of *sylva'* but which seemed to hold secret creatures definitely not borne from Nature's womb.

It was well past *yonev*, or midnight as you hearing this story would call it, when some of the creatures finally found them. Pale yellow eyes shown out from the night around the edge of their camp. First one, then two, and soon a small circle of them, staying just out of the protective circle laid down by the now-sleeping Candol. Shong, woken up from a brief nap by a slight noise made by one of the creatures, grabbed up his sword as he leaned over to talk to Bronto, whispering to him lest he wake up the others.

"How long have *they* been here?" he whispered, nodding over in the direction of the staring eyes.

"About a *nev* now," Bronto answered quietly back, "although they haven't done anything but sit and stare. Actually, we've gotten along quite well."

"Oh?" Shong asked.

"Yeah. I've even named one of them," Bronto pointed over to one pair of eyes, the twin yellow orbs winking back at them. "I've named that one 'Winky'. We've been talking about opening up a tavern together when this is all over."

"It *spoke* to you?" Shong asked doubtfully.

Bronto chuckled quietly as he placed a large hand on his friend's shoulder.

"At least you didn't completely buy that line like Lorel did," Bronto whispered back, a trace of joviality in his voice, "I had him going for at least a *diidlo*."

Shong smiled at the realization of his friend's little joke as Lorel just tried to ignore them and turned over for a quick nap. As he tried to catch a few restful moments, Lorel looked up at the night sky, looking at Gamri's fullness overhead shining down bright and blue upon the night.

He shivered, fearfully, while a hidden part within him leapt for joy. Lorel pulled his blanket up over his head, trying to hide himself from the full moon, as he quivered underneath.

Once or twice, one of the creatures would try testing out the barrier, charging at it only to have themselves thrown back away. A constant howling arose from all around them, low but constant, a murmur of deadly cries surrounding them, just enough to prevent Shong from falling back asleep again.

"Those guys *must* be tired," Shong commented. "I don't see how they can sleep through all this growling."

Bronto glanced over at the sleeping forms of Sabu, Mauklo, and the rest, resting peacefully upon the long grass.

"We had a long rise, what with doubling our pace and all," Bronto responded. "I guess wizards can just sleep through anything."

"Yeah," Shong smiled, "I guess wizards just aren't built for life on the road; even Eldar's asleep."

They glanced over at the elf's sleeping form, eyes closed peacefully against the night.

Another low growling was suddenly heard from within the night. Bronto glanced around sharply at the noise, Shong going for his sword. The sound seemed to be coming from beneath the blankets where Lorel slept, as a small figure squirmed beneath them.

Bronto sat back with a sigh.

"What triggered *that* now I wonder," Bronto sighed.

The blanket squirmed some more as Shong looked over at it.

"You don't suppose,…" Shong began.

"There's only one way to find out," Bronto raised up his voice to a hoarse whisper, aimed in Lorel's direction. "Schanter! That you?"

The wiggling stopped and then a moment later the blankets exploded outward. There stood a small green-skinned figure, clawed fingers slashing at the air, demented grin on his face. His face snapped around, looking quickly around him.

"Schanter want fun," he said in a loud screeching voice.

Bronto shook his head as the creature leapt around the camp sniffing at the ground.

"But, what triggered him?" Shong asked.

"As well as being insane, he appears to be a classic lycanthrope," Lindel answered as he walked over to them, "it's a full moon out tonight."

"Well, I guess that explains that," Bronto said. "So he's triggered by fire *and* a full moon."

"And probably stress," Lindel added.

"Just the quaint little maniac that we've all wanted to have," Shong commented.

"Schanter smell funny creatures," he said, sniffing around the edge of Candol's perimeter.

"Is he going to do that all night?"

It was Kilgar, walking over to them, knife in one hand, his other hand rubbing sleep out of his eyes.

"He woke me up," Kilgar continued as he sat down next to Bronto.

"I guess we *should* do something about him before he wakes up the others," Bronto said, putting an arm around the boy's shoulder, as he then looked up in Schanter's direction and whispered out louder. "Hey Schanter. There's some ghouls out there for you to chase."

Schanter spun around, looking at Bronto, then sniffing the air as he slowly turned around to the several sets of staring eyes around them.

He smiled.

"Schanter *like* funny stinky creatures," he said, licking his sharp teeth.

The ghouls continued to leap and howl, staying just at the edge of the camp. Schanter grinned as he then gave off a howl of his own. Crouching low, he suddenly sprang off into the darkness.

The sound of ghouls scrambling fearfully away was soon heard, along with the distant howls of delight from Schanter.

"That should keep him busy until morning," Bronto sighed.

"You gotta feel sorry for the ghouls, though," Shong smiled.

As the sounds got more distant, Bronto gave an almost fatherly hug to the boy's shoulders.

"Sorry he woke you," Bronto said quietly.

"It's okay," Kilgar responded, "all that howling kept waking me up anyhow. I don't see how the others can sleep with all this noise."

"They're just tired," Bronto said, "even Eldar's sleeping."

"We elves don't need sleep," Lindel put in, "at least not as do you Humans. We just sort of rest our eyes a little. Eldar wouldn't be asleep."

"Well he's doing a pretty good job of it right now," Kilgar said pointing. "He's over there dreaming with the rest of them. They're all even having nightmares; except Quickfoot."

Sudden concern came over the others' faces. They leapt to their feet, leaving the boy to wonder. Shong went over to Quickfoot, while Lindel bent down over the sleeping form of Eldar. Bronto went to examine the others.

They were all tossing and turning, eyes moving rapidly beneath their eyelids, as they each tossed quietly. Each, except for Quickfoot, who slept quietly. Shong roughly jostled the little one's shoulder.

There was a sleepy murmur from Quickfoot. Shong jostled him some more. Finally, Quickfoot's small hands came up to rub his eyes, as he stirred awake.

"Wha...?" he said sleepily. "Whas wrong? Jus lemme sleep; the big bad monster can come and kill me in the morning."

"Are you awake?" Shong asked.

"Of course, although I *shouldn't* be."

"Good," Shong ordered, as looked up for the others, "go back to sleep."

"Huh-wha...?" Quickfoot muttered. "You woke me up to *tell* me that?"

"The small one's okay," Shong said, as he got up to go over to Lindel.

"Eldar," Lindel was shaking his elven friend almost violently, "wake up! Come on!"

Shong sat down next to Lindel, watching him trying to unsuccessfully wake up the tossing form of Eldar.

"Any luck?" Shong asked.

"No," Lindel said, finally gently releasing his friend, "he's asleep and having some sort of nightmare. I can't wake him."

"They're *all* having a nightmare," Bronto said as he joined them. "I couldn't wake any of them."

"What's wrong with them?" Kilgar asked as he walked quietly up next to Lindel. "I was supposed to guard them."

"They fight something in their sleep," Lindel answered, "The same nightmare has taken hold of them all. A creature of dreams pulls at them, it was nothing you could have protected them from."

"What do we do then?" Kilgar asked, "We've got to do something."

"This may be something that only a wizard can fight his way out of," Bronto said, kneeling down next to the sleeping form of Eldar. "They are battling something that only they can understand. We can but wait, and hope."

Off in the distance they could hear ghouls howling in pain and fright and Schanter's distant screams of pain and joy mixing with the night. Nearer to hand, Sabu tossed and turned in his sleep, his hands moving as if he would cast a spell, while Mauklo growled angrily at some unseen indignity. Bronto, Shong, and Lindel sat down, holding guard around their sleeping friends, while Kilgar rested against Bronto's shoulder. Quickfoot was already fast asleep, ignorant of what

MARK ANTHONY TIERNO

went on around him. They watched as the sleeping forms struggled against unseen foes, tossing and turning as if in the middle of a life or death struggle. They waited in the quiet, its stillness broken only by the constant songs of howling and by shining blobs of light, peering balefully from outside of Candol's perimeter. But a single comment from Shong broke their silent vigil.

"Am I the only one to notice that the only ones sharing their nightmare are those with Hevon Gems?"

Night and day were the same. Swirling colors flashed like lightning around those gathered at the top of the hill of green. Below them gathered a moving forest, filled with trees that steadily walked up towards them. Trees with faces that grinned balefully as their tree-branch hands reached out for their quarry, marching steadily up the hill. A bolt of lightning leapt out from Sabu's outstretched hand, sizzling one of the trees into a charred stump, only to have it replaced by two more, crowding ever closer. The six of them gathered close together.

"But if this is all just a dream then," Candol was saying, "how can we *all* be in the same one?"

"Yeah," Eldar spoke up, "especially since I don't sleep!"

"Some sort of shared telepathic phenomena," Sindar answered, "sourced from some common foe no doubt."

"Something too cowardly to strike at us physically," Mauklo commented calmly, as a black bolt of energy leapt out from his hand off into the swirling green night beyond, "or too smart to."

"If it's just a dream, then why can't we just ignore it," Candol asked, "or even just wake up?"

"Dream it may be," Sindar answered, as Candol fought off an encroaching branch tearing at his priestly robes, "but believe me when I say that it is real enough for us; if we die here, then we *will* die."

"I'll take you word for that," Candol said, as he beat back the tree with a blast of fire from the Hevon Gem in his forehead.

"How do we *fight* a dream, then?" Eldar asked, sword in hand, as with it he tossed off firebolt after firebolt into the encroaching forest.

"The battlefield may not be of our choosing," Sheil-Bor(h) interjected calmly, "but perhaps the weapons may be."

"You got something in mind?" Sabu asked, as he readied his staff for another spell.

"The weapons are where this battle field cannot reach," Sheil-Bor(h) continued, "that which is within us all."

"He makes sense," Sindar said, as Sabu peeled off a cone of fire from his staff, "this dream already links us together mentally; we have but to use our combined efforts on a common goal."

"Well then let's pick something besides fire," Eldar said, as he stopped tossing out firebolts, "'cause they're starting to like it now."

The green carpet of trees surged around them, the trees seeming larger and more numerous than they had been but moments before, their thick bark now darker than before, looking almost stone-like as they casually shrugged off the varied bolts of fire.

"They've switched to petrified trees," Sindar observed. "They wouldn't be affected by fire, or electricity for that matter."

Mauklo stretched out an open palm, his Hevon Gem of Earth shining within him. Springing out from his hand flew a small rock, quickly growing in size until it was a large boulder more than twelve feet across. The rock landed on a large tree, smashing through its thick branches, flattening the tree as it landed. Mauklo looked on with a satisfied smile, but only for a short moment. Around the smashed tree, several more grew together, merging into a single much larger tree. They watched as the new tree picked up the boulder and crushed it between two branches as easily as one would crush a small clod of dirt. Mauklo frowned at the result.

"You can rule out earth now, too," he said.

"Perhaps then, a wind storm," Candol said, putting away a coin he'd just flipped as he stepped forward, then raising up his voice, arms stretching above him. "I call upon the mighty power of Indra to bring forth a storm of wind to hurl back our enemies. Splinter them unto matchsticks!"

But the only response he got was a loud peel of laughter upon the slight breeze around them. The trees below them only surged forward the faster.

"That should have worked!" Candol frowned as he brought down his hands. "It doesn't make sense."

"This is a dream," Sindar pointed out, "it doesn't *have* to make sense. It has it own rules."

"Indeed, it *does* appear to have its own rules," Sheil-Bor(h) observed, "if I may point out the one thing we all have in common that *has* worked consistently."

A brief moment of silence in the flashing green and purple night before several voices blurted out the same answer all at once.

"The Hevon Gems!"

"It would appear that the Gems are so connected to reality as to work properly even from within a dream," Sabu theorized.

"But we don't have any type that's had any lasting effect on the trees," Eldar pointed out. "Those trees keep changing: one moment they're normal, the next their petrified, then they're too large for even large boulders to affect. You never know what's coming next."

Sabu's eyes lit up as sudden realization hit him. Beneath them, the trees now pressed closer to each other, crowding around the larger tree.

"Ah!" Eldar brightened, seeing his friend's face. "I know *that* expression; Sabu has an idea that's goin' to let us kick some tree bark!"

"This dream does indeed have a consistency," Sabu proclaimed. "Everything used to thwart us has been some extreme variation on what types of *trees* it would take to withstand our assault. Our enemy has chosen a specific battlefield and must play within its own rules."

They backed up against each other, as the baleful ambulatory trees surged forward, just but a scant dozen feet away.

"Then," Mauklo continued for Sabu, as he picked up on the idea, "we just have to find something that will affect *any* tree, no matter how extreme."

"But it has to be something that our Hevon Gems can do, since they're the only things that work right in here," Eldar added, "but between our fire, water, and earth Gems, what is there that could truly be of use?"

"Whatever it is, we'd better think of it quick," Candol said, "for by the Face of Indra, that's a mighty big tree out there."

Sure enough, before them the malevolent trees were all merging, walking one into the other, growing larger with each such meeting, all combining towards a large central tree, its topmost branches growing higher and higher as it reached up past their hill. As all finished combining, an evil twisted face grew upon the large tree, as it now towered far above their high vantage point, the width of its trunk being greater than their entire hill. It grinned as it reached down immense clawed branches, ready to grab them up as if they were but small toys.

"Think fast guys," Eldar said, sword out defensively in front of him.

"It is said," Sheil-Bor(h) said calmly, "that there exists a Hevon Gem for Wood."

"As in woods and trees?" Eldar asked.

Sheil-Bor(h) nodded.

"That would be nice if we only *had* one," Mauklo sneered, "but we don't."

A grin spread over Sindar's face, while beneath them the ground shook from the giant tree's movements.

"Then, let's *get* some," he suggested. "Everyone, hold hands and concentrate."

"Are you saying," Eldar said, cocking an eyebrow in shocked realization, "that a *dream* can be a guardian?"

"It's possible," Sabu put in, as they all linked hands, backs to each other. "Why else would such a dream have such a consistent and strong theme of trees."

"Can it be done?" Candol asked. "To conjure up such Gems out of nothing?"

The giant tree hand reached closer.

"I know too little of the nature of Hevon Gems to answer that," Sindar said quickly, "but remember that dreams are of the mind, and that's *my* territory. Now, concentrate on the Hevon Gem."

The giant hand scooped them all up, hill and all. They tumbled around with the dirt and rocks of the former hill as the ridiculously huge hand swept them all up towards its huge twisted mouth. But still they kept their hands gripped tightly one to the other, a circle of one tumbling about in the huge hand. A deep rumble erupted from the huge tree, deep enough to shake the ground as if from a small quake, loud enough to be heard clearly throughout all the small dream world.

They concentrated, trying to ignore the reality of the dream world around them, the dirt in their eyes, the choking earth in their lungs, the nearness of the huge bark-like maw towards which they now tumbled. The hand brought them up to the large mouth.

Within each of them, their Hevon Gems glowed, filling their very being with a power that called out.

The huge hand stuffed them into its mouth. Teeth the size of oak trees chewed at its meal as it rumbled with laughter over its victory. Thunder echoed around it.

It stopped chewing.

Its twisted face looked puzzled. Two large branches grabbed at its midsection, as one would with a bad stomach ache. It rumbled out in pain as it stomped earthquake-causing feet around the domain of the dream world.

As it was holding onto its large tree-belly, several of its branches twisted down, weaving their way around its two main hand-like branches. The large tree looked up in astonishment as its own branches pulled against it. It plucked at the offending branches, but still more branches grew anew from atop itself, growing like ivy down the length of its immense height.

It was fighting itself.

It screamed and tossed madly on the ground, its own branches wrapping it up tight, squeezing it as if to crush. Several loud creakings were heard, the sound a large piece of wood makes when straining under immense pressure. The tree creature could barely rock itself back and forth now as its own enclosing branches encased it within a solid crushing shell of bark and wood. It screamed a loud muffed cry which shook the very ground it was laying on, as the shell tightened ever inward.

Thunderous crack, like unto Creation giving way, splintering asunder its hold upon Reality. Shower of wood chips, each the size of small trees, flying apart; an explosion of lumber. Thunderous peel, ringing out loud, echoing.

As the sawdust settled gently to the ground, in the middle of what had once been the large tree but was now a large scattered pile of wood and lumber, stood six figure, hands still linked, a greenish glow surrounding them like a large halo, faces aglow with victory.

Kilgar was just nodding off to sleep when he saw it; faint but definitely there. He watched as a small green gem appeared on Sabu's staff, its bright glow fading as it melded into the head of the staff. He looked over to Eldar to see a similar glow fading upon the elf's sword. Each of the others in turn saw their own faint glow of green as a new gem melted into each of their bodies. The sleepers' tossing and turning then stopped as they drifted off into a more natural sleep. Kilgar, tired but smiling, looked up at Bronto, whose shoulder he was still leaning against.

"It's okay now," Kilgar said.

"What?" Bronto turned his face down to the boy. "What'd you say kid?"

"They're okay now," Kilgar pointed out to the sleepers, "they made it."

As the boy, content that things were now okay, quickly drifted off into sleep, Bronto looked on as he saw Eldar stir awake. The elf stretched out his arms with a wide yawn. Lindel was quickly by his side as Eldar sat up.

"Are you okay?" Lindel asked, not bothering to whisper. "What happened?"

"Shh," Eldar put a finger to his lips, "you'll wake the others; you know how Humans need their sleep."

Bronto shook his head and chuckled quietly while Lindel puzzled at Eldar's casualness.

"I suppose," Bronto said quietly, "that you'll have to tell us what went on."

"In the morning," Eldar leaned back in the tall grass, "but let's just say that it was *different.*"

At the edge of camp, as Eldar looked up at the stars overhead, and the searching points of light streaked by through the night, Schanter walked back in, dragging the torn carcass of a ghoul behind him. It was then that Eldar noticed that there were no more pairs of baleful yellow eyes surrounding their camp anymore. He smiled as he watched the warty one tear an arm off the ghoul, biting into a repast that even the ghouls would find distasteful.

Eldar looked up at the stars while the night slept on around him.

Morning came, breakfast having with it a quick exchange of stories concerning the night's events, followed once more by an early start on their journey. Through the early morning and most of *solrise* they saw the same as before: endless grassy plains. *Degrise*, though, finally saw a welcome change of scenery. As the bright blue sun arched across the sky, they saw before them some trees.

Followed by some more.

A whole forest of trees, spread out before them, a horizon-embracing forest. Lindel fairly leapt for joy at the promise of cover, the tall forest trees perhaps promising better shelter from the valley's dangers.

For no reason that he would explain, Candol cringed at the idea of being surrounded by trees.

It was still daylight when they finally passed into the forest of the Valley Of Many Lights, marching past pleasant-looking trees with nary a suggestion of a nightmare about them; pleasing to the eye, innocent in appearance, yet perhaps still holding unknown dangers.

But then, thought Shong as they marched under the canopy of trees, so far that's the way this entire valley has been.

CHAPTER TWENTY-FOUR
Dwingale

R.K.: 9,990, 6 Monwïr:

    We have been traveling through the forest for several rises now. Kilio may be over, but still we are not safe from the peering eyes of what roams this land. We came here to try and find something with which to use against Miro, but now I realize that we were cunningly lead here. I haven't told the others my suspicions, but I begin to suspect that our lure here may have involved a plan as old as the fall of Thïr Tjorca itself; a plan going back thousands of rels! I cannot but guess of what else such a plan may entail, nor our own part in it, but I fear that any control we thought that we've had over our destiny has been a complete illusion. It may even be that the King's plan for recruiting us to fight Miro was unknowingly manipulated by Miro for his own purposes. We may all just be right where he wants us; or I may just be getting paranoid. I don't know.

    As for the forest, I'm certain that we are still being watched. From no source that even Sindar can pinpoint, it's almost as if the forest itself watches us; the very trees noting our movements, some of the animals trailing us, maybe even the winds carrying with them messages of our location. It's hard to tell. More than once have some of us heard faint almost-voices enticing one to leave or run, only to discover that no one else had heard them. No doubt a very effective use of simple illusions, but distracting nonetheless. It is perhaps a good thing that Candol made Quickfoot somewhat braver, for no doubt the small one would have long since run away from such ghostly voices.

    Evenings have seen more of the undead that seem to own this land, though not as many as during Kilio; perhaps only a dozen ghouls and one or two spirits a night. However, even the daytime has shown us a couple of spirits, powerful enough to brave the dim sunlight of this forest, but apparently not powerful enough to stand against Candol or Mauklo. Mauklo may be right; these encounters do seem to have served the purpose of moving us along faster towards whatever goal Miro may have in mind for us. I'm not sure; it's hard to fathom such subtle thinking.

The best we can do now is to press on with our original intent: that of finding something that we may use against Miro. We shall try to survive through that which he has ready for us, being ready for any opportunity to turn his plans to our own use.

Sindar has started having his visions again, his psychic visitations from our enemy inviting him to join. Eldar and I have had to join with him to fend off this latest assault. We have been successful so far, but if anything dangerous comes up then we may be too distracted to help the others. That may indeed be Miro's plan, but there is no helping it.

"There is an oppressive feeling to this forest," Lindel commented, as they walked across the needle-strewn terrain, "like unto a weighty burden that the spirit of the forest has carried for too long."

They were traveling through the forest, over a hilly ground covered mostly by blue-green colored pine needles but broken by occasional damp leaves, colored with the *orains* and *tairus* of late Fall. Daytime though it was, the forest still held a certain pallor, the high branches of the tall trees screening back the bulk of the day's bright sunlight, dim shadowy darkness being lord over their travels. The occasional small animal would scurry off in the distance as a lonely birdcall would go unanswered. They walked quickly but carefully through the thick forest, having to make their own path through its tortured undergrowth, Bronto hacking away with his greatsword as needed, Lindel just always seeming to find a way to slip through any thick overgrowth of plants no matter how extreme.

"Are you trying to tell us that a forest has a *spirit* now?" Quickfoot asked, unbelievingly.

"Maybe not as you would think of as being a spirit," Lindel answered as they started up a slight rise, "more like the collective of the spirits and life-forces of all of its plants, animals, and other inhabitants. In that sense, yes it does have a spirit."

"Okay," Quickfoot said slowly, with obvious doubt, "I think I'll just stick to what I can see for myself."

"And you can sense this spirit of the forest?" Shong asked curiously.

"Any good elf can," Eldar put in as he came up alongside of them, "although Lindel's a bit more attuned to it since he's of the forest elves."

"I didn't know there was a difference," Shong observed, "you both look like standard elves."

"You humans have different species among your kind that you separate according to skin color," Lindel explained, "we separate ourselves by differences other than just skin color. Perhaps those differences aren't as obvious to Humans, but they're there."

As they were talking, the dim light from above the trees had been gradually getting even dimmer, a slight mist rolling in around their feet, curling around in wispy streamers as they walked through it. The wind was also blowing, as it was wont to this time of the season, but perhaps just a bit colder than one might expect.

Sindar was getting an uneasy feeling.

"Something's wrong," he said to Sabu, as they walked next to each other.

"An enemy?" Sabu asked.

"A powerful one," Sindar nodded. "I can feel it looking for us, but its mind is not a living one."

"We're being trailed."

The voice came from Kilgar, who walked up next to them from out of the growing mist, knife in hand as usual. He had a serious adult expression on his face, which may have seemed mildly comical on the face of such a young boy for anyone that didn't know him.

"This mist isn't natural," the boy continued, "it rolls in with no wind to move it. And the light seems like twilight though it's but mid rise."

"The boy's right," Sabu said. "Tell the others."

"I don't think I have to," Sindar noted.

Sabu looked around. He saw Eldar casually taking out his sword, his special sense having already alerted him to the approaching danger, while Lindel's own forest skills had served as warning enough for the other elf. Mauklo always seemed to have his own ways of sensing such things, while the mist alone seemed enough to fuel Quickfoot's innate paranoia. Bronto and Shong always seemed ever ready, while Candol was no fool as he'd noticed the subtle preparations the others made. Sheil-Bor(h) could only be guessed at. Which left Lorel as the only one apparently oblivious to any danger.

Although Sabu wondered if, deep inside of Lorel, Schanter was already gleefully aware of what went on.

A low moan filled the air.

"Oh, how nice," Mauklo said to himself, "another wraith to add to my collection."

He discretely took out a small bottle from within his robes. Imprisoned within it were several small ghostly shapes swirling around as they moaned silently from within their prison, expressing a pain of spirit that they only thought they would give, not receive. Mauklo smiled as he carefully put the bottle away.

He'd never told the others what he *did* with the undead spirits they came across after he supposedly 'killed' them. He had plans of his own for these creatures, once they were out of this valley.

The moan got louder.

"It only sounds like one of them this time," Candol said. "Allow me to bring down the power of Indra upon this one."

"I don't know," Eldar shook his head as the priest made ready, "this one seems different. I sense it's more powerful than the others we've seen."

Directly in their path, the mist suddenly swelled up, swirling around as if to take on a shape. A vaguely human shape.

"I guess we'll soon find out," Candol replied, as he made his way to the front, planting himself squarely in front of it as the others stopped their marching.

The mist formed into a tall misty person. It towered more than a foot above Bronto's height, its cloak of mist clothing it like a large gown, its true sex not discernible from just visual appearance alone. The face that formed was a vague ghastly horror, making even the now-braver Quickfoot nervous. It rose up, ghostly arms to either side, looking down upon the priest that dared to confront it.

"Uh oh," Mauklo said to himself, as he saw the creature take form, "I think I may know of this spirit."

Candol boldly stretched up both his arms, ready to invoke the power of Indra.

"Hear me spirit," he intoned, "be gone to your eternal rest. By the power of Indra be dispelled. I command thee!"

It just looked down at him.

"Okay," Candol said, bringing his arms down, "so we try something else."

Candol thrust his right arm out towards the creature. From out of his open palm shot half a dozen balls of brightly glowing white light. They zipped through the air, impacting upon the spirit, each detonating with an explosion of light and the crack of thunder.

When the light cleared, it was still there, scowling its horrid face down upon the priest.

"That was my best shot," Candol muttered with more than a trace of futile exasperation.

Then the spirit reacted. A loud howl it screamed, its sound seeming to carry with it a sudden great force of wind as it came out as a narrow streamer of mist. It hit the priest with the force of a large solid fist. Some of the swift-moving mist seemed to lance straight through Candol's body, coming out his back as it speared through his soul, leaving his body unmarked. Candol cried out as the scream tossed him up and back through the air, landing him full into Bronto, the force tumbling them both solidly to the ground. Candol moaned weakly as Bronto tried to move the priest off from on top of him.

The creature then looked up at the others, malevolence in its gaze.

"This *could* be bad," Eldar noted.

"I was right," Mauklo said to himself.

"No one can do that to *our* priest," Sabu said as he raised up his staff. "It is time that this spirit was dealt with."

"Don't!"

Mauklo's shout came just a bit too late. From out of Sabu's staff came a tightly focused bolt of wind, slicing straight towards the creature, while Sindar cast forth his own bolt of energy. They collided with the creature in a single blast of power.

They then watched as both bolts of magical force bounced straight off of it, windy bolt and electrical jolt glancing off of the misty surface and ricocheting from it, to the trees, and around back to them. Everyone ducked as their own magic came back to hit them. An electrical bolt almost sizzled Eldar's ear as he gazed up in surprise.

"What in *Hades* was *that!*" he exclaimed, as both bolts of power dispersed on into the forest.

"It's the Spirit Of Shandeür!" Mauklo shouted out, a certain measure of his ever-present calm still in his voice. "Trust me on this when I say 'RUN'!"

As Bronto helped the weak priest up to his feet, the creature began to moan; a moan that they could feel in their souls, rising up through the forest.

"Mauklo's afraid of something," Lindel said as he looked quickly around for a fast exit, "that's good enough for me! This way!"

"I prefer to call it: well-placed caution," Mauklo corrected.

They all started running off in the direction the elf indicated, trusting to his natural forest instincts to guide them through, Bronto carrying the semiconscious form of Candol. Another howl burst out from behind them, a loud almost physical force that tore through the trees and into their ranks. They heard the splinter of a great tree, its life force blasted away to nothingness, its wood suddenly splintered, old and rotten. From behind them came another scream, as Quickfoot's body was seen to go flying through the air, landing on ahead of them in a cold heap. Beside him landed Shong, also tossed through the air by the same blast of death from Shandeür.

"Eldar," Sabu said quickly, "do you still have that haste spell of yours?"

"No sooner said then done," the elf replied.

"Mauklo," Sabu shouted out, "what *is* that thing?"

"A powerful spirit," the yellow-skinned one replied, "older and more powerful than any other spirit that I know of. If it screams its cry of death, then it will kill everything within miles of here."

"You mean, that *wasn't* it?" Lindel called back, as he stopped, along with Bronto, to help Quickfoot and Shong up.

"Among its many talents is the reflection of magic," Mauklo continued, "so I don't recommend casting any spells at it."

"*Now*, he tells us," Sabu sighed.

"The small one is dead," Bronto shouted out as the others caught up, "and Shong nearly so. That thing must be stopped!"

"I believe us without the capability to do so at present," Sheil-Bor(h) calmly offered, "but perhaps later, when we are stronger."

Another howl blasted over their heads. They watched as they saw a fifty-foot tall pine tree suddenly grow old and dead before their very eyes, its wood and bark rotting visibly, the wood starting to creak as it threatened to fall in of its own weight.

"Run!" Lindel shouted.

Bronto grabbed up Shong, to add to the burden of Candol that he now carried, while Lindel struggled with the quiet form of Quickfoot. The tree collapsed around them as they leaped on into the woods, rotten wood chips flying everywhere. Behind them, the spirit closed, floating along faster than any there could run, floating through the trees like they weren't there, each tree it passed through also rapidly dying.

It roared out another howl that streaked straight towards Sabu and Sindar.

"Got it!" Eldar exclaimed as he finished with his spell.

No sooner had Eldar uttered that phrase, then his spell took hold. They all suddenly found themselves running at several times their normal speed. Sabu and Sindar dashed away just before Shandeür's deadly scream would have hit them both. Trees zipped by in a blur as they trusted to instinct to not run into any while moving at such a great speed. But, as fast as they went, behind them they could still hear the howling of Shandeür.

"I hope we loose it soon," Eldar commented, after they'd been running for several long moments, "because my spell's about to run out soon, and I still hear it back there."

"Let's stop then," Sabu said thoughtfully, "maybe we can set a trap for it."

"Sounds fun," Eldar smiled, as he snapped his fingers.

Their movement slowed down to normal as Sabu called the others to a halt.

"Mauklo," Sabu began, as he faced him, "that immaterial wind you use to disperse spirits, can you set it up as a barrier that it would have to pass through?"

"Yes," Mauklo nodded as he caught on to the idea, "that way it couldn't be reflected because it wouldn't be coming *at* anywhere, rather he at it. Consider it done."

With a wave of his hand, the forest behind them seemed to shimmer. Mauklo turned around with a smile as the shimmering effect seemed to stay and float upon the very air itself. Meanwhile, Bronto was examining their wounded.

"I think Candol is okay," the big man said.

"Oh," the priest groaned slowly, "may the power of Indra…"

"He'll be all right," Sindar proclaimed, as Candol trailed off, "what about Shong?"

Bronto lay Shong on the ground, turning him over on his back. Several eyes looked down at the unconscious warrior.

He looked like he'd aged forty rels. His skin was withered, his muscles hanging loose and weak, his hair a pale grey. He tossed weakly as his eyes opened up slowly.

"By what magic be this," Bronto exclaimed in a deadly level voice.

"It's the work of Shandeür," Mauklo explained, "and that barrier will not stop him forever."

They all turned as they heard a howl behind them. Floating among now-dead trees they could see the form of Shandeür. It had stopped on the other side of Mauklo's barrier, howling its rage at the unseen wall, but not advancing. Not yet.

"If we can get time for Candol to heal, then he can take care of Shong," Sabu said, as he knelt beside the fallen one.

"What about Quickfoot?"

Lindel was holding the still, and rather pale, form of the small one. The look of death was upon the small face.

"I know he's always a nuisance," Lindel continued, "but he's still one of our own. We've all been through a lot together."

"Yeah," Sabu said, lowering his head.

"What's the problem?" Kilgar asked, in a combination of child simplicity and Destir practicality. "Candol raised up Shong from the dead once, he can do it for Quickfoot."

Sabu started to say something, trying to find the usual consoling words that an adult uses to explain to a child why something can't be done, why the world makes some things not possible. He tried to think of a way to explain the things that a child just couldn't understand about life.

And then stopped, as he found that he couldn't. He looked over at the kid.

"You know," Sabu began, "you're going to teach us adults a thing or two about life yet. Bring along Quickfoot's body; if Indra wants that we should continue, then Candol can just have him bring back the small one."

Lindel was moving a hand over Quickfoot's head as Sabu was saying this. When he was finished, Quickfoot's body took on a faint sheen.

"I've laid a simple preservative spell upon him, so he won't rot away before Candol can get to him," Lindel explained. "A spell I usually use to preserve meat while on the trail, but it should do for him."

"Good," Sabu acknowledged, "now, where to from here?"

Shandeür was slowly making his way through Mauklo's barrier, floating through it as if through molasses.

"He'll penetrate soon," Mauklo said, "and I have not the power to stop him."

"Perhaps I can use my psychic powers to..." Sindar began, and then suddenly put a hand to his forehead.

"Sindar, what is it?" Sabu asked quickly, concern on his face.

"I'm okay," Sindar waved off his friend, "Miro but sends his invitations to me at the wrong time. I can handle it."

"If you're sure," Sabu turned his attention back to the approaching form of Shandeür, "but with Sindar out of action, this limits our options a bit."

He looked up at the fearsome spirit, its malevolence reaching out towards his soul.

"I'm open to suggestions," Sabu said, swallowing a slight lump in his throat.

"Quickly, over here!"

They all turned to see the source of the whispered female voice. Standing in between two large oak trees stood an elf. Scantily clad was she, wearing only enough to protect what might be hurt by scraping and clawing branches, a little brown and green cloth around her chest, some around her middle, and some knee-high leather leggings. Five-foot-two was she, with milk-white skin and honey-blond hair flowing sweetly down to the middle of her back. Slim of build, though firm of body was she, with golden eyes sparkling out from a perfect face.

Eldar's eyes almost popped out of their sockets. Everyone else was caught a bit off guard by the sudden appearance of such an angelic vision.

"Come *on!*" she repeated. "Or it'll get you."

"*Saljesea;* and like out of a dream she comes," Eldar intoned, as he started to walk slowly towards her, "floating through the ether like unto an angel."

Eldar made a sweeping bow, ending kneeling on one knee at her feet. He raised up a hand in which to grab one of her own, bring the delicate back of it up to his lips.

"My lady," Eldar continued after he'd gently kissed her hand, "I do greet you."

"Me thinks he's smitten with her," observed Lindel.

"I don't blame him," replied the usually intellectually reserved Sabu, as his eyes played up and down her overly-feminine form.

The elf, barely looking as much more than a young girl, seemed momentarily caught up with Eldar's gesture. But one glance off into the woods beyond seemed to shake her out of it. She took her hand out of Eldar's and slapped him across the top of his head with it.

"Just hurry while that silver head of yours is still attached to your shoulders," she said a bit more sternly.

"I think she likes him also," Sindar smiled, still wincing from the effort of his own private mental battle.

"Then I suggest that we rapidly afford ourselves of the opportunity given us," Sheil-Bor(h) put in.

"What'd he say?" asked Lorel in puzzlement at Sheil-Bor(h)'s statement.

"Let's go," Kilgar shouted as he ran past the girl, Eldar still kneeling by her side.

"What *he* said," as Sindar followed the kid into the woods beyond.

Bronto followed next carrying Candol and Shong, with Lindel close behind with Quickfoot's body. As they passed by the new elf, Lindel stopped and gasped at her. But it wasn't her beauty that he gasped at.

"I thought them all extinct," he said quietly, in more than mild wonder.

His reverie, however, was interrupted by the nearby howling of Shandeür; it was starting to break through.

"My lady," said Eldar, as Lindel finally went on by, along with the rest, "I will not move until I have your name and a promise of gayer times to come."

"I'm Dwingale," she said in a voice as sweet as the color of her hair, "now go."

"Where do you take us?" asked Sabu, the last of them left, as Eldar got up.

"To an enchanted glade beyond the power of Shandeür," she said as she started to push them both along behind the trees, "now hurry."

Loud long howl, echoing throughout the forest. A soul-curdling scream, sapping the very essence of life out with its baneful chord. More than even the scream of a banshee, more like a choir of banshees did it sound. For miles around its voice echoed, filling every living thing with its cry of death.

"That's its big death cry," Dwingale said, with more than a trace of fright in her voice, "now are we truly doomed!"

"Not if *I* can help it," Sabu said, turning around, holding his staff up high. "You two get along with the rest."

"But Sabu," Eldar exclaimed, trying to urge his friend along beyond the trees with Dwingale, "Mauklo said that it *reflects* magic."

"That's what I'm *counting* on; now go!"

Dwingale urged the reluctant Eldar on beyond the trees where the others had gone, while Sabu concentrated on his magic.

"But he's my friend," Eldar said, "I've got to help him!"

"He's buying time for you and your friends," Dwingale replied, "now come on; don't let his sacrifice be a waste."

Eldar looked on to his friend, his staff glowing with all the colors of his Hevon Gems, an aura of magic filling the area in front of him as the horrid form of Shandeür finally broke completely free of Mauklo's barrier, shattering it in a single quick flash of light.

"Besides," Dwingale added with a smile, "it'd be a shame to see you hurt, especially after you did so well with everything else in the forest."

Eldar snapped a look at her, realization filling his face.

"You were watching us," he said with mild astonishment.

"I was watching *you*," she corrected, as she dragged Eldar along towards the others.

Sabu was charging up a lot of magic, his staff glowing with power. But its power wasn't directed *at* Shandeür but around him. Walls of magic did Sabu form around the creature.

"I hope this works," Sabu said a bit nervously, "I never tried to use more than one Hevon Gem at a time before."

The walls of magic surrounded him and Shandeür as the creature looked down at the young wizard. It seemed to almost laugh at the attempt to contain it.

Then Sabu's staff blazed white hot, sending forth bright colors of energy. The walls around them suddenly took solid form as fire, earth, water, and wood danced along within its field, only Sabu's magic keeping them at bay from each other. Encasing it all was then a final magical barrier, one which even Shandeür growled at. Sabu was pointing the glowing tip of his staff at the creature.

Shandeür pounded at his cage, but as much as he could reflect its magic away, so did it just reflect back towards him again.

"What's the matter," Sabu mocked lightly, "don't like your own power used *against* you? Good."

Shandeür faced back at the wizard.

"Then let's see what this does now."

Shandeür let loose with his deadly howl.

Sabu let loose with his staff.

Along the enchanted path, the others rapidly hurried, Dwingale guiding them in a hopeless run to get out of range of the deadly spirit's scream.

"We won't make it," Mauklo observed calmly, "and its scream will kill all but the strongest."

Suddenly the scream seemed to get muffled, as if thrown inside some container and buried deeply. Louder the scream tried to get, but still as if screaming through thick layers of cloth.

"What happened to it?" Dwingale asked at the sudden change in tone of the scream.

"My buddy Sabu happened to it!" Eldar smiled. "We've got to go back for him."

"No," said Bronto in a firm voice, as he gently laid down Candol and Shong, "if only the strongest survive it, then that shall be me."

No one dared argue with the big man when he was in this mood. They watched as he went back along the flower-lined path, back towards the source of the howling.

A double explosion rocked around inside of Sabu's barrier. He detonated the full power of his staff upon Shandeür, while the spirit's own deadly howl was contained within its prison. Instead of killing off miles upon miles of others around, it was all just focused down to within the cage.

Right where Sabu was standing.

Raw magical energy exploded out towards Shandeür as raw death imploded in upon Sabu from every side. Sabu's last sight was of the cage exploding apart from the forces it had contained, and seeing the misty form of Shandeür blown to the distant corners of this valley. Perhaps not destroyed, but at least, Sabu thought with some comfort, it wouldn't be bothering his friends again for a very long time.

The rumble of death that had focused in on Sabu had clapped down on him like a large metal gong. As sight and sound were quickly robbed of him, he felt himself flung through the air, his rapidly withering hands grasping tightly onto his precious staff. He dimly felt himself crash through several bushes and a tree. *If only I could have lived to see through to our destiny,* he thought with some regret as he came crashing down to the ground, *but at least I helped out my friends.*

Maybe Tinweril can show me around the Afterlife, he thought.

The last thing he felt, before consciousness and life left him, was a pair of strong hands lifting him up under his shoulders.

Dim point of light in the darkness, faint but growing steady. Vagueness coming into focus; shapes solidifying, light getting stronger. Flickering sight of a wooden room, a figure leaning over.

"Sabu, are you all right?"

Sabu slowly opened up his eyes, squinting as he did so, the soft light in the room still bright enough to momentarily hurt his eyes. When he focused, he saw Sindar leaning over him, sitting in an intricately carved wooden chair by Sabu's bedside. Around him he saw a room, perhaps twenty feet across, its walls a solid barrier of tree branches and leaves, appearing as if naturally growing in the shape of the room. The floors were a solid but smooth mass of living branches, their leaves all growing flat and smoothly together, as if grown to be walked upon. An arch of curved branches formed a natural door out into the bright light of the outside. Sabu weakly felt for his voice, finally finding it to speak to his friend.

"I should be dead," he said softly.

"You were," Sindar nodded, "just like Quickfoot. But you can thank the fact that Candol recovered and his Indra seemed generous that rise."

"How long?" Sabu croaked out.

"We've been in the elven village for about three rises now," Sindar answered. "Apparently that spirit took a lot out of you before it actually killed you, because Candol raised both you and Quickfoot up the very rise after we got here. Quickfoot came out fine, but you've been recovering ever since."

"What about Shong?"

"As chipper, and *youthful* as ever," Sindar said as he reached for a finely-wrought glass cup of liquid from a small nearby table, "another gift of Indra. Here, drink this; the elves here say it's worth two rises of rest."

Sindar helped his friend to sit up, and then to drink down the bluish liquid. When he was finished, Sabu propped himself up against the bed's backboard into a sitting position.

"Tastes kind of like blueberries and cheese," Sabu said licking his lips, "I'm already feeling better."

"Well, you should wait for about a *diid* or two before trying to get up," Sindar warned.

"Good, that'll give me time to ask the more obvious basic questions," Sabu started.

"The answer to your first question," Sindar said, anticipating, "is that everyone else is fine, although *you've* been worrying us for a bit. As for your second question, no, Shandeür isn't destroyed, but the elves assure us, after they saw what you did to it, that it won't be back for a while, and *no*, as powerful as it is, it isn't the master of the undead of this valley."

"It makes me wonder just what is," Sabu commented, "What about——"

"Eldar and Dwingale appear equally smitten with each other," Sindar answered, before it was asked, "he says that she's more beautiful than any other elf he's ever seen. Although, about that Lindel apparently has something he wants to say as soon as you're ready to hear with the rest of us."

"By the way," Sabu tried for a complete sentence once again, "did you note that——"

"Yes, they do actually *grow* parts of their trees into the shapes of their dwellings," Sindar answered the almost-spoken question. "This room here is actually part of the tree it's in. They use some sort of nature magic; Lindel could probably tell you more about the details of how it's done than can I."

"It's just so much fun having a conversation with a psychic," Sabu began, as he straightened himself up in his bed, "one just never has time to finish a——"

"I'm just trying to help you conserve you're strength," Sindar smiled, "Now, as soon as you're ready, the others will be happy to see you up and walking again."

The late Fall sun trickled down through the canopy of leaves when they finally walked outside, Sabu now strong enough to carry himself with just but a little help from his friend. The room he'd been in was indeed housed up in the branches of a tree, as were the others that he saw around them. In each case, did he see a small room or house, the branches of some immense tree growing around to form the needed shape for walls, roof, and floor. Even the doors and windows seemed grown by design. The carefully contoured leaves of the trees also seemed to hide the true size of a given structure, or in some cases the fact that it was even there. To top it all off, not one tool for sawing or nailing appeared to have been used in the entire village. Even natural bridges of interlocking branches formed between the trees, the branches of one tree running into and locking up with those of a neighboring tree, providing an extensive network of catwalks and pathways around the trees. Around this elevated city in the trees he saw elves, all dressed in earthen-colored clothes covering only what need be covered, all looking like young overgrown children at play as they skipped through the branches going on about their daily affairs. On the ground, some fifty feet below, he saw more elves at play and at work, amidst the flowery undergrowth that seemed to cradle all the trees. In the distance he saw a small stream trickling between the trees of the unusual city.

The sounds of elven children at play could be heard all around, as Sindar helped Sabu out along one of the tree catwalks. Sabu grabbed onto the naturally grown handrails, also made of living tree branch, as he was guided along it into a neighboring tree. As they rounded the walkways and headed in for the next tree, Sabu could see through the cloaking leaves the general shape of its ingrown structure. Several times larger than the small room from which Sabu had come, Sindar guided him up a bridge and towards a natural leafy door.

A small figure popped out from behind the door. No more than perhaps two feet tall, a tall brown pointed hat topped its smartly cut brown forest garb. In its mouth it sported a lit cigar, the tip of its one-foot length carrying a slowly expanding cone of ash. It walked up to the both of them, taking the cigar out of its mouth to tap off a small pile of ash before it spoke.

"I see he's finally awake," the creature said, in a gruff gravelly voice that a child might try to make. "Well, it's about time."

"You're a Brownie," Sabu observed.

"Oh, he's *real* smart for a Human," it replied sarcastically. "Was it the *hat* that gave me away?"

"This village houses all manner of the Faerie races," Sindar explained, "there's even a few nymphs around here."

"That ought to make Eldar happy," Sabu smiled.

"He's too smitten with Dwingale to bother," Sindar shook his head.

"That's not the Eldar that *I* know," Sabu replied doubtfully.

"But, he *did* once ask Dwingale if she'd make it a threesome with one of the nymphs," Sindar continued.

"*That's* the Eldar I know," Sabu smiled.

"Bronto, though, appears to be doing a good job of showing a couple of the nymphs a good time," Sindar said.

"Which would leave Kilgar with nothing to do," Sabu observed.

"Oh, the elven children are trying to show him how to have fun," Sindar replied.

"That should be an exercise in futility," Sabu stated. "I think it more likely that he would teach *them* better ways to fight."

"Ahem," they looked down to see the brownie tapping his foot as well as his cigar, "if you two are *quite* finished, they're waiting inside."

"Oh, sorry," Sindar apologized, "come on."

Together, they went up the bridge and on into the natural leafy door, the brownie taking a puff on his cigar before he trailed in after them. Inside was what appeared to be a large almost palatial room, the cunningly grown branches hiding its true dimensions as well as forming natural stairs and passageways to other rooms. Vines of ivy twisted around the ceiling in curving artistic designs, while elements of the branches in the ceiling seemed to emit the pleasantly bright glow that served as more than adequate interior lighting. Natural growths of branches served as chairs and benches, a low round table formed from the floor itself adorning the center of the large room, and a chandelier of glowing multicolored ivy hung down from the center of the ceiling. Spaced around the room were several elves, male and female alike. Hanging from smaller places up in the twisted ivy of the ceiling were smaller faerie folk, some looking like a cross between a brownie and a miniature nymph, others with long pointed ears and delicate pastel wings, still others with heads disproportionately large to their diminutive bodies. There was a general babble of talk, as elves and little creatures alike held a multitude of conversations.

As they came in, silence fell briefly as all heads turned to see Sindar and Sabu coming in. Sabu had a brief moment to be puzzled at this reaction before a chorus of cheers suddenly exploded out from the room. Several elven hands slapped Sabu on the back as Sindar lead him towards the central round table, as well as brief kisses felt on his cheeks by swiftly darting faerie forms no bigger than one's thumb. Loudest of all, though, was a voice coming from near the table.

"Well, it's about *time* you're back from the dead!" Eldar gayly shouted as he sprang up from a soft leafy couch beside the table. "It'd be poor form to use *death* as an excuse for leaving us. Things also wouldn't be *nearly* as fun."

"Yeah, well, I wouldn't want to spoil your fun just because I died," Sabu replied with a smile, as Eldar slapped him warmly on the back.

"Now you know how it feels."

Shong's cheerful voice came from where he sat across from Eldar. It was then that Sabu noticed that all of the others were also there, either seated near the table or scattered around the room, conversing with the various faerie folk assembled there.

"No, death is not an experience I would like to repeat," Sabu said over to Shong.

Seated next to where Eldar had been was the enchanting form of Dwingale, looking as young and beautiful as before. Eldar lead him over to a seat on the leafy couch, its substance giving way like stiff cotton as Sabu and Sindar sat down, Eldar next to Sabu, Dwingale to the other side of Eldar. As they seated themselves, one of the elves standing next to a bark-lined wall talking to Lindel came over to them. He gave a smiling bow as he stopped in front of them. Gold of hair and eyes, a merry twinkle set within his pupils, like all of his race he looked rather young, though he might be far older than any Human assembled there in that room.

"I am Fawsil," he introduced himself. "For what little we may have in the way of a leader may you call me such. I do honor to those that can face up to Shandeür such as you and your friends did."

"Not an act I'd like to repeat real soon, I assure you," Sabu replied, as Fawsil sat down in a chair on the opposite side of the table from them, "but I do thank you for the honor you do me."

"As the others already know," Fawsil continued, "you are all welcome to stay here for as long as you need to. Any enemy of the lord of this valley is *indeed* our friend."

"Which would bring me to ask," Sabu began, once again his inquiring self, "just who *is* the one who commands so many undead hordes in a valley long since forgotten by the outside world."

"Ah, now therein lies a tale," the elf sat back as his eyes lit up, "and since your friend Bronto has been so good as to regale us of the tails of your many adventures, we can but return the favor."

Sabu looked around and saw Bronto leaning against one wall, a scantily clad nymph on either arm. He smiled in Sabu's direction at the mention of his name.

"For other reasons should we hear this," Lindel said as he walked over to them from where he'd been standing when he was talking to Fawsil, "for there is much that would concern us here."

"Would this have anything to do with that which you would tell us?" Sindar asked.

"You will hear much of it in Fawsil's telling," Lindel replied, "and hear of what I saw in Dwingale the first I laid eyes on her."

"Hey," Eldar protested lightly, "she's mine."

"Have no fear," Dwingale said softly to Eldar as she gently stroked his long silver hair, "I knew I was yours 'ere you first entered the forest."

"So there *was* someone watching us," Sindar exclaimed. "I *thought* I felt something."

"More than our own eyes watched you," Fawsil warned, "there are many others that have watched you since first you entered this valley."

"Although," came a cry from another of the elves assembled, "Dwingale happily volunteered to watch you for us when she first caught sight of Eldar!"

Laughs rolled around the room, as Dwingale first blushed then sat up straight and proudly put forth her chin as she gave reply.

"I see no shame to admit seeing in Eldar the future of my life," she said firmly, "and I would stand up to anyone that would deny me otherwise!"

Another brief roll of elven laughter circled the room as Eldar beamed out happy pride.

"Feisty she is," Eldar said as he put an arm around his beloved, "definitely worth keeping."

"It will be most interesting to see who owns who in time," came Sheil-Bor(h)'s response from across the room.

"My vote's for Dwingale," came back Fawsil, "but you asked of the master of this valley."

"Yes," said Sindar and Sabu simultaneously, as they sat forward, interest on their faces.

"Long ago, after Thïr Tÿorca fell," Fawsil began, "the valley was left in a ruin. The forces that Beltor had gathered dispersed throughout the land as the people started to leave this once-fair valley. As they left, they sealed up the secret passes through the mountains so that none of Beltor's forces would escape. In fact, we were surprised that you made it through the mountains at all."

"It wasn't easy," came Quickfoot's voice from up in a ceiling nook next to one of the smaller faerie folk. "We would have been dragon chow if it hadn't been for me!"

A rotten tomato quickly found its way directly into the small one's face. From the other side of the room, Mauklo smiled at the result of his little conjuring spell.

"Why was it necessary to seal them all in?" Sabu asked of Fawsil, ignoring the outburst.

"Because of the nature of Beltor's army," replied Fawsil. "Beltor was a powerful necromancer. The more troops that were lost in battle, the greater grew his ranks. Beltor's was an army of undead."

"That would explain all the undead around here," Sindar commented.

"So you see," Fawsil went on, "the people were forced to abandon their home. Even after Beltor was defeated and sealed away, his armies still roamed free. Without Beltor to control them, they started to wander around at random.

There were too many for what remained of the Kingdom to destroy, so they were forced to seal up the valley forever."

"But, those of the undead that we have fought have definitely been under someone's control," Candol stated from where he leaned back in a chair to one side of the table. "Does this mean that Beltor has returned, perhaps undead himself, to lead his troops once again?"

"No," Fawsil shook his head, "Beltor is still sealed away. Perhaps still a danger if his tomb is ever breached, but it is not now him that rules this valley. Thousands of rels after the fall, another came here. The valley, hidden from outside eyes and filled with undead, was to his liking. He gathered the undead to him, all of them, and then started to multiply their numbers. Over the long rels their numbers swelled, till now this land has more than I care to count. Yet, of any outside place, he does not invade. He long ago discovered the sealed secret ways through the mountains, and could easily have opened them up once again, to lead his undead hordes out in conquest as Beltor did of old. But, he does not. He waits."

"What is the name of he who waits?" Sabu asked.

"He is a powerful wizard named Krey," Fawsil answered. "Mighty is he in the power of *yonsoodra*, and more powerful by far than Beltor."

"If he's so powerful," Lorel asked, "then how is it that you live so peacefully in his very midst?"

"It is not always as peaceful as it might seem," Fawsil answered, "and the magics that hide our home were cunningly laid long ago, before the fall of Thïr Tÿorca. But Krey seems to have designs of his own other than ourselves. He seems to wait, while he also holds council with the orkai deep in the mountains. We know not of what he waits."

"If he's working with the orkai then he's allied with Miro," Candol stated simply.

There was a low murmur at the sound of that dreaded name; a name that could spawn more fear than all the gods of evil combined.

"There is a devious plot at work here," Sabu stated, "and somehow we are a part of it."

"It is as I said," came Mauklo's calm voice from across the room, "we were lead here for purposes other than our own. It is perhaps that Miro *did* indeed arrange for the demise of Thïr Tÿorca, or at least make use of it, for his own plans of using its present undead legions as a convenient army."

"But, to wait five thousand rels for an invasion?" Lorel gasped, from where he stood amongst more of the elves. "How or why can anyone plan like that?"

"He waits for the Donjflou," Sindar stated, "the time when he can make his power the greatest."

"We know well of the Donjflou," Fawsil nodded. "Our people have seen its effects many a time over the long eons."

"There is one thing you have yet to explain," Mauklo observed, "and that is your own presence in this valley."

Fawsil paused, stood up, and started pacing around the table as he answered Mauklo's question.

"Our ancestors came to this land after their own kingdom had died," Fawsil started, "another victim of Miro and a Donjflou. Along their long journey, they encountered other elves, interbreeding with them before they came to this land. It was about ten thousand rels ago and the first of the Great Human Kingdoms had just started when they came to Catho to settle down. After some wandering, they found this valley. In the glory time of Thïr Tÿorca did they settle here, fast friends with those of the Kingdom for many long rels. When the people left to seal up this valley, we stayed. We'd found that we couldn't leave the land that we'd come to love so much, so we vowed to stay until the Kingdoms could once again be reborn. Perhaps a long wait, but we elves are immortal."

"If you're so immortal," came Quickfoot from up in his nook, face now free of tomato, "then how come none of your 'ancestors' are here to tell us this stuff themselves."

"For once," Eldar pointed out, "the small one makes a good point."

"Immortal yes," Fawsil continued, "but not invulnerable. Those that didn't die during the reign of Beltor, have seen slow death at the hands of Krey and his undead minions. The last of the old blood died out with Dwingale's parents."

Eldar cocked an eyebrow as he looked over at his beloved.

"What old blood?" he asked.

Dwingale shrugged nonchalantly as she hedged around a direct answer. Before she could speak, however, Lindel spoke up, excitement fairly jumping off of his face.

"They were thought to be all dead, extinct," he said with some excitement "that's why it surprised me when I first saw it within her. The blood of old shown forth through her every curve."

"*That* old blood?!" Eldar's eyes went wide, as he grabbed up both of Dwingale's hands with his own, "But why didn't you tell me?"

"We were too busy," Dwingale said almost shyly, "getting…acquainted."

"Would someone mind interjecting a *noun* or two into this exchange?" Bronto said, with some amusement.

214

"My mother was the last, before she was killed by Shandeür," Dwingale began, "I am half Evolin."

For long moments, silence seemed to take hold of the room, the import of that pronouncement sinking into the elves' guests. Finally, Sabu broke the silence.

"The parent race of elves?" Sabu asked, more than a bit incredulous. "The same ones that gave us such wondrous works of art and lost secrets of magic—*that* same Evolin race?"

"Their arts are lost to me," Dwingale said almost meekly, "but yes, I am of the very same blood."

An explosion of questions then seemed to arise from the visitors, even Bronto having heard of the lost elven race and the myths and stories of their legendary works. Dwingale seemed to shrink back from the cacophony until, with a sharp whistle, Eldar put a quick end to the barrage of questions.

"Hey," Eldar said, when the noise had dimmed down, "she's *still* mine!"

"Forgive us," Sindar apologized, "but to hear of such a race long thought dead…"

"It *is* dead," she said, "for I am the last of its blood."

"If only we had something of their lost arts," Sabu pondered. "Was nothing brought from the downfall of your Evolin ancestors? Nothing salvaged of their mighty works of alchemy and magic? The secret to their swords? Even a work of art or two?"

"Nothing was salvaged," Fawsil shook his head, "their knowledge is lost forever, and with Dwingale shall there be the last of that noble race."

"Not if *I* have anything to say about it!"

Eldar stood up, taking a step out from the leafy couch, one hand still holding lightly onto Dwingale's.

"I'm not one to make any vows, but here do I make this one," Eldar announced, uncharacteristically determined look on his face. "I will make it my life's work to find and preserve the lost knowledge of the Evolins, no matter what the cost. Likewise will I preserve all elven knowledge so that it may never again be so lost. Even should Miro wipe out every last elf on Maldene will I preserve their heritage! Furthermore, will I preserve and support every last elf and Evolin there be. The Evolin race shall not disappear from this world."

"A rather unusually fine pronouncement, especially for Eldar," Sabu wondered, "but how do you propose to preserve the Evolin race when Dwingale's the only one left?"

Eldar smiled.

Bronto's chuckle seemed to indicate him as the first to catch on; perhaps it was because of his way with the ladies that he recognized the look in Eldar's eyes. At any rate, as Eldar turned around and knelt to face his beloved, it quickly became apparent to all present what he had in mind.

"Dwingale," he said to the now-blushing elven maiden, "I know of only one way to preserve your mother's race. Be my mate for as long as the hills survive and the mountains soar high up into the sky."

There was a pause of silence as Dwingale considered; even the collected elves were quiet. Finally, a blushing Dwingale gave answer; the only answer that Fate would have expected.

"Yes."

Cheers exploded from around the large room; even Mauklo grinned at prospects only he knew of. But then Dwingale put up a gentle but stern hand for silence.

"But on one condition," she said.

"Uh oh," Bronto smiled, "here it comes."

"Anything," Eldar said seriously, and then gave a brief smile, "as long as it doesn't involve my giving up my gay personality."

"You have nothing to give up," she replied, "but only this one condition do I impose. My mother was a seer; she foresaw your coming and our falling in love."

"I don't suppose she had gold skin?" Eldar interrupted.

"No," Dwingale answered puzzledly, "why?"

"Never mind," Eldar waved it off, "continue."

"So, I know that you seek your Fate in Thïr Tÿorca," she went on, "I will marry you *after* you come back from your quest."

A large grin spread over Eldar's face. He kissed the back of her hand and then quickly stood up, practically shooting up to his feet.

"My lady," he said, "I shall be back with the heads of *both* Beltor and Krey!"

"Just bring back your own," she smiled, as some of those present laughed with mild amusement at Eldar's boast.

"And later, will I make you a goddess," he finished his broad boast.

"I know," she smiled a secret smile.

Eldar looked in surprise down at Dwingale, somewhat taken aback at her statement.

"Look," Lindel smiled, "she's already playing him like a lyre!"

Eldar then broke out in laughter with the others, laughing at his own reaction to Dwingale's little jest.

Only Mauklo, though, seemed to notice the look on Dwingale's face, a look suggesting that it was no jest and that she knew more than she'd said.

"Come," Fawsil said, standing up, "there is much in our city for you to see; perhaps some of it may be of use to you. Dwingale shall be your guide."

"We'd be honored," Sabu replied, as he and the others followed the elf's lead and also stood up, "you have a most interesting city here. A bright light shining out in this valley of darkness."

They filed out of the house in the large tree, out into the bright late Fall afternoon, Eldar and Dwingale going out arm in arm.

Dwingale showed them through a section of the forest they would not earlier have thought possible. In the midst of all the rampaging death throughout the rest of the valley, the small elven community shown like a small star. Hidden by magic from outside view, it was a garden of ivy-lined pathways, the ivy growing into natural contours as they shaped the paths, with a sprinkling of calm pools of clear water fountaining lightly up from the ground. Dwingale lead them through glades where naked elven children danced playfully with bear cubs and full-grown lions. The others had had a few rises to get used to some of this, but to Sabu it was entirely new.

"Such a wondrous place you have here," he commented, "one would never know it was here just to judge from what lies on the outside."

"We try to preserve what we can of the old times," Dwingale explained.

"And doing such a good job too," Eldar said, arm around her.

As Shong was admiring the scenery through which they walked, a brown streak suddenly whipped on past his face. Shong looked around for the source of annoyance, but another blurred form streaked past his noise, lightly brushing it as it passed by.

"I think you got some rather large insects around here," he commented, "'cause there's one about the size of a house-cat buzzing me."

"Oh," Dwingale replied calmly, "that's not an insect. Here, I'll show you."

She pursed her lips and whistled a high-pitched musical note, warbling briefly through the air. As a response, the brown streak flew to her side, stopping in front of her, its small winged reptilian form hovering rapidly in front of her.

"That's a Kozo lizard," Shong said, reaching for his sword.

"Stop that," Dwingale directed sternly at Shong, "you can put down the sword; it's tame."

"You can't *tame* one of those things," Shong answered, "we've encountered a swarm of those before."

"Yeah," Eldar agreed, "they were pretty vicious."

"Well, not with the right type of spell they aren't," Dwingale smiled, as she scratched it under its chin. "Besides, I have a knack for dealing with such creatures."

She cooed gently at the Kozo before sending it on its way. Then she smiled up at Shong.

"It shouldn't bother you again," she said, "it was just playing."

"The last kozos we found tried to strip us to the bone, they were so playful," Mauklo scowled.

Ignoring Mauklo's comment, Dwingale motioned them along. As they continued on along the ivy-lined path, Kilgar came walking up behind them. Bronto noticed a somewhat dejected look on the boy's face.

"What's the matter kid?" Bronto asked. "Didn't the elf kids want to play with you?"

"That's just it," he said, coming up next to him. "They kept trying to get me to play these silly games called 'tag' and 'hide and seek' but they couldn't explain the purpose to me. Now, I can kind of understand that 'hide and seek' one; it's good practice for sneaking up on an enemy, although they didn't seem too pleased when I jumped three of them. But, this 'tag' game I can see no use for. The purpose of the game didn't make sense. They couldn't tell me *why* we were supposed to touch someone on the shoulder. And then when they started tossing this large ball back and forth…"

"My boy," Bronto said, placing a hand on the boy's shoulder, "I think we've been neglecting your childhood. You're just supposed to have *fun*."

Kilgar just blinked at him, puzzled look on his face.

"You *do* know how to have fun, don't you?" Bronto asked.

"Yeah," Kilgar responded, "fighting the orkai was kind of fun, and then there was the time with the big golem back on Devoon——"

Bronto's chuckle interrupted the boy's listing of what constitutes 'fun'.

"Tell you what," Bronto said, pointing to one of the small ponds, "why don't you just relax and go for a little swim?"

"Oh, he mustn't do that," Dwingale turned around quickly, her sharp elven ears picking up the exchange, "at least not in *those* ponds."

"Why not?" Kilgar asked.

"Because those are magical ponds," Dwingale explained. "Come, I'll show you."

She lead them all over to a large glade, half a dozen ponds spaced around it, flower-lined foot-trails weaving their way around them. She knelt down beside one pond, its blue water shining peacefully in the sun.

"This one, for instance," she said, "has magical waters of healing. We used some of it to help Sabu recover."

"So *that's* what I drank," Sabu commented, "it tasted pretty good."

"Do you mind if I take some?" Lindel asked as he fished a small vial out of a hidden pocket. "It could come in handy on our journey."

"Help yourself," Dwingale offered, "if it helps to save a life, then its purpose will have been served."

Lindel knelt down to fill his small container as Dwingale continued.

"That one over there," she pointed to a pond with a slightly lighter shade of blue, "will cure lycanthropy of all types."

Sabu and Sindar glanced at each other, the same thought on their minds.

"You think maybe it'll work for Schanter?" Sindar was the first to ask.

"No," Sabu thought briefly, "I think even magical ponds have their limits."

"Hey, what about this green one over here?" came Eldar's shout from across the glade.

He was kneeling down beside a pond, its waters the green of new grass. Eldar had some of its waters cupped in his hands and was bringing it to his lips to drink. Dwingale leapt up in a sudden frantic leap.

"No!" she shouted. "Don't drink from *that* one!"

She got to his side just as Eldar had drank from the pond. Eldar was licking his lips, as if deciding on its taste.

"What have you done?" Dwingale exclaimed. "That pond is——"

"Shakoo," Eldar interrupted, "it *is!* I've been out of this stuff for ages!"

Dwingale looked puzzledly at him, as if fully expecting him to grow a third nose and wondering why he didn't.

"It has had no effect on you," she said, puzzlement and wonder both in her voice. "The waters of this pond should have had any number of——"

"I used to have a whole jug of this stuff," he replied, "I drank so much of it I became immune to it. Hey Sabu! Remember that jug of *special* wine I used to have back before we fought that dragon on Miro's island?"

"Yeah," Sabu replied as he walked over. "It did something different to the drinker with every sip. I seem to remember you trying to pass that stuff off on Lindel."

"And *I* seem to remember getting long ears and a bright blue nose!" Lindel chimed in.

"Yeah," Eldar smiled, "it *was* kind of amusing. But my jug got destroyed back with that dragon we fought. Hey, anybody got a jug? I could go for a refill."

"Don't let him," Lindel smiled, "or we'll *all* regret it."

"You know," Dwingale said, gently urging Eldar back up to his feet, "there *are* other places of magic in our forest besides these ponds. Other more *interesting* places."

"Oh?" Eldar had already forgotten about the green pond, much to the relief of all present. "Like what?"

"Well, there's a tree with magical fruit," she started, "then there's Cassandra's Grove, then——"

"If you would be so kind," Sheil-Bor(h) interrupted, showing sudden interest, "as to show us this grove of which you speak."

"A hunch?" Sabu asked quietly of Sheil-Bor(h).

"Possibly something of which I may have heard," was all he replied.

"Sure," Dwingale shrugged, "it even has a story behind it. Follow me."

An arm around Eldar's waist, she lead them through another path in the forest, telling her story as they went.

"It is said that Cassandra was a powerful conjurer and traveler of dimensions," Dwingale started, as they marched through the tree-lined path. "She traveled to many strange dimensions and even other worlds. One rise, it is said, she came upon another world that she found to be some sort of a sister planet to our own world; not an alternate to our own but more like the one planet that is the nearest to ours dimensionally. Well, she was so taken with such another planet that could be reached so much easier than the others that she'd been to, and so liked what she found there, that she used her magic to make a magical pathway. A way that one may walk through the dimensions and so on into this other world. The one end of that enchanted path is here in our forest: Cassandra's Grove. You have but to walk along its length to end up in that other world."

"You *can* use it to get back with, I hope?" Quickfoot asked.

"Of course, silly," she laughed as they rounded into a clearing, "and here we are."

It looked like any other normal grove of trees, a clearing perhaps two hundred feet across, sunlight shining down on the scattered wild flowers. Normal, except of course, for the golden path; it started in the center of the Grove and looked to recede on off into the distance. As the entered the Grove however, and started to walk around its perimeter, they could see that, from any other direction than from straight in front of it, the golden three-foot wide path could not be seen. From every other perspective was it just but a normal grove.

"As I said," Dwingale continued, "it is an enchanted grove and a magical path."

"So, what ever happened to Cassandra?" Kilgar asked, as he looked up the length of the golden path, trying to see what lay at its far end.

"That's the sad part of the story," Dwingale said. "One rise an evil lord came to power. Cassandra fought him all she could, but she finally died at the hands of him and his great dragon. Since then, no one who has traveled along this path has ever come back from that other world. Some even say this to be but a shadow of the real Path and Grove, one which will forever fade away when the sun finally sets on returning heroes."

"Sounds like a dimensional reflection," Sabu mused thoughtfully, "a by-product of the creation of the original, held in place only by the lack of a returning matter-stream to balance out the——"

"Um," Mauklo interjected, casual suspicion in his voice, "about this dragon; about how big was it?"

"Why, stories say that it is tremendous," Dwingale answered, "second only to Traugh himself."

Everyone except Lorel suddenly got the same expression, best summed up by Eldar's one-word comment.

"Uh-oh."

"What is it, beloved?" Dwingale asked of Eldar.

"This lord," Eldar began, "he wouldn't have a name by chance?"

"They just called him the Dragon Lord," she answered, "it was said he was an ally of Miro's"

"This path leads to Devoon," Sheil-Bor(h) nodded. "I suspected something earlier when I felt some small twinge of premonition at the mention of this Grove's name."

"Ah, then you've heard the story," she smiled, "of the sister world of Devoon."

"Let's just say that we've experienced it first hand," Eldar answered.

"Yeah," Quickfoot put in, "and that dragon of his was *still* too close for my tastes."

"You've *been* there?" she asked incredulously. "And *come back?*"

"All courtesy of *Tedelnosho* and the fine mind of Sabu," Bronto answered jovially, "and a grand adventure it was."

"Although those grey skies got kind of depressing after a while," Lindel remembered, "and we almost lost Shong to those two priests."

"You *did* loose me," Shong pointed out, "remember?"

"You *did* go there!" Dwingale exclaimed. "And faced up to the Dragon Lord!"

"Well, we didn't exactly meet him face to face," Sindar clarified.

"This Dragon Lord doesn't sound too difficult," Lorel said, his hand on the hilt of his sword strapped to his belt, "just another evil to be vanquished."

"This was before you came along, Lorel," Candol answered Lorel's boast, "and by the grace of Indra you *didn't* see that dragon!"

"That's an experience I hope not to repeat soon," Quickfoot said, as he sat down plucking random weeds from the ground.

"Have I ever told you how sensitive that my special sense has been getting lately?" Eldar said, thoughtful expression on his face as he paced around towards the front of the golden path. "Like for instance, I can start to sense the presence of Hevon Gems now."

Eldar stopped in front of the path and looked down its length, gazing meaningfully off into the distance.

"No!" Quickfoot said as he shot to his feet. "No more dragons. I refuse! We barely got out of there the *last* time!"

"Indra would seem to be pointing the way," Candol walked over to stand behind Eldar, "we can but follow his lead."

"If there's Hevon Gems there, then we must seek them out," Sindar reminded them, "although the rest of you need not be involved in this."

"Thank goodness," Quickfoot sighed as he sat back down.

"Hey, you know we aren't about to leave you," Bronto said. "If you have to go, then of course we're coming with you!"

"Well then," Sabu shrugged, "I guess that we can all—"

"Perhaps not this time," Sheil-Bor(h) cautioned.

"Your seer powers have something for us?" Sabu asked.

"Only that this is a small trip for only those that seek of Hevon," Sheil-Bor(h) nodded. "Others shall not only not be needed, but may actually come to unnecessary harm."

"We can hold our own!" Kilgar protested.

"Speak for yourself," Quickfoot added.

"Hey, I thought Candol made you braver now?" Shong asked the small one.

"He did," Quickfoot answered, "but I *still* don't like dragons."

"Sindar," Sabu asked, "what do your own abilities tell you?"

Sindar closed his eyes, as everyone waited, collective breath held. When finally Sindar opened up his eyes again, nary a sound was to be heard throughout the entire Glade.

"Sheil-Bor(h)'s right," Sindar finally answered, "perhaps more so than he knows. Beyond that path lies our route to more secrets of Hevon, but it is only a route that those of Hevon may survive; a journey that only those of us with the Gems can take. It is best if no others come."

"Fine by me," Quickfoot said simply.

"Okay then," Sabu said, "it's just Sindar, Candol, Eldar, Mauklo, Sheil-Bor(h), and myself. The rest can use the time to stock us up on supplies. It shouldn't take us too long."

"I'll post a watch by the path," Bronto stated, "just in case anything happens."

"Once again," Candol intoned, as he walked behind Eldar up to the path, "this humble servant of Indra has been given the privilege to do battle against His enemies."

Sheil-Bor(h), Mauklo, and Sabu soon joined the others at the head of the path. They looked down its long golden length, wondering. Kilgar came up to Sabu, tugging at his robes.

"None of you can come," Sabu said, looking down, "this includes yourself as well."

"I know," he said, "I just wanted to wish you good luck."

"Thank-you," Sabu smiled, "we'll probably need it."

"Well, let's go," Eldar smiled, as he drew out his sword.

They started down the path.

"Wait!" Dwingale came running up to them, her shout stopping them in mid-step.

She ran up to Eldar, standing directly in his path.

"I know naught of this Hevon that you seek, but I *do* know that you are the other half of my soul," she said, determination on her face.

"Sweet one," Eldar said, lowering his sword a bit, "I *must* do this."

"I know," she said. "Go into Thïr Tÿorca if you wish, for that is ordained destiny, but along this path, you will not walk without *me!*"

Eldar smiled.

"I *told* you she was feisty!" he grinned appreciatively. "Are you sure there isn't some way we can squeeze her in?"

"She is not one of Hevon," Candol pointed out, "she would be a danger."

"One more sacrificial lamb is fine by me," Mauklo smiled.

"We are two halves of the same soul," Eldar stated, "she *must* come."

Sabu looked at the pleading look in his elven friend's eyes, and then at the golden orbs of Dwingale, both having a look of need about them. Finally he turned to Sindar.

"You're the one with the precognitive powers," he said, "what say you?"

"I don't foresee too much trouble from just her presence," Sindar answered with a slight shrug.

Sabu thought a bit and then finally turned to Dwingale.

"Do you have a sword?"

A smile swiftly crossed both hers and Eldar's faces. She practically leaped up with joy.

"With life in this valley as it is," she answered, "always."

A twist of her wrist and a slim silver rapier appeared in her right hand, materializing out of nowhere. She took her place beside Eldar, the two lovebirds smiling at each other.

"I love a woman who can fight by my side," Eldar almost shouted. "Onward it is."

Bronto watched as the seven walked on down the golden path, receding off into the distance, while from any angle other than directly in front, the others saw that both path and those that walked it were not to be seen. It was as if they'd walked on through some invisible doorway, a doorway only visible from where the big man stood. Kilgar came up to his side, right hand fingering the curved knife at his belt. Bronto put a large arm around the boy's shoulder.

"Don't worry kid," he said, "they'll be back before breakfast tomorrow."

Kilgar looked up into the big man's face, trust in his word written all over his boyish look. Finally he spoke.

"Then we've only got a few nevs to get the new supplies together," Kilgar said in a practical tone of voice.

Bronto chuckled, turning them both from facing the path, walking, as were now the others, out of the Grove.

"Sometimes kid, I'm not sure which of us is trying to keep the other in good cheer."

As they walked out of the Grove, Bronto thought of Kilgar's trust in his words, and hoped that he had indeed spoken true.

They seemed to walk along a wooded path, gold though it may be, but through a seemingly normal forest nonetheless. The sun shown down bright and blue upon them, the air fresh and clear. Eldar and Dwingale were at the lead, swords out, twin blades of death in the sunlight. Pleasant though their journey might be, they knew enough to walk with caution.

"This seems a pleasant enough way to travel the dimensions," Sabu had commented after they'd been walking for almost half of a nev, "if a bit slow."

"I think we may not have much longer," Sindar pointed out. "Look up ahead; the sky turns grey, and the trees dark and dead. We near Devoon."

Sure enough, as they walked along, the sky began to take on the same drab greyness they'd seen when last they were on Devoon. The trees started to look blackened and dead, a thin cold mist curling in around their feet. Their golden path, now the only source of color in this bleak world, opened up into a wide Grove, as large as the one from which they'd started though as dead as the rest of their surroundings. Into the center of this grove their path lead them before it stopped, leaving them in a grey and bleak land.

"A bit gloomy for an enchanted Grove," Dwingale observed with a slight frown, "maybe this is the shadow of the real Path after all."

"This must be the other end of the path," Sabu observed, "another grove corresponding to the one we left."

"A less astute observation I myself couldn't have made," Mauklo said with pleasant sarcasm.

"Is he always that pleasant?" Dwingale asked Eldar, as they looked around.

"You should see him in a *bad* mood," Eldar answered back.

Around them, the grove of dead trees extended for perhaps a hundred feet in radius. Outside of that, they were surrounded on three sides by tall steep rocky hills, like tall stone sentinels reaching up into the distant heights. Ahead of them lay the source of the mist curling around their feet; a steam and mist shrouded region just beyond the dead trees.

"Be alert now," Sindar warned.

They walked carefully on through the Grove, coming to the edge of it as they looked on ahead. Like a line of demarcation, the trees cut abruptly off, ending at a rocky line. Ahead of them stretched a rough and stony terrain, marked in spots by small bubbling pools of this grey liquid, giving rise to the mist that curled throughout the area. Such bubbling pools lay scattered throughout all this rocky land, ranging in size from just but a foot across to more than a dozen feet in size. It stretched on ahead of them, a continuous land of damp rocks and bubbling pools, before getting lost in the mists after fifty feet.

"Acid," Eldar said, "I can smell it. Be careful of those pools; don't let any pop in your face."

Eldar at the lead, Dwingale just behind them, they walked carefully on ahead. Next came Sabu, conjuring forth his staff into his hand just before walking out of the grove. Sindar and Candol then came in turn, with Mauklo last. With careful footsteps, they walked out onto the mist-covered rocks.

Pools of acid bubbled and popped around them. Eldar carefully picked a way around the bubbling pools, the others following his lead. Dwingale walked delicately behind him, her light footsteps leaving nary a trace of her passage. As they walked through the slippery terrain, Sabu looked with some interest at the pools they passed by.

"A natural occurring spring of acid," he pondered. "It must be caused by a natural up-flow of spring water, percolating up slowly through the correct proportions of minerals in the surrounding rocks, thus yielding this rather caustic——"

"Is he going to start that again?" Mauklo asked pleasantly.

"Sabu," Eldar verbally nudged his friend, "this isn't the place."

"Oh, but I was merely wondering at the extraordinary circumstances that must give rise to——"

"Sabu!"

Sabu looked up innocently at Eldar's shouted exclamation.

"Oh, was I getting carried away again?" Sabu asked, almost absently.

"Just a bit," Eldar smiled.

"The acid *does* appear to be rather potent," Sheil-Bor(h) noted, "perhaps a bit more acidic than it should be."

"There is but one way to test it," Candol said as they picked their way carefully onward.

Candol took a small knife out from inside of his robes. Small, but thick of blade and made of polished steel. He gently tossed it into a nearby pool.

It landed in the pool with a soft plop, the pool's liquid being too thick to splash very far from such a small object. They watched, as within moments the thick steel knife dissolved into a spreading slick of quickly evaporating dark liquid. Between the space of one blink of an eye and the next, it was gone.

"Now *that's* what I call acid," Eldar commented.

"Yeah," Dwingale, holding tight to her rapier, "let's just not slip."

"Most interesting," Sabu said thoughtfully as they continued on, "for the occurrence of such an extreme acidity in a natural terrain setting."

"He's starting up again," Dwingale smiled at Eldar.

"Sabu," Eldar shook his head, "you're babbling again."

"Oh, but I'm not," Sabu responded. "This is an important observation of the chemical dynamics of——"

Sabu was interrupted by the sudden grabbing of his shoulders by Mauklo. The yellow-skinned one turned him around and looked him evenly in the eye.

"In three words or less," Mauklo said very slowly and clearly.

Sabu wet his lips, cleared his throat, and then spoke in just as slow a rate.

"It's...not...natural."

There was silence for a few moments as the others thought about this. They then began to slowly look around at the bubbling acid pits around them in a new light.

"Ever feel like you just walked into a particularly nasty trap," Eldar commented.

Crack.

They looked over at the source of the sudden sound; a crack had started across one of the large stones.

"Another observation," Sindar noted, "if the acid is strong enough to eat through the particular type of rock upon which we stand, or if it has been here long enough to weaken its structure..."

"Danger noted," Eldar acknowledged. "Anybody got any ideas."

Another crack was heard, coming this time from someplace off in the cloaking mists around them.

"Just one," Sabu said. "Eldar, you'd sensed that of Hevon earlier. I would suggest that now be a good time to locate the source."

Crack. Crack!

"And with all due alacrity," Candol added, as he saw another crack connect two of the bubbling pools.

"No sooner said," Eldar said as he concentrated briefly, "then..."

Everyone noted the sudden look of mild concern on Eldar's face.

"Eldar, what's wrong?" Sabu asked. "Are you having trouble sensing them?"

"No," Eldar shook his head slowly, "I'm sensing them just fine."

"Then where are they?" Sindar asked.

"Oh," Eldar smiled, "you might just say that they're right under our feet."

Eldar looked meaningfully over at one of the bubbling pools of acid.

"It figures," Mauklo shrugged, mildly sarcastic pleasantness about his demeanor, "and can we guess of what substance is the nature of *these* gems?"

The ground shuddered with the sound of several cracks running from pool to pool, runners of acid now advancing everywhere.

"It would appear that this sequence of events was triggered by our coming through the Grove," Sabu noted, while hopping around the spreading cracks.

"Perhaps the illusion of solid rock is only more of the acid in a solid state and not rock at all."

"You mean," Dwingale summarized, "that we're standing on top of a single large pool of acid?"

The sound of multiple cracks spreading rapidly around them.

"Apparently," Sabu said, as he danced around a newly forming pool, "the Dragon Lord likes his privacy. This may be why no one has yet come back."

A thin film of acid began to spread across the entire rocky surface, smoke arising from the soles of their shoes as it made contact. They danced up and down as they discussed what to do.

"Indra would deem less theorizing and more action," Candol said, breathing more rapidly from having to jump around the acid. "How do you stop acid?"

"With a good base," Eldar shrugged, as he himself danced along. "It turns the whole mess into salt. Any good alchemy student knows that. Hey, it's getting through my shoes!"

"At least your shoes aren't made of layers of woven flower petals and spun moon fiber," Dwingale put in, "extremely comfortable for walking, but rather useless against acid."

"I don't think we could find enough base material to counteract all of this acid," Sindar noted. "My psychic senses tell me that this pool goes on for at least a hundred feet in every direction; including down."

"Then first things first," Sabu said quickly as the acid started to roll in. "What is one thing that this acid *won't* eat through?"

Mauklo smiled.

"I'll bet *he* knows," Eldar smiled as he nodded in Mauklo's direction.

"The hardest known rock," Mauklo said as he brought his hands out, palms facing down, his brown-colored Hevon Gem of Earth shining forth through his palm, "and by my power, shall it be made."

There was a quick flash from his hands, and suddenly they were standing on a roughly hewn slab of white, almost pearly, rock, floating on top of the spreading bed of acid.

"Bedrock from our own world," Mauklo smiled, "if it's good enough for the walls of the King's castle, then it should do for us."

Several cracks sounded around them as their new stone boat lurched.

"Great, now how do you get it to *float?*" Eldar remarked as the stone slab started to sink.

A sudden torrent of air began to swirl around their rocky island. Faster and faster it went, slowly steadying their raft of rock, slowly lifting it. Soon, it was floating safely on the surface of the acid and rock stew.

"I hope that my humble magic will do for a small time," Sheil-Bor(h) commented, though no one had seen him move his hands to cast the spell with.

"Great," Eldar exclaimed, "now all we need is to figure out how to get those Gems."

"If I may offer a suggestion," Dwingale offered politely. "Eldar, you can sense them, and Sindar could move them with the power of his mind if he could see them…"

"Hey, teamwork," Eldar grinned, "that's why I love you. Well, I'm in for it."

"I'm ready," Sindar said, "just picture in your mind their location and I'll bring them up."

Eldar closed his eyes and concentrated. There was a final loud crack all around them as the last of the rock sank away, leaving them to now float on a single large pool of acid, its bounds lost in the thickening mists arising from its surface. Dwingale and Candol started to cough from the fumes arising, while Mauklo's robes began to form scattered acid holes from the vapors.

"A bit more speed if you will," Mauklo said calmly, "I refuse to loose another robe."

Eldar frowned. His face got the distant look of intense concentration as he increased his efforts. But still, his frown deepened.

"What's wrong?" Sindar asked, looking at Eldar. "Have you not found them yet?"

"We have a problem," Eldar said opening up his eyes. "I can't focus on them. It's like they're all around us."

"Maybe they're scattered in several locations," Sabu offered.

"No," Eldar shook his head, "it's more than that. It's more like the location of each of them *is* all around us. There is nothing for me to focus on."

The acid bubbled and churned around them, its fumes now starting to eat through everyone's outer clothing. Concern and worry passed from face to face as they pondered over this new obstacle.

"Then we *do* have a problem," Sabu agreed, "how do we get the Hevon Gems out of the acid if we can't even locate them?"

"It could be," Sindar theorized, "that if these Gems are indeed of acid then Eldar's senses can only detect them *as* acid. They would then blend in perfectly."

"Hmm," Sabu pondered, "that may be. In which case—"

"NO!"

Candol's cry interrupted them all. He was standing on one edge of their floating stone raft, the winds still whirling around beneath them. An almost fanatical look was on his face, an expression of pure determination.

"This is *not* a test of the intellect," Candol said, voice rising boldly upon the winds, as he knelt down on the rock, "nor of ability in combat, but of *faith!*"

Candol immediately plunged his right hand straight into the acid.

"Candol, no!" Dwingale's voice rang out.

Candol screamed as acid shot up his arm, almost as if it had a life of its own, but still he kept his hand in the acid. The others were immediately down by his side, trying to help the priest.

Except for Mauklo. Mauklo stood to one side, observing and thinking.

Before Candol could wave the others off from helping him, their stone raft gave a quick lurch, followed by a rapid sinking feeling. Like it was suddenly going down out of a large drain, the acid pool suddenly dropped by fifteen feet, the floating stone raft going with it as its riders tried desperately to hang on and not fly off into the distance. It stopped with a sudden plop, as if the drain had been cut off. The others got up, as Candol stopped his cry of pain and carefully stood up.

A grin slowly spread across Mauklo's face.

"Of course," he said to himself, "it *is* all around us."

Mauklo walked over to one edge of the raft and casually stepped on out into the acid, quickly plunging down beneath its surface.

"Are you all right?" Sabu said, as they helped Candol to his feet, "Why in the world..."

"By my faith in Indra am I alright."

Candol held up his right hand. Not only was it unscathed, but in its center was a greyish gem, the color of the acid pool.

"Of course," Sabu realized. "Eldar your senses were right!"

"Well I'll be," Eldar grinned.

"Where's Mauklo?" Candol asked, as he looked around behind them.

The pool gave another lurch, everyone hanging on for another sudden downward plunge.

"I think that answers your question!" Sindar shouted.

"I think we should get this over all at once," Sabu shouted, as the raft started to settle once more. "Dwingale!"

"Yes," she said, as she started to get up.

Sabu made a quick motion with his hand in her direction. A few moments later she started to float up off the raft, hovering in midair, her hair floating all around her, looking for all the world like an angel.

"Everyone on the count of three," Sabu said as they all stood up. "One, two,—"

"Just go for it," Eldar said, and then promptly dived in head first.

Sabu, Sindar, and Sheil-Bor(h) each calmly walked over the side of the white stone raft and down into the pool of acid. Dwingale and Candol watched as the surface of the pool stayed calm.

"I hope Eldar's all right," Dwingale said worriedly.

"Have no fear," Candol said with no doubt in his voice, "they are all better than fine."

It was then that the large pool started to swirl around, faster and faster. Candol tried to hang on for balance while Dwingale just floated in the air. Dwingale looked at the priest's predicament, wondering how to help. She tried pushing off against the air with her arms, thus discovering the means with which to control Sabu's spell of flight. As the pool swirled faster, she shot herself towards Candol, picking him up by the shoulders, straining to hold him aloft with both arms. As both were now airborne, they now looked down at the acid pool.

They watched as the pool suddenly swirled around into a violent whirlpool of acid, going round faster and faster as it dashed the raft around the unseen edges of the pool. A violent rushing of liquid it was, the sound of rocks splintering as the hard substance of the stone raft chipped pieces of the surrounding cliffs off in its wake. Down the pool went, draining rapidly.

"They're going to have a problem with that rock when it lands down on top of them," Candol noted as Dwingale struggled to keep them both aloft. "So, by the power of Hevon do I send it back."

One brilliant flash of light and the stone was gone.

"I can't keep us aloft much longer," Dwingale said in a strained voice as they began to sink down towards the pool.

"You may not need to," Candol noted, "look."

In a final splash and roar, the pool of acid drained away to nothing. As the mists then began to clear they saw five figures standing down at the bottom of the now empty pit.

"Come on down!" Eldar shouted up, as Dwingale and Candol floated downward. "The weather's fine!"

As they finally settled to the ground, Sabu canceling his spell of flight, Dwingale ran over to Eldar, throwing her arms around him in a tight hug. Candol joined the others as they looked around at their new surroundings. Mist was coming off of the now high sheer rocky walls that boxed them in from all around.

"Where to now?" Sindar asked. "There appears to be a rather limited choice of exits."

"Perhaps," Mauklo said, raising a hand in the direction of one of the sheer walls, "*that* way."

He sliced his hand quickly down through the air. As he did so the facing of the rock split. Large rocks tumbled aside as part of the cliff face started to part. Rock turned into sand as a doorway started to form in the wall. When Mauklo was finished, there was a nice wide opening in the wall, leading on into the mountain.

"It connects with a cave that I sensed," Mauklo explained. "Shall we?"

"You sensed it?" Dwingale asked, puzzled. "Eldar, I thought you were the only one that could sense such things?"

"An effect of the Hevon Gem of Earth," Eldar assured her. "On occasion it seems that we can sense that which is of the nature of a given Gem."

"These Hevon Gems sound rather useful," Dwingale agreed as they walked towards the new doorway.

They walked on into the wall. Beyond was a cave-like passage, slanting upwards into unknown darkness. A tap from Sabu's staff and their way was lit, as they started their upward journey. Upward they walked, up through the narrow cave.

"It's a bit cramped in here for my tastes," Dwingale noted.

"Well, you *did* want to see life on the road with me," Eldar reminded her with a wink.

"If you're trying to get rid of me," Dwingale smiled, "it'll take more than some dark cramped place."

"I believe I sense an open space on ahead of us," Sheil-Bor(h) commented, "maybe that will relieve your feeling of claustrophobia."

The light from Sabu's staff revealed a large cavern-like opening up ahead.

"He's right," Eldar said, taking out his sword, "and I sense a great source of energy along with it."

"Do I even need to urge caution anymore?" Sabu said as they walked on up towards the opening.

"Not really," Eldar shrugged. "Besides, it wouldn't do any good with me anyway."

The staff lit up the cavern as they entered it. It was a large cavern, filled with high rocky ledges and hidden recesses. As they walked across its open floor, they could sense a great openness about it, Sabu's light failing to reach the ceiling high overhead. The cavern echoed with their footsteps as they reached towards its middle.

"Anybody see a good way out?" Sabu asked.

Loud growl, echoing fierceness throughout the large cavern. Streak of lighting, blurred form come leaping down out of nowhere. Crackle of electricity blended with cat-like roar of challenge. Promise of death blocking their path.

"What in Indra's name is that?"

In front of them stood a large cat, perhaps six feet tall at the shoulders and almost ten feet long, its bright yellow fur dancing with electricity, its long sharp teeth dripping with menace. It crouched not but thirty feet away.

"Dead, would be my own opinion," Mauklo said as he calmly pointed both of his hands at it.

An ebony-colored bolt launched out of Mauklo's hands. A bolt of death, killing even the microbes unlucky enough to be floating in the air in its path, it shot swiftly towards the large creature.

The bolt was not fifteen feet away when it dispersed, its magic evaporated.

"Now *that* shouldn't have happened," Mauklo said calmly, cocking an eyebrow.

"Its presence appears to disrupt magic," Sabu noted. "I wonder if it..."

Sabu's musing was interrupted by the creature suddenly springing up through the air. Everyone dived aside, but the creature had no sooner leaped than it vanished. Before they could wonder to where it went, it reappeared behind Sabu, slashing out with its large claws, power glowing from its tips.

"Look out!"

At Sindar's sudden shout, Sabu whirled around, bringing his staff up in defense. His staff caught the claws in mid air, the substance of the magical staff holding back the claws, electricity from the creature dancing along the staff's length. But the force and power of the cat sent Sabu immediately onto his back. The cat lunged down at him, long fangs bared.

A bolt of earth suddenly hit the creature full in the chest, knocking it back several feet. The ground then swelled around it, encasing it in a solid casing of stone.

"It may dampen the use of magic while in its presence," Sindar said as he helped Sabu to his feet, "but the power of the Hevon Gems appears to be of more basic stuff than magic."

"Thanks," Sabu said as he got to his feet.

From within the stone casing they heard growlings and saw the rock flex as the creature sought its freedom. Sand sifted off its surface as the casing shifted and shuddered.

"It just doesn't quit," Eldar sighed. "Just what *is* that thing?"

"Of my humble self," Sheil-Bor(h) offered, "while I have never seen one before, I *have* heard of them. It is a Pugen Power Cat; powerful creatures from the continent of Puj, their ferocity is unmatched. You can see the energy they generate, as well do they disrupt the use of magic in their presence. This one, though, appears to be at least twice the size of any that I have ever heard tell of."

"I've heard stories of them," Sindar added. "It is said that if you catch them as young cubs, they can be trained as the most loyal of companions. Powerful lords and kings are said to seek them out."

The stone casing rumbled and cracked.

"A fierce creature indeed," Eldar admired. "Sometime, I'm going to get me a *pair* of those things. Now, wouldn't *that* be something."

Electricity arced off of the creature's fur, threatening to shatter the encasing stone with its power.

"This is all well and nice," Candol pointed out, "but I fear that we have a more immediate problem of it breaking free."

"It will not fall for the same trick twice," Sheil-Bor(h) calmly advised, "for it is said that they are as intelligent as any man."

With a fearsome ear-shattering growl, the stone casing shattered as the cat leaped free. Up into the air it arced, pouncing off of a convenient rocky ledge, onto another wall, and thence to land directly in front of them, in the same spot that it was when first it blocked their path. It growled at them, saliva drooling from its mouth.

"I say we hit it all at once," Mauklo said, readying the Hevon Gems within him.

"Okay then," Sabu said, "on the count of—"

"You men!" Dwingale exclaimed. "Always ready to kill something."

She calmly walked over to it, cooing gently, as she took a small pouch out of her pocket.

"Dwingale, no!" Eldar warned, concerned over his beloved.

"Can't you see," Dwingale chided, as she tossed some dried up bits of meat onto the ground in front of it, "it's just *hungry*."

The large cat bent down its large head, still growling low in its throat as it nibbled at the offered bits of food. In but a single gulp it swallowed it all, then looking up at Dwingale as if for more.

"If this is another one of your 'guardians' or some such," she went on, "then it's probably been here for ever so long with no fresh food for itself."

"Well I'll be," Eldar said, amazed. "I'm not sure which keeps surprising me more: the world in general or Dwingale."

"I think she's right," Sindar smiled at their own group male stupidity. "Hey Candol. Think you can conjure up some food for it?"

"By the mighty hand of Indra," he stated, "I shall conjure it up such a feast as it's never before seen!"

A few gestures from the priest quickly had the cat surrounded by piles of raw and cooked meat, fresh fruits and vegetables, and more food than even it might be capable of eating. It was soon purring out its contentment as it started to gorge itself on the offered feast.

"That'll teach us never to overlook the simple," Eldar chided himself. "By the way, I sense something over in that direction."

They walked across the cave in the direction indicated by Eldar, leaving the Pugen Power Cat happily at its meal behind them. Eldar had one arm around Dwingale, the other holding his sword.

"A fierce creature indeed," Sabu admitted, "I'm not sure if we would have fared well against it."

"Just be glad that we didn't have to find out," Eldar answered back. "There. Behind that rock."

They rounded a winding bend in the cave, slanting ever upward. Around and up they went, until they found themselves on an upper ledge, overlooking the large dark cave. Dark, that is, except for the bright glow of energy coming from the Pugen.

They looked around on the wide ledge in front of them. Strewn around them were the scattered bones of animals, and perhaps one or two people, gnawed and cracked by powerful teeth. At the far end of this rocky alcove was a large bed of old grasses and glowing yellow stones.

"This looks like its lair," Sheil-Bor(h) noted, as they walked carefully across its length, "although of note may be what it is that it uses to line its bed."

They went over to the grassy bed, looking down at the glowing yellow stones. Small electrical arcs seemed to flash around from within them, sometimes dancing off of their outer surfaces.

"It was using them for its bed," Eldar grinned.

"Well, you can't blame it," Sindar observed, "it *does* seem to like electricity."

Sabu bent down, picking one up in his hand. Dwingale watched, amazed, as the yellow gem seemed to melt into his hand like flowing butter.

"I thought that you usually put yours on your staff," Eldar said, as he touched his sword to another of the gems, watching it liquefy and flow up the sword's length.

"It makes no difference now," Sabu said calmly.

As Candol knelt down for his own gem, Sabu opened up the front of his robe, parting open the brown shirt underneath as he exposed his chest for all to see.

In the center of his chest was imbedded a ring of gems. The red of the Fire Gem, next to the swirling blue of the Water, the grey of the Acid, and the dark tones of that of Earth, with the new yellow Gem of Electricity now beside the bark-like green of the Wood Gem. They all formed a ring around a common center, with yet several gaps in its circle and an empty spot at its center.

"He's right," Eldar said, as now Mauklo and Sheil-Bor(h) collected their own gems. "I was too busy before to notice before, but I can feel them now; traveling through my body, becoming part of me. It's odd, but I think I'm starting to also feel my sword as but a part of me now."

"Bronto would just say that as being true for any good warrior and his weapon," Sabu smiled, as he closed his tunic and stood up.

"Judging from the arrangement of the Gems on your chest," Sindar said, coming up with the last of the gems, "I'd say that there are four more, not counting whatever it is that goes at the center."

"There is more to these Hevon Gems than any of us would think," Sheil-Bor(h) concluded. "One wonders what shall we be when they are complete. Of what greater whole are these small gems to be the sum of?"

"You can save the wondering for later," Dwingale reminded them, "because when that cat's finished his meal, it's going to come up *here* for a catnap."

"Right as always," Eldar agreed. "I think I see a way out over there."

Some quick searching around the ledge soon brought them to another tunneled passageway. Up and around its tortured length they traveled, through several more ledges and gradually upwards. Twisted passageway to twisted passageway, up and up. Finally, as one cave began to level out, they saw a grey point of light up ahead.

"Our way out, it looks like," Sindar noted. "I recognize the depressing grey of this world's skies."

"Great," Eldar said, "I'm getting tired of the inside of this mountain.

It was indeed outside. They came out onto a wide ledge, overlooking tall mountain peaks, and connecting to a small footpath that wound around their own mountain, to disappear around a curve overlooking what appeared to be an open valley. The skies shown their constant grey overhead while the wind was still as death. Outdoors though they were, but a stifling stillness did the air carry with it.

"Well," Eldar shrugged, "at least I *think* this is better."

"It looks like there's a valley over there," Sabu pointed out, as he started on towards the narrow footpath, "maybe we can get a good view of where we are."

"Anything to get away from the depressing feeling of this land," Dwingale said, holding her shoulders as if shuddering. "Glad would I be were we back in the forests of my home."

"*I* will even agree with that," Mauklo said, to the mild surprise of everyone present, as they started towards the end of the ledge with the footpath.

"NEVER SHALL YOU MAKE IT TO YOUR HOME AGAIN! NOW, HAND OVER THOSE GEMS; MY MASTER GROWS IMPATIENT!"

The voice boomed and reverberated throughout the surrounding peaks. As the echo faded off into the mountains, as a group did they slowly look up, towards the single source of the voice.

A hundred feet above them, on top of the peak of the very same mountain out of which they'd just come, crouched a dragon. A hundred feet in length with eyes that swirled with the look of raging winds and stormy skies. Its immense wings it spread to either side, giant reptilian head stretching forward, large mouth sprouting teeth the size of men. A wind seemed to whip continuously around the creature as it glared menace down at them.

"THE DRAGON LORD WANTS THOSE GEMS YOU STOLE FROM HIS LAND! THEN WILL YOU PAY FOR THE INVASION OF HIS HOME!"

"Boy," Eldar swallowed, his special sense telling him what the others had already guessed, "these guardians are just coming fast and furious today."

Kilgar sat cross-legged on a patch of grass, sharpening his long curved knife with a stone as he sat in the Grove. The leaves blowing lightly through the air had all the usual reds, yellows, and Trübs of late Fall. The Grove was silent except for the heavy footsteps of Bronto walking casually into the Grove.

"Any sign of them yet kid?"

"No," Kilgar said, while still sharpening his knife.

Bronto came over and sat down next to the boy, his usual friendly demeanor about him as he lightly tousled the boy's sandy-colored hair.

"Well, don't worry," Bronto said amiably, "they'll be just fine."

"But, what if they bump into trouble and need someone to guard their backs while they do their magic? You know how Sabu can get."

"He does need a shot of reality at times," Bronto grinned, "but don't worry.

I'm sure that at this very moment they're probably battling nothing more difficult than a late Fall storm."

Eldar dug his fingernails into the cliff-side, trying desperately to hold on. The wind that came out of the dragon's mouth was like unto a hurricane, threatening to blow them all off the ledge and scatter their shattered bodies throughout the mountains. Eldar looked back over his shoulder at the others, similarly trying to hold onto what part of their wide ledge that they could.

"So you say this thing's called a *storm dragon?*" Eldar shouted over towards Sabu. "*Sotüva,* I *never* would have guessed! Now what do we *do* about it?!"

Sabu's staff was plunged halfway into the side of the mountain with Sabu hanging from its end, feet flying up behind him. He looked up to see Dwingale holding on desperately to Eldar's legs, honey colored hair whipping about like a nest of golden snakes. Candol was to one side of the elf, restrained only by his legs wrapped around a rocky projection, the rest of his body bouncing up and down in the wind like a loose sock. Sindar was desperately holding onto the rock next to Sabu, while Sheil-Bor(h) was slowly sliding across the wide ledge, his fingers digging in deep. Mauklo was trying to flatten himself up against the mountainside, trying to go unnoticed by the tremendous winds but not quite succeeding.

"Well," Sabu shouted back, "we *do* have Fire, Earth, and Water, so it just figures that we'd be bumping into *this* sooner or later!"

"All nice and fine," Candol shouted above the winds, as his upper body bobbed up and down in the winds like some demented cork in an ocean, "but by Indra could you *do* something about it?!"

Eldar felt his grip slipping as the wind tore relentlessly at him. Around his legs, Dwingale hung on for her life, as the storm that was the dragon's breath came tearing down at them. Eldar's fingers slipped down some more.

"Hold on Dwingale!" he shouted down. "I think we're going for a ride!"

She looked up just in time to see Eldar's fingers slip completely off the rock, sending them both flying out through the air, over an open ravine, straight towards a spiky wall of rock.

"I don't know," Kilgar said, as he started sharpening the other side of his knife, "I just get this feeling that they might need some help."

"You're just worrying too much kid," Bronto said, as with another stone he now started to sharpen his own big sword straddled across his lap, "About the only thing that Sabu ever needs help with is reality. For such a big brain he sure has trouble focusing on current events."

Kilgar gave a little smile, turned his head and looked up at the big man.

"I guess you're right," he said. "What's the worst that could happen to them over there anyway?"

Eldar was now holding onto Sabu's feet while Dwingale was in turn holding onto Eldar's. Sabu, clutching onto the end of his staff, the other end still firmly planted into the rock wall, Sindar now also holding onto Sabu's staff for dear life, they made a desperately comical sight, as Candol went sailing by through the air desperately grabbing out for Sindar's legs. Sheil-Bor(h) was now a fingertip away from loosing the ledge, while Mauklo tried to dig his fingers into the rock behind him.

"Doesn't that thing *ever* run out of breath?!" shouted Eldar from somewhere beneath Sabu.

"I just wish that someone would shut that thing up!" came Candol's answering shout as his grab for Sindar's legs was successful.

"I would be *most* happy to oblige!" came the sudden shout of Mauklo.

The black-eyed wizard concentrated as best he could. Then, Hevon Gem of Earth glowing deep within him, he plunged his right hand straight into the rock wall of the mountain. His hand seemed to merge straight into the rock as he twisted and turned it as if feeling around. Suddenly, up on top of the mountain peak, a large stone hand, fully ten feet across, came reaching up out of the ground straight in front of the dragon. The hand reached up and closed itself around the creature's open mouth, clamping it shut with the solidity of solid rock.

The wind suddenly stopped as the dragon's scaly cheeks bulged outwards, storm-like breath still locked within them. The dragon started to claw frantically at the stone fist, chipping away small pieces of it as it held the mouth firm. The wind gone, Sheil-Bor(h) started to climb back up onto the ledge, while the others still dangled off of Sabu's staff. He got to his feet looking up at the dragon as a huge claw splintered the stone wrist, dislodging it from the mountain, and now started to work on the stone wrapping around its mouth. Another stone fist came lunging up out of the rock, but this time the beast leaped up into the air, spiraling upwards, before looking malevolently down at them. As Mauklo withdrew his hand from within the rock, Sheil-Bor(h) nodded his head, as if deciding something, while he looked up at their foe clawing away at its stony muzzle.

"Sometimes," he said calmly, "it is but the simplest of spells that is called for."

He gazed up at it, concentrating out his magic, willing his spell to work. Suddenly, the dragon's cheeks began to puff out, its body begin to spasm. It struggled even more desperately at the stone encircling its mouth.

It was about to sneeze.

"Yep," said Bronto, as they both put away their sharpening stones and started to get up, "they're probably just relaxing in some other grove just like this one, taking a little vacation away from all our troubles."

"You're probably right," Kilgar nodded his head, as they started to walk around the Grove, "but you can't blame them; all the magic and figurin' stuff they do, they *should* relax once in a while."

"I imagine this Hevon business has just got them all tired and restless," Bronto pointed out, as they walked slowly around the Grove. "Why, they probably just went over to some forest, grabbed up some more of those Gems lying on the ground, and have been just relaxing ever since."

"They're showing Sabu how to turn his brain off for a little while," Kilgar smiled as he kicked at a blade of grass, "instead of analyzin' everything."

They walked around for a bit more, the silence broken only by the distant call of a bird seeking its mate. As they passed by in front of the Path, looking down its empty length, Bronto looked down at Kilgar, a twinkle in his eye.

"Or maybe they're just trying to get Eldar and Dwingale a chance to be alone," he winked. "Perfect excuse, hijacking them to some other world and leaving them alone for a while."

"Girls," Kilgar snorted in reply, still at the age of treating them as a species to be tolerated at best. "Girlfriends just get in the way of things."

"Dwingale, you're in the way."

"Sorry love, but you're lovely rear is in the way."

Eldar and Dwingale were trying to climb over each other in an attempt to get over Sabu and back onto solid ground. Candol was already up on the ledge pulling up Sindar. Far overhead, the dragon was convulsing violently as it struggled to contain the sneezes building up within it.

"You're *both* in the way," Sabu called out, "and someone's foot is in my eye."

A thunderclap sounded overhead, silencing all discussion. Heads turned up to see lightning crackling from around the dragon. In full tribute to the storm dragon's kind, a true storm was building from around it, to match the storm building within it.

"Enough of this," Sabu said, as Eldar and Dwingale tried to squirm over him like ants.

Sabu gave a twist to his staff and the next moment they were all standing on top of the wide rocky ledge, nary a quick flash of light to show the transition of Sabu's spell. As they started to dust themselves off, a loud KABOOM sounded from overhead.

The dragon could finally no longer contain both the sneeze and the winds building within it. Jets of air went streaming out at supersonic speeds, coming out from its ears, nose, and exploding out through its mouth as the rocky clamp was finally shattered. It tumbled back through the air from the violence of the sneeze, the sky overhead crackling with large thunderous peels in response. As it tried to right itself, they could see the large pools of water welling up out of its eyes from the violence of the sneeze. Stunned, it hovered there overhead a moment, shaking its head to clear it.

"Well, at least that distracted it," Eldar acknowledged, "that one sneeze may have saved us."

Sheil-Bor(h) turned to the elf, expression of mild puzzlement on his face.

"One never said that it was to sneeze just the *once*," Sheil-Bor(h) attempted to clarify.

All eyes looked up as the huge beast made ready for another sneeze.

Thunderous crack, scaled dragon shooting out across the sky, lighting erupting from stormy skies in response. Second thunderous crack as once again a sneeze explodes out from a large toothy maw. Explosion after explosion, thunderous peel after thunderous peel.

"This show I like!" Eldar smiled, as they watched the hundred-foot dragon give sneeze after violent sneeze, tumbling itself around in the sky, unable to control the forces of the winds and storm at its disposal.

"I must admit to a certain originality in its use and implementation," Sabu nodded agreement.

"There's just one thing missing from it," Mauklo smiled almost evilly, as he reached up with a pointed hand to cast forth his spell, "and that would be if it had an *itch*."

"Do you think they'll be much longer?" Kilgar asked, as they strolled across the wide grove.

"Naw," Bronto answered. "Of course, you never know with wizards; they have their own time scale. They have stuff to figure that the rest of us couldn't possibly understand. You just have to trust them."

"The only thing I ever trusted before I met Sabu and Eldar," Kilgar said, as they walked along in the quiet, "was my knife. It never fails you and never leaves your side. It was the only thing that I had left after my parents died."

Someplace two songbirds sang forth their melodious tune while the breeze rustled through the trees. Bronto looked down at the boy, sudden appreciation at what the boy had been through in his young life.

"By the way," Bronto asked, "you never did tell us *how* they got killed or how you ended up on Cenivar. That's a bit far away from any desert."

"It was at the great desert on My-Thov," Kilgar answered, "some of those pig-faced orkai thought they could march in on our home. A thousand of those things came into our desert; none left. My parents were two of the five casualties."

"A *thousand* of those things," Bronto nodded in appreciation, "and only five lost? That's not bad."

"They didn't have those blue flaming swords back then," Kilgar shrugged, "and without those they were pretty lousy fighters. Even servants of Miro's must respect our deserts."

"How'd you get over on Cenivar then?"

"I wanted to track where the creatures came from that killed my parents," Kilgar said expressionless as he stopped walking and looked off into the trees, "so I followed their tracks out of the desert. But I was young, only six at the time, so I got lost and ended up as a cabin boy on some ship. When it finally docked at the Harbor in Cenivar, that's where you guys found me."

Bronto put an arm around the boy's shoulder, as Kilgar continued to look at distant images of times past that only he would ever see.

"That's quite some determination for such a young boy," Bronto admired.

"You guys have been the only family I've really known," Kilgar said, finally looking over towards the center of the Grove.

"Don't worry," Bronto said, following his gaze, the Path unseen from their present angle, "they'll be back."

The dragon groaned limply on top of the mountain peak, its body still twitching and convulsing from the intense itches, its eyes watery and nostrils quivering from some residual sneezing. Its great wings hung limply to either side, so tired was it from all the sneezing and itching. The others were on their wide ledge looking up as they watched Eldar fly up, courtesy a spell from Sabu, and land beside the large dragon.

"Adding in that itch was excessively cruel on your part," Candol was saying, "but, by Indra, it seems to have worked."

"Cruelty," Mauklo explained, in a pleasant manner, "is never a matter of having enough excessive force to apply, but knowing just *how* to apply but the minimum force needed to get the most…satisfactory results."

"It was cruel," Candol agreed.

They heard the dragon groan overhead, as Eldar knelt down beside its head. Too tired now to care, the beast just lay there and groaned while Eldar walked around it.

"Hey," came down Eldar's shout, "they're here all right."

"Good," Sabu shouted up, "just bring them all down."

Tear drops welled up out of the dragon's large round eyes. Trickling down its scaly cheeks, they dropped down to the ground, forming into swirling sky-blue crystals landing on the ground. Eldar scooped them up as, one by one, they fell out of the dragon's eyes. When he had them all, he shouted down at the others.

"Got them," he called down, as then he stood up and looked around. "Hey wow, what a view you get from up here."

"Just bring them down," came up Sindar's voice, "we must leave with all do speed."

"Hey, wait a *tid,*" he said looking around. "I can see for miles up here, why I can even—Oh great mother of all elves!"

Down on the ledge, the others caught the sudden shock in the elf's voice.

"What is it?" Sabu shouted. "What do you see?"

There was silence for long moments as Eldar just shook his head back and forth before answering.

"Just go along that narrow footpath and look towards the valley," Eldar shouted down. "I'll be down with the Gems."

"He probably just saw another lost village of elves," Mauklo said dismissively as Sabu leaped across the ledge.

"No," Sabu pointed out, as he edged his way along the narrow footpath. "That dragon *did* seem to try and keep us from going over here when it attacked. Its wind blew us *away* from this direction remember."

Back on the ledge, Eldar landed, handing out the newly found Hevon Gems as Sabu slowly made his way along the narrow path. Slowly, the valley it overlooked began to come into view. A desolate and bleak countryside he began to see, with a couple of far scattered villages just as scattered as the land upon which they were built, grey skies hanging a pallor of bleakness over it all. Farther along he walked, being careful not to slip, as more of the wide valley came into view.

Then he saw it.

In scattered clumps sitting on the ground, in groups of twos and threes in the air, spread all throughout the wide valley in front of him, there they were.

Dragons.

Hundreds, perhaps thousands, of them, stretching throughout the valley, farther than the eye could see. Sabu just stared at the sight, unmoving until Sindar came up behind him.

"Here's your Storm Gem," he said, putting one of the Gems into Sabu's hand, "the others already have theirs."

"Fine," Sabu said absently, the Gem just melting into his palm. "What do you *think* of that?"

Sindar turned to finally look at what Sabu saw. His eyes widened as his brain strove to take in the massive quantities laid out before him.

"There must be thousands out there," Sindar said quietly, "maybe more."

"Now we know why he's called the Dragon Lord," Sabu said, just as quietly. "There's no telling how many more lay beyond our sight."

"With all those dragons under the Dragon Lord's control," Sindar said, "there's no one on this world he couldn't invade."

"He already owns *this* world though," Sabu pointed out, "so who would he invade with such an army?"

They looked at each other as, a moment later, they both came to the same conclusion.

"He *is* allied with Miro…," Sindar began.

"But, how would they bring them all through?" Sabu wondered. "The path of Cassandra is too narrow for even one of them, and *Tedelnosho* is too uncontrollable."

"Unless they have their own portal erected," Sindar suggested, "but then who would they invade?"

"With Traugh and *his* dragons to team them up with," Sabu theorized, "and the other forces that we've seen evidence of Miro gathering, there isn't *anyone* on Maldene that he couldn't invade. Even the King would be in danger."

"We've got to get back to the others," Sabu decided, as he started to move them both back along the ledge.

"This just doesn't seem to get any better," Sindar added, as they walked back around towards the wide ledge.

"Guys," Sabu called on ahead, "we have a problem!"

Lindel came walking on into the grove, shining golden bow slung over his shoulder. Kilgar and Bronto were sitting down at the front of the Grove, glancing down, from time to time, at the golden path before them. Lindel walked over to them, unslinging his bow from over his shoulder.

"Hey guys, what do you think?" the elf asked. "I've gone through so many bows lately, that some of Fawsil's people helped me make a new one."

"It looks pretty good," Bronto said, eyes admiring its delicate form as he ran a light finger along its length, "like no bow I've ever seen."

The bow gleamed golden in the late afternoon sunlight, its smooth curves looking almost seductive. Even Kilgar was entranced by its magical form.

"I designed it myself," Lindel went on, "had it made special."

"It looks great," Kilgar said in slow awe.

"You ought to see the way it shoots," Lindel smiled, "they even gave me a few new arrows to go with it."

"Good, because we're going to be needing it."

Three heads turned around to see the source of the voice. Standing at the head of the Path stood Sabu, Eldar coming up behind him, followed by Dwingale, Candol, Sindar, Sheil-Bor(h), and Mauklo.

"You're back!"

Kilgar leaped up to his feet and ran over towards Sabu and Eldar. His short boyish reach tried unsuccessfully to embrace them both as they walked out into Cassandra's Grove. Bronto got to his feet, as he sensed an urgency about those coming off from the path. His feeling was confirmed by what was said next.

"We've got to leave immediately," Sabu said, "get the others; we leave at solrise."

"What'd you see over there?" Bronto said, all seriousness, as they walked out of the Grove.

"Let's just say, that coupled with what we saw over in Devoon," Sabu answered, as the whole group walked out into the approaching evening, "whatever Krey's up to in this valley, *can't* be good."

The Path faded away behind them, the Grove now but a normal glade, as what was apparently a shadow of the real Grove after all was lost with the setting sun.

"*You* just remember your promise and come back!" Dwingale chided Eldar.

They were all assembled at one edge of the elven community, Fawsil even present along with several of the village's inhabitants. Elves, brownies, and all manner of Faerie Folk, survivors of a better age, surrounded them as they faced out towards a forest path leading off into the distance. A small multitude of faerie voices sang and twittered out through the early morning daylight as they saw the group off. Many a new friend these strange new visitors from outside the valley had made, and perhaps at least one new love. Shong was checking his sword, and Lorel his backpack full of new supplies given them by the elves, as they made ready to leave.

"At least wait until we're *married* before you start nagging me," Eldar smiled. "Don't worry, I'll bring you back Krey's head as a wedding present."

"This path," Fawsil was saying to Sabu and Sindar, "dates back to the times of the Kingdom. Its magic will get you to the site of Thïr Tÿorca, safe and unobserved. Deviate not from its path and even Krey will not find you until you reach its end."

"It's that 'end' part that's kind of got me," Lindel commented, as he slung his new bow up over his shoulder.

"We wish you luck on your trip," Fawsil said, grasping both Sabu's and Sindar's hands in his own. "I'm sure that at least our Dwingale looks forward to your success."

"Here," Dwingale stepped forward and passed out a couple of small leather pouches to Eldar and Sindar, "the food contained within these pouches is of our own make; it will sustain you for many a long rise if need be."

"We thank-you," Sindar acknowledged politely, "and there is something that we would like to give you."

Sindar nodded at Bronto, who stepped forward in response. The big man looked out into the small crowd of faces, large and small, winged and not. The clearing of his voice seemed a signal to the others to quiet down, as a relative silence quickly came down over the forest. Bronto spoke, his voice booming out loudly for all in that hidden village to hear.

"I've been told that I am of the old blood," he began, "if so, then so be it. Hear me then as one of the old blood when I say this: if the Kingdoms be reborn again, then not in this valley shall it be done. History has passed it by and left it with the taint of evil. No, Thïr Tÿorca shall never arise from this valley again. But, this one offer do I now make. We have ourselves an island, hidden off in the Sea Of A Thousand Islands. It is safe, and temperate of clime, and has more than enough room for all of you. When we come back, and we *shall*, we invite you to leave with us to live on our island and start a new Kingdom."

"Great," Mauklo said to himself, as a knee-high faerie went flying by his head. "That's all we need is a bunch of these foot-tall flying *gnats* around there."

Silence seemed to be the response of those gathered around them, as Bronto looked around the crowd for any reaction or surprise to his offer. Only Fawsil stepped over to the big man, his youthful elven face shining gayly in the bright blue daylight trickling down through the trees.

"As your coming had been foretold," Fawsil gave as answer to Bronto's offer, "so also had been the offer of which you now make."

"Let me guess," Eldar interrupted, turning to face Dwingale, "your *mother* foresaw it."

"Actually, no," Dwingale answered, slight smile curling about her mouth. "*I've* inherited some small measure of my mother's talent."

Eldar smiled to himself at what small surprises his beloved kept offering, as Fawsil went on.

"As much as we have loved this valley, and its people of old," Fawsil went on, "we also realize the truth of your words."

The elf paused as he looked around at his people gathered around them, before looking back at Bronto and continuing.

"If you are successful," he said, "then when you return, we shall leave with you, to end the final chapter of Thïr Tÿorca as we start life anew. But, we only ask of you this one favor: cleanse this old land of the evil that has taken hold within it, that the Valley Of Many Lights may some rise be able to renew itself."

"A promise we make with great pleasure," Bronto replied jovially, as he took Fawsil's hand and shook it almost violently.

"It's like I keep saying," Eldar winked, "Krey, head on a platter, wedding present, the whole bit."

"It's time we left," Lindel said, looking up at the sun, "the sun gets higher in the sky."

"He's right," Sabu said, as the others started to turn towards the magical path behind them. "We must leave, but we will see you upon our return."

As they started walking down the path, Dwingale blowing one last kiss to her beloved Eldar, Fawsil waving them off as those gathered shouted out a last chorus of 'good-bye', Dwingale couldn't help but wonder. The figures on the path walked out of sight around a bend in the path, and the crowd that had gathered round began to disperse back to their daily lives, but Dwingale still absently held her hand still aloft as if waiting to wave again. She gazed off down the path, lightly chewing on her lip, as she worried about them all.

For you see, Dwingale had inherited somewhat more than just a bit of her mother's gift of foretelling, and had foreseen what was to happen at Thïr Tÿorca.

And it frightened her.

CHAPTER TWENTY-FIVE
Thïr Tjorca

They traveled for four rises along the magical pathway through the forest, keeping strictly to it, not even Quickfoot wandering off from its course. Overhead they could see winged harpies that searched the day and deadly spirits that scarched the night, but of the enchanted path of Fawsil's people nary a sign did they give of its sighting. To the outside world the travelers may as well have just dropped completely out of sight.

Arüdwo had always been known as the windy season and this time was no exception. Around them they could see the wind picking up in strong gusts, tossing the painted leaves of Fall around in colorful dust devils traveling through the forest, but on the path they followed, nary a wisp of wind was felt. They traveled in pleasant comfort during the day, and slept along the path at night. Thus it was, almost two kevs after they'd first entered the valley, that their path finally exited upon the base of a large hill.

The hill rose up its tall steep sides before them. Off in the distance they could see the large lake, waves pounding in the distance, stirred on by the rising winds. As the path opened up into a small clearing, they could now feel the cool wind in their faces, carrying with it the promise of a cold winter soon to come. Tall trees carpeted the hill for as far up as they could see, with a thickening of bushes and tall grasses lying low to the ground. They walked over to the hill, poking along its base for a bit in a search for the best way up.

"I don't see any sign of a city," Quickfoot complained as he kicked a piece of gravel along with his foot.

"It has been five *thousand* rels since Thïr Tÿorca fell," Sindar pointed out, "there may not be much here for us to find."

"You mean we could have come all this way for nothing?" Quickfoot kicked again at the dark gravely chunk as they walked along through the trees.

"If it were of nothing to be found," Sheil-Bor(h) put in, "then of interest would there be naught."

"*He's* about as bad as Sabu," Quickfoot said, kicking his black pebble on again. "What'd he say?"

"He means," Sabu translated, "that if indeed this bodaln had nothing left that would be of interest to later generations, then the minions of our nemesis wouldn't be showing as much alacrity in their endeavors to connect us with the goal of our quest."

Quickfoot stopped short and looked up at Sabu, complete puzzlement on his face, as he uttered one word.

"Huh?"

"If Krey wants something here," Eldar simplified, "then there's gotta be something here for him to want."

"*Now* someone's making sense," Quickfoot said, and then drew back his foot to give one last kick of his pebble.

"Wait," Sindar's mind reached out and stopped the small one's foot in mid-stroke.

Sindar came over, Quickfoot balancing on one leg, and bent down to pick up the small black pebble that Quickfoot had been kicking. He slowly stood up, turning the pebble over in his fingers, Quickfoot's leg still dangling in midair.

"Hey!" Quickfoot complained, trying to keep his balance. "If you wanted to kick a rock so bad you could have gotten your own stone! Now get my leg down."

Sindar casually released his mind's hold upon Quickfoot's leg, the small one almost stumbling to the ground as his leg came free. Sindar, still examining the small black rock, walked over to Sabu and Eldar.

"What do you make of this?" Sindar asked, showing it to them both.

Sabu took the pebble, turning it over in his fingers, rubbing the old crumbly black stuff between his fingers.

"It's asphalt," he finally pronounced, "of the kind used in——"

The three made mutual eye-contact as they uttered the last two words together.

"Paved roads."

"Quickfoot," Eldar said quickly, looking over at the small one, "where'd you get this?"

"It's just a rock," he answered, "they're all over this place."

They slowly looked around them, at first seeing only scattered patches of smooth black gravel poking up from between the weeds, and then drifting their vision on up the steep hill before them. To the observant eye, it may have been more than just a coincidence that, in an almost straight line from where they stood to the top of the hill, no tall trees grew, only tall grasses and a few small bushes, for a width of perhaps a couple dozen yards. Like an old scar, it stretched on up towards the top of the hill.

Smiles slowly spread across several faces as all but Quickfoot realized what they were standing on.

"The luck of Indra is upon you," Candol said, slapping the small one on the back.

"What?" Quickfoot asked, looking around at the scattered smiles. "What'd I do now?"

"Its construction must have indeed been masterful for it to have lasted this long," Lorel nodded in appreciation.

Quickfoot scratched his head in puzzlement.

"Behold, small one," Bronto said, catching Quickfoot's eye as he pointed out ahead of them, "a road. And where there's a road, there's a city!"

"Last one to the top of the hill is a Miro-lover," Eldar smiled playfully, as he started jogging up the hill.

"That would probably be you," Kilgar said to Mauklo as he jogged on up after Eldar.

Mauklo just grinned to himself as the others started on up the ancient road.

"Who's to say," he said softly.

The hill stretched over a dozen miles across, its top being a tangle of tall trees, ivy-covered boulders, and tall bushy grass. To either side of their road rose tall ivy-covered rocky projections, some merely wide flat slabs standing tall against the wind, others round towers of stone broken off at the top.

"Some city," Quickfoot commented.

"Give it hope," Eldar urged, as they trudged on along the old weed-choked road, "there *has* to be more than just meets the eye after all."

"Like roaches?" Quickfoot offered.

"No," Lindel put in, as they rounded a slight bend in the large road, "like *that.*"

The road ended abruptly a dozen feet before them, along with the trees and bushes that choked the surrounding terrain. Ahead of them, with but a few scattered bushes and weeds to clutter it, lay the stone ruins of a city. They walked on up to where the road ended in a pile of scattered rubble and looked out at what lay before them, eyes looking on in wonder at the goal of their long quest. Even the birds were quiet, the wind stopping briefly its rustling through the trees, offering them a quiet stillness as they looked on. Kilgar, boyish form standing towards the front, was the first to utter the name of their hard-won goal, speaking in an almost soft whisper.

"Thïr Tÿorca."

The ruins went on for as far as they could see. Rubble lay scattered through the streets, the paved roads of the city sporting an occasional statue struggling to stay atop its pedestal, weeds growing in cracks in the wide walkways. Tumbled piles of rubble marked where old buildings once stood, while others stood only in half ruin, a wall or two still standing to mark the rough dimensions of an old structure. Most of the buildings, though, still seemed to be reasonably intact, their stone walls rising defiantly against time, their curved roofs shining brightly in the sun.

Several of the tall structures still shone bright and polished, gleaming a dull white against the ravages of time. Occasional glints of gold and silver shown forth from some of the roofs, the remains of valuable metal sheeting still lining curved arcs. From what could be discerned from the intact buildings, this city's architecture was that of curve and arc, structure and purpose combined with beauty and form. Tall gleaming towers rose a hundred feet into the air, to be each capped by a curved roof, pointed steeples lancing up through their centers. Even in death, this city had a look of grandeur about it.

Kilgar was the first to step forward, to place his foot upon the tired soil of Thïr Tÿorca, stepping over the rubble as he walked out into the open avenues. The others followed, looking around at the ruins of the legendary city.

As they advanced farther, they could now see that, all along the edge of the vast ruins ran a wall. Cracked and tumbled in several places it was, but of its course there could be no doubt. It ran off to either side of them, stretching far away, dotted with tall curved towers every hundred feet or so. Ten feet thick was the wall, and more than thirty feet high, taller still its towers. In its flecked and chipped surface could be seen the remains of a polish and smoothness that spoke of a people that cared even of the make of their walls. A caring for art and appearance lost for many a long rel.

"By Indra," Candol said in amazement, "this place goes on for miles; and it's all stone."

"I haven't seen this much rock since the Harbor Of The World," Eldar admitted, as they walked slowly on down the central avenue, "and the whole thing's *walled* as well. Does that thing go *all* the way around?"

"Yes," Sindar nodded, "I can feel its length going on for many miles. It seems to wall in the entire top area of this hill."

"You mean, this city's *that* big?!" Shong exclaimed. "*I'm* impressed."

"That is why the prefix of 'Thïr' has not been used for a city in so long," Sabu explained, as they picked their way along the rubble-strewn main avenue, "although even mere size does not merit one of that title; a city must be truly grand of stature and influence to be so named."

"I think," Lindel looked on at a gold and silver covered pinnacle, "this one qualified."

"The art and knowledge that must be lost within these shattered walls," Sheil-Bor(h) commented, "indeed a precious thing."

"More than you know," Sindar said, pointing to one of the walls. "On all of these walls have I not seen a single seam or place of joining. However the method of their construction, they left nary a seam or blemish to mar the beauty of their homes."

"Indeed a shame was the loss of this place," Lorel agreed, "but where now do we head in such vast ruins?"

"How's about there?"

Bronto was pointing on towards the center of the city, where, in the distance, there arose a tall pointed spire, rising up tall above all the other buildings, even part of a golden roof curving out from its base being seen above the other rooftops.

"For people that build so proudly on such a scale," Bronto continued, "could they do no less for their main castle?"

"Center of town it is then," Eldar agreed.

Thus, they struck out towards the center of the ruins. They passed by many a tumbled building, past statues that once adorned the sides of the streets but now lay tumbled and broken, and over streets once smooth and straight but now broken by time. They passed by a small park, its trees and plants once a place of beauty, now but a dark overgrowth of fear. But the plants in the park did not stray from their boundaries; in fact, nowhere, but for a few weeds, did Nature's growth overtake what was once its own, as if paying tribute to the lost city.

"There must be a magic about this place that preserves it," Sabu noted as they walked along towards the central tower, "or else the trees would have long ago overtaken here. Thousand of rels is more than enough time for Nature to reclaim her own."

"The old Kingdoms lasted for five thousand rels," Sheil-Bor(h) pointed out, "they built their city to last forever."

"That must mean that there's still some treasure left?" Quickfoot asked hopefully.

"No," Candol disagreed, "I'm afraid that the people probably took it with them when they left, so long ago."

"Then what's the use?" Quickfoot said, kicking at a stray stone.

"We'll soon find out," Bronto announced, "because we're here."

Before them lay a palace. Stretching on for hundreds of feet, its polished blue-grey walls shone in the sun, a tall curved tower arising from each of its four corners, with a larger central tower soaring up high from its middle, the roof curving down, delicate and graceful, between each of the towers. The roof seemed to be lined with polished platinum, pounded down to an almost cloth-like smoothness. The tops of the corner towers curved back, an opening looking out upon the streets below. Large windows looked down from several scattered positions about the grand walls, with many small doors and openings marking its base. The center of the side facing them was marked by a pair of large double doors inlaid in gold. As they walked closer they could see that these massive doors were more like gates, fully twenty feet high, yet standing out as small against the scale of the palace.

Nary a scratch was on the palace, not a single sign of ruin or decay, not one piece of rubble out of place.

"Five thousand rels, and that building still looks grand," Bronto admired.

"If Man can but build like this, there may still be hope for the species," Sheil-Bor(h) agreed.

"Even the small one is silent in the presence of such grandeur," Lorel smiled.

"Silent, or absent," Lindel noted. "Where is he?"

Quickfoot was nowhere to be seen. Around them lay large stands of strewn boulders and walls of rock, but no Quickfoot.

"He's probably wandered off to peel some of the platinum off of that roof," Lindel smiled, "you know how he is."

While everyone else was almost ready to agree with Lindel's pronouncement, Kilgar's knife suddenly appeared in his hand, the boy standing in a crouch, tense and looking quickly around.

"We've got company," the boy said, "very tall and smells like garbage."

"Okay, now that we don't have to guess what happened to Quickfoot," Eldar said, pulling out his sword while scanning around with his own special sense. "Where is he?"

"There is one way to find him," Candol said, lifting up his arms as he gazed skyward. "Mighty Indra, let the small one be revealed to us like unto the popping of a cork."

A loud 'pop' sound was heard, followed by an ear-splitting scream, as Quickfoot came flying up from behind a large pile of rocky rubble.

"AAAAAAAAAAAAAAAk"

"I got him."

Bronto went running over to where the small one looked to land, putting out his large arms as Quickfoot arced downward. With a soft jolt, Quickfoot landed in Bronto's arms.

"AAAAAAAAAAAAAAAAAA."

"You can stop screaming now," Bronto said, "you're safe."

"AAAAAAAAAAAA."

As Bronto looked down at the screaming wriggling form, he could now see several gaping wounds in Quickfoot's arms and torso, as if bitten out by large teeth. Blood was gushing out from his wounds as he tossed back and forth feverishly.

"Candol," Bronto called out.

The priest came over to Bronto's side and looked down at the small form, as Bronto put him carefully down onto the ground. Candol placed a hand on Quickfoot's forehead while the latter continued to scream and wriggle.

"He's badly wounded and with fever," Candol said, "but I can help him."

Candol closed his eyes in brief concentration and then opened them again. Quickfoot stopped screaming and closed his eyes as if sleeping.

"He shall sleep while he heals," Candol explained, "he will be fine after about a couple of diids."

"Then we've got to get whatever did this," Bronto said as he stood up.

"I shall take care of this unseen foe," Lorel announced, drawing his sword and walking over to the pile of rubble that Quickfoot had popped out from behind of.

"No," Sindar advised, "I sense great strength and danger in its presence."

Ignoring the others as they called out to him, Lorel disappeared behind the large pile of rubble.

All waited, as for a brief moment there was silence.

But this was quickly followed by a stabbing scream that lanced out through the air.

Which was in turn followed by the scrawny form of Schanter flying out through the air, screaming out in gleeful pain as he came down to land hard against a single standing rock wall.

"Well," Eldar commented, "now we know that pain and trauma *also* triggers Schanter's presence."

"Is there anything that *doesn't?*" Lindel asked.

"Well, enough of this," Sabu said, pointing his staff towards at the large pile of rubble.

There was a loud zapping sound and the pile was instantly reduced to a small pile of sand. Standing behind the pile was a creature that could be described as Human in name only. A man it looked to be, but demented in form. It was eight feet tall, with scraggly hair hanging down past its shoulders. Its fingernails stood out like claws, eyes agleam with hunger. Arms rippled with muscles, looking like it could rend stone with its bare hands. Old rags it wore for clothes, clawed feet bare to the ground. It looked up at them, the shock of its sudden exposure quickly passing.

"Schanter want again!"

The green scraggly one was standing himself up, blood dripping from his forehead. He wiped a warty hand at his head, taking some of the blood off with it. When he looked at the blood on his hand, he jumped up and down with glee.

"Is that thing Human?" Shong asked doubtfully.

"Maybe once," Lindel shook his head, "but not anymore."

"It looks as strong as an ogre," Eldar commented, "and not too friendly."

The creature growled as if in challenge, flexing its muscles and gnashing its fang-like teeth.

"This one's mine," Bronto said, stepping towards the creature.

Bronto walked towards it, with only his bare hands as his weapons. The creature growled at him as he came up to it.

"Now come on," Bronto said, almost amiably, hands on his hips, "you don't want to put the bite on people anymore; it's not nice."

It slashed at him, claws raking a jagged tear across Bronto's dark-colored furs, but on Bronto himself, there was nary a scratch. The big man looked calmly down at the tear in his shirt, and then back up at the creature growling at him.

"Now I'm going to have to get a new shirt."

It growled in anger, its big muscles bulging, as it then leaped straight at Bronto. Bronto nimbly stepped aside, catching the creature by an arm and a leg and turned the creature's leap against him, as he spun quickly around once and then released the creature, sending it flying up over the ruins, landing far off in the unseen distance. Bronto walked calmly back to the others.

"I hope that didn't strain you too much," Eldar quipped.

"Naw," Bronto waved it off, "just a minor pest."

"Speaking of pests," Mauklo spoke up.

A loud screech broke the silence of the ruins. They looked up at what Mauklo indicated and saw a winged horror swooping down out of the sky. Leathery of skin, even its wings a dull grey leather, its tail whipped back and forth behind it as it extended six-inch talons in deadly greeting.

Rings of light came streaking out from Sindar, encircling its arms and legs, binding back its wings, while a burning steel coil flew out from Sabu, snaring it about the head as it squeezed tighter. Though deprived of the use of its wings, it still hovered there in the air, struggling at its bonds.

"It looks like one of those things we encountered in the mountains," Lindel commented as he notched his new golden bow.

"Not quite," Mauklo said mildly. "I can assure you that this breed is much worse."

With a flex of its muscles, it shattered the bonds, just as Lindel unleashed his arrow. The flying menace straighten itself just as the arrow hit head-on with its forehead. But the arrow promptly shattered. Lindel glared up at it in frustration.

"I am real *tired* of everything being unaffected by arrows!" he exclaimed. "I might as well as give up the art for a plot of good farmland!"

It streaked down towards them, just as Mauklo aimed his own spell at it.

The creature stopped its flight as its skin suddenly began to bubble. It hovered in the air, puzzled, as it watched its skin begin to ripple and crawl. Then, as if a living thing unto itself, as a whole did the creature's skin begin to peel and crawl off, sliding down along the contour of its muscles as it began to slide off of its body. The creature's scream of pain was possibly the only thing more sickening, just then, than the sight of its leathery skin crawling off, leaving blood-coated muscle behind. It screamed and struggled, whipping about through the air as its skin sought refuge elsewhere. Completely forgetting about the intended targets below, it went fluttering off into the distance, its cries echoing throughout the ruins.

"That was sick even for you!" Shong exclaimed, wiping some stray drops of the creature's green blood from his shirt.

"I'll take comments of gratitude later," Mauklo smiled calmly, "but for now, that creature was sent by Krey; as were those."

Mauklo pointed up in the sky. Off in the distance were what looked to be a flock of creatures like unto the one that they'd just seen. The creatures flew over the distant ruins, making a straight line for where they stood.

"We can't handle all of them," Sabu noted, "there's got to be over fifty in that flock. We need cover."

"The palace," Sindar suggested, "it looks secure enough."

"The palace it is then," Sabu said quickly, "come on."

Candol grabbed up the still-sleeping form of Quickfoot, as they ran across the rubble towards the large double door that was the main gate. As they ran, they could hear the distant screeching of the creatures getting closer. They ran across a wide open area in front of the palace, past old and bent trees that once served as adornment for the palace grounds. The screeches got closer, the vile faces of the creatures now discernible, as they ran up to the palace gates.

The golden doors were carved with stylized figures and strange markings, its top towering up more than the height of two men above their heads. In its center appeared to be a single golden ring, attached to the large door like a handle.

"I hope this isn't as heavy as it looks," Shong said as he grasped the ring and gave a pull.

The door wouldn't budge. Shong gave another hard tug.

"It's locked," Shong said, "and probably bolted from the inside by the feel of it."

"From the look of those figures carved on it, it looks to be held closed with magic as well," Sabu said. "And from the looks of its potency, it's no wonder that Krey hasn't yet gotten to whatever it is that he seeks in this place."

The creatures were now well under half of a mile away, and closing fast, their screeches now loud and clear, their fangs shining in the late afternoon sun.

"Hurry, those flying *turenyo* are getting closer!" Lindel exclaimed.

"We'll never get them open in time," Shong said, drawing his sword, "we'll have to fight them."

"Fight, fight, Schanter love fight!"

Bronto shoved his way by the others, going for the door and its single ring.

"Let me try," he said quickly, grabbing onto the ring.

He was all ready to give forth with a strong pull, but when he grabbed onto the ring, the door gave a loud creak and drifted open a crack. Several tense faces looked at Bronto and the door in puzzlement.

"Its magic must have been triggered by your ancestry," Sabu theorized quickly. "Perhaps only those of the old blood can open its doors. Bronto give it a good tug!"

The creatures now swooping in for a dive, there was no time to argue. Bronto gave a strong heave at the golden doors. At his touch, they slid open as easily as if greased and as silently as a feather drifting upon the wind. Attached to just the right-hand side of the gate though it was, as he pulled back on the ring both halves of the huge gates parted and opened up. As they opened, their three-foot thickness could be seen, as well the precision of their workmanship.

A net of electricity did Sabu shoot forth from his staff, ensnaring the creatures flying in front, slowing down their charge.

"That won't hold them for long," Sabu said as the creatures struggled about in the net, apparently little affected by its electricity.

"Got it!" Bronto shouted, when the gates were open far enough. "Everybody in!"

They ran into the palace, just as the creatures broke free. Quickfoot moaned sleepy awareness, stirring in Candol's arms as the priest ran through the opening. The last to enter, Sindar stopped as he then saw the formation of clouds overhead; a face was forming, the same face they'd seen on the night of the magical storm soon after when they'd first entered the valley. Its large puffy lips seemed to be forming words.

"MY CURSE WILL YOU FIND. RUN, BUT YOU SHALL NEVER LEAVE THIS VALLEY!"

"Come on!"

Bronto's shout snapped Sindar out of it. He looked up to see the creatures flying down at them again, not more than a hundred feet overhead. Sindar ran on in after the others, just as Bronto heaved at the door from another gold ring on the inside of the great doors. When everyone was inside, with a loud groan of effort, Bronto gave a tremendous heave on the heavy doors that were as but feather-light to his touch. The first of the creatures was just swooping down into the doorway, aiming its sharp claws straight at Bronto.

Bronto leaped straight back when he heaved at the doors, just as the screeching creature was reaching out for him in mid-flight. Like a tiny sparrow propelled by the tremendous power of a Roc's great wings, the gates practically flew shut, slamming swiftly closed with a loud crash that was heard all over the ruins.

The creature's claws were but an inch from Bronto's eyes as the great gates slammed shut on it, catching it full across the middle, reducing its midsection to pulp as the front of its body gave a surprised quiver and landed at Bronto's feet.

The creature looked up at the big man, face filled with shock and pain, as it tried to reach a hand quivering with death out towards its foe. It didn't make it though, as it gave one last shudder and died, what was left of its entrails dangling out behind what used to be its lower chest, blood streaming out onto the floor. Where the gates had met, closing in on the creature, was a small stain of blood dripping down the central seam, the only sign as to the rest of its body. Outside, could be heard the dim screeching sounds of the rest of its kind, scratching vainly upon the outer door.

"Now *that's* what I call timing," Bronto said, as he turned around to join the others.

They were in some sort of antechamber, the walls being a blend of polished turquoise stones interlaced with sheets of silver, relief drawings of kings and warriors embossed in its surface. The grey stone floor had an inlaid pattern of red stones arranged as a large sunburst, with each of its different rays pointing out towards one of its six exiting corridors. The ceiling, some twenty or more feet above, was a curved dome, paintings of clouds and sky swirling around its borders, colors still vibrant as ever, even after so long a time. A dim light seemed to come down from the tall ceiling; enough apparently, to adequately see by. Bronto walked over towards where the others were gathered at the room's center.

"How's the small one?" he asked, at the sound of Quickfoot's groaning.

"He's coming round," Candol answered, "he should be fine in a few moments."

"Ow, what happened?" Quickfoot asked as he slowly came awake, no sign of any wounds upon him. "All I remember is a wall of muscle and teeth."

"I think we ought to just call him *lightning rod* for all the trouble he seems to attract to himself," Shong commented.

"Funny," Quickfoot said sarcastically, as he sat up rubbing his arm. "I'll remember that the next time you die."

"Enough," Sindar said calmly, "we need to get to the matters at hand; like which way we should go. There's six corridors to choose from."

"We shall let the wisdom of Indra guide us," Candol said, producing a small gold coin from inside a pocket.

"Now *how* is a *two-sided* coin going to help us decide which of *six* ways to take?" Lindel asked.

Candol just smiled and flipped the coin up into the air. It whirled up high into the air, tumbling round and round, and then came straight down. It bounced once off the ground, arcing up into the air again, to finally land directly in front of one of the corridors along the right-hand wall, landing flat and still on one side, not so much as vibrating in the normal way of a falling coin.

"Ask a silly question...," Eldar began.

"Well then," Sabu shrugged, "if Quickfoot's well enough to walk again, that corridor it *is* then."

The small one got to his feet as they gathered themselves together and started on towards the chosen corridor. As Candol bent down to retrieve his coin, Lindel came up to him, puzzlement on his face.

"Just what is it that Indra is god *of?*" Lindel asked, "Luck or flamboyance?"

"There's a difference?"

The corridor was a normal stone hallway, though lined with the occasional fresco depicting some long-past battle or event across its walls. Light seemed to come from glowing spots along the upper parts of the walls, as if individual spots of the wall were set with Sabu's own spell of light. Though many millennia old, nary a speck of dust did mar the floor upon which they walked. Bronto and Shong were out in front, swords out, ready for anything.

They walked past rooms, large and small, abandoned for so long, their functions were now only to be guessed at. One room had a large meeting table, its carved wood, and even the maps pinned to the stone walls, still amazingly intact. Another room seemed to hold an office, papers and quills scattered all over the floor. Past a branching corridor they walked, its short length leading down into a wide room, an immense sunken pit giving evidence that this was once some sort of public or private bath, its finely carved marble lining now but home to some unseen form that seemed to slither through its dark murky waters. Past a room filled with paintings and statues, all almost alive and new as if but waiting for the next visitor to admire them.

"Amazing how the magics of this place have survived all these long rels," Sabu looked around himself as they walked onward. "The wall-paintings are still intact, the place is evidently self-cleaning, and still no seams do I see in these walls."

"Definitely a marvel of magic and engineering," Sindar conceded.

"Not to lessen the majesty of this place by interrupting your well-placed admiration of this domicile," Mauklo said calmly, with mild sarcasm in his voice, "but we should concentrate on more immediate concerns."

"You had something particular in mind?" Eldar asked as he tread lightly down the corridor.

"Perhaps the concern of what Krey wants in this place would do for a start," Mauklo said, as they walked by a small wooden door, "and the observation that out of all the groups of people that he could have chased into this place, we just *happen* to be the ones capable of getting into a palace whose defenses have thwarted him for hundreds of rels."

"It *does* seem a bit of a stretch to attribute it solely to coincidence," Sabu admitted.

"Hold it," Eldar interrupted them as he stopped in mid-step in front of the wooden door, "there's magic behind this door; old and somehow familiar."

"Let's check it out," Bronto nodded to Shong, as he and his friend went over to either side of the door, weapons ready. "Quickfoot, how's about that lock?"

Quickfoot padded over to the door, the last vestiges of his healing sleep finally just leaving his eyes. He rubbed at his eyes with one hand as he bent down in front of the door, putting his eye to the lock, scrutinizing it quickly but thoroughly.

"Well," he said, just a trace of grogginess still in his voice, "this door appears to…"

He took a long thin pin out of a pocket as he spoke, pausing in his speech as he stuck it into the keyhole, turning it around a few times until a faint 'click' was heard.

"…have *been* locked," he finished, as he stood up and put his pin away, "Doors like that aren't even worth the effort."

He stood back as Bronto carefully grabbed hold of the doorknob. Nodding to Shong, weapons ready, he flung open the door, flattening himself back against the wall. When nothing came out, he leaped through, followed immediately by Shong.

"Well I'll be," came out Bronto's voice a moment later, "I think we found the armory."

Eldar was the first to step through, the others following behind. Inside he saw a large room, its full size hidden by the many racks of weapons standing about, piled almost to the ceiling. As they entered the armory, they could discern many styles and makes of weapons, from small slim daggers to curved longswords, to large greatswords that even Bronto would be proud to use. They spread out through the aisles, looking at the arrayed weapons, admiring their work. They all shone polished and in good repair, as if someone had been careful to take care of them.

"Shong," Sindar called out from one of the aisles, "what's your expert opinion on these weapons?"

"Well," replied Shong, as he picked up a shortsword and examined its length, "good workmanship to begin with, kept in excellent condition, by magic I'm guessing…"

He took a couple of test swings with the blade, before continuing.

"It would serve well in a battle," he pronounced. "Good for your average troops in the field. There's probably enough here in this room to supply an army of about five hundred."

"Are you thinking that we should take these along?" Sabu asked.

"We should start to prepare for the future," Sindar nodded, "and good weapons such as these may come to be in short supply. Perhaps we could collect them after we have dealt with the more immediate business of Krey."

"Fine by me," came Eldar's shout from one of the aisles, "but I'm taking *this* one now. Come over here, you've *gotta* see this."

When Sabu joined his friend, he saw the elf standing in front of a tall glass case, piled almost haphazardly against one far wall. The others stopped and looked as they saw the blades contained within the case.

One, maybe three or four feet long, was delicately curved, its blue and gold length shining bright in the dim light, its hilt studded with tiny gems twinkling brightly.

The other sword, about a foot longer, seemed to be made of one material from tip of sword to the base of its hilt, as if from one single cut of material. The sharp edge on the blade reflected keenly in the light, the rounded curve of its hilt carrying its own bright twinkle. The whole length seemed a bright crystal color, the facets of its colorings swirling into intricate shapes.

The two swords gleamed invitingly at the onlookers.

Eldar placed his hand on the front glass of the case. When he did so, his hand glowed red hot, the case melting away at his touch. When the blades were exposed, his hand stopped emitting its heat and he reached in. Taking out the blue and gold sword, he held it before him, pride and awe in his face, his voice.

"I told you I sensed a magic both old and familiar," he said, "this blade was worked by the Evolins of old. Its make hasn't been seen since many thousands of rels before Thïr Tÿorca fell."

"It certainly looks like a good sword," Shong admitted, "are you sure it's an Evolin blade?"

"Sure?" Eldar responded. "Light, perfectly balanced, sharp enough to cut through the despair of humanity; there can be no mistake."

Eldar looked lovingly at the sword of long-dead ancestors. He then gripped it firmly in hand, and whirled quickly around, slashing swiftly at a row of a dozen long swords standing up on the ground, propped up against another shelf of weapons. The stroke was fast, and seemed to go through the swords, but when the others looked, the blades seemed untouched.

"I think you missed," Quickfoot pointed out.

Eldar just smiled and nodded down at the swords. Slowly they began to bend in upon themselves, each splitting at the now-visible cut that sliced across them all. They fell to the ground in a clatter, each sword cut neatly in two.

"Yup," Lindel nodded agreement, "that's an Evolin blade alright."

Eldar smiled at his find, sticking it carefully through a loop in his belt.

"I shall carry it as a tribute to those who made it."

"That's not the only rare blade in this glass case," Shong said, as he brought out the other shining sword, "if I'm not mistaken——"

"That's diamond!" Quickfoot hopped up and down. "Solid diamond; I'd recognize it anywhere!"

"A diamond blade?" Candol asked in wonder.

"An art long lost," Sheil-Bor(h) explained, as Shong turned the sword around in his hand. "Made from a single cut of diamond, their workmanship a tribute to both beauty and purpose."

"I've heard legends about these swords," Shong began, "to find one here…"

"This must be the royal armory," Sabu said, "that would be the only place they would keep such things."

"I think we'd best move on," Bronto said, "as much as I admire a good strong blade, I think finding what Krey wants is more important."

"Right," Shong said, snapping out of it as he picked up a sheath for the sword from off a shelf and strapped the diamond blade around his waist. "I saw another door at the other end of this room."

They walked on down the room, coming indeed to another door at its far end. Bronto once again opened up the door, leading them all beyond. This time they found themselves in a barracks, long double rows of beds lining the room as they walked down along its length.

"This must be where the royal guards stayed," Sabu said, as they walked through the room, left it through another door, and came out into another hallway.

"Apparently, they're *still* staying here," Sindar said, pointing out in front of them as they entered the wide corridor.

Directly in the middle of the hallway, blocking their way as it floated twenty feet in front of them, was an apparition. Looking somewhat like a man dressed in metal scale armor, sword in hand, they could see through him rather clearly. His ghostly form drifted out in front of them, mouthing unheard syllables, as it waved a spectral sword in front of them.

Quickfoot shifted nervously from foot to foot, his new bravery working against his innate instincts. He gazed over towards Candol, having sudden fond memories of hiding behind his robes and trying to think up an excuse for doing so now.

"In a place as old as this," Eldar offered, "there must be hundreds of spirits still hanging around here. Still going about their old duties and whatnot."

The spirit slashed its sword menacingly in their direction, not advancing but not moving from its post.

"I know a little something about disposing of ghosts," Mauklo offered with a smile, "perhaps I could——"

"No," Bronto said firmly, "he's only an old soul, still serving his post. That's something to be admired, not destroyed."

"Perhaps, if it's still following its last orders," Sabu suggested, "one of the old blood could relieve him of his duties."

"I'm never going to live down that 'old blood' thing am I?" Bronto smiled.

"Probably not," Eldar answered.

"Well, I guess it's worth a shot," Bronto said, as he walked over to the spirit.

The ghost put up his sword defensively, as if he was ready to strike at the approaching man. Bronto sheathed his sword and stood not two feet in front of it. Ghost and man regarded each other.

"Well old man," Bronto said, "it looks like you've been here for a while."

The ghost seemed to take a closer look at Bronto, as if looking for something the others couldn't see. Then, as if finally seeing something, it straightened up, bringing his sword down by his side, standing at attention as it floated there, inches above the ground.

"So, it seems as if I have some authority around here after all," Bronto nodded. "So be it. Attention!"

The ghost snapped to attention as best as its ghostly form would allow it. It rose up its misty chin with a pride to his duty that was rarely seen anymore.

"I have new orders for you and any others still here at their posts," Bronto said in a firm military voice. "First, let it be said that you have done your Kingdom proud with the long faithful service that you have performed, staying here at your post for so long."

The ghost seemed to look a bit taller and straighter, holding its transparent head higher.

"You have done yourselves proud," Bronto continued. "A service that can never be repaid. But, the Kingdom is now long dead; we have come here to reclaim what we can and give final tribute to the great name of Thïr Tÿorca. The spirit of the old Kingdom shall sometime rise again, but not here in this place. You are hereby relieved of duty; discharged from your service with full honors due you."

A ghostly tear seemed to run down the silent apparition's face as it listened to Bronto's words.

"I and my friends shall now take charge of Thïr Tÿorca," Bronto said, "you and yours are hereby dismissed. Have a good rest; you've earned it."

Bronto gave a smart salute, snapping his heals together, hand launching towards his forehead. The ghost returned the salute, pride and relief in its vague face as Bronto snapped his hand back down to his side. It then relaxed its stance, gratitude showing on its face as it smiled at Bronto and then faded from sight, disappearing like smoke upon the wind.

"It would have just been easier for me to destroy it," Mauklo shrugged, "instead of all this excessive emotional melodrama."

"I'll remember that the next time that *you're* an old ghost waiting to be relieved of its burden," Bronto almost snapped back. "But then, you probably don't know anything about personal honor and duty."

"I am *quite* sure that my own code of honor is extremely different from your own," Mauklo smiled back, "and for that am I exceedingly grateful."

A rumbling of distant howls interrupted them, filling the air with ghostly voices, getting louder, getting nearer.

"What's that?" Shong asked, new diamond sword ready.

"Offhand," Eldar said, nodding off down the corridor, "I'd say it's the day-shift getting off."

Streaming up the hallway, like joy given flight, spirits flew. Spirits by the dozens, spirits by the hundreds, coming up out of the floor, coming down out of the ceiling, all coming straight towards them.

Mauklo flattened himself up against the wall, readying a spell that he might use against such hordes, while Candol held firmly onto his priestly sigil. Shong held cautiously onto his sword, while Schanter jumped up and down at the prospect of pain and death at the hands of such a multitude of spirits. Bronto just faced the onrushing ghostly hordes and stood firm, no weapon in his hand.

The ghosts all did have one thing in common; they were all dressed in ghostly armor, ghostly swords strapped to their sides, military bearing about their transparent visages. As the spirits streamed on past them, each in turn saluted Bronto, then soon disappearing after it flew past, as if through some unseen door. Bronto stood facing them as they did him honor, head up as he watched every one of the thousands of spirits fly on by, lost souls now relieved of their duty to go on to a well-earned rest.

The last spirit to pass by seemed to be a bit larger than the others, the vague insignia on his uniform a bit different somehow. As this last spirit passed on by, it saluted and then dropped a large ring of keys at Bronto's feet, before it too flew on by and disappeared.

As he bent down to pick up the offered keys, Bronto looked over towards

Mauklo, the black-haired Sileen slowly releasing the spell he'd half prepared. Bronto grinned over at him.

"And what would you have done against so vast a horde of spirits," Bronto jovially pointed out, "if not for my *excessive emotional melodrama?*"

A slight scowl was Mauklo's only response.

"Wow," Eldar exclaimed, "I've heard of haunted before, but this place was *loaded!*"

"And those were only the *good* ghosts," Sabu agreed.

"You mean there might be more?" Quickfoot asked, somewhat nervously.

"Schanter want more!"

Eldar leaned in close to Lindel, speaking quietly to the other elf.

"Why is he still Schanter?" Eldar asked. "Isn't he overdue to change back?"

"I don't know," Lindel shrugged, "I'm giving up trying to figure that creature out."

"So what'd that last ghost give you?" Shong asked.

"A gift from their Captain of the Guard," Bronto said, holding up the chain with its dozens and dozens of keys, "the keys to the castle."

"Hmm," Sabu thought, "apparently, since you relieved them of duty, the spirits feel that they now belong to you. Their Captain has put the castle in your charge."

"A duty I shall not abuse," Bronto responded as he attached the keys to his belt.

"This way," Shong motioned down the wide corridor from where the ghosts had come, "they were guarding something from this direction."

They walked down the hallway, wide enough it was for six men to stand abreast, its walls hung with tapestries and banners from times long gone. As they walked through the dim light, they could see on up ahead a large gate. When they got closer, they saw that the gate was almost as tall as the twenty-foot high arched ceiling. Layered with sheets of finely pounded gold, it bore several stylized designs traced in gems, and leaves of turquoise along its edges and down its center. In the middle of it, about five feet above the floor, was a single gold ring at the center of the large door, a small keyhole just below it. They approached the door, admiring the workmanship of such peoples as had built this place, Quickfoot running his small hairy hand along the smoothness of the delicately wrought gold.

"Well, I think we know how this ring-and-door thing works by now," Lindel said as Bronto walked towards the door.

"Yes," Bronto agreed as he brought out the keys, "but which of these hundred keys fits this door?"

Quickfoot took a brief break from his admiring of the valuables on the large door to glance once at the keyhole on the door, and then over at the ring of keys that Bronto now fumbled with.

"That one," he said, pointing to one of the keys on the ring.

"Now how do you know that?" Bronto asked with some amusement.

"Hey, you know weapons, *I* know locks," Quickfoot replied. "Trust me on this one."

Bronto shrugged, took the key and fitted it to the lock. One quick turn and a loud click was heard. Quickfoot smiled as the others looked at him, Bronto shaking his head in mild amusement at the odd talents the small one sometimes displayed. He pulled back on the gold ring. The door opened with the same ease that the earlier one had, likewise opening up in two equal halves, the left side swinging open as well, as Bronto pulled back on the ring attached to the right side. Returning the key to his belt, with a steady pace Bronto opened up the large door wide, revealing what lay beyond for the first time in five thousand rels.

A light, brighter than that they'd yet seen from the rest of palace, shone out from the large room revealed beyond. Slowly, they stepped past the double doors.

"It's the throne room," Kilgar said, child-wonder peppering his cautious battle senses as he held his curved knife tight, "it *has* to be!"

Before them lay a vast room, hundreds of feet long and maybe half that wide, its domed ceiling arching up fifty feet or more overhead, brightly glowing stones sprinkled amongst the reds, blues, and golds of its intricate star-burst design. Round marble pillars stood everywhere, their tops connecting up with sweeping arcs in the ceiling high overhead. The walls held tapestries the likes of which no one there had ever seen; as high as the room was tall, and more than twenty feet across, the dark cloth of these tapestries was woven with bright gold and silver threads tracing out their designs of kings, queens, and wizards. Even the very floor they walked on, as they entered the immense room, was polished granite, a seamless expanse of black-flecked grey that one could almost see one's reflection in. If this room be called anything, then 'grandeur' was its name.

"*Shakoo,*" Candol exclaimed, in slow appreciative awe.

"I'm with him," Eldar thumbed towards the priest as they walked on in.

"A guy could get used to this place," Shong said as he gazed around.

As they walked on in, their footsteps echoing quietly in the distance, they could now see something else at the far end of the large room. A central dais rose up, circular steps going up its ten-foot high rise. At the top of this dais was a single throne, tall golden chair, the top of its back dusted with a glittering of small gems, colors ranging the entire rainbow. They quickened their pace over towards the throne, Quickfoot and Schanter being the first ones to reach its marble steps, the others following quickly behind.

"Can I take it home with me?" Quickfoot asked, greed gleaming in his eyes.

Schanter apparently had other ideas. He ran up the circular steps, to the base of the large throne, and tried biting violently at one of its feet.

"Schanter want burn it. Burn!" he said when he broke a tooth on its gleaming surface.

Eldar looked a question at Lindel, who just stopped him with a raised hand.

"I gave *up* trying to figure him," he said, "remember?"

"I'll get him," Shong said as he ran up the steps.

"Whatever Krey wants," Sindar said, as Shong ran up the steps, "has to be around here."

"Agreed," Sabu said, "maybe some hidden compartment or chamber."

Mauklo carefully thought to himself, his sly mind considering possibilities that the others hadn't yet thought of. Possibilities that might just change what they did. But for now, the sly one just kept everything to himself.

"Schanter want hurt self," Schanter complained as Shong lifted him up away from the throne. "Throne hard, break teeth."

"You call *this* hard?" Shong baited the warty-one. "Why, that floor down there is solid granite; you can't get much harder."

Schanter stopped, as if suddenly considering the possibility. Then he struggled out of Shong's arms and went leaping down the steps for the floor.

"Schanter want hurt self on granite floor. Hurt real bad."

Schanter flung himself down on the hard floor, pounding a fist down violently on its surface as if testing it. His fist hit the floor with a loud *crack*. Schanter screamed out as the bones in his wrist shattered, and then began to smile in glee as he started pounding down with his other wrist, the bones on the first wrist already beginning to mend.

"I really wonder about that one," Shong said, shaking his head.

He then looked around from where he stood, the ten-foot rise of the dais affording him a perfect view of the entire throne room. The others were down below, the wizards planning out what to do, Bronto and Kilgar keeping alert for any danger that might offer itself, everyone ignoring Schanter's antics.

"Nice view," Shong said as he stepped over to the throne.

"I wonder," he said musingly, as he turned to sit down on the large throne, "what it would be like to be a king; especially in a place like this."

He sat back in the throne, placing his hands on the armrests, thinking about what it must have been like.

Black inky flash of light, death aglow. Scream of pain as Death reaches out from the blackness and in towards one's soul. Golden throne glistening brightly with the glow of death, shining out for all to see.

Bronto looked up at the sudden scream to see Shong, seated on the throne, but the throne now glowing with a deep black light. Shong's hands gripped the arms of the throne tightly as his body went rigid with the dark energies coursing through it, his face rigid, his eyes wide, staring straight ahead as if looking at Death himself. Bronto leaped up the steps, reaching the throne in two bounds. He reached quickly into the globe of black light and pulled hard at Shong, yanking him free of the golden seat.

When Shong came to his senses, Bronto was holding him by the shoulders, his strong jovial face peering concern into Shong's eyes. Shong shook himself free of the effects of the throne, its black light already gone, as he struggled to stand on his own feet.

"I'm okay," he said.

"And here we thought we'd have to bring you back from the dead again," Bronto smiled. "What'd you trigger?"

"I don't know," Shong answered as the others came up and surrounded him, the incident even getting Schanter's attention. "Maybe only kings can sit in that chair or something."

"You probably triggered some sort of defense mechanism," Sabu explained, "designed to keep others away from the throne."

"Perhaps…," Mauklo said to himself, a bit of doubt in his voice.

"Well, I assure you it is not something I would like to repeat," Shong smiled as he shook his head clear.

"But it only happened when you placed *both* arms firmly on the arm rests of the throne," Sindar noted, "not a common position for most people sitting there. Perhaps it is a defensive device designed for something a bit more specific than just sitting on it."

"Like for hiding a hidden switch?" Sabu continued the train of thought. "But if none of us can get to it without ending up like Shong…"

"We'll soon see about that," Bronto said, stepping over to the throne.

Before anyone could say otherwise, he sat down on the throne, placing both arms firmly down on its armrests. They waited a brief moment, tense, expecting at any time for something to happen.

What happened wasn't the black light that they'd all feared. With a slow grinding noise, the throne slid aside, revealing a passage behind the throne and a series of stone steps leading downward.

"Well," Eldar said, as Bronto got up out of the chair, "it appears that the old blood strikes again. I think maybe that beyond lies what Krey seeks"

"There's only one way to find out," replied Bronto as he stepped on into the dark recess and down the stone steps.

"Now, we may finally find out what this is all about," Candol commented as he followed the big man down, "and what in the name of Indra is so important about this place."

Weapons drawn, spells ready, the rest followed carefully down the steps.

Down into the darkness the steps went, no magic stones around to light this passage, the dim reflected light coming in from the entrance being their only source of light. The stone steps spiraled down, winding down a hundred feet, until Bronto finally stepped onto a wide flat surface, the end of the spiral of steps. As he did so, a bright light finally lit up, revealing what lay before them as the others came down after Bronto.

It looked to be a circular room, no more than about fifty feet across, with five doors spaced equally around its perimeter. The polished grey floor had another red sunburst design inlaid into its surface, its rays pointing to each of the doors. The doors looked to be of simple mahogany and fine woods, but carved in an intricate and decorative way. The ceiling, this one no more than about ten feet or so high, curved up into another dome, its inside lined with a shiny blue metal that was giving off the light that now illuminated the chamber. They walked into the center of the room, looking around.

"My guess would be the king's private chambers," Eldar said, as they walked around to the various doors.

"You're probably correct," Sindar said, "which would mean..."

Sindar paused as he concentrated briefly, before continuing.

"That door leads to his private bed chambers, that door to some sort of dressing and ready room," Sindar said, pointing to each door in turn, "leaving the others to contain some more interesting stuff."

"I'll take this one," Eldar said, going over to one of the doors.

Eldar tried the handle but it wouldn't turn; he pushed on the door, but it wouldn't budge.

"It's stuck," the elf called over his shoulder.

"Here," Sabu raised up his staff, "allow me."

Sabu tapped his staff once on the ground; immediately three of the five doors clicked open as they unlocked.

"I thought we'd leave the king's private chambers alone," Sabu nodded towards two of the remaining closed doors.

Eldar tried the handle again, and this time it opened. He opened up the door and entered the room beyond, Quickfoot scurrying in after him. Likewise, Mauklo went over to one of the other doors, something within him telling him which one to choose, as he too turned a knob and entered a room. Bronto and Sindar went over to the remaining door while the others stood ready.

Eldar was greeted by a library; small room, its tumbled shelves filled with books, a single table with a scattering of papers on it in the room's center. The room was small and cramped, made even more so by the disarray of its contents. What walls they could see through the tumbled piles of books had black scorch marks on them, while the ceiling overhead was pitted with deep gouges to mar its smooth grey surface.

"It looks like there was a small war in here," Quickfoot commented as they walked in.

"I quite agree," Eldar replied as he went over to the table.

"But, if this was one of the king's chambers, who would want to do this?" Quickfoot asked, kicking at one of the books lying on the floor.

"Remember who the last king was," Eldar prompted as he shifted through the papers.

"That Beltor guy?"

"Right," Eldar said, producing a key from amongst the scattering of papers. "This must have been where they finally cornered him when he was overthrown. I'm surprised most of these books are still intact; it must have been a quick battle."

"More books," Quickfoot grumbled, kicking at a leaning shelf.

The shelf he kicked trembled in response, the contents of its shelves sliding off on top of the small one. Quickfoot gave a short scream, covering his head with his arms, as dozens of books pelted him over the head. The wooden shelf, eight feet tall and already leaning, creaked as it gave way, angling down another foot before coming to rest against another bookshelf. When the books stopped falling, Quickfoot carefully looked up, slowly taking his hands away from his head when it looked like no more books were going to fall.

Eldar was laughing.

"You know," the elf grinned, "after all you've been through, it'd be a shame if you got killed by a *bookshelf.*"

"Hey," Quickfoot said sharply, "I *told* you books are dangerous for you!"

"Yeah," Eldar said, as he walked over and picked up one of the fallen books, looking at its title, "especially these. This was Beltor's library alright; these books look to have stuff that only Mauklo would like. Matter of fact, he'd probably give his eye teeth for some of these."

He tossed the book over his shoulder as Quickfoot freed himself of the books that had piled around him.

"Hey, I know," Eldar smiled, "what say we *don't* tell him about these?"

"Fine by me," Quickfoot replied, dodging one last book that had decided to fall from the slanting shelf, "as long as he doesn't ask me a direct question, I won't say a thing. That guy frightens me."

Eldar shook his head in amusement. As he looked up, his eyes rested on what lay on the section of wall that the shelf's movement had now revealed.

"You appear to have done it again," Eldar said, stepping over to the new section of wall as he held up the key that he'd found on the desk, "I think I know where this key goes that I just found."

The small one looked over to see what the elf was referring to. There, imbedded in the wall that the shelf had just revealed, was the door to a small wall safe, a simple metal door no more than a foot across, with a small keyhole and a latch handle. Eldar fitted the key into the lock.

"I'm not sure what it is that I keep on doing," Quickfoot said, as Eldar turned the key, "but I'd sure like to know how it is that I keep on doing it."

"The key fits," Eldar said, turning the handle with a click, "time to see what's inside."

The small door opened, revealing the wall safe beyond. Eldar reached in with a hand and fumbled around for what may lay inside. After a few moments he finally produced the safe's only contents.

A rolled up scroll.

"Well *that* doesn't look too exciting," Quickfoot noted.

"You never know," Eldar said as he brought out the scroll.

The scroll had a thick layer of dust on it, but as Eldar brought it up out of the safe, the dust immediately slid off as if repelled, leaving not a speck of dust on the almost new-looking paper.

"This doesn't feel like any paper I've ever seen," Eldar noted, walking back across the room as he unfurled the scroll.

Eldar chewed on his lip as he pondered at what he was looking at, puzzlement now filling his face. Quickfoot went over to his side to get a look at what puzzled the elf so.

"What is it?" the small one asked, trying to get a peek.

"I'm not sure," Eldar replied, as he rolled up the scroll again, "but definitely something for the others to see."

As Eldar rolled up the scroll, Quickfoot ran a finger along its surface. Immediately he drew back.

"That's not paper," Quickfoot said, "and it's not cloth."

"I know," Eldar agreed, "and that's not the least of what's puzzling about this scroll. Come on."

Mauklo entered a dark round room, walls painted red, floor covered with an engraved pentagram inside of a circle of strange markings. Mauklo smiled as immediate realization came to him.

"I like this room already," he said, the door closing behind him at a gesture of his hand, "now let's see. If I was Beltor, and I had to leave my conjuring room and all its contents whenever I was away, then…ah."

Mauklo looked at the door directly behind him, and the pentagram directly in front of him. At the other side of the pentagram, the far side of the room held a work table, strange paraphernalia of conjuring and dark magics covering its surface. Mauklo smiled and took a few steps to one side.

The pentagram started glowing, puffs of dark mist coming up from the edge of the pentagram. In a quick flash of dark smoke and black light, something appeared in the center of the pentagram. It was a large man, maybe half a foot shorter than a full seven feet tall, his dark complexion and black hair almost blending in with the equally dark plate mail armor that he wore. His face wore the dark passion of evil, an ugliness that went far beyond mere looks. Power, old and evil, radiated from his every look, his every movement, his very countenance being one that would strike fear into the heart of he who just but looked at him. In his hands he held a pair of shiny black swords, over a yard long each, wide and curved were they. His eyes glowed a dark purple light as, with a battle cry that sounded like a cross between a large jungle cat and a gorilla in heat, he brought down both of his swords right in front of the doorway where Mauklo had been standing. The swords cleaved deep slices into the tough stone ground.

"Hmm, I've only *heard* of your kind, *night devil,*" Mauklo said calmly, as the creature looked over towards the voice, both puzzled and angry that its target hadn't been where he was supposed to be. "That would make Beltor quite a conjurer to snare one of *your* kind as the guardian of his conjuring room."

The creature drew up its swords again, growling menace at Mauklo, as it turned to face him.

"Oh, I'm quite sure that it is presently far beyond my power to match you in physical or magical combat," Mauklo said, calm as ever, "or to find any spell that could even *harm* you, much less dispose of you."

It came slashing down with both of its swords, slicing at the calm unmoving form of Mauklo.

"Except for *this* spell of course," Mauklo said, calmly snapping his fingers on the word 'this'.

A light, bright as day, appeared directly in the creature's eyes. Like small burning suns, the light appeared as twin orbs, each no larger than the creature's own eyes and each directly in front of them, twin blazes of white threatening to attach themselves directly to its retinas. The creature stopped its downward slice, dropping the swords in the pentagram as it screamed and brought its clawed hands up to its eyes. Green blood could be seen oozing out from the corners of the burning eyes as it screamed out its rage.

"Now," Mauklo said, all calm and business like, "before your own powers dispel my little spell, hear me when I tell you that your master Beltor has been long dead and your services are no longer required. I therefore intend on freeing you of your binding to this pentagram, and for just but a small price."

The creature screamed, a dark light shining out from under the bright daylight covering its eyes. With a sudden dark flash, the bright lights were gone, the creature's eyes now once again revealed, though puffy and oozing of green ichor.

"What price?" came the dark gravely reply.

"Ah, cooperation," Mauklo said pleasantly, "the stuff that alliances are formed of. My price is merely that you take a message down to some of your friends back home. For but that small task, I shall destroy this pentagram that binds you here. I know of your particular species, and have full confidence that once your word is given, you will stick to an agreement."

"As long as you stick to yours," added the deep gravely voice.

"Of course," Mauklo smiled pleasantly.

The creature thought, dark smoke coming up from its muscular shoulders, an evil radiating from it that was almost palpable. Finally, it answered.

"Very well," it replied, "I agree to take down your message if I am freed from here."

"Good. Oh," Mauklo said, as if adding an afterthought, "and none of this, you kill me then take down my message, stuff. I fully expect to live through this and do business with you again sometime."

The dark-armored man smiled as he looked eye to eye with the dark-hearted human before him. Then it roared out a laughter that would have sent most people cowering, so deep and dark was it. Mauklo just returned his gaze, even and level.

"Very well," it said, "I see that you are almost as sly as Beltor was."

"What do you mean, 'almost'?"

Mauklo's expression got serious, becoming somehow expressionless yet quite deadly at the same time. He stared the devil straight in its eyes, playing the creature's own lethal game of matching gazes. It stared back at the Sileen wizard, pouring out its darkness into the gaze, welcoming the opportunity to flood its evil will into his soul, wrenching away Mauklo's will and making him its own puppet. It poured its dark evil into this gaze.

But, its gaze was met with a gaze equally as dark, and perhaps even less forgiving. Its will was matched by a will equal to its own, perhaps even a bit greater. It learned surprise to find such a dark heart in a human; it learned shock to find such force of will in the mere mortal.

It began to learn fear.

The creature averted its gaze, turning away from the darker gaze that was Mauklo's.

"Now," Mauklo smiled slyly, "are you ready to deal?"

"Very well," it answered, as it straightened itself up, but never again looking into Mauklo's eyes, "what is your message?"

"Hey, Sabu," Eldar called out. "Have a look at this."

Sabu looked over to see Eldar and Quickfoot coming out of one of the five rooms, a rolled up scroll in the elf's hands. Eldar unrolled the scroll as he came up to his friend, handing it over to the young wizard.

Sabu looked it over, feeling the strange texture of its surface, looking at what was written on it. As he did so, Candol, Sheil-Bor(h), and Shong came over, Kilgar being kept busy trying to keep Schanter from chewing on a doorknob. Mauklo came quietly out from the room that he'd gone in to, closing the door behind him.

"It looks like some sort of map," Sabu said, looking it over. "It seems to be depicting continents of some sort—this could even be Catho over here—but these markings...Sheil-Bor(h)?"

Sheil-Bor(h) looked down at the map that Sabu now showed for all to see. It was indeed a map of some sort; with continents drawn in colorful greens, the light blue of oceans, concentric circles spiraling inward towards the center of some of the land masses, widening rings over the oceans. But what caught the eye were the markings. All over the map, like strange hieroglyphs turned in upon themselves, odd assortments of angles and curves, picturesque stick drawings, some of the markings almost looking like an expression, if an emotion could be put to paper.

"Of several languages can I speak and read," Sheil-Bor(h) replied, "and of several more can I recognize. But of what language is this, I know not."

"Some of it's almost recognizable," Eldar pointed out. "This symbol, for instance, looks like some standard elven lettering, except for that last bit on the end of it, that looks sort of dwarven."

"I too, see elements of Sileesh, Darnese, Osan, and even Hydwaun," Sheil-Bor(h) noted, "but also many an unknown element."

"Like someone mixed them all together and added their own stuff," Shong summarized.

"A parent language perhaps?" Sheil-Bor(h) suggested.

"But for so many languages?" Eldar said. "Some not even human or elvish."

"What about those circles," Candol said, pointing to the concentric circles drawn faintly on the map.

"Well," Sabu said, "If that land mass there *is* part of Catho, then the more tightly nested ones would correspond to known mountains peeks. That would make the land-circles elevation lines, and the ones in the ocean depth indicators."

"That only brings up more questions," Eldar noted, as he saw the density of some of the faintly-drawn ocean lines, "because *nobody* has ever measured the ocean's depths with the accuracy that those lines would indicate. It's impossible!"

"All very puzzling indeed," Sabu replied thoughtfully, rolling up the map again, "but something that shall have to wait until we are back on our island; we have not the time for this here."

"Come back here!"

Kilgar was chasing Schanter across the room. Schanter had hold of the boy's knife, trying to chew on its hilt as the boy chased him across the small room. Schanter screamed delight at the chase, until he looked on ahead of him and saw who he was going to bump into.

He was headed straight for Mauklo.

Schanter immediately started to try and skid to a stop, tossing Kilgar's knife in back of him, the boy catching it just as Schanter was about to land into the wizard. Mauklo calmly pointed a finger, releasing a thin line of flame; just enough to hurl the warty one off to one side, slamming against a wall instead of into the wizard.

The beam also reflected off of Schanter's green hide and across the room…hitting the map in Sabu's hands.

"The map!" Eldar exclaimed, as the tongue of flame hit it. "How——"

But, just as worried glances quickly passed around concerned faces, just as quickly did they turn to wonder, as they looked down at what Sabu held in his hand.

The map was untouched.

"It's not even warm," Sabu said in mild amazement, as he brought the map up for a closer look, "or even scorched. I wonder…"

"Uh oh, he's going on another intellectual trip again," Quickfoot sighed.

"Shong," Sabu said, stretching out the map between both hands, "see if that diamond blade of yours can cut this."

"Are you crazy?" Eldar asked, shocked. "I thought we were going to study it."

"We *are*," Sabu answered, "now slice."

Shong thought that this time Sabu had busted a brain cell or two, but he did as asked. He ran the sharp diamond edge up along the edge of the paper, slicing up half the length of the sword.

The paper was untouched.

Puzzled, Shong sliced harder. Still nothing.

"It won't cut," Shong finally gave up.

"Nor will it burn," Sabu said, the gleam of curiosity aroused in his eyes. "This is most interesting. If we have the time, I'd like to——"

"I think we found the royal treasure chamber," came Sindar's interrupting call.

At the sound of 'treasure', they all immediately rushed over to the central door which Bronto and Sindar had gone to check out. As Sabu rolled up the map again, Eldar whispered a quick aside to him before going over with the others.

"We're *definitely* going to have a better look at that map later on," Eldar said. "You've got *me* curious now."

Bronto and Sindar were standing in front of an open wooden door. Beyond it could be seen a short passage, ending at a single large iron door, on either side of which stood an immobile suit of black plate armor, metal from head to toe, standing silent sentry.

"Even after your spell that opened up the other doors, there was still a powerful magical barrier holding it shut," Sindar explained, as the others gathered round. "It stopped any spell that I tried. I thought it unopenable until Bronto tried the doorknob himself."

278

"It must just be that *old blood* thing again," Bronto grinned.

"To but follow Mauklo's own earlier supposition," Sheil-Bor(h) offered, "if this be the only door here that need have Bronto's touch to open, then what Krey desires no doubt lies beyond."

"Then we have to get it before Krey does," Candol decided. "We must see what it is that he wants."

"For once, the priest is right," Mauklo said in his calm sileesh accent. "We must put this all to an end."

"Very well," Lindel agreed, "then if Schanter's finished playing around, we might as well get started."

Schanter gave a pouting look, looking as a child caught at doing something naughty.

"One thing first though," Sabu came up to Sindar, holding out the rolled up scroll before him, "of what do your psychic powers make of this."

Sindar closed his eyes, as Shong and Bronto drew out their swords in preparation for entering the treasure chamber. Sindar swayed back and forth as he concentrated, his strong mental powers trying to delve deep into the nature of the simple-looking scroll. Then, he stopped.

His eyes popped wide open, as if in extreme shock. Sindar nearly fell back, Eldar catching him by the shoulders.

"Sindar, what is it?" the elf asked, as he tried to lightly slap his friend awake.

Sindar put a hand to his temple as he tried to rub the shock out from his brain. Eldar helped him straighten up as he answered.

"It is old beyond belief," Sindar said, "older than any history that I know of. Its age can probably be measure in *dorels;* not a length of time I can easily fathom. Where did you get that?"

"A subject for another time, perhaps," Sheil-Bor(h) suggested. "As interesting as that map may be, of even more interest is our present circumstance. The map will wait."

"I suppose," Sabu said, reluctantly putting the map away in his robes.

"I'll go first," Bronto said, as he started to step into the short hallway.

"Wait," Quickfoot said as he scurried over to Bronto's feet, "can't you people see *anything?*"

They watched as the small one took out one of his many daggers and casually tossed it into the hallway. It landed halfway down the short twenty-foot stretch, clanging once or twice. Immediately a shower of pellets began spitting out from tiny holes in the walls on either side of the hallway, landing against the walls and on the ground. Upon impact, each pellet broke open, releasing a bubbling fuming liquid.

"The small one's innate *meuwmen* does seem to have its uses at times," Mauklo commented to himself, watching the rivulets of bubbling liquid.

"Acid," Eldar said, as he casually strolled in, "you act like that's a problem,"

Eldar went in, walked partway down the hallway, and bent down, casually scraping up some of the acid onto his finger, putting it to his mouth as if to taste it.

"Hmm," he said, licking his lips, "pretty potent too."

"If I might point out," Lindel said, leaning in the doorway, "some of us don't *have* Hevon Gems."

"Details," Eldar shrugged as he brought out his sword.

He aimed the sword down at the acid trickling along the floor, the acid pellets still shooting out of the walls, impacting upon the elf but just washing off of him. As he pointed, a stream of yellow liquid jetted out from the tip of his sword. Like a hose, he sprayed it around the floor and walls, spraying it into the tiny holes out of which the pellets shot. When he was finished, the liquid around him was no longer bubbling or smoking. Instead, a fine white crystalline ash was forming along the floors, coating as well all down the walls.

"Did I mention that our Acid Gems also do alkali?" Eldar smiled.

"He means," Sindar answered the puzzled expression on Quickfoot's face, "he just turned it all into salt. It's quite safe now."

Bronto stepped in first, fresh salt crunching under his heavy footstep, Shong following close behind. Eldar, already partway down the hallway, turned to skip down towards the door at the far end.

"Eldar," Sabu shouted out, his voice stopping the elf but five feet before the door, "I'll give you odds on those suits of armor."

Eldar stopped, turning a thoughtful expression towards the twin suits of dark plate, looking like the ghostly remains of long-dead knights.

"Hmm," he said, sheathing his old sword and taking out his new Evolin blade, "perhaps you're right."

Cautiously, he approached the large iron door. Two steps closer did he take, when both of the suits came to life. They turned to face him, drawing millennia-old swords out of their scabbards, black pools of night now filling their empty faceplates. Eldar dodged as one sliced down at him.

"Need any help?" Bronto asked, coming down the hallway.

"Naw," Eldar grinned, as he sliced down at the one on the left, "this is fun."

His blow cleaved through the armor at the shoulder, separating the metal arm at that point as it was sent clattering to the ground. But, when Eldar looked up at his foe, there were now *three* suits of armor, two of them with only one arm.

"Now *this* could get tricky," Eldar admitted, as he leaped back from three swinging swords.

He slashed at the one with the two good arms, this time slicing off its head. But the only result he seemed to produce was the presence of four of the suits of armor, two of them without heads, but fighting just as efficiently all the same.

"Uh, guys," he said, backing up, "I'm open to suggestions."

"I just have one," Sindar said, raising up his hand, "in that metal is rather conductive."

A stream of half-seen force seemed to go from Sindar's outstretched hand, around Eldar, and on towards the four suits of armor. They all seemed to briefly glow with a faint luminescence and then quiver. Realizing what was about to happen, Eldar leaped back towards Bronto just as all four suits came flying towards each other. They impacted at a common center, the force of their impact causing their number to once again double, but still leaving the entire group as a single magnetized heap wriggling upon the ground. Eldar smiled at the sight.

"I like that one," Eldar said, eyes twinkling silver-blue, "but what about the pile? It's kind of blocking the way."

"Allow me," Bronto said, as he walked on past Eldar.

The big man went over to the struggling pile, and placed a hand around either end, as if he were going to lift it all up. Instead, he pressed inward, carefully crushing and bending the struggling suits. He then moved his grip, crushing inward from a different location, and then repeated this, squashing and crushing, reducing it all into a smaller and smaller pile. When he was finished, all that was left was a compact metal ball no more than two feet across.

"There just *has* to be a way he can make money doing that," Eldar commented as the others came up to join them.

They walked up to the iron door, Sabu surveying its work. All along its surface were glyphs and magical runes carved into it. Nary a gold ring did this one have, but a simple flat plate at its center. Sabu looked the magical writings up and down, while Eldar gave a slow appreciative whistle.

"If these runes are as potent as the magic I feel coming off of this thing," Eldar said, "then this door is *not* coming open!"

"I can assure you that those runes *are* indeed potent," Sabu noted, "but its solution is all but an intellectual problem. For instance; notice the flat plate at the door's center."

Sabu walked over to stand beside the door.

"It is obviously no larger than one's hand," Sabu continued, finishing up by looking at Bronto.

Bronto shrugged and stepped over, putting away his sword as he drew up his right hand.

"Sure, it's worth a try," he rumbled goodnaturedly, "by the power of the old blood and all that."

He placed his right palm against the flat plate. At first, nothing happened, but then a loud crack was heard, resonating throughout the short hallway. Then a slow grinding, as if of long unmoved gears grinding slowly awake for the first time in eons. Then, the door began to part down the middle, straight down the center of the flat plate, as it drew apart, recessing slowly into the walls, Bronto brought down his hand, readying his sword again as the door slowly parted wide enough to admit them through. Eldar, Bronto, and Sabu stepped forward.

A glittering spectacle were they admitted into. A room filled with the wealth of Thïr Tÿorca, from chests brimming full with bright shining gems, to shelves of ornate scepters, chalices, silver platters, golden candlesticks, and other valuable knickknacks. Gold was piled almost haphazardly around, making neighbors with small statues of marble and gems, propping up old forgotten paintings. Quickfoot ran right past the others and into the lavish room.

"Wow!" he exclaimed, as he dived into the nearest pile of treasure. "This *has* to be what Krey wants. I know *I* want it."

Sabu shook his head as the rest of them entered the large room.

"No," he said doubtfully, "this *can't* be just about money."

"Maybe it's about *that* then."

Kilgar was pointing to what lay in the very center of the room: a tall crystal table, topped by a dome of glass. Sabu, Eldar, and Sindar walked over to what Kilgar had found, the others fanning out through the room. As they approached it, they could see what lay under the transparent case.

"It looks like the crown jewels or something," Eldar said, as they looked down at it.

Inside, they saw a short golden staff topped with a small blue crystal ball, a crown of gold and jewels, and a small ceremonial dagger encrusted with a multitude of small gems. They looked down at it, each sensing it in his own unique way.

"There is great power about those items," Eldar remarked.

"As well about the case that protects it," Sindar added, "any magic that could get through that case might also harm that which lies within."

"I found another door over here," Bronto said, walking over to them, "but this time it won't open for me."

"Hmm," Sabu said thoughtfully, idea forming in his head, "I wonder..."

"Here it comes," Eldar grinned, catching the look in his friend's eye, "we all know *that* look."

"Bronto," Sabu said, "why don't you take a try at this dome casing, and then we'll try that other door."

"Something just occur to you?" Sindar asked, as Bronto came up to the case.

"Yes," Sabu answered, "and I've a sneaking suspicion that it has already occurred to Mauklo's devious little mind a while back."

"Here goes," Bronto said, grabbing either end of the small round dome.

The moment he touched it, the dome started to glow a bright yellow. When the light faded a moment later, so had the dome, exposing the items underneath it for all to see.

"Hey," Eldar said, as he grabbed up the gem-encrusted dagger, "I've always wanted a knife that was too fancy-looking to be practical."

"I'm sure useless accouterments suit you just fine," Sindar said, mild mocking in his voice, as he picked up the crown.

"Hey," Eldar replied, swinging his new dagger around playfully in the air, "I resemble that remark."

"Now," Sabu said, as he picked up the short staff, "where's this door?"

"Over here," Bronto directed.

They walked past piles of treasure, around shelves of old artwork, and over to a wall with but a single door at its center. No handle was there upon this door, but more of a stone enclosure was it, a seal, as if someone wanted to wall in what lay beyond. Overhead was mounted a dark metal plaque, its lettering engraved in bright gold.

"That seal is quite a bit younger than the surrounding wall," Eldar noted.

"And made of a different texture of material as well," Sindar added, "it was definitely added a good while after Thïr Tÿorca was built. As well does it have the feel of *deg soodra* about it."

"That plaque is written in an old variant of Selgish," Sabu said, looking up at the caption, "but I think I can read it."

Sabu cleared his throat, his voice ringing out loud and clear; the others in the room stopped looking around to hear what was to be said.

Mauklo just smiled to himself, watching as his own conclusions were being verified.

"'Disturb not that which lies beyond,'" Sabu intoned, "'let rest the Black One in his burning crypt of night.'"

"Sounds like they don't want anyone going in," Quickfoot said after Sabu was finished. "Okay by me; all this lovely gold will do nicely."

"What Krey wants, lies beyond," Sindar said. "We must get to it before he does."

"I just *knew* someone was going to say something like that," Quickfoot complained.

"And I know how to open it up," Sabu said.

Sabu brought up the short golden staff, its blue crystal top now swirling bright. Sindar followed by putting the crown up on his head, Eldar holding the dagger in his hand.

"But, what if it only works for a specific person?" Eldar asked. "I don't even think Bronto's heritage would do it on this one; it doesn't look like they wanted just *anyone* to open this up."

"That's why we're going to supplement," Sabu said, as he brought up his own staff in his other hand, "with Hevon."

Sabu's Hevon gems began to show brightly on the tip of his staff, arranged in their half-formed ring around its top. Then, he slowly brought the gold staff of Thïr Tÿorca to his own staff, touching them both together. There was a flash of multicolored light as they met, intense concentration showing on Sabu's face as he tried to control the opposing forces as they mixed and strained against one another. When they light had faded, only Sabu's staff was there left, only now with a faint golden sheen to it, the Hevon Gems already fading back down into the staff.

"If I'm correct," Sabu explained, "that seal can only be personalized to open for a specific person if these items are so specific to one person."

"But," Sindar picked up on the thought, "if the nature of the items was changed to be keyed to another person, *then* it could work for that other person."

"And, only with Hevon would there be the power to change them without harming them," Eldar finished up in a quick intuitive leap, "by merging them with the power of whatever it is that is Hevon. Sounds great!"

Eldar quickly pressed the small dagger to his own sword and then, as an afterthought, took out his Evolin blade and pressed that to both of the other two. When the flash of colored lights was gone, Eldar was holding just the one sword.

"There," he commented, "that should save on equipment as well."

As for Sindar, they watched as the crown upon his head simply melted down into him, seeming to merge with his skull until it was gone.

"*Shakoo*," Kilgar voiced, as he watched the display.

"I'm with you kid," Bronto agreed.

Even Schanter was too caught up in watching the three to do anything but stare.

"I think," Sindar said, facing towards the sealed door, "that afterwards we are going to have to do some more research on just what these Hevon Gems are all about. Their nature would seem to go far beyond that of magic."

The three turned and faced the door, linking hands with Sindar in the center, Sabu on the left, and Eldar at the right. They looked at the sealed door, concentrating their efforts, as if willing the seal to break. Sabu held tightly onto his staff, Eldar to his sword, while Sindar just stared directly at the sealed door. The magic of the seal felt the power of the items which would open it, felt them and something more. For, the three weren't actually *using* the items so much as they now *were* the items.

The seal became a wash of colored lights, not only the golden power of the items found under the case, but also glowing with the prismatic colors that were of Hevon. The others watched as the seal became a cascading rainbow of color, washing down the surface like liquid light. As it washed down, the colors seemed to take with it the grey stone of the seal. The light ran off into little pools, quickly evaporating into the stone floor. What it left behind was not a seal, but an opening.

An open portal, wide enough for a single man to walked through, with carved stone steps, covered in layers of mildew, leading downward. As the three relaxed their concentration, as well their grips upon one another, the others approached cautiously, Kilgar, knife in hand, peering cautiously into the darkness that lay beyond.

"So, what's in there?" Shong asked, as he poked at the darkness with his diamond blade.

"That which Krey seeks," Sheil-Bor(h) answered, "and of what we must find."

The smell of moisture came drifting up from the open portal, as did the faint sound of lapping water. Candol went over to the edge, looking down into the darkness beyond.

"If indeed Krey wants what lies beyond, then in the name of Indra should we seek it out, whatever it is."

"Let's hurry then," Lindel said, readying his bow, "we don't know how long those palace gates up there can hold out against Krey since our going through them. We may have opened up the magics that kept him out."

"Agreed," Eldar said, stepping towards the darkness, "we've got to hurry."

"What is it, though," Shong asked as they all walked over towards the dark portal, "that could be so valuable to him in there?"

The sound of Mauklo's laughter caught them all off-guard. All eyes turned to see the dark-haired Sileen laughing a laugh that sent nervous chills up Quickfoot's spin, almost breaking Candol's spell of bravery.

"What's so funny?" Eldar asked. "I suppose *you* know what Krey wants in there?"

"Of course I do," Mauklo said more calmly, smiling as he stepped over to the front of the portal, "I know exactly what he wants. I figured it out before we finally found this lost city."

Mauklo looked suggestively down into the dark depths, and then out at the others, slow smile curling upon his lips.

"He wants Beltor."

CHAPTER TWENTY-SIX
Beltor

"But, Beltor has been dead for thousands of rels now," Candol asked, as they walked carefully down the wet slimy steps, "what in the name of Indra could Krey possibly want him for?"

"Beltor, my good priest," Mauklo answered calmly, his sileesh accent carrying out into the damp quiet of the cavern they now walked down into, "was a necromancer, and a pretty good one. Now, it is said, that good necromancers never truly die. That alone would make Beltor a good ally."

"But," Shong asked, walking a few steps behind them in their single-file trek down the stone steps, "then what *does* happen to a good necromancer when he dies?"

Mauklo just smiled.

"Okay," Quickfoot put in, a little taken aback by Mauklo's pleasant but unnerving smile, "I never thought that a smile would tell me more than I wanted to know."

They were walking down the carved stone steps that the opening of the portal had revealed; steps that hadn't been used for thousands of rels. The steps were wide but wet and slimy, leading down through a narrow tunnel, the sound of lapping water coming up from below. Cold drafty air came up the steps, lending a chill to the dark dampness. After about a hundred of the steps, the walls to either side gave way, the cold draft now taking on the feel of a much larger open area, though all they could see was darkness. Then, one by one, they each finally came to the bottom of the steps and on to a wide flat platform of rock, the sound of water lapping now about their feet. Sabu tapped his staff once on the stone floor, immediately causing a ball of light to shine forth from around the tip of his staff, illuminating the darkness as if with the light of day. They then just stood there for a bit, all looking around at what surroundings were revealed.

A fluttering of small creatures, both winged and crawling, went scurrying quickly away into the shadows at the sudden appearance of Sabu's light. The steps had brought them to a wide stone platform, but a few inches above the surface of the dark waters that stretched around them. They were in a large underground cavern, the ceiling stretching forty feet up as it curved and arced around, moistly gleaming stalactites hanging down from the ceiling in colorful arrays, Sabu's light glittering off their damp surfaces. The water lay before them like a small lake, a tall cavern wall defining its opposite side some fifty feet away, the sides of the water curving away like a slow river as it flowed away and around other openings in the cavern. >From their left they could see the water coming gently through a narrower reach of the cavern, while to their right it split into two, meandering around the tall walls and rocky projections of the slowly twisting cavern.

In back of them, the steps came out of a large cavern wall, a narrow ledge near the base of the steps leading off into an open flat area in the rock wall, a foot above the surface of the water. In front of them the water lapped gently around a long rowboat, old and wooden, tied off at a stone projection at the base of their platform. It bobbed slowly up and down, as if inviting use.

"The water must somehow come in from that large lake," Sabu said, gazing around. "It probably filled up these caverns long before Thïr Tÿorca was even built."

"Maybe that's why it was built here," Lindel pointed out, "it makes for a nice emergency exit."

"I should point out," Eldar warned, "that if the *water* comes from the lake, then whatever creatures that *live* in the lake may also be around."

"Then we'll just have to be careful of them while we search for Beltor's tomb," Sabu agreed.

"At least we have an enchanted boat in which to search these caverns," Sindar observed, as he walked over to the small boat.

"How do you know it's enchanted?" Quickfoot asked.

"It's a wooden boat that's been here in a damp cavern full of water for thousands of rels without decaying and rotting away," Sindar answered, "how could it *not* be enchanted?"

"Good point," Quickfoot admitted.

"Is that thing big enough for all of us?" Bronto asked, as they all walked over to the longboat. "Some of us need a *bit* more elbow room."

"We should all just about fit," Sindar answered, sizing up the small boat with his eyes. "It looks long enough, and my guess is that its magic will allow it to keep us all afloat."

"Well, we're about to find out then," Bronto said, while getting into the boat.

"Just one question," Shong asked, as the others started to follow after Bronto, "if these caverns connect with the lake outside, and Beltor is buried somewhere *in* these water caverns, then how come Krey just hasn't used these caverns to get in and find Beltor's tomb instead of waiting for someone to open up the palace?"

"Hmm," Sabu pondered, while stepping into the boat after Shong, "it may be that Krey doesn't know about these caverns-although after a few hundred rels of him being in this valley looking for a way in that's hard to believe-or some other reason that we don't yet know."

"More unknowns," Eldar said, as he untied the rope, the last one to get in. "Life just keeps getting better all the time."

"If these caverns are as large and extensive as I suspect," Sindar said, as Bronto and Shong each grabbed for an oar, "then finding the tomb could be quite a lengthy process."

"Not at all," Sheil-Bor(h) replied, "the boat knows the way, let *it* guide us."

"I'm almost afraid to ask how a *boat* can know," Quickfoot groaned.

"Simple," Sabu explained, immediately catching onto Sheil-Bor(h)'s idea. "This boat was obviously used at least once in getting Beltor to his place of rest. Therefore, the boat has been there and knows the route, or rather, residual sympathetic and psychic emanations of its travel would be left on the boat. We can simply tap into these emanations and use them to guide our way."

"I think I like *his* explanation better," Quickfoot nodded towards Sheil-Bor(h), as he held his head between both hands as if in pain.

The boat gave a sudden jerk away from the stone pier, moving away without benefit of help from either Bronto or Shong.

"The spell has been cast," Sheil-Bor(h) explained, "the boat shall now be our guide."

The small boat seemed to then take on a heading of its own. Heedless of currents, the boat drifted on through the water, heading off to the left of the stone pier, floating stately out into the caverns. Around a bend in the rock wall it went, down another side-channel, around a curve of gently flowing waters, and through a narrow section of cavern. The boat floated at a steady gentle pace.

Eldar looked bored.

"Hey," he finally said, after they'd gone through several caverns of colorful stalactites, "you think maybe with these Hevon Water Gems we have that we could put a bit more *speed* on this trip?"

"Eldar's right," Bronto agreed. "I feel like I'm on some rich man's pleasure cruise and not hunting after a dead necromancer."

"I think it can be managed," Sabu answered, "but let's not try for too fast; these caverns are rather twisted."

Sabu nodded to Sheil-Bor(h) and a moment later the small boat was picking up speed. Faster and faster it went, speeding around the bends in the watery caverns, sometimes almost threatening to scrape against the walls. Quickfoot held onto Candol, seated right in front of him, as the boat splashed through the water. Down watery rapids, past glittering cavern walls and raised muddy expanses of dry land, through tunnels so narrow that the stalactites overhead almost touched down upon Bronto's lowered head, and around pointed rocky projections coming suddenly up through the water.

Eldar just put his face into the wind and screamed with delight.

Schanter mimicked Eldar, but with one minor difference; Schanter *tried* to catch his head upon the passing rocks, actually *hoping* to maim himself on the swiftly passing terrain.

Quickfoot hung on for dear life.

"*Karu!* Now *this* is a ride!" Eldar exclaimed. "I'd pay *money* for a trip like this!"

"I'd pay money just to get *off!*" came Quickfoot's immediate reply.

"Maybe you'd better slow this down a bit," Sabu shouted over to Sheil-Bor(h) above the roar of their passage.

"As you wish," Sheil-Bor(h) shrugged.

The boat slowed down to a more acceptable pace, much to the relief of Quickfoot and the disappointment of Eldar and Schanter. They found themselves sailing through another long watery cavern, Sabu's light reflecting green off of the ceiling far overhead.

"That does it," came Quickfoot's immediate comment, "I now hate dragons *and* fast rides."

"Uh, just a little question," Shong asked, looking up, "but should that ceiling up there be glowing that particular color?"

Lindel looked up, squinting his sharp elven eyes for a better look. Covering the entire ceiling he saw a thick green carpet of moist fuzz, coating the ceiling, hanging from it in ragged strips.

"It looks like some sort of moss," the elf answered, turning back to Shong. "I can't tell what type though. It's probably harmless."

"Why does that almost sound like a cue?" Quickfoot moaned to himself.

One of the ragged strips chose that moment to tear off from its loose moorings, falling down towards their small boat. With a sudden plop it hit the edge of their wooden boat, catching the tip of the prow in a sizzle of green foam as it ate through the enchanted wood, turning it in turn into even more of the strange green growth. When it hit the boat, part of the green foam splashed onto Bronto's right arm, eating straight into the exposed flesh it found, foaming and sizzling as it also turned the flesh into more of itself.

Grimacing in brief pain, Bronto quickly took out a knife and scraped the green stuff off from his arm. The green growth tried to ooze up the knife as Bronto threw the blade across the cavern.

"Uh oh," Lindel said, "*now* I know what type it is."

Quick as thought, Sindar's mind reached out and yanked the growth off of the boat, throwing it far off into the water. Then, with the fires of his mind did he cauterize the green stain upon their boat, being careful to only burn through that which was no longer wood. Then, just a quickly, he turned the fires of his mind onto Bronto's arm, cauterizing any of the green growth that was left there, the big man grimacing as he tensed the arm against the brief moment of pain.

"What *is* that stuff?" Candol asked.

"It's a form of moss or slime," Lindel answered quickly, "it'll eat through anything organic."

"I can testify to that," Bronto agreed as he rubbed his arm.

"Considering how much of that ceiling overhead is coated with it," Lindel continued, "we may want to put on a bit of speed."

"I agree with the elf," came Quickfoot's nervous voice, as he suddenly pointed. "Look!"

It was then that they noticed something else about this particular stretch of water on which they sailed. Floating upon its surface, in scattered green clumps, was more of the strange green moss. All around them the moss floated, coming slowly towards them with the lapping of the waves.

"This looks bad," Eldar said.

"Schanter like!"

The small green one had dipped his hand into the water, producing a handful of the oozing green stuff. It dripped out from between his fingers but did him no harm. He reached out with a long warty tongue, licking up the oozing green mass from off his hand.

"I think I'm going to be sick," Quickfoot groaned, as he watched Schanter's display.

"It figures he'd be immune to the stuff," Eldar sighed. "It probably doesn't like how he tastes."

"Fire kills it," Lindel offered, "but the amount of fire it would take to kill off this much of it would also kill our boat."

Another green mass plopped down into the water near their boat.

"Suggestions?" Sabu asked around.

Plop.

"Just one," Sindar answered. "Air is for flight."

Sindar thrust out his palm, the swirling light blue of his Hevon Gem of Air showing forth. Their boat then picked itself up out of the water, hovering a foot above the surface of the water.

"Hold on," Sindar said.

With a crack of thunder, their small boat roared out of the cavern. Down under the long green ceiling they flew, Quickfoot holding onto the priest once again, strips of green peeling down from the ceiling in the wake of their sudden passage. They rounded a watery bend in the cavern as the wave of green surged beneath them, then turned into the new passage ahead of them, flying fast enough for the boom of their flight to reverberate throughout the caverns.

A sudden shape loomed into view ahead of them. The gaping mouths of a large twin-headed snake, looming high up out of the water, a mass of tentacles coming up out of the water in front of it, dozens of feet long. Long tongues hissed greeting as hungry eyes looked down at the prey speeding straight towards them, as it blocked their only way through.

"Hydraswit!" Lindel shouted out, pointing.

"We don't have *time* for this now," Sindar said, pointing his free hand out towards it.

There was a sudden loud 'squeak' and a 'pop' and the large hydraswit was suddenly reduced to the size of a clenched fist, hanging momentarily in the air before it plopped down into the water. They sped on past the puzzled creature and into clear water.

"I think we're clear of it," Sabu said, as he looked up at the ceiling for any traces of the dripping green carpet. "You can put us back down into the water now."

At a gesture from Sindar, their boat lowered down onto the water, their speed reducing substantially. They floated along the currents, the boat once again leading them onward.

"Hey," Eldar suggested, "do you suppose we can make money for this ride. I know people that would *pay* to go through some of what we just did."

"Bad idea," Lindel said, "it would never catch on."

"Pity," Eldar responded.

"I think we have other things to worry about just now," Kilgar said, pointing on ahead of them.

Ahead of them, the water started to slope downward at a steep angle. Their boat was heading into its current, being drawn down as the cavern that it sluiced into seemed to slope at a gradual downward spiral.

"It looks like we're going down to a lower set of caverns," Sabu said thoughtfully as their boat picked up speed from the current. "A second series of caverns right beneath the first; most interesting. To be almost totally separated from each other but for through a few select egresses, the geology of their formation would have to be——"

"Sabu!"

Sabu jumped with a start at the unexpected shout of Eldar's voice directly in his ear. He looked around to see everyone holding on to the sides of the boat, the water ahead of them now running downward in a wide but rapid spiral, as if down through the drain of a giant bucket. Cavern walls rose on either side, channeling the water into its deadly curving passage.

"Oh. Yes," Sabu said, grabbing onto the boat himself as he was brought back to reality, "another time then."

Down into the bowels of the watery deep they went, down deeper beneath the ground. The water spiraled round and round, deeper and deeper, faster and faster, everyone now holding on for their lives to the small boat. To make matters worse, the sides of the spiraling cavern now bristled with a scattered array of spiky formations of rock; one little brush with just one of these deadly spikes at this speed would splinter their boat and tear half of its inhabitants in two. Watery grave before them, rocky death around them as they tumbled about and down, Sheil-Bor(h) used his magic to straighten their course as best he could.

Quickfoot looked up to see a particularly large spike coming straight for them, the boat on a collision course for death. He covered his eyes in fright and waited for the painful end.

When it didn't come, he dared a peek up. Sheil-Bor(h)'s magic had steered them clear of it at the last moment, as he now concentrated on the next approaching projection of rock.

They careened down about the treacherous water-slide, Sheil-Bor(h) trying his best to steer them safely around, sometimes their small boat only narrowly missing a brush with death. They spun down faster and faster.

With a roar, they finally shot out onto open level waters once again, skidding along the surface like a stone. When they had slowed down to their normal steady pace once again, they looked around at their surroundings.

"It looks kind of like the previous caverns," Sindar noted.

"With one exception," Mauklo voiced. "I can now feel the presence of Beltor's minions down here."

"I thought they got *rid* of all of his undead army," Candol said, turning towards Mauklo, "or is there something you haven't been telling us."

"I think you ought to narrow that question down a bit," Eldar smiled, "like to *which* of the several things he hasn't been telling us about."

"My dear compatriots," Mauklo smiled with just a trace of venom, "any *suspicions* that I may have are still not proven to my own satisfaction and hence will not be voiced until then."

A distant ghostly howl interrupted the exchange, echoing throughout the caverns so that the direction of its source could not be told. A lonely cry echoing over the dark waters.

"Sounds like one of your friends," Eldar said over to Mauklo.

"We can discuss this later," Sheil-Bor(h) pointed out, as their boat floated onward. "That is, if we want to survive to have the discussion."

"He's right," Bronto said. "Candol, there's something you should handle up ahead."

Floating out from the watery gloom rose seaweed-covered ghosts; spirits with the look of long-dead vagueness about their green glow. Rising up by the score from the murky depths, their long lonely song spoke of a different sort of ghost than those faithful that had haunted the palace of Thir-Tÿorca, now far above them. They rose up to block the boat's path.

"Stragglers from Beltor's old army perhaps," Candol said, bringing up the sigil of Indra from around his neck.

"Hey, get back."

A glance back showed a slimy moss-covered form, humanoid of appearance but the light of life having long since left its dead eyes. It was trying to climb up into the boat, long green claws reaching out for young tender flesh, for Kilgar. The boy was stabbing at it with his knife, taking deep gouges out from where its heart should be, but to no avail.

You can't kill something that's already dead.

"Candol," Eldar said quickly, "I can sense many more where these came from. Almost like this place could be the *source* of all the undead in this valley."

"Hmm," Candol said, fingering his sigil.

While Lindel joined in with stabbing at the creature coming at Kilgar, and Sabu used the brightness of his light to try and keep the ghosts at bay, Candol reached into a pocket and took out a small coin. Flipping it up in the air, then catching it, he turned it over onto the back of his hand and looked at it.

"Heads it is," he said, and then raised up his voice, loud enough for all to hear. "May this boat be blessed by the power of Indra, free to sail its cargo through the seas of death!"

There was an inhuman scream as the creature clawing towards Kilgar was sent flying out into the air to land several dozen feet away in the water. A dim glow seemed to encompass their small boat and its occupants. Dim but apparently bright enough, for the ghosts ahead of them started to part way for them, floating aside as the boat came on through them. Expressions of fright covered their vague faces as they lined themselves on either side of the boat, more and more coming up from the watery depths to form ghostly walls on either side. Like an honor guard of death, they quietly watched as the small boat sailed on by. Watching and waiting. A mix of eagerness and fright on their ghostly faces.

"There's gotta be hundreds of them," Sabu observed. "Eldar, I think you're right."

"But, why all in this one specific place," Shong asked, "in all these twisted watery caverns?"

"I think we have our answer," Bronto nodded.

Ahead of them was a solid bank of fog. Fog so thick it looked like an impenetrable wall. Their boat, still following its own course, sailed straight into the fog.

Moments seemed like long rels, each foot a mile. The fog swirled in around them, so thick they couldn't even see their own hands, so stifling they couldn't even *feel* their own hands. Worse than fumbling around in the darkness, this glowing white fog, for at least in darkness you could still feel when you stumbled against something. Not so in this fog. All sound was stifled, deadened by the fog. Quickfoot tried to scream, to at least hear his own voice, but no sound could he hear coming out of his mouth. A deprivation so complete that one could go insane and not even know it.

Then, like suddenly bursting through a bubble, they were clear of the fog, sound suddenly washing in around them like a heavy force. Several hands grabbed at their ears, so akin to a deafening roar was the sound that pounded in around them, so sudden the sensation of feeling once again.

Gradually, they lifted their hands from around their ears, as they began to realize that the deafening sound was nothing but the simple quiet lapping of the water about their boat. A flickering red light lit up the large cavern before them as they each shook their heads free of the effects of the strange stifling fog.

"That's not something I want to experience again too soon," Eldar said, feeling the tingle of warmth flowing back into him.

"I don't know," Sindar said thoughtfully, "such total deprivation might be good for meditation; under controlled circumstances, of course."

"That plaque," Bronto said from the front of the small boat, as he looked out in front of them, "it *did* say something about 'let rest the Black One in his *burning* crypt of night'?"

"Yes," Sabu said, looking up. "Why?"

"Then we've found Beltor," Bronto replied, looking straight ahead of them.

He looked at the source of the red flicking light in the cavern. Ahead of them, but thirty feet away, roared a great wall of fire. It danced upon the surface of the waters, its flames not affected by the wetness upon which they fluttered, nor giving any sign of abating. A large round circular wall of fire they formed, around a single island not more than thirty feet across, the island also alight with flames. But big enough was this island for a single cave in its small rocky hill.

Around the cave they could see tall, almost man-like, creatures, their lower bodies being roaring tongues of flame upon which they stood, their red muscular arms holding long sharp glaives, bladed dark-metaled polearms with which they stood their guard.

The flaming water too held its own guardians, at each of the four compass points around the island, standing upon the flaming water. Body like unto a giant snake, with dark green scales and swishing tail, but with the head of a woman, was how they looked. Like true snakes, no arms had they, but a look that promised death did they stare out with as they stood their grim guard, the hot flames leaving them untouched.

"I think you're right," Sabu said, straining for a better look around the others.

"Even in death did they so fear Beltor," Candol said as the boat drifted closer to the flames, "that they would guard him thus."

Everyone was staring at the flaming sight, almost entranced by its hypnotic effects, before the soothing heat snapped Shong out of it.

"Sheil-Bor(h)," he snapped, "your spell. We're still drifting into the fire!"

Sheil-Bor(h) nodded, the boat then drifting to a motionless stop in response. The flames danced high, up towards the rocky ceiling far overhead, reflecting heat in their faces as they floated now not ten feet from its reach, one of the strange woman-faced snakes directly in their path.

"The snakes in front," Sabu pointed out, "are naga; guardian spirits. They will use their magic to prevent us from entering."

"I recognize those on the island," Mauklo added, "they are a sort of fire elemental. The fire they emit is said to be hot enough to turn hardened steel into a liquid puddle upon contact."

"A trap made to keep anybody from entering," Sindar said thoughtfully, "anyone who *doesn't* just happen to conveniently have a Hevon Gem or two to guard their passage through. I am beginning to appreciate your unspoken paranoid suspicions, Mauklo."

"I am glad to know that my presence may *finally* be appreciated," the sileen nodded, "but as to a solution…"

"We go on," Sabu decided, after a brief pause. "I want to see what's at the bottom of everything that we've been lead through; the reason why we're here."

"Once I see what is inside the tomb," Mauklo offered, "I may be able to provide an answer."

"Good," Sabu replied, "and then we'll see if we can turn this whole thing back at the one that's using us."

"We need to get past the naga first," Bronto pointed out. "How do you want us to handle it?"

Before they had time to decide what to do, however, the naga decided for them. A screeching like unto the high-pitched scream of a banshee sang out from the snake-like creature, filling the air with sonic death. The little boat shuddered with the force of the sound, cracking and splitting. They were caught between bailing water out of the boat or covering their ears against the sound. But covering one's ears does no good when you can feel the intensity of the sound down to your bones.

"I think that answers our question!" Shong cried out, as he tried vainly to cover his own ears.

Lindel and Eldar both screamed out in pain, their sensitive elven ears especially affected by the high-pitched attack. Schanter cried out in both pain and pleasure, while Quickfoot just cried. In the midst of the screeching could also be heard the firm female voice of the naga, softly but somehow still heard clearly above the sound of its attack.

"Enter not this place of death. Disturb his rest only at your own peril!"

Then the naga wiggled its snake body once and the water around their boat seemed to rise up, swelling up into a wave that threatened to push them back into the strange fog through which they'd come. Their boat rose ten feet up into the air, the sound still permeating through the boat.

"Hold on!" Bronto called out, as they all fought for purchase on their quickly-disintegrating boat. "We're in for a ride!"

The boat shuddered, finally flying apart in an explosion of enchanted wood, just as the water smashed them down like some large watery fist. Quickfoot screamed in sudden fright, Schanter in demented joy of pain, as the entire boat and its occupants were plunged down into the dark watery depths. As the waters calmed down to a smooth peaceful ripple, the naga looked on sternly, satisfied that it had once again done its job.

But before the waters had completely calmed down, the naga saw them start to swirl around. Round and round like a small whirlpool, faster and faster. When the naga looked over at the whirlpool, she saw something rising up out of the center of the whirlpool, standing on the surface of the water as if it were but hard ground. Something that she didn't expect.

The occupants of the boat.

Several watery Hevon Gems glowed about the circle of people, while those without such Gems stayed at the center, supported by the power of their friends. Several stern faces looked back at the naga, returning her stare.

As well, did Quickfoot nervously look down at his feet, standing there on the water, hoping that whatever magic it was that held him there wouldn't give out.

The water swirled around them, forming a large round boat of solid water, held in place only by force of will. The watery boat floated there as they regarded the naga.

"There shall be an end to this," Sabu said sternly, "you shall let us pass."

With a wave of his staff, the circle of fire around the island died down and vanished, revealing four naga spaced around the island's circumference, looking around in puzzlement.

"*You must not pass,*" the naga warned again, "*he must not be freed!*"

The other three naga swam round the small island to join with their sister. Four naga now faced up against them.

"We will pass," Sindar said calmly.

"*Then you shall die.*"

Magic now swirled around the four naga, as a misty magical barrier swirled up around them, expanding to circle around the island. A barrier of force, standing against those that would enter.

"That barrier is proof against both sword and spell," Sheil-Bor(h) observed.

"That's what *they* think," Eldar said, drawing out his sword. "Let's see what that fancy dagger can do."

He walked across the surface of the water, facing up against the misty wall of force, regarding it while he fingered his sword, the same sword with which he had merged both his Evolin Blade and the jeweled dagger found with the crown and staff in the king's chambers through which they'd come. The four naga regarded him, looking him sternly in the eye as they enforced their magical barrier.

Eldar swung at the barrier with his sword.

Upon contact there was a flash of fireworks, the barrier trying to maintain its integrity as the naga tried to support it. But Eldar's sword sliced through it easily. In a rapidly expanding explosion of light that quickly encircled the entire small island, the barrier was gone, evaporated like smoke in the wind.

Then, before the naga had time to react, thick metal cables lashed out from Sindar, encircling them, drawing them tightly against one another as their snake bodies tried to wiggle free. But the young wizard had tied his knot too tight. With a gesture from Sindar, the squirming bundle lifted up into the air, flew across the cavern, and on into the thick fog that surrounded the entire area around the island. They screamed out their cries of warning until the strange fog cut them abruptly off.

The watery boat floated gently towards the burning shore, Eldar walking on across the surface of the water ahead of them.

"What about them," Lindel pointed towards those guarding the cave as he was notching his bow. "And there's still fire on the island."

Eldar looked around at the fire covering the small rock of an island, and on towards the four creatures guarding entrance to the cave. He sliced through the air once with his sword. Immediately the eternal fire on the island vanished.

"Those creatures are conjured," Mauklo smiled, "leave them to me."

As the others got off their watery boat, its watery form disappearing back down into the depths from which it was formed, Mauklo walked calmly across the island, straight towards the creatures and their sharply pointed glaives, muttering arcane syllables under his breath. The creatures pointed their weapons at him, making ready to fight, while Mauklo held up his right hand as if in greeting.

The creatures never had a chance to fight. A swirling blackness came spinning out from Mauklo's upraised hand, encompassing all four creatures in a spinning vortex. It spun quickly about them till none could be seen, and then vanished, leaving no trace of the four creatures behind.

Mauklo's left hand, hidden by his dark robes as he faced his back to the others, held a bottle which he was now discretely stoppering. Inside the bottle were four creatures, their bodies each ending in a tongue of flame, each holding a small metal glaive that they tried to beat against their glass prison with. Mauklo tucked it quickly into the many folds of his robe as the others came up from behind him.

"That took care of them," Sabu said as he walked towards the cave, "now let's see about this burial chamber."

They walked the short distance towards the cave. The cave appeared rather nondescript, just a normal hole in the side of the small hill of a tiny island. Weapons drawn, spells ready, they walked down into the darkness. As they entered, Sabu doused the light on his staff, reducing it to minimal torchlight. Bronto in the lead, they followed the cave's downward path, going even deeper into the bowels of the earth.

Their shadows curled along the walls, dancing around rocky projections, floating along the ceiling, and bobbing along in response to the light from Sabu's staff. The cave went down, steep and curved. A long while they traveled, tons of rock and earth now above their heads.

Nary a noise did this cave make, not a creak of settling earth, nor the squeak of some passing rodent. But it wasn't an unnatural silence; the footsteps of those that now traveled down its course could be clearly heard echoing along the walls, the breathing of those that walked a faint echo. No, this silence was natural, but it was almost as if nothing *wanted* to make a sound in this deep cave. The very ground even lending silence to a place that it didn't want a part of, a place better left alone. If silence be death, then this place was long dead.

It was not physical exertion then that played at their limbs as they walked down hundreds of feet, but the psychological that played at their souls; the oppressiveness that weighed down upon them like the untold tons of ground above their heads. Ready for an instant's reaction, adrenaline keeping them tense and aware of every little sound, every little rock. Thus they walked for an endless eternity. Muscles threatening to tire just from the effort of maintaining such readiness for so long, yet with no relief of a real threat.

It was after such a long downward trek that they finally came to the gate.

"It's about time," Quickfoot complained, relief in his voice. "I think I'd rather get it over with than take that long trek again."

"More fearful than a danger, can be its expectation," Sheil-Bor(h) agreed.

"Not to mention, the *teya'* of this place *is* rather oppressive," Candol added.

"How far down are we?" Eldar asked.

"A thousand feet straight down beneath the island," Sindar answered.

"Boy," Lindel commented, "they really wanted this guy buried deep."

"So, what about this gate?" Bronto asked.

The gate was just seven feet tall and but five feet wide, a single iron door sealed with no lock, no handle. Runes covered its edge, magic the only seal it would need. Sabu and Sindar walked up to it and studied the runes, quickly looking up and down the gate at the magical writings that covered it.

"Hmm," Sindar said thoughtfully, "potent magic. Forcing it open won't do any good."

"Maybe there's a key?" Kilgar offered.

"No child," Candol answered patronizingly, "I'm afraid that it doesn't work that way. There's not even a keyhole, nor handle to open it with. This involves matters that—"

"Oh, but the child is right," Mauklo corrected, "there *is* a key."

All heads turned to the wizard, Mauklo just standing there, calm as ever, pleasantness about his face. Expectant faces waited in the sudden silence.

"Well?" Eldar finally asked.

"It is so very simple," Mauklo continued. "Shong was correct in questioning why Krey just didn't take a shortcut down here and get to Beltor long ago, thus avoiding the palace altogether. Unless, of course, there was something *in* the palace that was needed to open up this gate. Something he couldn't get to."

"Like a key?" Candol asked.

"Like *three* keys," Mauklo corrected the priest once again.

"Of course," Sabu snapped his fingers in sudden realization. "The staff, dagger, and crown that we found. Obviously used by the king as his crown jewels, they also have their own powerful magic. Magic powerful enough to have been used to finally seal this gate with. They would be the key to opening it up."

"And they're *part* of us now," Eldar continued, "but what if it only works if a king uses them?"

"As you said," Sindar replied, "we *are* those items now; they are within us."

"Then, let the crown jewels choose the new king of Thïr Tÿorca," Sheil-Bor(h) suggested.

"That works for me," Eldar said, as he stepped over beside Bronto.

Sabu then stepped over to Bronto's other side, Sindar behind him. Each of the three placed a hand on the big man's shoulder, concentrating some of their energy through the warrior.

"Consider yourself crowned," Eldar said, "now just try knocking."

Bronto placed both hands upon the sealed gate, palms flat. He then raised up his eyes to the gate, as if looking someone in the face.

"In the name of Thïr Tÿorca, I command thee," he intoned. "Be open!"

His voice rang through the cavern like thunder, echoing along its long length. It was then that some noticed that it was not Bronto's voice that thundered, but the gate itself. Slowly, the gate that had been sealed for five thousand rels began to slide open. With a slow grind of iron against stone, it slid sideways into the surrounding wall. Long moments passed while it opened, but finally there was nothing in front of them but an open darkness.

"I would say that worked," Eldar said, as each of the three took their hands off of Bronto. "Who's first?"

"I think we could do with a little more light," Bronto said as he stepped in.

At a flick of Sabu's fingers, a ball of light went streaking out into the darkness beyond. With a flash, the darkness was suddenly dispelled, revealing what lay beneath it.

They walked into a single room, not fifty feet across. The walls were filled with hieroglyphics and pictures; colored drawings depicting scenes of battle, conquest, and betrayal. The ceiling overhead was inlaid with a golden sunburst, a single round dark spot as its center. The dust of millennia lay about the floor, Bronto's being the first footsteps to mar its smooth coating. At the opposite end of the room was another gate, silver of face but inlaid with a golden starburst. A single statue stood in front of the other gate, as if on guard.

The statue looked like a gargoyle, but with four arms, large black wings folded to its sides, and two long black horns growing out of its forehead. Long thick claws sprang from hands and feet, a thick tail ending in a needle-like sword coiled around behind it. It was all black, with a hideousness that no normal carver of rock could possibly induce into stone. A sense of evil pervaded the lifelike carving.

"That statue gives me the creeps," Quickfoot shuddered as he backed over against a wall.

"The guardian of the tomb," Mauklo explained, "a powerful daemon held prisoner to guard this place."

"You mean, that statue's going to come to life?" Lindel asked, notching his bow ready.

"Well,..." Mauklo started.

A ripping of stone sounded, as the statue started to move, to stretch its stone-like muscles and lift its dark gaze out at the intruders.

"...yes," Mauklo finished.

302

The beast breathed in a large gulp of air, ready to give out its cry of challenge.

Instead, it screamed in pain. A golden arrow lay buried deep in its left eye socket, slender shaft sticking straight out.

"Finally!" Lindel exclaimed, as he reached for another arrow. "Something not immune to my arrows!"

The creature ripped the offending arrow out of its now-dead eye, tossing the shaft aside, as it reached back a large claw to grab at the nearest intruder.

But the claw the arm was attached to promptly fell to the ground, severed and bleeding black blood. It reached out with another claw, only to have that one also sliced off.

Bronto stood to one side of it, the Dragon Sword drawn, while Shong stood by its other side, diamond blade in hand. The daemon had just enough time to roar out its anger before two more swiftly-placed cuts sliced through it.

The daemon's body collapsed as its severed head rolled along the floor. A smell of sulphur began to pervade the room as the body slowly began to disintegrate.

"Enough playing," Bronto said as he stepped over the body, "get this other gate open."

A beam of light lanced out, hitting the gate as if with a great force. The gate exploded inward, its shrapnel flying into a large room beyond. Bronto looked back to see Eldar, Sabu, and Sindar, linking hands, Sabu's staff pointed towards the gate. As they released their grips on each other, and Sabu lowered his staff, Bronto entered the tomb, Shong close behind him.

And indeed, this was the tomb. Dark and foreboding it was, even with the benefit of Sabu's staff. Their footsteps echoed lonely on the smooth black stone as they entered. Two hundred feet long and a hundred feet to either side of their gate, its ceiling rose up into the unseen darkness. As they looked around in the dimmed light, they could see the walls lining either side: coffins, each standing on end, shoulder to shoulder, their dark wooden cases forming twinned walls of death. The far end of the tomb held a wall as black as night, blending in with the blackness that seemed to pervade the very air itself. Shoulder-high pedestals lined that opposite wall, as well as the wall through which their own gate had come, each of these pedestals holding upon it a small round globe of blackness, a dark void almost seeming to hang there rather than to rest on the pedestal.

Tall marble pillars glistened in the soft light, four marble behemoths spaced around that which lay at the center of the great room. Carved serpents curled around the pillars, winding on up its length in an eternal embrace. As they walked across the wide room, they could see what lay between the pillars.

A large platform, raised up high above the floor on a rectangle of black stone steps, its flat top towering twenty-five feet up. Its base fifty feet long and over half that wide, each corner held a tall ceramic pillar capped by a round golden ball. At the top of this platform rested a long oblong box. But not made of wood was this box, but a crypt of obsidian, blacker than night, dull yellow runes covering its lid. The ceramic pillars seemed to gleam with an inner light all their own.

"Now *this* is what I call a tomb!" Eldar exclaimed as they looked around the vast cavern-like room. "But what's with all those other coffins?"

"Not to mention all those other globes along the walls," Sabu added. "Definitely interesting."

"Uh," Quickfoot said nervously, "Candol, could you give me another shot of that bravery thing? This place feels *real* creepy."

"I think we share the same thoughts," Candol replied, gazing around. "This tomb would have Indra being cautious. Very well."

As Candol placed a hand on Quickfoot's forehead, Shong walked up to one of the ceramic pillars. He lightly tapped the pillar with the tip of his sword, causing sparks to run up and down its length, electricity curling around the golden ball that capped it. He then took a dagger out of his pocket and tossed it between two of the pillars. A quick zap of electrical power went flashing from one pillar to the other, hitting the dagger in a sizzle of ozone. Metal ash crumbled down to the ground, the only remnants of the knife.

"That's what I call protected," Shong said to himself.

"Ooooh, Schanter want sparkly."

As Kilgar tried to keep Schanter from throwing himself against one of the ceramic pillars, Sindar turned to Mauklo.

"Okay," Sindar said, "I believe you said you'd be able to voice your suspicions now. Why does Krey want Beltor."

"Well," Mauklo said, slowly strolling over towards one of the coffins lining the walls, "aside from the fact that whatever lies left of Beltor in that coffin is most likely a powerful undead by now, waiting to be released, just simply observe all that is around you."

Mauklo gestured first towards the coffins, and then towards the black globes floating each on its own pedestal. The others gazed towards where he gestured.

"Coffins for the material," Mauklo continued, "dark globes to the nether reaches for the immaterial. Hundreds of coffins and a dozen globes, each not a single chamber but a doorway to many such chambers. Why, just feel the darkness coming from each coffin, each coffin a doorway to many."

He spun around on heel, facing towards the others, gleam in his eyes.

"That which we encountered in the valley are but the barest remnants of Beltor's army of the dead," he said, raising up his voice. "They buried his entire army here! With Beltor himself!"

Mauklo's voice echoed briefly in the darkness as the full implications of what he said sank into the staring faces.

"Krey wants Beltor *and* his army," Sabu stated, "combined with his own armies of the dead and demonic, he would wash over all of Catho, and thence on to Cenivar."

"And he needed the combined efforts of all of us to get the tomb open for him," Sindar added.

"Which means," Eldar finished for them, "that he can now get in here and free Beltor, his armies, the whole bunch."

They looked back at the gate through which they'd come, now open for anyone to come through.

"It's too late to close the gate," Candol said quickly. "By Indra, must we destroy Beltor before he awakens, then dispose of his armies forever."

Explosive concussion, pyrotechnic roar echoing through eternity. Electricity arcing madly about, sending streamers of lightning in fingered greeting. Hand of concussive force slamming all to ground. Footsteps quickly running.

"What the heck was *that?*" Lindel asked, looking around as he started to pick himself up off the ground.

"Over there," Kilgar pointed as he got to his feet.

One of the ceramic pillars was smashed, cleaved in two by a single sharp slice, the wreckage of its form lying smashed on the ground, mad arcs of electricity lashing out from the other two pillars that it used to connect to. Running up the steps towards the black stone coffin, diamond sword in hand, was Shong.

"Shong, what are you doing?" Sabu shouted out.

Shong reach the top, turning quickly around. In the dim light, his eyes flashed out clear for all to see. They held no pupils nor any whites; Shong's eyes were a solid black. The black of deepest night, the black of despair. He paused for but a moment before swinging up his sword, ready to come down on the coffin's lid.

"He'll free Beltor," Eldar shouted, "stop him.

"The throne!" Bronto shouted back, as he ran over towards the platform. "The blackness possessed him."

"It *wasn't* a defensive mechanism," Sabu quickly realized. "As the last king of Thïr Tÿorca, the throne was *Beltor's*. That black light possessed Shong."

Just as Bronto reached the base of the tall platform, Shong's sword came down with a resounding crash, cleaving the lid in two.

A wave of force exploded out from the cracked lid, flinging Bronto and the others back like rag dolls, but leaving Shong standing by the coffin, facing outward, sword at his side, as he stood ready to protect the coffin against any that would approach it. The two pieces of the lid flew off towards opposite ends of the large room, splintering themselves against far walls. A purple light shone up out of the open coffin, a wind soaring swiftly up out of its unseen depths, a wind that carried with it the stench of death and decay. The room rumbled as hundreds of other coffin lids flung themselves open, rocked as a dozen void-like globes pulsed a deeper black, shaking themselves awake. The whole room shook about them, as if a thing awakened from a long sleep.

As Bronto struggled to his feet he looked up at Shong, standing high above him, the dark blackness of someone else's soul behind the gaze of his good friend's eyes. Shong stood at the edge of the coffin, sword held defensively before him, as Bronto saw what rose slowly up out of the stone coffin behind him.

Beltor!

Almost skeletal in form, with bones as black as his heart and tatters of old decayed flesh hanging from his arms, the bulk of his aged flesh was mummified to a tautly-drawn stretch over his bones, and then blackened as if with splotches of dark soot. His hands were almost like talons, his teeth but sharpened points coming out of an almost skinless skull. Stringy brown hair came out in straggled dried lengths going down to bony shoulders. His eyes were sunken black orbs, no color or substance to them at all, yet an almost unseen black radiance coming from them as he gazed out below him. He wore the tattered remnants of an old burial garb, its remaining strips hanging about his thin body. On his fingers he wore several large and almost gaudy rings, while his right hand held a tall staff topped by a skull, its eyes glowing a deep red. A single amulet hung about his neck, small blue-crystal medallion hanging on the end of a simple gold chain. Evil and power seemed to wave off from him like the light from Sabu's staff, fear to radiate from him as a palpable force.

Beltor looked down at them, regarding each in turn, as he stepped out of his coffin. Shong stayed by his side, eyes still filled with blackness as he took his place as Beltor's bodyguard. Bronto looked up at his friend, concern and anger both on his face.

"Shong, fight it!" he shouted out.

But it was useless. Shong was now fully Beltor's, his highly skilled sword arm now at the Black One's disposal. Shong just glanced his black eyes down at Bronto, sword poised ready to fight and kill his friend should he come near.

Quickfoot just looked on ahead, rigid with fear, unable to move or speak, while Lindel just stood there quivering, the elf unable to take his eyes off Beltor's horrible visage. Even the brave young Kilgar had collapsed to the ground, a huddled mass of fear, unable to even reach for the dagger that he'd dropped on the ground just by his feet. Candol swallowed hard as he grabbed onto his priestly sigil, while Eldar tightened his grip on his sword. Schanter just stood in place, fear quivering through his entire demented body. Even Sabu was nervous at just the very sight of Beltor.

"I'm not sure if we're up to this," Sindar said doubtfully.

Beltor raised up his skull-topped staff, speaking as he did so, his voice coming out as a low crackly rumble. If they thought just the sight of him was enough to put fear in a brave heart, then his voice was even worse. Quickfoot went catatonic, Candol's spell of bravery not withstanding.

"I am free once more," Beltor said, *"free to unleash my power upon the land. And this time, I shall not fail; I am eternal!"*

He looked down at those arrayed below him, regarding them as one would mere lesser forms of life.

"You will join my minions," Beltor said, stating it as a predetermined fact and not as a request or choice.

Beltor then spread out his arms, skull-staff held high, as his voice rang out. *"Be free my armies; come to me, your lord and master!"*

The hundreds of open coffins then quivered and shook, the dozen black globes to pulse brightly. A rumbling shook the room, a rumbling that turned into the march of many hundreds of feet, a rumbling that had the sound of an army marching.

Out of each of the coffins stepped a skeleton, but not just a single one for each coffin. As the first one stepped out, another one followed behind it, then another behind that. An endless stream of skeletons marching out of each coffin, an impossible number to fit inside of them. As Eldar looked around, he saw several of the coffins also emitting other types of undead. Ghouls crawled out, slavering and gnashing their rotten teeth; large pale humanoids, muscles the size of the strongest man, fangs dripping hate; zombies, their dead rotting eyes staring out as they mindlessly obey the summons of their master; rotting corpses with a coldness of soul about them unmatched by the frozen wastes of the Northern Wastelands. An endless array of walking dead.

The black globes were also quite busy. The high-pitched howl of death emanated from them as a river of spirits streamed out of them. Ghosts, wraiths, spectres, large shadowy forms that could sap one's soul, silvery filaments of light that could rob your mind of thought, all endlessly pouring out in long streams of death straight towards their lord Beltor, swirling around him in protective circles of moaning and screaming apparitions. The large room filled with the screams of the immaterial and the marching of the material.

Fear clamped down on everyone like a heavy hand, surrounded as they were by hordes like they'd never seen before. The room was filling with hundreds upon hundreds of undead, and still they came.

"This does *not* look good," Eldar understated.

"Shong," Sindar said, "we must free Shong; he is the closest to Beltor. I can use my mind to——"

Sindar stopped, grabbing his head in his hands, gritting his teeth as if against a large headache.

"Not now!" he screamed. "The visions return; Miro invites!"

Inviting mental fingers swirled around in Sindar's mind, as visions of colorful enticement swam before his eyes.

"*Really* bad timing," Eldar said as he went to Sindar's side.

"Or planned," Sheil-Bor(h) suggested.

"I'll take care of him," Eldar said to Sabu, "you take care of those undead; its beginning to smell in here."

"Right," Sabu answered, as he turned and pointed his staff towards Beltor.

"*You would dare!*"

Beltor pointed his own staff, his eyes glowing brighter as a red spray of light flashed out. The effect was immediate: strength was sapped from limb and bone, energy evaporated out of their bodies. The paralyzed Lindel collapsed to the ground, Eldar quickly getting too weak to hold up Sindar as the latter found it harder to fight his battle of the mind with his body suddenly giving out. Even Mauklo cringed in pain and weakness as he strove to not sink down to his knees. Sheil-Bor(h) trembled with weakness as the undead marched in around them.

Four ghouls piled in on the curled up form of Kilgar, still reaching for his knife. Sabu watched helplessly, fighting his own weakness as the ghouls hid the boy from sight, gnashing down with their teeth, a fresh meal at their mercy as they dragged him into the horde around them. More ghouls crowded around Quickfoot and Lindel, taking the helpless forms from sight as still others tackled the fear-ridden form of Schanter.

Unfortunately, fear seemed to have a somewhat different effect on the insane one.

Schanter burst out from the pile of ghouls around him, spitting out a severed ghoul-hand in the process. He then jumped up on top of the head of a nearby zombie and started running and leaping across the heads of the more material undead, making a straight line for Beltor.

A dozen spirits swooped in on Bronto, sapping his strength, weakening his resolve. The big man tried to get up to his knees, failed, and then tried again. He looked up at Shong, still guarding Beltor, and then slowly struggled to his feet.

"This must not happen," he said weakly, as wraiths tried to suck out his very soul.

He looked at the remaining pillars, electricity still sparking off around them, then stepped onto the first step of the large rectangular platform. He looked over at how the others were doing, but couldn't see much with so many undead in the way. He thought he saw Sabu tumble to the ground, ghouls piling in on top of him, but he couldn't be sure. He looked back up the platform and took another step up.

Schanter came running along the tops of the undead as if he were skipping along from stone to stone across a river. Beltor looked over at the quickly approaching figure.

"A minor nuisance," he said, pointing his free hand at Schanter.

Streamers of black light went shooting out from Beltor's hand. Like a dozen lances of light, they cut through Schanter, slicing through him in several places. One moment Schanter was leaping across another ghoul's head, the next was he a collection of loose body parts, several arms and legs falling down, three halves of his torso, a hand, his head cleaved at the neck, all neatly cauterized by the dark light, scattering in amongst the ghouls as they fell to the ground.

Bronto took another step up the platform. Electricity from one of the pillars now arced over him from one of the ceramic pillars, hitting him full in the back. He fell to his knees, grimacing with pain and weakness, another wraith flying through him. He struggled harder as he got to his feet once more.

Eldar and Sindar were buried under a pile of ghouls, Eldar too weak to move, Sindar still engaged in his mental combat, as the ghouls clawed and scraped at their bodies. The world was a blur of decaying flesh and clawed hands as Eldar began to loose consciousness.

Sheil-Bor(h) tried to weave a protective spell about himself, but the effects of Beltor's staff was making it almost impossible for him to concentrate. Two spectres came wailing at him, their cry trying to draw the strength from his limbs. He inhaled in deeply as he summoned all the power of his mind, all the strength of his meditation. He closed off the world around him, ignoring the death and pain of his friends, ignoring his own pain as the spectre came at him with its cold touch of death.

Mauklo felt his knees buckling as a multitude of spirits swarmed in around him. A dozen wraiths, ghosts, and spectres diving in for his soul, angry malevolence in their vague faces as if they would take revenge on the Sileen wizard for his acts against their kind. They buffeted him, sapping more and more of his strength, as Mauklo raised up a hand to try and cast a spell.

Beltor looked down at his gathering armies, looked on as they piled in on the would-be heroes, slowly shaking his skeletal head as Shong stood guard beside him.

"So much for the riffraff," Beltor's voice echoed quietly, *"now to plan my conquest."*

Several of the ghouls walked up the steps towards Beltor, stopping halfway up. They carried with them several bodies, dumping their still forms onto the steps. Bronto looked on as he saw the limp and torn form of Kilgar dropped down like a sack of wet flour, watched as Quickfoot was lumped beside him, his small face frozen in a permanent grimace of fright. He watched too as they dumped the torn and unmoving form of Lindel, golden bow still gripped tightly in his hand. Beltor looked down at the bodies more than a dozen feet below him.

"Ah," Bronto heard Beltor's voice echo, *"the first new additions to my army. Arise and serve your master."*

He pointed his skull-staff in the direction of the unmoving forms, its eyes glowing brighter once again as it caressed its red light over the bodies. Kilgar's body was the first to quiver. Bronto mustered his remaining strength to take another step up as he watched the boy slowly start to stand up. Kilgar's complexion was pale with death, his eyes fixed trance-like at a point that no one could see as he stood up. Like a puppet he slowly faced up to Beltor, his skin beginning to turn a pale ghoulish green. His arms hung loosely by his sides as small claws started to sprout out from his fingernails, fangs to grow from his mouth, his eyes becoming cat-like slits.

"No!" Bronto said weakly. "Not the boy. This cannot happen!"

Taking an deep breath and concentrating as hard as he could, Bronto summoned up all of his remaining strength. Adrenaline surged up through his body as anger swelled within him. Anger at the plight of his friends, anger at Beltor, anger at the sight of young Kilgar becoming another one of Beltor's undead minions. An explosion of will burst out from Bronto as something snapped within him.

Beltor looked down as Quickfoot and Lindel also started to quiver on the ground in transformation. He was most pleased; he was free and there was no one to stop him.

Explosion; mighty cracking and shattering. Ceramic, stone, and metal grinding and ripping, tearing loose from longtime foundations, electricity arcing madly. Wild power shorn from its moorings as a cry rings loudly above the endless march of undead. Cry of despair, cry of anger.

Beltor turned to see one of the ceramic pillars torn completely off its base, electrical fingers arcing madly about it, as but one man held it up in his hands. One very *angry* man.

It is said that Bronto's battle cry was heard all the way up to the faraway surface, causing even the birds in the trees to run for cover. True or not, his anger was heard loud and clear within the cavern, as he heaved back the large ceramic pillar and tossed it high overhead, putting the last remainder of his great strength into its throw.

As the pillar was tumbling through the air, Beltor turning his staff towards it, something else happened.

Flash of light, peel of thunder. Bang of creation turning ghouls to grey dust, zombies to decayed piles of old rotting flesh. Inhuman screams, flying spirits blown to tattered bits upon the wind. Expanding globe of life, undead falling to its holy touch.

"INDRA IS WITH ME, I SHALL NOT FEAR!"

Candol, robes tattered and torn, several fresh claw marks over his face and arms, was standing straight up, left hand around his sigil, right hand in front of him. A globe of white light was emanating from around him, as he walked slowly forward. The undead started to back off at his approach as they realized its deadly touch to their kind. Beltor turned his head towards the priest as the pillar arced down towards him.

At the same time as Bronto's cry rang out, Sindar was fighting his own battle; and loosing. Weak was he physically, his battle against the invitations of Miro were gaining ground, making their way into his soul, starting to win him over. Even Eldar's added strength wasn't enough, as the elf too was weak from Beltor's attack.

But then came Bronto's anger. Sindar felt it as a physical force, as only a psychic can. He felt the strength of its anger, the resolve of its will. He felt it as a source of power on which he might draw.

"Bronto," he said quietly to himself, as a ghoul tried to tear at his face, "I need your strength."

As Bronto threw the ceramic pillar, Sindar used the power of his mind to tap into the tremendous well of psychic power that was the big man's great anger. Tapped it, and turned it out against his own private enemy.

The pillar came down as Beltor pointed out a hand towards the priest. Shong, blackness still in his eyes, leaped in front of Beltor and swung at the pillar, his blade of diamond arcing smoothly through it.

The room shook with the explosion, the force flinging Shong back across the room as the pieces of the ceramic pillar fell in a scatter around Beltor. Shong landed down hard in the midst of some skeletons, shattering them into piles of bones with the force of his landing.

"You will die, priest!"

A cone of dark light shot out from Beltor's pointed hand, hitting Candol's own globe of bright light. The two fought each other, the pyrotechnic flames of their battle showering throughout the room. Candol's faith in his god was great, his resolve firm, but Beltor was powerful. Slowly the bright light began to give way to the dark as Candol weakened.

Wind of spirit, wind of soul. Swirling maelstrom of night, sucking spirits into its deadly void, spinning around faster and faster.

Mauklo, weak and almost to his knees, was now surrounded by a whirlwind of night. A whirlwind that gathered in the spirits and spectres upon itself, destroying them and adding their essence to the strength of the protective wind.

"I am really sick of these indignities," he said, gathering his strength in the brief period of rest that his spell now afforded him.

A ghost came flying in upon the meditating form of Sheil-Bor(h) as he stood there, eyes closed, relaxed concentration upon his face. The ghost, seeing an easy prey, raced in upon the helpless victim.

And was immediately surprised when a hand lashed out and grabbed it by its ghostly throat. Surprise registered on the ghost's face as Sheil-Bor(h) opened up his eyes; surprise that a material mortal could grasp onto an immaterial spirit. It struggled helplessly as Sheil-Bor(h) looked steadily into its vague face.

"One should never underestimate one's opponents," Sheil-Bor(h) said calmly, "as one may just happen to have a new spell that he has been waiting to try."

Sheil-Bor(h) flung the ghost back over his head, then put himself into a ready battle-stance. He faced towards the spectres that surrounded him, hands ready as he stood in a martial arts stance.

"Now let us how well do you battle," he said calmly.

The last thing the spectres ever saw was something that rarely crossed the ever-calm visage of Sheil-Bor(h).

He smiled, ever so slightly.

Sabu slowly got to his feet, brushing off the dried ghoul-parts that Candol's passage had left. He looked quickly around, seeing Beltor waving his staff about, seeing ever more of the undead pour out from the coffins and black globes, and finally seeing young Kilgar turning into a ghoul, now almost completely transformed.

"Too much to handle," he muttered to himself. "Those portals have to be destroyed to stop the undead, but Kilgar and the others are in trouble. And then there's Beltor; if he's a lich, then I've got to remember what I know of them."

He looked around at the swiftly moving events.

"Eldar's right; I *do* loose track of reality," he finally decided, as he raised up his staff.

Fire, hot as a small star, streaked out from Sabu's staff, straight towards the large platform on which Beltor stood. A burning deluge, it engulfed the entire top of it, sending flames out in an explosion that threatened to shake the entire crypt. Flames engulfed the platform, racing down its length.

Down towards Kilgar and the others.

"LET THE SPIRIT OF INDRA PROTECT YOU ALL!"

Candol's globe of light reached out towards where the priest pointed, reaching around those on the steps. Kilgar, now almost completely a ghoul, screamed out in pain as the light hit him, smoke exploding off of his green skin as he collapsed to the ground. Quickfoot and Lindel, quivering on the ground as they too started to turn green, also screamed out briefly as the light encompassed the three.

The green tinge already fading from his skin, Lindel's eyes suddenly flickered open, gleaming now with the light of life. Still on the ground, he looked around him to see the still form of Quickfoot and the shivering form of Kilgar as his green flesh burned and smoked. Then he looked up.

And saw a ball of white-hot fire coming straight at him.

"I hope this doesn't hurt much," he said weakly.

The fire encompassed the entire platform, turning it into a raging inferno. Large electrical explosions also rang the room as the fire overcame the two remaining ceramic pillars, turning them into broken and burned bits of scorched pottery. Fire flamed as electricity arced wildly over the platform.

The flames parted in the middle, revealing a single figure still standing there, holding onto his skull-staff.

Beltor.

"No mere ball of fire can destroy me, mortal," Beltor said.

"Then I just suppose that we'll have to do better!"

Eldar was standing up in the midst of a pile of charred ghoul bodies, helping

Sindar to his feet as the platform blazed brightly. Sabu walked over to his two friends as Sindar straightened himself up.

"How are you feeling?" Sabu asked quickly.

"Fine," Sindar answered, "Bronto's anger gave me strength."

"Enough for some group effort?" Sabu asked.

"Anything to put ugly up there away for good," Eldar said as he brought up his sword.

They joined together their power, aiming it as a single bolt of magical force straight at Beltor. It ionized its way through the air, hitting the lich directly in the chest.

Beltor just laughed, shrugging the effect off with a wave of his hand, sending the three crashing to the ground, as his undead hordes gathered protectively about him, more and more of the spirits circling around him.

"He's too powerful," Sabu said as he struggled to his feet, "and there's too many undead guarding him."

"We've got to do *something,*" Sindar said as he stood up.

Several spirits suddenly went flying out past them, but this time fleeing in fright.

Walking up behind them came Sheil-Bor(h), calmness ever about his face.

"If it is strength that you need," he said, as the three stood up, "it may be that there is strength in Hevon, if one but reaches beyond the mere appearance of the Gems."

"Tap into them," Eldar said, "sounds good. Come on then."

Sheil-Bor(h) joined in with them as they concentrated their efforts once again. Meanwhile, the flames covered the platform, raging out as they covered Candol and the three on the step from view. Mauklo, flickering vortex of spirits still swirling around him, was finally recovering his strength as he looked with cunning eyes at the situation about him.

"First things first," he said, finally abandoning any attempts at getting his torn robe straightened.

He looked around, his eyes resting briefly on the roaring fire, and then over towards the coffins with their endless rows of undead coming out of them.

"Yes," he smiled, "that fire will do rather nicely."

He raised up his hands, concentrating as a flaming red Hevon Gem shone forth on his palm. He concentrated on what he desired, adding the magic of his own spells to the power of the Hevon Gem.

Roaring pillar of fire, turning black stone steps to runny liquid. Swirling wind, unseen hands guiding flames around. Round and around, spinning maelstrom of fire. Circling out, ever faster, ever wider. Ring of fire, ring of expanding death.

Beltor looked around as the fire about the large raised platform suddenly began to spin round. It gathered up, into a circle, until it was all a single large wall of fire encircling the base of the platform, soaring high up towards the distant ceiling.

"This trickery will not hurt me," Beltor's voice rang out, his right hand pointing out his staff, his left holding onto the amulet chained around his bony neck.

As they focused their powers, Sabu's gaze fell upon the flickering image of Beltor between the leap of the flames as he grasped onto his amulet.

"Now I remember the secret behind a lich," Sabu said. "It was mentioned in one of those dimensio-books."

"So," Eldar said quickly, "just don't stand there; tell us!"

The circle of flame now began to expand outwards, spinning out wider and wider as it expanded to fill the room. A widening circle, passing through the ranks of undead.

"LET THE HAND OF INDRA SMITE OUR FOE!"

Candol was standing near the base of the platform, watching the flames come down. Weak though he was, his bright shield of light now completely gone, destroyed by Beltor's dark light, he held onto the sigil around his neck, his faith in Indra summoning up the last of his strength as he added his own special twist to Mauklo's spinning fire before he collapsed to the ground.

The flames suddenly turned purple.

More than just an effect for the vain, the nature of the flames had now changed. As it expanded out through the undead ranks, besides burning through the running forms of the more material of their kind, the wraiths and other deadly spirits found that now they too were affected by the roaring flame. Ghouls and spirits alike went running away from the expanding flames.

"Fools," Beltor said, pointing his staff down at them, *"I shall just make more undead. Starting with you!"*

They could feel the irresistible wave of Beltor's power as he concentrated his rage down upon them, power that fought against their own. Beltor smiled evilly as his own magic sought to conquer their own combined efforts.

The circle of fire gained speed, expanding out, wider and faster, catching up with the fleeing undead as its widening circle raced across the hundreds of feet that was the room's width. Beltor looked at the racing wall as he suddenly realized where it was headed.

"NO!"

His cry carried throughout the room as the flame headed straight for the room's walls. Straight towards where the coffins stood on end and the small black orbs floated upon their pedestals.

"Oh *yes,*" Mauklo smiled pleasantly, "you mummified lout."

The wall of purple flame hit the walls, burying the hundreds of coffins in a wall of flame, engulfing the black globes in spiralling twists of fire. In a single simultaneous crash of sound, the coffins all exploded, wooden bits exploding outwards in splinter-filled fingers of flame, hot translucent tongues wrapping around the undead that were marching through them, licking inwards at the open portals. The portals in the coffins all suddenly gave way to the flaming wall, collapsing as a one.

As well did go the black spheres; one moment untold numbers of spirits and wraiths were streaming out of them, the next moment the strange purple flame was about them. Like a glass bubble bursting, so did the black orbs. Flashes of night exploded upon the flames, destroying forever their access to the darker places of the spirit world.

The walls of the room were now alight with purple flame, roaring their screams of flaming hunger as they ate their way past the burning remnants of the coffins and seemed to sink into the very walls of the room itself. Anger crossed Beltor's face as he watched the flames sink into the walls, leaving not a trace of coffin, black orb, or undead behind.

"For that, you die!"

He singling out the wizard that had started the destructive circle of fire, pointing his staff at Mauklo, its eyes glowing a bright red, the crackle of dark-colored power forming at its tip. The eyes then flashed black as an ebony-colored bolt of power raced out.

Crack! Splintering of wood, sudden shattering of power. Red-eyed skull exploding in black power now unrestrained.

The two halves of Beltor's staff clattered to the ground, broken, useless, and now without power. Beltor turned around to face the one who dared so offend him.

Bronto stood to his side, Dragon Sword raised up in both hands, ready for another blow.

"The next one's for the kid," he said, anger and the look of *yora'zaugh* in his eyes.

Beltor screamed and lunged for Bronto, hands going straight for his throat.

A wash of power interrupted Beltor's charge, as Sabu and the others focused their own wrath upon the lich. Beltor turned as the energy washed off him like water off a furred pelt. He just laughed his dark laugh, and turned back towards Bronto.

"Aim for that amulet!" Sabu shouted. "It's the secret of his kind's power; every lich has a secret place for its soul, and I'm guessing that that's his!"

Bronto dropped his sword as he went for Beltor with his bare hands, large meaty arms reaching out for the bony throat, while Beltor's strong skeletal hands sought the death of the large warrior.

Swift sound of racing wind. Dull thump of impact, metal-tipped courier bringing home it message.

A single dagger was imbedded in Beltor's chest. Of no harm did it to he who was already dead, but of its true target perhaps more might be said. The dagger was long and curved, its small curved handle sticking straight out of Beltor's chest. Under its blade though, lay a severed golden link; the link to a chain about Beltor's neck.

Bronto spared a quick glance at the source of the knife. Off down the steps, Candol, weak though he was, sat with three patients in his care. The youngest amongst them now sat up, weak and still pale, resting against the steps as Candol laid his curative spells over him, his skin now significantly less green, his boyish face looking up at Bronto, hand still raised from the dagger he'd just thrown.

Bronto smiled, a grin of resolve, as both he and Beltor looked down at the chain holding up the amulet as it lay broken about Beltor's neck. The chain slipped from around his neck, the amulet slowly falling to the ground.

Beltor screamed and dived down for the amulet, but Bronto's large fist came racing up for his jaw. The impact sounded like a hammer hitting stone, as Beltor took the blow, staggering back on his feet, facing Bronto. The amulet flew to the ground, rolling along the top of the platform, dragging the chain after it.

Beltor raised up a hand, magic ready at his fingertips, power enough to turn Bronto into a pile of ash. But, as he opened up his mouth to cast the spell, he was interrupted.

A single golden arrow, sent through his mouth, sticking out the back side of his head. Beltor staggered back as he struggled with the arrow, pulling at the deeply imbedded offending shaft while Bronto ran over to the amulet.

"That should shut him up," Lindel said, his wounds already healed by Candol's ministrations.

The amulet rolled to a stop against a particularly large boot. Bronto looked up at Beltor, determination on his face as the lich saw final death now before him.

"And *this*," he said, raising up his foot, "is for the kid!"

His heel came down with a hard resounding crack upon the amulet, the force of his crashing foot instantly reducing it to powder. Beltor cried out with a soul-wrenching scream just as Sabu, Eldar, Sindar, and Sheil-Bor(h) hit him with their full combined power.

Beltor exploded in a white-hot incandescence just as Bronto leapt off the platform, jumping twenty-five feet down as the lich exploded behind him. An explosive scream of death sounded behind the big man as a wave of force reduced the entire top of the large platform to a molten slag of melted rock. The sound of Beltor's final death, that which not even the last of Thïr Tÿorca had accomplished, echoed up through the deep cave and out into the water caverns beyond.

At some place in the strange fog that encircled the island above them, finally struggling free of their bonds, four naga heard the death-knell. They heard it, and were relieved; satisfied that at last Beltor was gone and their duties finished.

The explosion had sent everyone to their knees, hands protectively covering heads as white-hot death screamed out overhead. When the bright glare of light finally cleared, and the echoing sound of destruction at last dissipated, several heads looked cautiously up, ready if need be, but seeing only the bubbling rock that was the large platform's top; lich no more upon its molten surface.

Bronto picked himself up as Sabu came over to him. The large room was quiet now, empty of all sound except the fading resonance of Beltor's death scream.

"Are you okay?" Sabu asked his large friend.

"I'll do," he waved off the question, "how's the kid?"

"I'm fine," came the weak reply from the base of the steps, "but I think I'll have to get that dagger replaced."

Bronto walked over to where Candol now nursed the groaning form of Quickfoot and sat down beside the boy. He put a fatherly arm around the boy, straining to hold back the weakness that strained his every movement.

"Maybe we can get Quickfoot to loan you one; it's not like he has a lack of them... So, how's it feel to almost become a ghoul?" Bronto asked with a smile.

"Not something I would try again," Kilgar replied, "but you should let Candol look at you; you're ready to collapse!"

"Naw, there's others worse off than me."

"You should be looked at," Sindar advised. "I don't know where you got the strength from after you threw that pillar, but you're too weak and tired now. We aren't finished yet, and you'll need your full strength."

"Yes mother," Bronto mocked with a tired smile.

"I'll take care of Bronto," Lindel offered, as he took out a small vial from amongst his tattered robes, "I still have some of that healing water from Fawsil's village."

"Good," Sabu nodded, as Lindel went over and sat next to Bronto, holding the vial up to his lips. "Who else needs help?"

"Shong," Sindar nodded over towards the far end of the room, at a quiet figure lying on the ground, diamond sword still gripped in his hand, "Beltor's control will be broken, but his mind must still be healed."

"Do you think you can help him?" Bronto asked, concern for his friend showing on his face, Lindel's potion slowly returning strength to his body.

"It will take a while," Sindar replied, as he walked over to the still unconscious form of Shong, "but I believe that I can free him of any influence that the throne had over him."

"That will be good," Bronto said with relief, leaning back against the steps. "When we're out of here, I shall have to treat him to a good woman and a tall tankard; teach him never to sit on strange thrones again."

"What about Schanter?" Eldar walked over and asked Candol. "The poor insane creature got sliced to bits."

"Yes," Candol said as he looked up from the now-conscious Quickfoot, "strange creature that."

"Don't tell me he survived?!" Eldar gasped.

"Well, his wounds were cauterized and sealed by Beltor's spell," Candol continued, "and he *does* have some regenerative powers. When I started placing his limbs next to each other in preparation for a spell, they started to heal together, trying to reattach themselves. Slowly, but definitely doing it. It only took a little bit of help from Indra to get him in one piece again."

Candol pointed towards a humanoid form lying quietly by the base of the platform.

"He's over there," Candol said, "all but healed, though I think when he wakes up he'll be Lorel again."

"It may be that such extreme damage takes a lot out of the Schanter side of him," Sindar theorized, as he knelt down beside Shong, "and needs time to rest before it can surface once again."

"Well," Candol put in, "if he hadn't been Schanter that time, he never would have made it."

"We still have some unfinished matters," Mauklo reminded them, strolling over as unperturbed as ever.

"Yes," Sheil-Bor(h) agreed, "Krey awaits us in the valley above."

319

"Yeah," grinned Eldar, "and he isn't going to be too happy about what we did to Beltor and his armies. I don't think they're as *intact* as he wanted to have them."

"We'll have a battle on our hands then," Sabu nodded.

"Battle?!" Quickfoot sputtered, apparently feeling much better. "We barely survived *this* one!"

"Actually," Eldar pointed out, "you *didn't* survive this one."

"Krey must be stopped," Sabu said, "for more reasons than I can count, his being an ally of Miro being not the least among them."

"We must rest first," Lindel stated, "or we *won't* be ready for him."

"Our present abode appears perfect for this prospect," Sheil-Bor(h) offered, "it would be unwise of him to seek us down here."

"Yeah," Eldar agreed, "too much trouble him coming down here, all he has to do is wait for us; he's stopped us from using a spell to just teleport out of here, so he knows we'll *have* to come out sometime."

"Perfect. We'll rest here then," Sabu decided, as he walked over to the base of the platform. "We must be fully alert when we face him."

Sabu sat down at the base of the steps with a heavy tired sigh, using his staff as a brace as he did so. He then looked over at Candol as the priest stood up and stretched himself, his healing work finally finished.

"Hey Candol," Sabu asked innocently, "do you think that Indra can spare us some conjured food? Fighting the hordes of the nether world *really* works up an appetite."

CHAPTER TWENTY-SEVEN

Showdown

"Hey," Shong said apologetically, as they walked across the stone floor, "I'm sorry for whatever I did; I was aware of everything I did, but I just couldn't control myself.

"You *already* apologized enough," Eldar said, "so stop repeating yourself; we know it was Beltor, not you."

"Just don't sit in anymore thrones in the future," Lindel advised with a grin.

They were in the original ante room that they'd come into when first they entered the palace, walking across the red starburst inlaid upon the floor. They had rested for a full rise down in the place of Beltor's crypt, regaining their strength, tending to their wounded. Now they were ready to leave the Palace and face whatever might await them. Their trip back up from the deeply buried crypt had been uneventful, as if events patiently awaited their concern elsewhere.

They came up to the main gate that they'd first come through. Bronto kicked aside the already decaying half-corpse that was still in front of the gate, the blood along the gate's central seal now but a dried stain. The group faced around towards each other, swords being drawn, bow being notched, magic at the ready.

"Is everyone ready?" Bronto asked.

"Does it make a difference?" Quickfoot shot back.

"Not really," Eldar grinned.

"We know that Krey and his minions are out there waiting for us," Sindar explained, "and he has seen to it that this is our only way out."

"Our Fate is forced upon us," Sheil-Bor(h) said, "as is often the case with such things."

"There goes that word again," Quickfoot sighed, "if I ever get my hands on this 'Fate' guy…"

"Enough talk," Lorel said, once again himself and ignorant of his activities as Schanter, "we must vanquish this foe once and for all."

"If he uses the word *vanquish* one more time," Mauklo said quietly, "our foe isn't going to be the *only* thing that's going to be vanquished."

"Eldar," Sabu asked his friend, "does your special sense pick up anything outside the gate?"

"No," Eldar shook his head, "all's quiet. Still as death, as it were."

"I wish he hadn't phrased it that way," Quickfoot moaned.

"Very well," Sabu decided.

Sabu, staff in hand, nodded to Bronto. The big man grabbed hold of the large gold ring on the inside of the door and gave a tug. Slowly, the large double doors opened outward, letting in the light of a late afternoon. The large palace's courtyard lay spread out before them, silent and peaceful.

"Well," Lindel said, as Bronto stepped outside into the light, "here's for a quick death."

"I just love walking into traps," Eldar said, as he walked out, sword ready in his hand.

The ruins of Thïr Tÿorca stretched out before them, miles of broken rock and fallen edifice in every direction. They walked out into the wide courtyard, once a place for ancient celebrations, holiday festivals, and armies ready to serve their lord, now a battlefield in waiting. They walked out into the center of the large open area, looking carefully around them, tense at every small noise.

It was quiet; not even a lonely bird chirped nor loose stone tumble down to the ground. The only sound heard was the slow heavy footsteps of Bronto as he walked across the open ground. When they came to the center of the courtyard they stopped, looking around for any sign of movement.

"So how long's he going to keep us waiting?" Lindel asked. "I'd rather get this over with."

"Yeah," Eldar agreed, not quite as cocky as usual, "I've got a girlfriend waiting for me after this."

"I don't think we'll have to wait long," Bronto noted. "Look."

Tall misty horror, ghostly visage floating low above the open ground. Image of dread come down as the hand of vengeance to smite onlooking mortals. Howling, lonely and promising of death.

"It's Shandeür," Candol said, his voice level, his gaze straight.

"Not *him* again," Eldar sighed. "We barely survived him before."

Nervous faces glanced around at each other as the ghostly horror slowly approached across the open courtyard.

"I can try what I did before," Sabu offered, as he raised up his staff.

"No," Candol said firmly, stepping forward, "I must deal with him. Shandeür has blasphemed upon the word of Indra and called to question the worth of his humble servant. I must make amends to Indra and face this. I will not run."

Candol walked forward, placing himself between Shandeür and the others as he started walking towards it.

"It'll kill you!" Lindel called out. "Remember, it's unaffected by magic."

"It is not magic with which I shall face it," Candol called back, as he walked slow and straight across the courtyard, "but my faith and the power of Indra."

From where he was, Kilgar could see the bright light that blazed out of the corner of the priest's eyes; a flash of bright blue light and determination that bespoke of more than mortal determination in Candol's eyes. The wind picked up as the creature came towards the priest, his sandy-colored hair tossing about in its breeze. The others watched, tense and ready, as their friend marched slowly towards the creature that even Sabu couldn't best when first they'd met it.

When he was halfway across the courtyard, Candol stopped. He faced the deadly spirit, his left hand holding onto his priestly sigil, his right hand facing the palm out towards Shandeür. The two seemed to regard each other for a brief moment.

"You have done us grievous harm," Candol intoned, voice rising above the growing winds, "as well as untold others before us. This will be no more. I stand against you."

The creature reared up its vague ghastly form, towering up tall above the priest as it presented a visage that had poor Quickfoot quivering as they watched. Candol just kept facing it, looking full on into its face. It then raised up its howl, loud shriek of death, blasting down full upon the priest. A mist-filled wind seemed to stream down upon the priest, its howl shaking the very ground upon which he stood. Streamer of swift-moving mist come lancing straight out for Candol's heart, swift promise of death as the priest just stands there facing it.

The misty streamer hit Candol, erupting out and around him as if it had hit some invisible barrier, grey foggy tendrils of air exploding around the priest just as the howl hit him with the full force of a large hammer. The ground around the courtyard quaked with the force of the impact; the shaking of an earthquake and the boom of thunder, as the full power of Shandeür hit.

Mist and fog littered the courtyard for but a brief time, Shandeür's vague form being the only discernible sight. Then a wind whipped up, spinning around like a miniature tornado as it quickly dispersed the winds before it too faded away.

Candol still stood there, unmoving, facing directly towards Shandeür. Tense faces watched, looking for any sign of life from the priest. Sabu watched and wondered if indeed Candol was still alive, or if his soul had been destroyed by the evil spirit, his body now but a shell. Eldar reached out with his sense, trying to see if indeed the unmoving priest was alive or dead. But a brief tense moment had passed, though it seemed a lifetime.

Eldar smiled, his senses having touched upon a welcome target.

Candol's head faced up towards the floating spirit, regarding his full frightful form. Shandeür howled his rage at him, surprised and angry that the priest lived.

"Vile spirit," Candol's voice rose even above the sound of Shandeür's howl, his right arm still straight out, as if he would stop the spirit with a gesture, "you face not the weak form of this humble servant of Indra, but the full wrath of his Lord."

A faint blue light rose up around the priest, flickering beacon against the waning afternoon, growing stronger. A wind seemed to whip up around Shandeür, a wind that only the spirit could feel. But this wind was not of its making, coming it did from Candol's outstretched palm. The wind curled around it, trying to pull at the powerful spirit, trying to enclose it.

Shandeür thrust out his ghostly arms, bursting out of his airy cage with ease as it then howled down upon the priest. Angry at such impudence, Shandeür raised up its fatal howl, a howl that echoed across many miles, a howl that would kill all it touched. Lindel and Quickfoot tried stoppering up their ears against its deadly tones, but a gesture from Sindar warned them off; the mere blocking off of its hearing would do no good. It would kill regardless.

The blue flickering light around Candol then shot up his arm and out through the air. Swift as thought it sailed out, wrapping itself around the floating form, curling around, binding it tight. In but a moment, like faint blue ribbons, it held the struggling form of Shandeür, the sound of his howl suddenly diminished as if that too would be contained by the faint bands of light. It howled its rage down at the priest, giving out a stare that would have turned strong men into withered husks. But Candol was unmoved.

"I banish you spirit!" he intoned above the raging scream of Shandeür, "In the name of Indra do I turn thee; by His power do I smite thee."

The blue bands of light began to flicker as another light shone out from Candol's eyes. A stream of pure will went out from the priest, through the sigil clutched tightly in his left hand and out along his outstretched right hand. Will given force, force given form. It wrapped around Shandeür like a large enclosing hand.

"BE GONE!"

Candol's final pronouncement echoed loud and clear throughout the hilltop that was Thïr Tÿorca. As well did the screams of Shandeür; screams that spoke of rage and death, screams that had killed countless souls over the long millennia. Screams that now saw its own end.

The force of Candol's will and faith closed in around Shandeür, clamping down tight and strong. Shandeür glowed a bright blue, his will striving to fight against that of the priest. Striving, but weakening. In a sudden bright flare of light, Shandeür's ghostly form exploded upon the sky, tattered bits of his misty essence scattering suddenly through the sky, the deadly scream cut abruptly off. Flaming bits of Shandeür soared pyrotechnic overhead, the last display that Shandeür would ever give.

"Now *that's* what I call a show!" Eldar whooped out, as he ran out towards the priest.

"Are you okay?" Sindar asked, walking over with the others.

"Yes," Candol said, firm expression still on his face, standing tall as his body shook from the exertion. "I have redeemed myself in the eyes of Indra."

"You did more than that," Eldar exclaimed in a merry tone, "you *flattened* that thing! You killed the unkillable."

"It is just but——" Candol began.

A single lonely clapping was heard, as if of one person slowly clapping his hands together in a tired applause to a show he cared not to see. Heads turned as they looked around for the source of the mocking applause.

"Who——" Eldar said, looking around.

"I see that you have survived your trial by fire," came a voice from high above them.

They looked up, towards the high roof of the Palace behind them. Standing atop the roof, by one of the towered pinnacles directly above the gate from which they'd come, stood a single man, slowly clapping his hands together, as he smiled down at them. His dark hair tossed in the wind, the setting sun reflecting off his black eyes, his purple robes wrapped around him as a red cape fluttered behind him in the wind. The wind, having gradually grown stronger since Shandeür had appeared, now seemed to have a central point, as they raced around him, gaining speed with each passing moment as he lowered his dark gaze down at them.

Lindel needed not Eldar's special sense, Sheil-Bor(h)'s foretellings, nor Sindar's psychic powers to tell him who now faced them with such calm malevolence in his eyes.

"It's Krey," the golden-haired elf said calmly.

"His face looked better when it was up in the sky," Eldar quipped quietly.

"I am *so* glad that we finally get to meet," Krey said, his voice grating upon their souls, "I hope that you enjoyed your little training session."

"Training?!" Eldar cried out. "I think hanging out with all those undead has dried out your brain. We *defeated* that which you had sought for so long."

"We have destroyed your would-be ally Beltor," Bronto said, holding six feet of sword tight in his hand, "and his undead armies are no more. Your long wait for his freedom has been for nothing."

"We overcame that which you faced us with," Sindar shouted out, "you won't get what you came for."

"Oh," Krey replied with a smile, cocking an eyebrow, "won't I?"

Krey started to float above the roof, slowly floating up higher and higher into the sky as he spoke.

"You think that it was to free Beltor that you were maneuvered into this lost valley?" Krey continued, as he floated high up above their heads. "That it was his power and undead hordes that I truly sought?"

Krey started to laugh, his laughter echoing upon the now-fierce winds. Quickfoot looked nervously up at Candol, and Kilgar clutched at the fresh knife he'd borrowed from the small one's collection, while the laughter sounded among the wide ruins.

"Either he's cracked," Quickfoot offered, "or he knows something we don't."

"It was not for Beltor or his hordes that I sought," came Krey's voice down from above. "I can make numbers of undead greater than any Beltor ever dreamed of."

"Why *don't* I want to hear what comes next," Shong said, diamond blade waiting for combat.

"It was *you* that I wanted!"

Krey's statement rang down like a pronouncement, sinking into their souls like water into the ground, as its implications echoed through the air. Stunned faces regarded each other and the distancing form of Krey. Silence reigned over the courtyard as Krey finally stopped his rise up through the sky, almost a mile up, his voice somehow coming down from above to be heard clearly by those below.

"All this was set up to *train* you," came Krey's voice, "to prepare you for service in my own armies."

"Us?" came Candol's astonished reply.

"A war comes upon the horizon of time," Krey's voice said, "one greater than you would know. The part that you shall all play in it has already been foretold, and it is a part that you shall now play for *me*. For my master!"

Krey's voice echoed down upon the courtyard, the winds high above seeming to whip around into many solidifying forms.

"For Miro!"

The name seemed to echo almost endlessly throughout the secluded valley, resounding amongst the scattered ruins as those assembled heard its utterance like a final pronouncement; to be told that you had indeed been helping the very one whose destruction you had sought.

"Many have been recruited into my army," Krey said, the vague forms in the wind now forming definite solid shapes floating all throughout the sky overhead. "I gather those that show true promise in His service. Those like yourselves; seekers of His destruction, turned to come and *serve* him instead. An army of heroes! And you shall be amongst his *finest* warriors."

The shapes had now taken full form, a small army of individuals floating upon the sky overhead. Not only did they see the vast numbers of Krey's army of undead, wraiths and spirits floating upon the darkening sky, but also of people. Humans, Elves, Dwarves, even Felinians and other lesser known races. A wide scattering of people, darkness now filling their eyes and souls, service to but one person engraved upon their essence. Warriors, wizards, priests, and more. Elementals and Genies floating upon the clouds, demons given human form, darkly angelic hawkmen soaring high. An army of minor gods it seemed; an army born such as themselves, out of the fires of Miro's evil, seeking after his dark forces, now faithfully serving that which they so hated, their hate and fanaticism turned against them.

Loyal minions of Krey and his master, Miro.

"Come now; join with your brethren," Krey called down. "Just but reach up to me and take your place at the head of this army. An army that will some rise crush that foolish King that would send you out against my master. Sindar, you especially have been invited into His service; perhaps you can convince your friends in the wisdom of joining."

"No!" Sindar almost shouted out. "I have fought the visions and will not give in to them. And I will never betray my friends into Miro's service."

Eldar came over and stood on one side of Sindar, Sabu on the other. They clasped onto their friend's hands, lending him their strength.

"He has our strength to help him," Eldar said, "the visions will not overcome him. We three are one."

"Ah," Krey's voice could almost be heard to smile, "but that's what I'm *counting* on!"

Sindar suddenly doubled over with pain, grabbing at his head like something would stab through it. Before they could react, Sabu and Eldar also doubled over, feeling the backlash of their friend's pain through the indelible connection which they three shared. Candol raced over to help them up, while Krey's laughter came down.

"Now," Krey continued, "who shall be the first to come up. Or shall I send some of my servants down to fetch you? The result will be the same in the end. You shall serve."

"We've been tricked," young Kilgar said through gritted teeth.

"I fear that we have been maneuvered more than even *Mauklo* had suspected," Sheil-Bor(h) agreed.

"I *will* not serve an evil lord," Bronto vowed, "nor anyone not of my own choosing!"

"We must not give in," Sindar said between clenched teeth, as he tried to draw his own pain away from his two friends.

"Such an army would surely be unstoppable," Sabu said, as he tried to use his staff to get up with.

But Sindar's pain was great; it occupied not only himself, but Eldar and Sabu as well, bringing them all down to the ground in helpless gasps. Sheil-Bor(h) walked over to Sindar, inscrutable calmness upon his face as he looked down at the concentration upon the young wizard as he strove to master the pain.

"Perhaps," Sheil-Bor(h) offered calmly, "a lesson from meditation can help."

"Anything," Sindar said, as even more beings materialized overhead.

"Do not seek to master the pain, or to let it master you," Sheil-Bor(h) advised. "Rather, live *with* it. Move alongside of the pain and dwell with it in harmony."

"That's easy for *you* to say," Eldar said, gripping his head in sympathetic pains, "you don't have a stampede of pugen power cats going through your head!"

"Your answer now!" Krey demanded. "I have invested much in your training; it is now time for you to serve your true master!"

"I'm not sure," Sindar gasped, "it is too much, and I have not your meditative training."

"Then I shall join in with you," Sheil-Bor(h) said, bending down beside Sindar.

"No," Sabu gasped, "you would be drawn into the pain too."

Sheil-Bor(h) ignored Sabu's objections and just calmly placed his hands upon Sindar's forehead. He put himself into their link, sharing the bond that the three had. His mind linked with theirs, drawing part of the pain out to himself, guiding their minds in the ways of his meditation, lending them his strength of mind and will. He helped them forge the bands of their link into a stronger whole, helped them calmly ride the waves of their pain, ignore the strength of Sindar's unwanted visions. He became a catalyst to the forging of their whole.

Sindar stood up, pain no longer upon his face. Eldar and Sabu stood up to either side, Sheil-Bor(h) behind them. Calmness was upon their faces and a smile upon Eldar's lips. The pain would bother them no more, the invitations upon Sindar's mind serve their purpose no longer.

Sabu looked up at that gathered about them. The sky was filled with spirits by the thousands and fallen heroes by the dozens. The ruins around them now crawled with the careful footsteps of other creatures: ghouls, ghasts, and wights; skeletons, spectres, vampires, and other creatures too twisted to view in the light of day. They were all around them. Surrounded, and the nearest form of cover long hundreds of feet away.

He looked around as he saw Bronto and Shong standing battle-ready, Kilgar waiting with his knife. Candol clutched onto his sigil, his faith in Indra now unshakable, while Lindel readied a bow. Lorel drew his blue sword of flame, his form slowly shifting to that of Schanter, while Mauklo grimaced up at the distant form of Krey. Even Quickfoot fingered a knife, fear no longer on his face, as if he'd finally passed a threshold of courage; a final barrier where fear finally becomes determination.

Sabu looked back up at Krey, hovering high upon a cloud, the winds swirling around him, his servants and armies all about him. Sabu raised up his voice loudly, so that there would be no mistaking his tone.

"You have your answer," he called out, "we will not serve you!"

"Besides," Eldar called out, a smile creeping out from the side of his mouth, "I promised someone your head on a platter."

"VERY WELL!" Krey boomed down. "If not willing, then unwilling. But serve you shall! Take them!"

At Krey's pointed finger, those gathered up in the sky, heroes and armies, black of heart and soul, turned as one to those below them. Weapons of both steel and spirit were drawn, forces gathered about them. The creatures hidden about in the surrounding ruins sharpened their claws against the large stones as they crept closer, closing in like a large vise.

"Well," Eldar swallowed, falling into a battle-crouch, sword ready, "here goes nothing."

"*That* has to be the biggest understatement I've ever heard," Quickfoot sighed as he fingered his knife.

In another faraway section of the surrounding forest, Dwingale looked up, almost as if knowing of what deadly peril the others suddenly faced. She stood up from where she was kneeling next to the small green pond and looked on into the distance towards Thïr Tÿorca as a name of love escaped silently from her lips; a wish for luck to the one she loved.

On a small island in the middle of the Sea Of A Thousand Islands, one island amongst many, now empty but for its single cliff-side castle, a large ogre walked out of his cave, several old heads hanging from his belt. For no reason that his conscious mind knew, he was drawn outside, to look up into the evening sky with sudden anxiety. Thoughts of his friends came suddenly upon his mind, concern for their well-being. He knew naught of what had drawn him out, or why he should know of their jeopardy; it was enough for his dim mind that they were in danger, the only ones that had befriended him without any concern for what he was. A single large tear rolled down his hairy cheek, as he realized that on this battle they were alone, that he could do nothing to help them. So, he did the one thing that he *could* do.

"Blag-ak wish luck to friends," he rumbled silently.

As he stood at the mouth of the cave, the ground dropping far away below him, gazing up into the starry sky, he heard a sound coming from back in the cave; the sound of a large dragon egg rolling about in its nest of rocks as it cracked and strained, something within it moving.

Blag-ak sighed, as he turned around and went back into the cave to care for his eggs.

"Sir, what is it?"

330

A soldier was trying to politely nudge Starke as the latter just stood there staring off in the direction of the rising sun. His vortex sword was in hand, the body of another orkai lying dead at his feet. The sounds of battle were all around them, scattered throughout the surrounding forest. Starke shook himself out of his sense of foreboding and brought his mind back to the matters at hand.

"I just had the strangest feeling," Starke finally answered slowly, "that they're in trouble; at a crossroads of their own making."

"Who sir?" the soldier asked.

"Never mind, soldier," Starke gave out a tired smile. "I'm sure we'll hear about it later. For now, all we can do is wish them luck."

"If you say so sir," the soldier replied doubtfully.

"But now," Starke said as he snapped back to his professional solider attitude, "we've got this orkai raid to clean up. Let's move it!"

The wave of spirits soared down at them just as the creatures hiding amongst the ruins charged across the open courtyard. Ghouls, ghasts, demented humanoids, and things that could only come out with the setting sun. As one did they charge out, innumerable numbers washing out across towards their trapped prey. The growing night sky lit up with the wail of spirits, blackened with their descent. Above them, fallen heroes took out spell and weapon, aiming them at those below while Krey's hordes kept them busy.

A tall red-haired man, eyes the black of night, standing proud and strong, took out his large sword as he floated upon the sky. Strength enough in his arms to crush a solid metal sword between his fingers, he looked down at his chosen opponent, smiling a dark evil grin as he anticipated the coming joy of combat. Yes, good indeed; he would present their limp bodies at Krey's feet. With a wave of his sword, he vanished.

Large blue-skinned man, blue cap fluttering behind him, raised up his arms in the direction of the large lake, just but a few miles away. With a minor act of will, he stirred its waters, moving them, molding them to his desires. The lake's surface seemed to form into a violent watery fist, ready to launch itself across the short miles separating it from the hill of Thïr Tÿorca. With a gesture, he launched the watery conjuration through the air, soaring like a rocket given sudden flight, through the short miles towards the hill.

In rels gone by, a former life it seemed now, the elf had tried to stand up against Krey, to stop him and the slaughter of his people. But now, that was of no matter; he would use his magic for whatever his master Krey desired, and at present that was to capture those that would thwart his will. As he fluttered high upon his cloud, he cast down his spell, conjuring up a cage of glowing bands of light to hold them all prisoner, containing them for his master.

Two dwarven warriors leapt down from the sky, battle axes in hand as they waved them overhead, they flew straight down towards the biggest man they saw. Darkness reflected in their eyes, a darkness that covered any memory or care for the dwarven hold in the mountains that they both used to hold so dear; the dwarven hold that they themselves helped to destroy as their own axes cleaved down upon their friends and family.

Three human wizards, joining their magic in an effort against Krey's enemies. They sent forth their power, power that would encase them in bubbles of force and deliver them unto their master. Three wizards, friends for a long time, once with dreams of changing things and fighting evil, now only with dreams for their master. Dreams once of a hidden haven from which they might fight Miro, but now a haven for his servants. With the enthusiasm of true fanaticism, they poured in the full force of their magic.

Bronto and Shong stood back to back, a bit away from the others as the ghouls charged at them. A single swing of Bronto's large sword cut through three of the creatures, but more just came up after them. Shong used his diamond blade almost like a rapier, so precise was its balance, piercing one creature through its dead heart, neatly cleaving off the head of another. Bodies piled up quickly around the two, but still more came. Clawing ghouls tried launching themselves at Bronto in an attempt to bury him in sheer weight, but the strong man held, clenching his teeth as he heaved back the pile of them and swung about with his sword once again.

A small leathery-skinned warty creature leaped out into the midst of the charging hordes, blue flaming sword in hand, lighting itself afire as it also cleaved all about it, a flaming dervish of death. Schanter shouted in pain and glee as he leapt up and out into the air, curling himself into a spinning ball of flame as he cannonballed straight into the thickest nest of the creatures coming at them, a flaming ball spinning through the air, blue sword spinning along with it as it shot out a whirling tongue of flame.

Lindel notched a golden arrow into his bow while he looked quickly about. Kilgar stood by his side, knifing any creature that came near them, while Lindel looked around for a good target.

"Forget the ghouls," he said to himself, "there's just too many of them. But, about those guys up there in the sky…"

His eyes rested upon the blue-skinned human, and then panned over as he saw the large watery fist coming through the sky straight for them, the blue-one maneuvering it with a gesture.

"If that thing hits us," he said, pulling back on his bowstring, "we could have problems."

The spirits wailed down upon them, a storm of fright and death. Wraiths, spectres, ghosts, and more came at them. Candol held forth his arms, his Hevon Gems and his own priestly power sending forth a blast of translucent purple flame through his outstretched arms, pouring out upon the charging hordes from the sky. Flame washed through a hundred spirits, reducing their wails of death into wails of fright as they were blasted away into ectoplasmic bits. More spirits rushed in behind them, soaring down upon the small group, rushing in at them, reaching for their souls. Several were coming directly at Kilgar, Lindel, and Quickfoot; one swipe of a wraith's deadly touch would leave the boy dead, two touches would take care of Lindel, but a dozen or more-that would be too much. Candol tried, but he was unable to handle them all.

A sudden blast of wind surrounded them, a wind that only the spirits felt. It reduced the spirits in their mist to nothing, just as they were about to make contact with Kilgar and Lindel. Candol looked over to see who had lent the timely assist.

Mauklo smiled back at the priest, a smile that might unnerve even a wraith but now gave Candol hope. The spirit wind emanated from Mauklo, spinning around them all to hold back the worst of the immaterial opponents.

Quickfoot leapt out upon the nearest ghoul, avoiding its paralyzing touch as he knifed it in the back of the neck. As it dropped, he took out another of his many knives and spun around. He launched the knife straight out, almost without aiming.

The knife hit another large hairy creature straight through the throat, just as it was a mere five feet away from the small one. As it fell heavily to the ground, Quickfoot could see that it was quite like the large eight-foot tall man-like creature that had attacked him when first they'd come into the ruins.

"I thought I recognized that awful smell," he said as he pulled his knife out of the ghoul.

A thick wall of thorns suddenly sprouted up in the charging path of some others of the ghouls. Tall and high it rose, and sharp were its thorns, as the ghouls found out when they ran straight into it.

Sheil-Bor(h) looked on at his handiwork, nodding at the result.

"To remember a similar situation," he said, holding out his hand, "it just but needs one thing."

His palm produced a small ball of flame, which he then lightly tossed over towards the thorny wall. The ghouls screamed as the large bush exploded in flames.

Eldar swung about with his sword, flame dancing along its length as it stabbed through both spirit and ghoul alike. He tried to keep them away from Sabu and Sindar, to let the wizards work their magic.

"We're going to have to do something rather large scale for this," Sabu was saying, "there are just too many."

"Agreed," Sindar nodded, "perhaps it's time that we see what *all* of our Hevon Gems can do."

"That may be just the thing," Sabu responded, as his own Hevon Gems started to glow within him.

Bright light exploded down upon them, sending rays of itself down around them all. A cage of light did weave itself quickly around them, its brightly glowing bars woven tight as it embraced the ground. A cage that also seemed to restrain the bulk of Mauklo's immaterial wind, so that several of the spirits tried once again to seek a way through. Bronto cleaved at the bars with his large sword, swinging with all his mighty strength.

The bars of light cut straight through his immense six-foot sword, leaving Bronto to hold but a short length attached to the hilt while the other half rattled down upon the ground. He tossed away the now-useless sword.

"It won't cut," he shouted out to the others, drawing out the Dragon Sword.

"We'll just see about that," Eldar shouted back, then his own sword lit up with all the forces he could conjure from his Hevon Gems.

The ground suddenly shook, as a sound like unto a sonic boom reverberated about them. Eldar lost his balance as Quickfoot was thrown back towards the glowing bars, catching onto Candol's robes in an effort to stop his tumbled flight; he smelt the sizzle of his hair as he stopped but a breath away from the deadly light. Kilgar was knocked to the ground, but a tumble and a roll brought him just as quickly to his feet. Lindel brought down his bow as his line of sight was blocked by the brightly-glowing roof over their heads.

A cry of battle turned Bronto's attention quickly towards the bars. He brought up the Dragon Sword just in time for it to block a large battle axe tumbling at him through the bars. With a bright spark of magic, the sharp axe hit the sword as Bronto held it firm, cleaving in two as it made swift contact with the edge of his sword, the two halves falling to either side. From where the axe had hit Bronto's upraised sword, he could tell that it would have hit him right in the middle of his head.

He looked up to see two dwarves charging straight for him, one of them drawing out another axe, blackness shining forth in both their eyes. They cried out while Bronto stood trapped behind the bars.

Sabu brought his staff up in defence against the next bubble of force that hit them, the boom of its explosion once again resounding throughout the courtyard. He looked up to see a group of three wizards hovering far up in the air, throwing their combined force out against him. Sindar threw in his own magic just as the second bolt hit, a bolt of pure power that rivaled their own.

"What was that?" Eldar asked, as he regained his balance from the first blow.

"We aren't the only ones that combine their power," Sindar said as he pointed up towards the other three.

"Three on three," Eldar said as he stepped in beside them. "Sounds fair to me."

Candol blasted out with the light of day, contained though it was by the cage that surrounded them, as he struggled to stop the spirits from entering. Ghouls clawed at the cage of light, their claws making occasional contact with flesh and bone. The priest fought with the blue fire of Indra in his eyes, while Sheil-Bor(h) stood nearby, calmly examining the glowing cage.

"The magic of this cage is too strong for me to pierce," Sheil-Bor(h) observed. "A rival to any of our own, and yet it is from but a servant of Krey."

A ghoul came diving in between the narrow bars, his dive narrowly avoiding the closely-spaced bars as it came straight for Sheil-Bor(h), claws and teeth ready to tear and rend. Sheil-Bor(h) looked down just as a sword point came out of nowhere and pierced it neatly between the eyes.

Sheil-Bor(h) looked up at Shong as the latter drew his sword out from the creature's skull. No time even for thanks, Shong ran over to another spot in the bars where another ghoul was trying to make it through.

Then the cage began to shrink.

The bars drew closer together as the width of the cage came in upon itself, the bars tightening, the ceiling getting lower. They backed up towards their common center, ducking lower as they were surrounded by light, all trapped in a shrinking cage.

All except for one sword-wielding ball of warty flame still clawing its way through the worst of the ghouls and creatures about them.

Sabu's gaze lit upon the flaming form of Schanter, a sudden idea popping into his mind as he backed away from the sizzling bars.

"Eldar," he said over his shoulder to his elven friend, "your sense; who does it tell you that the energy of this cage originates from?"

Eldar concentrated but briefly before he answered.

"That Elven one up there on the cloud," he pointed through the rapidly closing bars.

"Good," Sabu said. "Sindar—"

"Got it," Sindar said, saving time by taking the idea straight from his friend's mind, "and working on it."

Sindar's mind reached out towards the flaming form of Schanter, his regeneration somehow keeping up with the damage done to him by his own flame, his screams of pain, pleasure, and battle blending into one. Sindar's mind picked up the small leathery creature, rising him up above the ghouls as it spun him round and round. A spinning ball of flame and sword hovering above the ghouls' heads for but a brief moment, before Sindar launched him up into the air.

Straight at the elf on the cloud. The elf turned his head, his concentration upon containing those within his magical cage. For a brief eternity he saw a flaming pinwheel screaming through the air straight towards him, blue flaming sword spinning along one side. The living pinwheel screamed out joy and suffering as it slammed into the elf.

From where they were, Sindar and Sabu saw Schanter hit the elf like a fireball, exploding as he went through the elf, screaming ball of flame enveloping the entire cloud as bits of elf were scattered throughout the sky. They watched as the ball of fire that was Schanter then went plummeting down towards the distant ground, screaming in pleasure as he saw the possibility of his own imminent death.

The glow of the cage started to weaken, its shrinking slowing down. Sabu tapped his staff firmly on the ground, a quick crack of thunder from its base dispelling the cage in an explosion of light. They were free of their prison.

Free just in time to hear a rumbling from high overhead. Eldar looked up to see a large watery fist coming down out of the sky towards them, large blue-skinned man riding its crest.

"This is going to hurt," Eldar sighed.

Golden missile of light, reaching swiftly through the air. Pointed contact made with blue-skinned prey. Sudden deadly impact, as gravity seeks to reclaim its own.

Eldar blinked as he saw a golden arrow suddenly spring out of the blue-skinned one's forehead, the man's eyes growing suddenly wide and lifeless, his concentration and life both broken. He tumbled swiftly towards the distant ground, the large watery fist loosing its shape as it fell down upon them in buckets. A large splash of water, it came down upon them, but no force was there now behind its plunge, other than that given to it by gravity. Quickfoot sputtered, almost drowning in the deluge as Lindel notched another arrow.

A blast of force hit Eldar unawares, sending him flying into Candol who was still holding back the many spirits. He caught the priest in the stomach, knocking the breath out of him and breaking his concentration. Spirits started to flood in around them, ghouls to dog-pile on them all.

Bronto and Shong turned quickly around as the sound of twin axes cleaved through the air. Bronto blocked with the Dragon Sword as the dwarf's other hand came in with a knife to his belly. The second dwarf lunged at Shong with more speed than one would expect from one so short and stout.

Bronto grabbed the dwarf's other hand, getting it before the knife reach him, crushing the bones in his hand into a fine powder. The dwarf screamed in pain as he tried to free his large axe from its lock with Bronto's sword. Bronto released his grip upon the pulverized hand as he brought his fist straight into the dwarf's face.

The dwarf's scream was cut short as Bronto's fist caved in his skull.

The second dwarf had lunged at Shong, blade heading straight for his neck. But, with a speed that amazed the dwarf, Shong suddenly wasn't there; he had time enough to look up with mild puzzlement and see the point of Shong's sword coming straight down through his eye as he landed upon the dwarf.

Force impacted upon Sabu and Sindar once again, as large hairy creatures came leaping at them from out of the night. A bolt of lightning from Sindar disposed of the beasts, but more came, including now a large felinian, twisted sword in its hands, malevolence in its grin, as it walked steadily towards them.

"We have to do something about the riffraff," Sabu said to Sindar.

"Agreed," Sindar said, as he placed a hand upon Sabu's staff.

"Count me in too," Eldar said as he staggered over to join them.

Kilgar stabbed at yet another ghoul as he ducked the passing attack of a wraith. He looked over and saw Quickfoot also battling, his thrown knives always hitting their marks. As the boy was stabbing at yet another ghoul, a large figure suddenly loomed over him.

"Out of my way *boy*," rumbled a tall red-haired main, eyes black as night.

A large hand swiped at the boy, hitting his small wiry frame full in the chest. Kilgar was sent sprawling far across the courtyard, impacting straight into Quickfoot as they were both then sent flying. Through the air they went, their flight to be interrupted by the sudden appearance of a standing wall of rock a mere hundred feet or so away. The two impacted with a sickening crunch upon the rock, the force of their impact starting the wall to rocking as their limp forms slid down its length. The wall toppled back and forth before it finally fell forward onto the two bodies. Quickfoot, lying on top of Kilgar, had just enough energy to look up and see the large wall of stone coming straight down upon him, blackness and the bliss of eternity being the only thing he saw after that.

Bronto turned around in time to see the large red-headed man swinging at him with his large sword. Blade contacted blade as Bronto blocked the blow, though the force of it almost sent him to his knees. Bronto growled defiance as he heaved all his strength against the big man.

"We seem to have a challenge here," the red-headed man rumbled mockingly. "You're almost as strong as me."

"What do you mean," Bronto growled between gasps, *"almost!"*

Bronto heaved against the other man, but they were indeed almost a match for each other. They ground against each other like two mountains in heat.

"Think you the *first* one to get so strong?" the red-head laughed, his rotten breath breathing into Bronto's face. "We were here long before you; another group also bent on destroying Him, and now look where we are."

"I won't give in like *you*," Bronto growled as he pushed against his opponent.

"What do you mean *like* me," the red-head rumbled, as he pushed away from their combative embrace, "you *are* me!"

The sudden comparison threw Bronto off; he looked up at the one as strong as himself, then glanced over at the three wizards that Eldar, Sindar, and Sabu now confronted, then around at some of the others that now came down out of the sky at them. The similarity between themselves and the ones they fought was just too close for coincidence. His mind reeled as the true subtlety of Miro's game dawned upon his mind.

Bronto doubled over as a sudden blow to his stomach took him unawares. His opponent came down again, his fist smashing into Bronto's face as he brought his sword around in a last mighty swing.

"You *will* become us!" the red-headed man said, as his sword came round.

"You're almost there right now! Pity about the kid though, but he just got in my way."

Under half a ton of rock, Quickfoot's eyes flickered weakly open. He was face to face against Kilgar, close enough to see blood streaming from several spots in the boy's broken body, though his own was not much better off. Quickfoot tried to groan, but all strength was gone from him, the pain from innumerable broken bones overwhelming; he saw his death before him and knew it was time to give up.

Then he saw the boy's eyes flicker open, slowly and almost imperceptibly did they flutter. But something else did he also see flicker. A trace of blackness, seeping slowly across Kilgar's eyes as it sought mastery over the helplessly dead child.

"No!" Bronto shouted, as the sword came down towards his head. "He will not be yours!"

Anger rose up in the big man, as he suddenly brought his sword up to meet with the oncoming length of steel. Magical sparks flew from both swords as swift contact was made. Steel strained against steel, as Bronto strove to rise up from his knees. Equally matched they were, but anger gave Bronto the additional strength he needed; anger about the boy, anger about the fate that his opponent now presented to him. He was determined that their fate would not be his. He powered his way up, crying out all his fury as he pushed the large man away. Blackness swelled up in his eyes, anger in his heart. He swung out his sword with all his strength.

The Dragon Sword hit the other man's large sword with a loud crash, cleaving straight through its thick magical steel like it was but paper, the force of Bronto's anger driving it home. As the pieces of the other's sword went flying out, Bronto drew back for another strike, the look of *yora'zaugh* now full upon his soul, the blackness seeping slowly across his eyes.

As the red-headed man looked up at his approaching doom, he smiled, chuckling a silent joke to himself, as if almost waiting for the sword to strike.

But Bronto's sword strike never came, nor was it ever needed. Bronto looked down, sword ready to strike, and then saw the man's chuckle suddenly turn silent. His eyes bulged wide with surprise as a metal tip erupted from his chest, straight through his heart. The man fell to his knees and thence to the ground as he slid off of the slim diamond blade, falling to the ground dead. Fury still in his heart at his kill having been taken from him, shaking with rage, Bronto looked up.

Shong stood there, wiping his blade off on the dead man's back, calmly looking up at Bronto.

"If you had killed him, you would have become like him," Shong said calmly, as Bronto's anger broiled up in confused swirls in his mind. "Your eyes are already turning black."

Bronto looked down at the dead man's black eyes, seeing within them the hatred and anger that had been turned against him, that which had been his own undoing, that which had almost been Bronto's undoing. Like a release valve being opened, Bronto's anger suddenly left him, purged from his soul as if he'd suddenly seen himself charging towards a precipice and had finally stopped. He lowered his sword as he looked up at his friend, the blackness rapidly clearing from his eyes.

"They were once like us, weren't they?" Bronto asked.

"I had just noticed that when you two were going at it," Shong answered. "Seeing you two going head to head like that, so similar but for the eyes. Then, when the blackness began to creep over your eyes too, I finally saw it."

"Krey would use our rage against us," Bronto said, once again his calm self. "Some wizard's trick to get into our souls."

"Apparently a rather effective trick," Shong observed, "to judge from by the others."

"Well, we can still fight without the rage of anger," Bronto said as he brought up his sword. "Thank-you, my friend."

"Watching each others' backs is what sword-mates are supposed to do," Shong shrugged nonchalantly.

Sabu's staff glowed brightly, Eldar and Sindar also holding onto it, as another wave of force came down upon them. Their Hevon Gems stirred within them, mixing with their own magic and force of will. The full force of the three opposing wizards hit them just as they let loose with their own power.

A world of fire, heat and power. Explosion of force against force. Ball of lightning, rain of fire, exploding upwards to meet the sky. Stone ruins turning to rocky shrapnel as the winds of their desire sweep through them. Streamers of acid slicing through both creature and structure alike. A large hill erupting like a volcano.

The explosion lit up the night, its fires washing through hundreds of ghouls and creatures that crawled through the ruins, blasting through stone and flesh alike, but leaving certain others untouched. It washed around Bronto and Shong, left Candol and Lindel unharmed, and went around the others. When

Mauklo and Candol saw the flames coming, they both had the same simultaneous idea; more magic sailed forth as both priest and wizard lent their own support to the raging storm of fire and lightning.

The flames turned purple as the lightning now flashed blue across the dark sky. Wraiths and other spirits screamed sudden pain as the lightning now slashed through them as well, the flames to now burn upon their very essences. A storm of screams arose from the hill, burning all that it touched, as thousands of spirits flashed out of existence like disintegrating fireflies. Fire reached high into the sky as lightning crackled far across the heavens.

When the fire died down, several spots around the courtyard still burning as piles of ash now surrounded them, they looked around. The bulk of the ruins were now leveled, though the main Palace of Thïr Tÿorca still stood, untouched by the raging storm, a monument against the night. In front of Sabu and Sindar stood the felinian, unharmed but for a few scorch marks, fangs showing as he grinned back at them, twisted sword still in his clawed hands. Lindel looked up to see four other warriors, human and elven alike, holding out glowing swords ready to do battle. Candol's own roaming glance came upon a large demon, red skin and pointed horns, standing in front of a fallen stone wall, while an elemental of swirling winds swept across the courtyard towards them. Sheil-Bor(h) walked over to the priest as a single hawkman circled high overhead, while the three human wizards still floated high up in the sky, facing off against Eldar, Sindar, and Sabu.

"So," one of the three wizards called down, "you *are* like us."

"Although you appear to have more of Hevon than did we," another said. "A whole lot more from the looks of it."

"They're like us," Sindar said in sudden realization. "Three of them, three of us; all seekers after Hevon, all sharing their power."

"You are indeed correct," the third one said, "though I would think *myself* to be more intelligent than your Sabu."

"The parallel is just too disturbing," Sabu agreed.

"You have been such a nuisance, future comrades in arms," the first one said, "it's a good thing that our master Krey can replace the lost armies in but a kev."

"Now it's time for you to all come along with us," the second one announced. "Our mutual master grows impatient."

"You see," came down Krey's voice, "history not only repeats itself, but it does so on a boringly regular basis. We have been through this all before, just the names have changed. You are far from being the first to challenge that which you shall now serve."

Candol grasped hard upon his sigil, indignant anger upon his face as he sought the best form for the wrath of Indra to take. Rage swelled up within him as he concentrated his power. Sheil-Bor(h) tapped him lightly on the shoulder just as blackness was about to take root in the priest's eyes.

"My friend," Sheil-Bor(h) whispered in his ear, "there needs be something more immediate that calls out for your priestly attentions."

"We don't have time for this now!" Candol objected angrily. "Indra must have his vengeance upon——"

Candol's speech was interrupted by Sheil-Bor(h)'s quiet whisper in his ear. The inky blackness creeping into Candol's eyes was replaced by concern, as all anger suddenly left the priest. Candol nodded in response as he reached once again for his sigil, but this time much more calm and controlled. He muttered a quiet incantation, humble and hopeful.

"No," Sindar was saying, "you would seek to use our own anger to poison us with, to turn us into these other lackeys that you have twisted over the rels."

"Only in your anger can you find the strength to truly defeat us," said the first wizard. "Without that, we are more than your match. So you see, either your anger will be your undoing, or we will."

"You expect *me* to get angry in the heat of battle?" Eldar grinned with mock surprise. "Boy, do you really have the *wrong* elf. I just have too *suave* a personality to go for that sort of thing."

"And, my good friend Sabu here," Eldar continued, gesturing casually to his friend, "he's just too much the intellectual to even *notice* an emotion, much less know what one is. And I won't even *start* on Sindar's failings in the emotional department."

"I think I object to that statement," Sindar said calmly. "I mean after all, there was that one time when——"

"Not now," Eldar whispered harshly out of the side of his mouth.

"And I do too know what an emotion is," Sabu chimed in, "I'm just not in the habit of——"

"Not *now*," Eldar whispered more insistently.

"Oh, sorry," Sabu realized, "another time maybe."

"Will you still be this way when all of your other friends have been turned against you?" the second wizard asked, "Even now, the young boy becomes such as ourselves."

"In the name of Indra, this must stop!"

Candol stepped forward, anger on his face, sigil held up before him. Mauklo, the visage of calmness having never left him, looked over at the priest.

"That holy *rik* of Indra will do us in yet," Mauklo said quietly to himself, as he started secretly making magical gestures with his fingers.

"Candol, no," Shong called out. "You must not approach them in anger."

"I know what I do," Candol said, anger rigidly on his face, thrusting up both arms in incantation, "when I say this: may the mighty Indra bring his justice down upon the truly deserving; from the plight of innocence shall come his vengeance!"

Candol gazed skyward, face contorted with rage as he awaited the result of his incantation.

Nothing happened.

"See," the felinian grinned as he stepped a bit closer to Sabu, "already his powers leave him; his god has forsaken him. He is ours!"

The felinian took one step closer and then stopped. In mid-grin, he fell straight to the ground, long knife sticking straight out of the back of his neck. Eldar smiled when he saw from where the knife came.

"I hate being dead," Kilgar said almost tiredly, his eyes free of blackness, sitting on top of the fallen wall as he rubbed the back of his neck.

"Well, he *did* say from the 'plight of innocence'."

The demon standing in front of the fallen wall turned swiftly around, claws reaching for the young voice that it heard behind it. Its gaze was met with, though, by a long kitchen knife, sticking straight out of its right eye. It screamed in rage as it tried to angrily pluck the offending stick from itself.

"A priest of Indra must have many talents," Candol said smiling, no trace of anger now about his face. "Among them, the art of *acting.*"

The first of the three wizards looked down upon them, expression growing cold. He pointed his finger down at them as if in final judgement.

"Get them," he said.

The four warriors started to advance, swords slicing out in front of them, as the hawkman came diving down, spear in hand charging for them. The elemental came whirling straight for Mauklo, the wounded demon to advance upon Quickfoot and Kilgar, as the three wizards focused down their power.

Meanwhile, Krey stood back upon his cloud and watched. His cloud, now black as night, was starting to form into a shape. So busy had the others been that they hadn't noticed the slow convergence of the clouds above as they went from random bits of grey puffiness to the organized form of a more lethal shape. Krey smiled as he watched the show, waiting for the cloud to obtain its final shape.

343

Golden shaft, a streak of pointed light. Swift crack, soaring through the flames of retribution. Flaming shaft, like a bolt of fire come down from the heavens to wreck its vengeance upon sinful mortals. Twin screams of death, as deadly shaft hits its mark not once, but twice.

Lindel had sent out his arrow with a small paper pouch wrapped tightly to its tip. It went soaring through one of the still-sizzling walls of flame that lay scattered about the courtyard, catching fire as it went. A streaking bolt of bright flame, it went straight through the chest of one of the four approaching warriors, came out the back side, and firmly embedded itself in the heart of the next warrior just behind him.

Lindel had killed two with one arrow.

"That's not a bad shot," Lindel congratulated himself, as he looked on approvingly at his handiwork while notching his next arrow.

The demon, green ooze dripping from the ruin of his right eye, lunged out towards Kilgar and Quickfoot. Weak though they both were from the results of Candol's curative spells, especially young Kilgar, they clambered back up along the fallen wall. The demon advanced, claws popping out to their full twelve-inch length.

"Stop there, foul beast!"

The demon turned, as did Kilgar and Quickfoot, to see the source of the new intruder, the one that would dare interrupt the demon just before his intended meal.

"Lorel?" Kilgar said with more than a little disbelief.

Lorel stood there, tree branches sticking out of his torn and battered armor, ragged scars all about his limbs, leaves scattered throughout his hair. He held his steel-blue sword in his hand, his lungs heaving as if from recent exertion.

"What does it take to kill him?" Quickfoot wondered. "Or rather, Schanter; or *is* it Lorel?"

The demon took a step towards the new intruder, just as he leveled his sword at the creature. A bolt of blue flame shot out towards the demon.

And promptly washed off of his thick hide. Lorel looked at his sword in puzzlement and then back up at the approaching demon.

"Come on," Quickfoot shouted out to Lorel, "even *I* know that fire doesn't hurt a demon!"

"It doesn't?"

Javelin of steel, now javelin of light. Streak of lightning come swiftly down from the heavens to strike full upon its target.

The electrical jolt sent Sheil-Bor(h) sprawling across the ground. Lightning danced off of him in great arcs as the hawkman readied his next spear. His clothes were singed almost to tatters, his skin blackened with soot.

Sheil-Bor(h) stood up. Lightning still arced off of him as he calmly examined himself, observing the minor fact of his continued life.

"Hmm," he said. "It would appear that another benefit of the Hevon Gems has spared me. Well, as Eldar would no doubt say, 'waste not want not.'"

Just as the hawkman raised up his next spear, Sheil-Bor(h) pointed out his hand. The lightning dancing across his body suddenly collected around his arm, gathering swiftly around his hand into a single ball. Resting not a moment, the lightning shot back up through the sky, a larger bolt than when it had hit Sheil-Bor(h), now racing back up towards the hawkman. The bolt hit just as the second lance was about to leave the feathered one's hands, detonating the lance to add to its own great electrical roar.

Flash of light, crack of thunder; startled squawk giving way to the sound of doom. Flash of fireworks, brightly lit display around an explosion of feathers. Flaming bits of flesh coming down like an expanding bloom of colorful shooting stars drifting down upon the wind.

Sheil-Bor(h) looked up at the falling debris that had once been the hawkman, nodding at the results.

"A most satisfactory display."

The elemental came whirling its way straight towards Mauklo, the force of its twisting winds enough to rend the wizard apart should it ever hit. Like a whirlwind given life, it came at him.

Mauklo smiled.

"This is going to be too easy," he said in a calm mater-of-fact voice. "I don't believe that I have an elemental in my collection yet; of course, I'll have to destroy its mind before I can get it to serve me."

Mauklo took out a small vial from within his robes. He then looked up at the approaching creature as he unstopped the vial. Magic arising within him, he said but one word to let it off.

"In!"

"AAAAAAAAAAAAAAA!!!"

Lorel went slamming hard up against a charred stone slab, his bones crunching beneath him, so hard had been the demon's slap. A single set of claw marks lay streaked across his chest, ripping shreds through the metal plate that had covered him. The creature approached Lorel, fire now dancing from its claws. Lorel looked up as it approached, his sword lying too many feet away for him to get to it in time.

A single coin tossed up through the air, tumbling end over end to finally land down upon an open palm and turned over onto the back of another hand.

"In the name of Indra, I banish you back to the foul pits from whence you came!"

There was a sudden crack of thunder around the demon. It turned around in time to see Candol pointing his hand directly at him. With a sudden roar of power, the demon felt himself pushed away, back to his own plane of existence.

Clap of thunder, roar of flame. Demonic wail rising upon the winds, soon to be heard no more. Bright flaming explosion, a pyrotechnic banishment leaving nothing left to mourn.

Candol walked over to help Lorel up, while Kilgar and Quickfoot came out of the rubble to join them. Quickfoot came over to the priest and looked up, question on his face.

"What was the coin toss for?"

"Well," the priest shrugged, "I had to decide if I should kill it or just banish it."

The two remaining warriors charged ahead, swords out, running straight towards their intended targets.

Unfortunately for them, they chose Bronto and Shong.

The two just looked at each other, in the silent communication that only professional warriors that are also fast friends seem to share. Bronto looked down at the broken hilt of his old sword, lying by his feet; broken though it was, it was still the length of a good longsword. In one swift motion he picked up the sword and hurled it through the air like some large knife, while Shong leaped straight up.

The warrior on the left was caught full in the chest by Bronto's throw, as three feet of broken sword plunged straight through his chest, the hilt even embedding itself in past the ribcage. The force of the blow not only stopped the warrior's onrushing charge, but threw him back across the courtyard, his crumpled body landing in a heap over a hundred feet away.

The second warrior's charge was interrupted by the sudden landing upon his shoulders of an uninvited guest. His charge turned into a tumble as he tried to catch himself from the sudden additional weight. As he tried to balance himself, he looked up to see Shong dancing upon his shoulders, sword coming down. The warrior sliced up with his own sword, trying to block the attack.

But just as Shong's sword would have hit, he leapt off from the warrior's shoulders, somersaulting around through the air just as the warrior's own sword came up smashing himself in the nose. Shong landed directly in front of the warrior, just as the other was screaming out the pain of his own wounding, and sliced across with his diamond blade. Before he had time to bring his sword around to bear, the warrior fell into two pieces, severed cleanly at the waist.

"You know," Shong said as Bronto walked up next to him, "I really don't think that they're making fallen heroes like they used to."

Thick strands of wire went streaming down for Eldar, Sindar, and Sabu, wrapping their way around them. Eldar slashed out with his flaming sword, cutting through the strands like they were but string, but still more came down from the three wizards. Sindar stabbed out with his mind, using his great mental power to try and crush the mind of one of the three, but his effort was thwarted; one of the wizards blocked Sindar's mind with his own mental power. Sabu sent up a bolt of force from his staff, but it was only met with by another such bolt from above. Every move that was made, was matched.

"They can counter every move that we can make," Sindar said, "defend against every magic that we have, predict everything we might do."

"We appear to be equally matched," Sabu observed. "Suggestions?"

"Yeah," Eldar said, as he hacked at another weaving metal strand, "how's about something completely random."

Eldar quickly took a small vial from out of his earthen-colored tunic. As he opened up the vial, Sabu smiled at recognition of what it contained.

"You aren't going to—" Sabu began.

"Of course I am," Eldar smiled, as he held the vial in one hand, pointing out towards the three with the other, flaming sword in hand. "You know how I always like a good party."

His sword took on a watery color, its flames dying down as the Hevon Gem of Water arose from deep within Eldar. The liquid in the vial suddenly emptied, as if draining directly into Eldar's hand through the base of the vial. Just as it was emptied, Eldar's sword flashed with the multiple colors of a new liquid pouring into it. As Sabu fended off another bolt of force, Eldar shot a streamer of rainbow-colored liquid straight up at the three wizards.

347

The water hit them full on in the face, exploding into a shower of colored rain that swirled around them. The three threw their magic defensively around themselves, but then saw that the water had done no harm, its force not enough to hurt them, its light rain nothing but a nuisance. They faced back down towards Sabu and the others once again.

"Ha!" the first wizard called down. "Your magic weakens; that little trickle of rain did nothing."

Sindar leaned over to Eldar, whispering in the elf's ear.

"That's water from one of the ponds back in Fawsil's village," Sindar noticed.

"Yeah," Eldar smiled, "the one I wanted to refill my old jug from but no one would let me. I snuck some out when no one was looking. This ought to be real interesting; I gave them my full supply."

The first wizard looked angrily down as he thrust out his hands for his next spell, certain to kill them this time. But something was wrong, the magic wouldn't come. He looked down at his hands.

They were flippers.

Now, the ability to manipulate magic by the intricate movements of one's fingers assumes that one *has* fingers. The first wizard looked around at his two companions for help.

The second wizard was growing several feet of purple fur out from every surface of his body. Fur ballooned up underneath his clothing, expanding around his body in tangled twists. The second wizard struggled as hair covered his eyes so he couldn't see, grew long over his hands so he found it difficult to grasp anything but more hair, and started growing out of his mouth and over his tongue so he couldn't talk. A muffled noise was all that the second wizard was able to emit.

The third wizard was of no help either. His head was lolling from side to side as he danced around in the sky in a staggering walk upon the air. His skin went from blue to pink to orange, as he grasped at imaginary objects in the air about him.

"That third one's drunk," Sabu noted.

The third wizard grabbed hold of the first wizard's two flippers as if he would dance with him, and then kissed him full on the lips, whirling around in a drunken tangle as the first wizard struggled to keep his feet from becoming flippers also.

"Drunk nothing," Eldar beamed, "he's stoked to the gills!"

"A most interesting drink you favor," Sindar commented, as they watched the display.

"You should see the stuff at parties," Eldar grinned widely.

"But we should now use this opportunity," Sindar continued, "to finally be finished with them."

"I think it would be a mercy-killing at this point," Sabu put in as he raised up his staff.

Three joined together as one, their powers unite; three in the sky, their powers in chaos. A bright star lights up the night, expanding white and hot in the heavens. Bright bringer of doom shining high over the hill, its luminescent energy reducing all it touches back to the stuff of creation. As a small sun did it glow for several long moments, visible for miles around, before it faded down into the stillness of the night. Gone.

Mauklo walked back up to the rest, discretely putting a small vial away within his robes, while the others gathered together from their various individual combats. Eldar gave a loud whooping cheer as the three wizards became no more than a memory, while the others walked up in tired relief.

"We got them all!" Eldar shouted out in glee.

Laughter rang out from high above.

"All except for one," Lindel said, aiming his bow up at the sky.

"I almost forgot about him," Shong said, bringing his sword back to a ready stance.

Krey hovered high above them, standing atop a large dark cloud that moved and churned beneath him, slowly forming into an almost complete shape of a large dragon, dark cloudy claws reaching out like vast islands of black mist as the cloud that would be its head slowly floated into position.

Concern crossed Sabu's face as he saw this.

"Hey," Eldar said, gazing upwards, "have you noticed how that big cloud up there looks like——"

"Yes," Sabu interrupted, "I know of the spell that he casts; I read about it in the dimensio-book of magic. He means to shape that cloud into a large creature that will wipe out everything within a mile of where it attacks. We can't let him finish that spell."

"If we attack him all at once, we can beat him," Lindel said, aiming his bow.

"Right!" Sabu shouted out, as he raised his staff up high. "Now!"

Energy coursed out from Sabu's staff, while Sindar's mind sought a crushing blow upon Krey's. Flame and lightning leaped out from Eldar's aimed sword, Lindel unleashing his golden bow. Flaming black tendrils flew out from

Mauklo's arms, racing swiftly through the air, as a long windy dart launches out from Sheil-Bor(h). Candol summoned down a bolt of lightning from the sky, glowing brightly with Indra's power. Much energy did they expend on keeping their spells on course, so far away was Krey, even Lindel expending what magic he himself had to allow his arrow to fly true for the long mile towards its target.

They came at him all at once, heading towards him as one. And it is a certainty that they would have hit their target true.

Thirty feet away from Krey, just when it looked like Krey's demise was a certainty, it all dispersed into the air. The energy from Sabu's staff and the flame from Eldar's sword both discorporated into harmless flickers of light, while Mauklo's black reaching tendrils turned to dust to but float upon the wind swirling around Krey. Lindel's arrow turned to golden ash while Sheil-Bor(h)'s bolt of wind dispersed into vague little dust-devils. Even Candol's bolt from the heavens crackled and strained, surrounding Krey in a globe of lightning sixty feet across, but did not penetrate. They all looked up in astonishment at the lack of any sort of result.

Krey laughed, his laughter rumbling across the dark sky as he then made but a single casual gesture with his hand.

Several bolts of black lightning arced off from his hand, racing through the air as they quickly slammed against the hill. Bronto and Shong were both knocked into the hard stone of the courtyard, the large man's form crashing a full foot deep into the now-shattered stone. A bolt arced through Candol, pinning him to the ground as he suddenly felt all strength drained from his limbs. Ebony-colored lightning threw Lorel aside like a rag doll as he leapt in to shield Kilgar from harm. Quickfoot was tossed straight into Lindel as they were both slammed hard against the distant Palace gates. Another bolt went up Eldar's sword and straight through his arms, plunging the screaming elf back hard against the back-flying form of Sabu, as another bolt raced up the young wizard's staff. A black bolt lanced through Sindar, leaving a black mark upon his chest as he was thrown to the ground, left weak and near death. Sheil-Bor(h) flew through the air, to be crumpled up against a wall of the Palace, back broken in several spots as he fell to the ground beside Lindel. Even Mauklo was tossed through the air to land far across the courtyard.

Krey laughed at the broken bodies strewn below him, his cloud's shape now almost complete.

"You see," his voice came echoing down, "there never was really any contest in the matter. You *shall* work for my master, willingly or not. I give you one chance; who shall volunteer before I deal with the rest?"

"Eldar," Sabu groaned weakly, "can you sense—"

"An amulet," Eldar coughed, charred hands trying to point but failing, "around his neck. I sense it protecting him."

"We're too far away," Sindar said faintly as he coughed up large gouts of blood.

"Even Bronto couldn't throw that far without getting hit by Krey," Eldar coughed again, his body now starting to shake from the aftereffects of the charring it had just taken.

Shong lay unconscious while Bronto, weak though he now was, tried to pry himself up out from the rocky bed in which he was now embedded. Candol tried to grab hold of his priestly sigil but was too weak to clutch his fingers, the effort almost draining him of the last of his strength. Kilgar, shielded as he had been by the now unconscious quivering form of Lorel, crept quickly behind a fallen slab of stone, determined not to get killed a second time in the same evening while he waited for any opportunity to make his skills useful. Over by the Palace Lindel picked up his bow, still in hand, and reached back in his quiver for an arrow.

Only one arrow had survived Krey's onslaught. He slumped back weakly against the wall with a heavy sigh, then looked over at Quickfoot laying beside him. The small one was unconscious, bleeding from his head by a wound caused by his sudden impact upon the Palace gates. He looked over at Sheil-Bor(h), his vague wisdom now doing his broken body no good. Lindel dragged himself over to Sheil-Bor(h), pulling out a vial as he did so. He undid the cork with his teeth and began sprinkling its liquid contents upon the broken body.

"I hope you got some useful advice when you come to," the golden haired elf said, "'cause we need some way of getting close to Krey without getting blasted again."

"Well," Krey's voice came down, "what is your answer?"

The silence over the courtyard was broken only by scattered gasps of pain and effort. Darkness settled over the silence as Krey's cloud neared completion.

"I will join you!"

Several weak eyes turned to see Mauklo slowly standing up, tattered and blackened robe drawn about him, facing up towards the sky.

"It figures that *piëgo* would join," Kilgar spat out, fingering his curved knife.

"What's he up to now?" Eldar grimaced in pain as he tried to get his charred hands to unclench their frozen grip around his sword. "He doesn't like us anymore?"

"He probably," Sabu groaned with effort as he reached towards the now unconscious form of Sindar, "doesn't like your sense of humor."

"Now who," Eldar tried to force a smile from out of his world of pain, "would *not* like my sense of humor?"

"Sindar's unconscious," Sabu said, as he checked the other wizard's eyes, "probably trying to use his mind to heal himself again."

"I see clearly now which side shall win!" Mauklo called out, as he stepped across the courtyard. "And I always wish to be on the winning side."

A thunderous chuckle came down from the dark sky.

"Ah," Krey said, "now why did I know that you'd be the first to see it *my* way?"

Mauklo shrugged and gave a pleasant smile.

"Perhaps it was inevitable," he said.

"Very well," Krey called down, "come up to me and together we shall dispose of the rest."

"As you wish, my lord," Mauklo said humbly, putting out his arms to either side, palms outward. "I am but your humble servant."

Mauklo rose up on a cushion of air, floating up above the hill, heading slowly up towards Krey.

Sheil-Bor(h) coughed as Lindel helped him sit up, his broken bones slowly mending.

"How are you feeling?" the elf asked.

"This humble one has felt better," Sheil-Bor(h) answered, "but it shall do for now. What has happened?"

"Mauklo's gone over to Krey," Lindel answered, "and I'm too far away for my bow to do any good."

Sheil-Bor(h) glanced over at Mauklo's slowly rising form as it headed up towards Krey, supplication on the Sileen's face. He regarded the scene for a moment and then turned back to Lindel.

"It is quite dark," he said, "can you still shoot well?"

Lindel gave him a look as if he'd just said something infinitely stupid.

"I'm an elf," Lindel cocked his head to one side, "I can see as well at night as you can during the day. But I only have one arrow left; I have to get real close."

"I shall arrange for that," Sheil-Bor(h) said weakly, "just ready your bow and wait until the amulet around his neck is gone; it protects him."

"Figures," Lindel said, as he gathered up his bow. "It seems like every wizard around here has a magic amulet of one sort or another. But he's not going to just take the thing off."

"Never mind about that," Sheil-Bor(h) said, "just have your arrow ready."

Sheil-Bor(h) raised a hand up towards the elf, making weak magical gestures in his direction. A slight breeze seemed to gather around the elf, weaving in and around him. As Lindel looked at his hands he seemed to fade from sight, not becoming invisible but becoming one with the wind, his body loosing its solidity as he faded from sight. He felt himself rushing with the wind, as airy and indefinite as was the breeze that blew around him, and yet he could still feel his own body, could still feel the bow in his hand, the arrow notched in its string. He could still see with eyes that weren't there and touch with hands that couldn't be felt as anything but a late Fall breeze.

"By what magic——" Lindel began, his voice coming out in slow windy gusts.

"Speak not," Sheil-Bor(h) cautioned him, "and he will not hear you. Now go; I will take care of the small one."

Lindel looked over at the unconscious form of Quickfoot and then back over at Sheil-Bor(h), lying weakly against the Palace gates. He then turned towards the rising form of Mauklo, hands out in supplication as he rose up higher still. Lindel grabbed firmly onto his bow of wind and turned towards the courtyard.

He floated up with the breeze, being nothing more than a faint updraft.

Candol's hand finally found its weak way to his sigil, as he lay gasping there upon the ground, eyes faced up towards the rising form of Mauklo.

"I come to thee, my new master," he heard Mauklo say as he rose up. "I pledge thee all the loyalty due your superior magnificence."

"Indra," Candol whispered weakly to himself, "do not forsake this, your imperfect servant. Give me the strength to vanquish my enemy."

Candol tried to hold onto his sigil for several long moments, but his body finally failed him. With a sigh, his head fell back to the ground, his sigil slipping from his grasp.

"Shong," Bronto weakly nudged at his friend, "you okay?"

Bronto had pulled himself up out of the hole his fall had caused, and was lightly nudging the unconscious form of his friend. Shong groaned absently, but would not wake up. Bronto looked up into the dark sky.

"I guess it's just me then," he said to himself. "You rest there my friend. Now, what can I use..."

Bronto looked around at the wreckage that his body had made of the courtyard's ground, the large boulders carved loose by the deep hole that he'd finally crawled out of.

"Boulders?" Bronto's face lit up.

A large smile spread slowly across the big man's face.

"Eldar," Sabu said, as he tried to weakly prop himself up with his staff, "get ready."

"For what?" Eldar asked with dismay, his sword finally pried loose from his charred grasp. "I can't even hold my sword."

"You don't need to," Sabu said, as he tried to stand up. "Hevon is *within* you; you need not your sword to use it, nor *any* other external accouterment."

"I guess so," Eldar said doubtfully, trying to rise to his feet without using his hands. "But, what about your staff? You use *that.*"

"Hey," Sabu protested, "all wizards need a staff; it's good for the image."

"Then you *don't* need the staff?"

"Not really."

"And how long has *this* been going on?"

"I haven't really needed my staff since we got our Earth Gems," Sabu said, finally getting to his feet with a gasp of pain, "and haven't needed it at *all*, since our visit to the king's treasure chamber."

"And were you planning on keeping this a secret much longer," Eldar said with more than a little exasperation in his voice.

"You never asked," Sabu shrugged weakly. "Now get ready."

"Okay," Eldar said, "but we're going to have to have a long talk some rise."

"Come to me, my new servant," Krey motioned, his cloud now but moments away from completion. "Come and be at my side, that I may take you into the service of Miro."

"As you wish, my lord," Mauklo said, eyes lowered, hands spreading out to either side as if in supplication.

Mauklo floated up towards Krey, now a full mile above the distant ground. Unseen to either, a gusty breeze hovered just out of range of the dark cloud, watching and waiting, its unseen windy bow drawn tight, unsure which of the two to yet shoot at. Mauklo approached, coming closer to his new master. He raised up his empty arms, palms spreading open before him, as Krey beckoned to him.

"I come but to serve you," Mauklo said with an unnerving smile, floating nearer.

Mauklo came to within thirty feet of Krey, passing through into the area shielded by Krey's amulet. The windy figure changed its target, knowing now that the traitorous Mauklo was beyond his grasp and that only the death of Krey could now bring him to justice. Lindel carefully drew back on his bow.

Mauklo slowly brought his hands up to either side of his head, empty palms open for Krey to clearly see. He floated to within ten feet of the dark wizard.

"I come to you with open hands," Mauklo said, "that you may know my intensions are true."

Mauklo smiled pleasantly as Krey motioned him closer, his cloud now just completing itself. Deep within the empty palms, a dim green glow began to pulsate; the color of trees, the glow of nature, tiny crystal buried deep within the center of its glow.

The glow of Wood.

Twin missiles of wood, slim lances longer than a man is tall, sent flying swiftly through the air. Wood sent speeding faster than lightning, its aim held true by the very air upon which it flew. Long splinters of death streaking straight for their target, wooden fingers clutching towards the dark heart of evil.

Krey cried out in pain, his scream echoing far upon the dark winds. One of the wooden shafts had hit him full in the stomach, bouncing off as if from having hit something harder than itself but doubling Krey over in pain nonetheless. The second shaft had pierced through his left shoulder, dark blood spurting out in its wake as three feet of shaft lanced through his body. Krey screamed his pain for all the world to hear.

As fast as his Hevon Gem of Air could carry him, Mauklo flew over to Krey's side, evil grin on his face as he ripped the amulet off from around Krey's neck.

"I see that you haven't figured out who I'm *really* loyal to," Mauklo smiled pleasantly, as the winds that bore him carried him swiftly away from the necromancer.

Like a bomb, several things immediately went off. A fast moving shaft of air went slicing up through the air, solidifying into a single golden arrow just before it pierced Krey straight through the heart. Then, like a display of fireworks, bolts of every form of energy at their disposal came rocketing up from the hill below. Just as Krey was staggering from the arrow, trying to use his necromantic powers to yet survive the well-aimed shaft, a bolt of fire hit him full in the face, followed quickly by another bolt, then by lightning and a sudden blast of cold. Krey was pelted about with hit after hit, becoming the centerpiece in a maelstrom of magic and power as he tumbled about in the sky.

Mauklo watched as the crowning touch was a single boulder, thrown up from but one man, hurtling up with an unnatural velocity to catch Krey full-on just as the retribution of Indra came down at him from his other side, a red bolt of death aimed at what was left of the wizard.

A scream blew high upon the wind, singing through the trees as Dwingale came out of her home in the trees. The battle in the sky had drawn the attention of everyone in the village, and probably everyone in the valley. She ran out to the ledge in time to see a tremendous explosion lighting up the night sky.

If a dragon doesn't die quietly, then a necromancer with the power of Krey dies even less so. Though it was many miles away the explosion was almost blinding, as Krey's power was unleashed in one mighty death throw that lit up with all the colors of creation. Wind howled through the trees, threatening to shake them off from their foundations with its violence. As Dwingale grabbed onto a nearby railing for support she saw a distant black cloud, its form resembling that of a large dragon, suddenly explode outwards in a gigantic belch of black steam, sending the gathered bits of itself scattering far out upon the winds.

As the winds calmed down, and the other elves scurried about trying to find out the source of the display, only Dwingale then knew just what had happened. She smiled up into the night sky, suddenly the most pleasant evening that the Valley Of Lights had seen in five thousand rels, and thought of her beloved.

"I just hope that he remembers to clean that head off *before* he brings the drippy thing into our new home."

On a mountain cliff at the southern boarder of the Valley, a lone hawkman kept vigil over the quiet night, his blue-streaked wings folded back behind him. Quiet, that is, until a sudden explosion caught his attention. He looked up to see the bright flare of light; over a hundred miles away and still could he see it, its luminous incandescence a bright star in the night. He could think of but one cause for its making.

The Kÿecian's beak curved, as best it could, into a satisfied smile. He flapped back his colorful wings, the streak down his feathered back shining out in the night, and took to the air.

The others will have to be told, Narudwa thought as he squawked out his joyous message into the night, *the unthinkable has happened.*

The spirit of Thïr Tÿorca shall be reborn.

Cheers rose up from the hillside as Lindel solidified and Mauklo settled down to the ground; self-congratulatory cheers at having beaten a millennia-old evil. Cries of 'Karu' echoed over the battle-torn hill, cries given loud and clear despite the exhaustion felt by all; a release of the soul, a final purging of despair. Candol staggered over to help Eldar's charred arms as Sheil-Bor(h) came over carrying the slowly-stirring form of Quickfoot. Sindar carefully sat himself up as his body had finally healed itself enough for him to move about, if rather slowly. Kilgar came over, the limping Lorel beside him as he helped him to walk. Sabu collapsed upon the ground, completely spent, while he waited for Candol to come around to him.

"You tried to save me," Kilgar was saying to Lorel, "a Destir never forgets a debt."

"You know," Lorel grimaced, "I think I've finally learned enough about you to treasure that debt. I wonder what the *adults* of your people are like."

Kilgar just smiled, the only true smile that Lorel had yet seen the young boy make.

"And thank Schanter for me too," Kilgar added.

"Who?"

"Never mind."

"I hope I can find enough of Krey's head left to piece together," Eldar smiled, as he flexed his newly-healed hands.

"You aren't *still* going through with that, are you?" Sabu said with exasperation as Candol now tended him.

"Yep," Eldar grinned, "I'm going to keep my promise and bring it right to her, dripping and all."

"Just don't do it around me," Quickfoot said tiredly, as he stirred on the ground next to Sheil-Bor(h). "I'm tired of seeing bloody body parts; especially when they're mine."

"Don't worry, small one," Sindar said, his own body continuing to quickly repair itself, "our adventure in this valley appears to be at an end. You shall soon have plenty of time to go and steal yourself all the food and knives you want."

"Even pastries?" Quickfoot perked up.

"Oh, we're *far* from finished," Sabu quickly said. "There's the armory that we found in the Palace to salvage, and Dwingale's people to get moved over to our island, and surely there must be some old books in the Palace that no one has seen since the last Donjflou."

"Enough," Eldar interrupted his friend tiredly, "save it for when my ears stop ringing from that last explosion. Besides, we still can't use your teleport spell to get all that stuff out of here."

"Krey's power over this land was broken when you destroyed him."

The voice came from the direction of the Palace gates. Everyone looked over towards the new intruders, tired but ready to jump towards their weapons if need be.

"And that includes his blocking of your powers," the voice continued. *"Your powers will work now to get you away from this valley."*

From out of the shadows walked three figures, white-haired men dressed in long white robes flowing down to the ground, the night making seem more solid the transparence of their forms. A dim glow of light surrounded them as they walked the short distance across the courtyard. Eldar was the first to recognize them as they came out of the night.

"Hey, it's those nameless guys that we met earlier."

"I would think 'unwanted spirit guides' to be a more apt description," Mauklo quipped.

"When we met you before," Bronto said, as he thought back to their previous encounter, "you mentioned that you would be our allies if we completed our quest."

"Yes," Candol said, standing up from his tending of Sabu, "and that you would need our Hevon Gems with which to be free."

"They also said," Sabu said, standing now without the help of his staff, "that it would happen when our quest is complete. I have a strange hunch that we never knew truly what our quest was when we started this journey."

"Ah," said the one on the left, *"then you have learned."*

"And, have you also figured out," continued the one on the right, *"what you are and what you might be?"*

"We are not servants of Miro," Sabu said with mild firmness in his voice as he looked over at them, "therefore we are his enemies; there can be no in-between in this world. But beyond that, I fear that we may never really know."

"For once the brain here is right," Eldar said, thumbing in Sabu's direction. "What we *are* is what we *do*, and that changes every moment of our lives."

"Eldar getting philosophical?" Lindel mocked. "Truly this is a sign."

"We've all changed," Sindar said, "not only in what we've learned about magic and combat, but about our selves and our limits."

"The quest for one's self is a never ending journey," Sheil-Bor(h) added, "a voyage into an inner eternity."

"You still have much to learn," the man in the middle said, *"for there is a reality beyond Sheil-Bor(h)'s philosophical arguments, a reality in which you can truly know yourself, with no restrictions upon your soul."*

"It's real comforting to know that for *once* one of Sheil-Bor(h)'s little founts of wisdom might be a bit off," Shong smiled.

"But, you must have the confidence to know yourself, to realize what you truly are," the one on the left said, *"for only then can you* Become, *be more than what you seek. But let not confidence be confused with false pride, you must know yourself precisely; no more, no less."*

"But, to answer your question," the one on the right said, *"allies we promised, and allies we are. As we guide your destiny, so shall you one rise free us of our prison."*

"But, we have a lot of Hevon Gems now," Eldar offered. "Maybe if we——"

"You have not a complete set," replied the central one, *"nor any real knowledge of what they truly are. When the time is come, then shall we be free."*

"Just one thing," Kilgar asked, as he walked up to face them. "Do you have any *real* names?"

The three men started to glow brightly as their voice drifted upon the wind, their forms to grow fainter as they answered the boy's simple question.

"We are the Nameless Ones," the central one answered, *"beyond that we cannot answer until the time of our freedom. But be patient; the time of your coming has been long in the waiting, its fulfillment close at hand."*

As they faded from sight, their forms dissolving down into three fading points of light, their last words could be heard with the blowing of the breeze.

"To fight He who cannot be beat, you must become that which truly knows of itself."

As the three Nameless Ones faded from sight, concern grew over Sabu's face, thoughtfulness to fill his mind. Eldar interrupted his reverie with a slap on his friend's back, a merry smile dancing about his cheeks.

"Hey, this is all just a bit too philosophical for now," Eldar said. "Why don't we just celebrate and worry about the philosophy later."

"That is what worries me," Sabu said, as he turned to Sheil-Bor(h). "Sheil-Bor(h), in all the theories of philosophy, is it ever written that one can *ever* really know one's self completely?"

"It has always been said," Sheil-Bor(h) answered, as he walked over towards where the three Nameless Ones had disappeared, "that there are different degrees of knowing one's self, but that one can never truly know one's own soul. People are always changing, always adding new things to their soul, and that is why one can never really know. Time changes one's self and therefore one's perceived knowledge of one's self."

"But," Sabu persisted, "is there any sort of theoretical type of being that can truly know itself; past, present, *and* future selves; encompassing *all* that one may become?"

Sheil-Bor(h) thought for several moments, all eyes following his slow walk around them as he thought the question through. Finally, he stopped and looked up at the stars brightly speckling the sky overhead, as he gave his answer.

"Yes."

"That's what I was afraid of," Sabu said, as he faced up to the others. "I know now what it is that we must become."

"You do?" Lindel asked.

"Yes," Sabu looked up at the stars shining down brightly from overhead, "and that's what frightens me."

CHAPTER TWENTY-EIGHT
The End of the Beginning

R.K.: 9,990, 20 Monwir:

Our long quest with Thir Tjorca is finally over, although I know now that we never truly knew of what our quest was about. Whatever the Nameless Ones are, they are right in that our destiny lies with something much greater; much more fearful. For now though, I shall take Eldar's advice in just worrying about the present.

There is a saying: Remember the Past, think towards the Future, live in the Present. Advice I shall hold closer to my own heart from now on.

It has been little over a kev since we left the Valley Of Many Lights, but already are Fawsil's people making themselves at home on our little island, that which we now call Haikldalnsa. If Lindel showed miracles in initially bringing the local forest back to life, then it is indeed wondrous what a whole village full of forest elves can do for it. The trees blossom and prosper as they shape their growth into the natural tree houses that are to be the elves' new home. The forest have they filled with many rare and enchanted creatures that they bring with them, including even a unicorn or two, a friendly forest giant, and a few enchanted trees. They bring much life and gaiety to our home.

Eldar tries to help Fawsil's people as much as he can, questioning them about any stories they may have about their ancestors as he does so. He has made it his goal to bring back long lost elven arts, including those of the Evolins. What a blessing for the world it would be indeed if he could! The abilities and knowledge of the Evolins has been legend since long before the first of the Great Human Kingdoms was even founded. The resurrecting of such old knowledge would be a truly worthy achievement.

Dwingale is the only one of Fawsil's people to not live in the forest; Eldar's seen to that.

She has taken up residence in our castle, although she won't move into Eldar's room until she has been properly courted; much to Eldar's impatience. As such, Eldar has been lavishing her with all sorts of little gifts, and promises to arrange for a proper wedding with a wedding ring worthy of his love for her. Lindel says that she's just having sport with him, that all a forest elf wedding amounts to is the couple getting together in a forest and exchanging vows with only the trees as witness; end of wedding. I say she's playing him like a flute.

We also have some new guests living in the seaside cliffs; some of Narudwa's people have come to live on our island as well. Apparently impressed by the final display against Krey, and remembering Bronto's ancestry and his promises to them, they appear to have taken us as a new focus for the future, especially Bronto. Well, so be it then. Although, our island is getting a little crowded now.

We have made many allies along our journey, many new friends. We have found that there are many people out there, and indeed whole societies, that have lain hidden and dormant, too fearful of Miro's wrath to poke their heads up into the sunlight. Bronto is right in saying that people have cowered under Miro's name for too long, and if we be the catalyst that brings a new age into this world, then it is a fate that none of us would now refuse. I hope, though, that as we lead them into the light, that the light doesn't make of them a target for an old evil.

I have also thought of some others that we have met, some whose place in things is doubtful at best. Po-Adar for instance; undoubtedly a powerful wizard, but also prone to a sort of insanity that looks to be even more dangerous than that of Lorel. Sheil-Bor(h) tells me that we shall meet him again, his prophetic abilities telling him that Po-Adar indeed has a place in what is to come, but of what that may be cannot be said. A most interesting person, I hope we are more ready for him when next we meet.

On a happier note, we have apparently come back in time to see the dragon eggs hatch. Blag-ak is running all over like an expectant father, which for an ogre of his size is quite a sight indeed. Lindel is helping to make sure that their hatching goes safely, and even Bronto is eager to observe; he has gained a new liking of dragons since our journey began.

We have all changed on this trip, gained a new respect for not only what lies out there but for ourselves as well. I remember well what the Nameless Ones said that we must become and I have figured out what it is, as I have no doubt that Sheil-Bor(h) has also. I haven't told the others though, as that very knowledge could very much influence their actions. It is something that each must figure out on his own, and come to terms with.

There are too many questions that lie open before us, unveiled by our recent journey. There is much more going on in the world than I think even the King suspects, much more than need be done before the coming Donjflou.

I hope that we are up to it.

Narudwa looked down upon the spreading green and *orain* of the forest below, knowing that below its innocent-looking canopy of colorful leaves lay an entire elven village, even now using their magic and skills to turn the island into a sylvan paradise, hidden from the dangerous gaze of the outside world. He ruffled his wings out behind him as he clucked his beak in appreciation. Standing atop the cliff-side peak, he noticed Bronto making his way up to him along the treacherous rocky hillside.

"You should not come up here to me," Narudwa called out, "lest your blood of old spill itself all over the rocks below. I would have gladly come down to meet you."

"It *would* be a bit disappointing," Bronto chuckled loudly as he climbed nearer. "After all I've been through to be killed from slipping off from such a small *tadalnsa* as this."

"I suspect you would only be happy if you were killed by at *least* Traugh himself," Narudwa jibed as Bronto came up beside him.

"Oh, at the *very* least," Bronto said, his chest barely heaving from the exertion, his skin not even sweating.

He paused for a bit as he looked down at the view spread down around him. To his back the Sea Of A Thousand Islands lapped vigorously at the far bottom of the rocky cliffs, while beneath him the small mountain range stretched around half of their island's perimeter. The forest spread out for most of the island, while the flat beach at which they'd first set foot upon this small land was now sporting the beginnings of a dock; being built by a mix of elves and hawkmen, lead by the hard-working Shong.

"Now I know why you like to fly so much," Bronto breathed in deep of the sea air, "you like the view."

"It is indeed a secret that the likes of dwarves seem unwilling to come out from their underground caves to learn of," Narudwa answered. "But what brings you up here; surely not just the view?"

"The eggs are hatching," Bronto answered. "I thought you'd like to see dragons born free of either the Dragon Master or Miro's influence."

"That would indeed be a sight to remind this feathered heart of times of old, when dragonkind traded as friends with my people."

Narudwa spread out his wings in back of himself as he continued.

"Yes, I would indeed like to see that," he said. "Would you like a lift down?"

"Naw," Bronto waved him off, "getting down is the easy part. I'll even race you."

"I fear the sun has baked your brain, my friend," Narudwa chuckled. "My wings would give me a *slight* advantage in such a race."

"You think so?" Bronto cocked an eyebrow as he gave a mischievous smile.

Bronto walked over to the edge of the thin rocky ledge and looked down. Far below him was another rocky ledge, its narrow length leading on towards Blag-ak's cave. With a slight bending of his knees, Bronto launched himself up and out into the air. Narudwa watched in sudden fear as Bronto disappeared down below the ledge to the rocky ground far below. He ran over to the edge to look down, fully expecting to see his friend a flattened bloody mass below.

He was just in time to see the big man pick himself up and dust himself off. Narudwa smiled as Bronto waved up at him from a couple hundred feet below him and then started running on up the narrow ledge towards the cave.

Narudwa's laugh was heard as a sort of loud chuckling whistle, echoing out as he shook his head at Bronto's display. The hawkman spread out his wings and took to the air, still in wonder at the daring young Human.

"I will *not* be beaten by a groundling," he called out as he sailed down after him.

The large egg rocked back and forth in its rocky nest, cracking one slow bit at a time. Bronto walked into the cave to see Blag-ak, Quickfoot, and Lindel already peering down at the hatching wonder. As he went over beside Lindel, he saw a triangular snout poke itself out through the egg, struggling for freedom. A small claw soon followed, striking away at its confining prison. It struggled free of the egg, small unsure legs carrying it out across the rocks, moistness dripping from its hide, wings still slicked back to its leathery green hide. Cheers went up at the advent of its final freedom, even Quickfoot getting into the act.

It was the size of a large dog.

The other eggs also began to rock back and forth, several cracks now appearing in them as their occupants decided that it was time to be born. Blag-ak rumbled a large lopsided grin as he saw his charges fumble uncertainly across the cave floor. Quickfoot went up to the first one, hand reaching tentatively out as if to try and pet it.

"Well," he said, "I guess they aren't too bad when they're this small."

"Be careful," Lindel warned, as Quickfoot tried to scratch it behind the ears.

"It seems okay," Quickfoot replied. "What's to-Yow!"

The baby dragon nipped at the small one's fingers, Quickfoot just barely getting his fingers away from the reach of its teeth in time. Bronto's laughter rumbled through the cave as Lindel grinned.

"As I was saying," Lindel said, "it hasn't fed yet, and even this young, they eat *meat.*"

"*Now* you tell me!" Quickfoot said as he ran over to Blag-ak.

"Little friend be careful," the ogre scolded.

"Great!" Quickfoot said, as he nursed his finger in his mouth. "The big dumb *rik* is giving *me* advice now."

"Here," Lindel said, opening up a pouch at his side, "I brought something for the newborns."

Lindel reached into his pouch and brought out some dried strips of meat, tossing them to the rapidly hatching newborns. They watched as the little dragons greedily snapped up the offerings, two of them even getting into a little tug-of-war over one piece.

"This island shall soon be swarming with dragons," Narudwa said as he walked up behind them. "Maybe you should think of raising some sheep to feed them with."

"Blag-ak feed them. Make good mother."

"You do that, my large friend," Bronto said, "but as for myself, I have other plans for when they're grown."

Bronto looked down at the hatched eggs, watching the little ones at play as they scrambled around on the floor, stretched out their drying wings, and got into playful fights with each other. The big man's eyes lit up, a smile crossing his face.

"I'm going to *ride* them."

"Can I at least get it *bronzed?*"

"Just so long as that drippy thing stays *out* of this castle. This place *definitely* needs a woman's touch around here, and I *don't* mean that Kilinir person."

Eldar was walking down a hall in the castle, Dwingale at his side. He was holding a small sack, a bulge the size of a large melon at its bottom. Light came down from the ceiling, emitting from several small stones spaced throughout the rock; more of Sabu's improvements based on what he'd seen at Thïr Tÿorca. The empty hallway echoed with their footsteps as Eldar strove to keep up with Dwingale's increased pace, mock anger on her face.

"Or, you could just start a trophy room if you're going to keep bringing these things home," Dwingale suggested. "I'd rather not wake up every morning with him staring me in the face."

"Hey, I could make him into an ashtray?" Eldar offered. "But what makes you think I'll be having enough of them for a whole trophy room?"

She stopped in mid-stride and turned around to face him, her golden eyes staring up into his silver-blues. A slight smile crossed her face as she regarded the bold elf, now almost helpless before her. *Why is it that men always seem to loose any trace of a backbone when in the presence of their beloved,* she thought, *oh well, he's sweet enough.*

"Hey," she said, "who do you think is the seer in this family?"

She put both arms around Eldar, Eldar responding by hugging her close. She looked up into his puzzled face as she continued.

"You shall fill up the room with all manner of trophies," she said, her eyes briefly getting a somewhat faraway look, "maybe even ones that will surprise you."

"Hmm," Eldar wondered, as they stood there, hugging each other, Dwingale resting her head against his chest, "maybe a trophy room might not be half bad. Is there anything else you can foresee, my love?"

"My powers are limited, unlike those of the gold-skinned gypsy that visited our valley once before I was born," she said, as surprise crossed Eldar's face. "But this can I say: after we are married, before the Donjflou has passed will we have a baby boy; one of three children whose destinies will intertwine with our own."

"A son?" Eldar's eyes widened. "Hey, how soon? A rel? Two? When? And what's this about *his* destiny? Come on Dwingale, can't you tell me more?"

Dwingale just smiled to herself and said nothing. Eldar's questions just faded off, as if with distance, as she just stood there and hugged tight up against her love.

Mother always said that sometimes a little doubt was good for a relationship.

"I hear that you guys had quite an adventure after we left," Kilinir said as she and Kor-Lebear entered the dark room.

"It had its moments," Mauklo answered from where he sat at his worktable, large book open before him, several small vials laid out in front of him, "but how about yourselves? Did it go as we'd thought?"

Kilinir sat down at a chair that Mauklo offered, Kor-Lebear preferring to stand, always ready, always suspicious. At a gesture from Mauklo, light rose up in the room, illuminating the shelves of vials and beakers before him, and a large pentagram behind them, still smoking of recent use. When Kilinir was seated, Kor-Lebear answered the wizard's question.

"A wizard named Bedor now works with us," he said. "He's good at conjuring up creatures and the occasional illusion. We travel as a small carnival wagon specializing in acrobatic displays."

"And pretty good from what I hear," Mauklo said, while examining a vial with several small squirming shapes in it.

"But it's our *after-job* work that has really paid off," Kilinir smiled. "We've gotten a certain...reputation...in what we do now."

"Has anyone seen you in this after-job work, then?" Mauklo asked, as he put down the vial and picked up the next one.

"Of course not," Kor-Lebear said levelly, "we're professionals; we don't even allow ourselves the dubious pleasure of letting our faces be the last thing a victim sees before they die."

"Yes," Kilinir sighed, "if one is to become the best in this profession, one must sacrifice certain things; personal recognition is one of them."

"From what I hear there is recognition enough in what you do," Mauklo said, almost absently as a small wraith struggled vainly to break out of its imprisoning bottle.

"Certain calling cards have helped," Kor-Lebear responded. "But what about yourself; what have you done for your own part in this?"

"I have made certain...contacts; allies for the future," Mauklo said, putting the vial down as he turned around in his chair. "As have I not been idle."

Mauklo reached for a small vial, vague ghostly mist floating about within it. He held up the vial in his right hand as he regarded the undefined form within it.

"It was called Shandeür," he said thoughtfully, "before our favorite priest of Indra blasted it back to creation. I managed to harvest enough of its remains to make for some rather interesting uses."

"You're going to bring it back?" Kilinir asked.

"No," Mauklo said, putting the vial down, "Shandeür was too unstable and uncontrollable a creature for me to risk that. His essence, however, can have many uses for the imaginative."

"A lack of imagination is *one* thing that I won't fault you with," Kor-Lebear said, a slight grin crossing his shadowed face.

Mauklo sat back in his chair, a slow smile crossing his face that perhaps only the two others in this room would not be unnerved by, as he thought of the future.

"Yes," Mauklo finally said, "when the Donjflou comes, I shall see to it that I have no shortage of allies."

Mauklo glanced down at the vial of swirling vagueness that had once been part of Shandeür as he continued.

"Even if I have to *create* them myself."

The tall darkly-robed figure walked down the stone hallway. Roughly hewn, it was more of a long cave then anything constructed by tool or implement. A hood covered over his head, leaving his face cloaked in shadows. The figure's head nearly scraped the ceiling as it walked down, another much smaller figure hopping alongside of him. The smaller figure was no more than three feet tall, its green eyes almost matching the color of its skin, thick scraggly shoulder-length hair tossing about as it bounced alongside of the one to whom its loyalty would never die.

"You look good now master," it said cheerfully, "ugly enough to scare away demons, yes."

"Yes my faithful Jumpit," the tall figure said, "perhaps even ugly enough to reflect the pain the world has given me. Ugly enough to force respect upon others."

As they walked along, the taller figure's footsteps echoing down the long cave, Jumpit could see a glimpse every now and then of what lay beneath the hood. A thin pale worm-like tendril would stir beneath the covering hood where an eye would be, or almost-seen waves of dark movement rolling across beneath the shadow of the face. The figure lifted up a single robed arm, but it was not a hand that it ended in, but rather a large crab-like claw, with a foot-long tentacle coming off the back of it. With this appendage, the tall figure pointed down the hallway, towards where a light indicated the nearing end of the tunnel.

"I shall build upon my armies, Jumpit," it said, "build upon them, and then shall I show the world the danger of what they have spurned."

"Yes master, Jumpit like. Show them all!"

Jumpit jumped up and down as they came up to the mouth of their cave-like hallway. They walked out onto a wide ledge as the hallway opened up into an immense cavern, sounds of many impatient voices assembled within it. The ledge overlooked the bulk of the cavern and what lay gathered below as they walked out and stopped at its edge.

"With this," the tall figure waved out with his tentacled pincer, "shall I show them to *respect* the name of Po-Adar; teach them to *fear* it!"

Jumpit watched as the claw that Po-Adar gestured with casually shifted its shape, the tentacle withdrawing back into the skin, the pincer melting away into separate fingers and yellow-splotched skin. Po-Adar waved out with his now normal-looking hand as he gazed down at those gathered in the cavern below.

Long-nosed goblins by the thousands, dour-faced elves with skin the paleness of moonlight, ghouls crawling in amongst the others, a dozen wraiths floating about, with even the occasional sharp-toothed figure with the taste for blood in his mouth to be found. All gathered about, their numbers sprinkled with an occasional unidentifiable race, varying in ugliness and function, a result of Po-Adar's own experimentation. They all filled up the large cavern, thousands gathered below the feet of Po-Adar, if feet they still be. They drew quiet, more out of fear than of respect, as their master gazed down upon them.

"Yes Jumpit," Po-Adar shouted out, his voice echoing through the cavern, "all these and more shall I make an army out of. Mutants such as they've never seen; creatures to fill their cherished dreams with dread indeed. Creatures to trample their smooth faces into the muck. I'll show them what true ugliness is! Let no one use poor Po to then just toss him away like that King did."

"You want to conquer the King, master?" Jumpit asked eagerly, dancing now from foot to foot.

"No!" Po-Adar's voice echoed throughout the large cavern. "Not conquer, but destroy. And not just that King; even Miro would use poor Po for his own ends, that much I have foreseen. No Jumpit, they *all* must pay; equally and at my own whim."

"These armies," he slowly gesture with his hand, as it now slowly shifted into a single long tentacle, "shall grow vast indeed. Vast and horrible. I shall teach them to respect their nightmares, to dread the unknown."

He looked up towards the ceiling, hands, or rather hand and tentacle, rising up as if to greet a higher power. His voice carried out through those gathered below him; loyal to him they all were, their minds each twisted by the demented will of Po-Adar. They listened to his speech with the attention of the fanatic.

"I shall be the punisher of those who would abuse the Night!"

Cheers, growls, howls, and other cries boomed out through the cavern in response to their master's declaration, echoing their master's insanity. Po-Adar looked down, both pleased and angry at the same time, his emotions straddling both extremes. Darkness hid any expression on Po-Adar's face from even Jumpit's view, as his master looked down at him.

But he needn't see his face to know his master's heart; tonight Po would seek out a beautiful young maiden and honestly fall in love with her beauty. Before the evening would pass Po would drive her to near insanity as he had his way with her, and then would he change her into some twisted contortion of humanity with his alchemy, saying it to be for her own protection, that he did it out of his love for her. But before the light of morning would pass, he would be angered by the new ugliness that he would put upon her and just toss her out into the cavern with the others, just another mutant to loyally follow him in her broken insane mind. Yes, he knew his master well.

And that didn't matter, Jumpit thought, I shall stay with him no matter what.

Po-Adar looked down at Jumpit as the crowds in the cavern cheered and growled his name. Another small pale tendril came weaving its way out from Po-Adar's hidden face as his tentacle-hand shifted once again, now becoming a large furry paw.

"They shall do for now, my friend," he said quietly down to Jumpit, suddenly calm once more. "They *shall* do."

"Captain Starke," the tall well-muscled youth called out, his fair hair matching the clean shirt he now wore.

"Yes, your highness," Starke snapped to strict military attention, his yellow-brown skin shining in the sun, his long mustache neatly combed, his shoulder-length hair tied back behind him.

The youth walked across the open courtyard towards where Starke stood by one of the statues that guarded the entrance to the garden path. Tall pearly white buildings rose all about them, the sun reflecting brightly their walls to the streets far below. People went about on the streets and walkways around them, each going about their own business but none paying particular attention to Starke as the Prince approached him.

"Now you know it's just Filmar when you're not in front of your troops," Filmar smiled as he came up next to him. "You called me by name before you ever knew of my parentage."

"Yes, your highness, I mean," Starke struggled between form and friendship, "it's only proper that—"

"Never mind, Starke," Filmar smiled, "this isn't official business anyhow. Just pretend we're in the pub for a diid."

"Pub rules: no titles," Starke quoted as he relaxed a bit.

"Right," Filmar replied.

Filmar glanced on up the garden path that Starke stood in front of and then drew his attention back to Starke.

"Why don't we take a little walk," Filmar suggested, his hand motioning on towards the path.

"As you wish- Filmar."

"Ever the military professional," Filmar shook his head smiling, as they walked on into the grass-lined path. "That's probably why you'll go far, and probably why your men like you-aside from the fact that you treat them like real people instead of just grunts."

They walked around a tree-lined path, their leaves glistening silver in the sunlight as the path curved through them. They talked as the sounds of birds whistled overhead.

"I just remember what it was like to be a fresh recruit in someone's army," Starke answered, "Discipline is necessary in any army, but it does no good if the men don't respect you."

"Some of the men are even getting impressed with the company you used to keep," Filmar went on, "now that the stories of what happened at Thïr Tÿorca are starting to circulate."

"Yes," Starke sounded almost wistful as he thought of his former companions, "Sabu and Eldar and the others. I need no soothsayer to tell me that they shall rise up higher than any heights I shall ever attain."

"So," Filmar said, as they came out into a small clearing of grass and small flowery bushes, "you think that their destiny puts them out of reach of your friendship then?"

"No, Sire," Starke answered. "They shall always have my loyalty and my sword; I just realize that their concerns shall soon be beyond those of a mere individual. I will never fault them for it, I just realize it to be their own duty in life, as mine is to be a soldier."

"So, you think that they can't by dutiful and companionable at the same time then," Filmar said as he stopped at the edge of the clearing. "Maybe you should ask *them* what they think."

At a nod from Filmar, Starke looked up at what lay in the clearing. A single stone bench there stood, with but a single person now standing up from sitting on it, rune-covered golden staff at his side.

"I think," Sabu said, "that you should stop being the loyal soldier so often and start being the close friend that reminds us for what we fight."

"Sabu!" Starke broke out into a wide grin as he walked towards him, Filmar following behind. "I heard the stories and *knew* them not to be an exaggeration."

Sabu and Starke firmly clasped arms, admiration deeply imbedded in the solider's eyes as he vigorously greeted Sabu. Filmar stood a few feet away in the clearing, letting the two talk on their own.

"It probably *will* be an exaggeration by the time people are finished telling it, though," Sabu smiled as they released their clasp. "But what's this about you thinking that we'd forget you when we've gotten to wherever it is that we're going?"

"I just realized that those with a destiny such as yours won't have time for——"

"You can stop right there, Starke," Sabu smiled as he put a hand on the soldier's shoulder. "In all the wide universe there is no such thing as too small. I'm sure Kilgar would say something like 'once a friend always a friend', so you can stop thinking in terms of loyal henchman and start thinking in terms of just being a friend."

"In other words, 'pub rules, no titles'," Starke quoted with a smile.

"Just don't brag about knowing me too much," Sabu said as they walked over to the stone bench, "it'll make me feel a bit self-conscious."

"As you wish it," Starke said, as Filmar came over to sit down with them, and then brightened up with a new thought. "Maybe you could tell me and some of the men the true tale of Thïr Tÿorca."

"Before exaggeration has its way, you mean," Sabu said. "No, storytelling is more for Bronto; maybe you could get him to do it. Him and Shong came along with me."

"They're both here?" Starke asked.

"Yes," Sabu answered. "As a matter of fact, I think Shong is presently showing a certain sergeant just how much he's learned since their last fight together."

"It shall be good to see them again," Starke said, with just a trace of wistfulness in his voice, "as it is good to see you now."

"It shall be friendships such as what you and the others share that will get us through the coming rels," Filmar finally spoke up. "As what my father would call, the most precious of things."

"I know not what is to come," Starke said, facing Sabu, "nor is it my lot. I am but a soldier; I go where my lord would command and follow a true soldier's code. But this do I know: while what would truly change our world must be born from the hearts of men, it will be such as you and the others that must guide us all there. Greater, by far, than the masses will you be, that you may guide their hopes and dreams."

"If I didn't know better," Sabu said, standing up, "I would say that the Nameless Ones told *you* of what it is that we must become, for you talk like you know."

"No," Starke shook his head as he stood up and walked beside Sabu, "I need not anyone to tell me of what destiny Fate has in mind for you; I've known since before we came back from the island of Miro's dragon."

Puzzlement crossed Sabu's face as he stopped and looked Starke in the eye. Starke stood tall and proud, almost at attention as he faced Sabu.

"But, how could you have seen?" Sabu asked. "We ourselves hadn't even known, and only myself and Sheil-Bor(h) have yet figured out the meaning of the Nameless Ones' words."

"To watch the way that you all work and fight together," Starke answered, as the sun reflected off of the silvery leaves around them, "to see you in action against whatever odds you face, to see you determined to win against any foe that the forces of Miro would put against you…"

Starke paced out to the center of the clearing and turned back around to face Sabu before he finished, head held high.

"No," he said, "for such as what I saw in each of you all, there can *be* only one conclusion that I *could* reach. Only one answer to the Nameless Ones' puzzle of which you speak."

Starke placed his right hand firmly on the hilt of his black-bladed vortex sword, now resting peacefully in its sheath, as he continued.

"And I will personally deal with *anyone* that gets in the way of that destiny!"

She looked to be in her mid twenties, her golden hair flying with the wind, as blind golden eyes looked down from the hill atop which she stood. Her skin reflected its golden color in the light, her colorful gypsy dresses flowing down around her. A large bird stood by her side, almost as tall as was she. She watched the sun reflect off of Thïr Glomdäitaÿor's tall color-streaked golden walls, but a few miles away from where she stood. Blind though she was, she somehow seemed to be seeing something out in its direction, while her right hand absently scratched the large bird under its beak.

"My lady," a voice called out from behind her, "it is a fine day that you choose to be atop this hill. The sun shines out brighter than it has in a long time."

Armor reflecting in the afternoon sun, cape flowing behind him in the breeze, Lo walked up beside her, standing on the opposite side from her as did the large bird.

"A longer time than you would think," she said, not turning to face him. "Many a dorel has passed before a day this bright has dared to shine out."

"They have done well then," Lo said, as he too gazed out towards the faraway castle, shining like a beacon in the bright light.

"They have just but started upon their path," she said, blind eyes still fixed at some point that only she could see, "and a treacherous path it shall be, but at least it is more of a start than I have seen in many a long rel."

"I shall watch after them," Lo said, "but as you have earlier advised, I shall only make my presence known if truly needed."

"They must indeed make their own way," she said, as the wind tossed her golden hair in front of her face, "but a little guidance through the rough spots would be appreciated."

They watched as the sun began its long slow descent towards the horizon, their shadows lengthening slightly as they watched distant wagons and horses make their way along the main road to the castle. Finally, the golden-skinned one spoke up, a bit of light-heartedness now in her voice.

"My time as a gypsy is at an end," she said, "this disguise is now no longer needed."

"If I may ask, why did you choose to pose as a gypsy in the first place, my lady?"

"It was a convenient disguise," she answered. "A form that people don't look at twice in the streets, but one that also serves the role of foreteller that I must perform. It has served me well over the last few hundred rels."

"A disguise which you must now abandon," Lo finished.

"Besides," she said as she broke into a smile, "I was getting tired of appearing old anyhow. And the colors must surely appear garish on me."

"Not to these eyes, my lady," Lo answered with a smile. "In Truth, there is beauty enough for those that would but behold it."

She smiled as the bright blue sun worked its way down towards the horizon, its trüb haze glowing around it as it slowly arced through the orain sky. Their shadows grew long as they stood there in silence, each regarding the brief moment of peace afforded them, putting off the future for just one more rise, delaying its inevitable approach for but a moment of silence.

"My lady," Lo said, as the sun settled towards twilight, its blue-gold rays now but peeking out from over the horizon, "how will it all come out?"

She just shook her head, not even her own formidable powers of foretelling able to pierce through the veil of night that lay before them.

"I don't know."

EPILOGUE

The dark-faced assassin walked briskly down the black corridor, his chin a stubble of recent growth, his clothes brown and dingy, knife at his belt, as he walked along the black stone towards the tall platinum door before him. The door opened before him as he approached, closing behind him as he walked by it into the dark room beyond. The room's expanse could not be known, so dark was its interior to more than just mere light. But the assassin knew his way about and stopped at what he knew to be the room's center. He stopped and knelt down to one knee, darkness now all around him, no sign of the door that he'd come through but moments before. He knelt and bowed his head, hands clutched over his heart, as he awaited to be spoken to.

"Speak."

The voice was level in tone, but somehow struck nerves at the soul that not even the fearful sight of any demon could do. But this loyal servant was made of tougher stuff than the two wizards that had previously been in here; fools that had quaked in fear before their master. He would not quake or shake as had they. He served his master in heart and soul; if he had displeased Him then he would die and no amount of shivering in one's boots would ever stop that. No, he proudly served that which now spoke to him.

"Krey has failed," the assassin said, "his army lies in ruins, and those he has recruited for you over the ages are no more. They have bested every challenge that has been put in their path."

Most people would have expected Him to be angry at such news, cowering in the corner as they delivered the report of His enemies' continued survival. But the assassin knew his master better than that, knew that nothing ever truly disturbed the dark thoughts of his thinking.

Mild chuckle from out of the dark. Quiet laugh, able to send shivers down the spine of any creature of the night.

"I am pleased," the voice finally said, *"it all goes according to my plan."*

"Krey was your loyal servant for many thousands of rels," the assassin replied, a bit puzzled by this revelation, but eager to hear his master's answer, "his death was *part* of your plan?"

"Yes my loyal one, all part of a plan I laid down many thousands of rels ago, back before Thïr Tjorca fell."

The assassin grinned inwardly as he began to appreciate, yet once again, how truly devious his Master was. But concern was still in his heart, concern for his Master and His plans.

"But Master, they grow in power and knowledge. They could yet find out too much and become a threat to your power."

The mild chuckle returned, its dark laughter now a bit louder than before, as if the assassin had just read off the punch-line to some mildly amusing joke.

"Have no fear, my servant," the voice came, *"I always have every contingency planned for, and this is no exception. There is one secret to my plans that they know not; one that will put them right into my waiting hands."*

The assassin lifted his head up to the darkness, as if he would look beyond it to see the visage of his Master. Hope and appreciation lit up in his dark heart, love and loyalty to shine out in his eyes, as he once again drew pleasure to see his Master at work.

"And what is that, my Master?"

Laughter seemed to close in with the darkness, around the assassin like a grasping fist, but a fist whose touch the assassin indeed welcomed as his Master gave response.

"That brave group of intrepid adventurers," the voice said almost mockingly, *"so determined to seek forth their Fate and defeat me; so foolish indeed."*

The voice paused briefly before continuing, as if considering something, or perhaps just for dramatic effect.

"One of them is under my COMPLETE control!"

A smile curled up around the edges of the assassin's mouth, as he appreciated the true inspiration of his Master's genius, gained immense joy as he realized the nature of the joke that his Master's laugh now echoed throughout the dark room.

He smiled widely as he asked the one question now in his heart and upon his lips.

"Who?"

APPENDICES

Appendix A:
The Maldene Alphabet

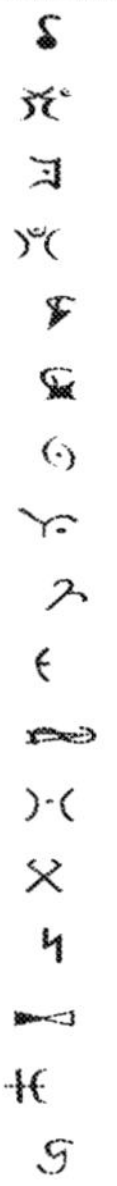

Maldenese	English Equivalent	Maldenese	English Equivalent
	A		SHP
	AIR		SHT
	a		SWH
	AuW or aH		T
	AuGH		TH
	B		U (Y-OO)
	D		UI (YOU-E)
	E		UM (Y-OO-M)
	EUW		UN (Y-oo-N)
	e		V
	eR		W
	F		X (KS)
	G (as in 'ga')		Y (Ya)
	H		Z
	HWEY		TZH
	I		DZH
	i		ZH
	J		
	GN (JN)	Special Symbols-	
	DJU		
	K	Prefixes:	
	CH (hard sound)	II	CH O: the
	L	>	C O M: one who

	M		ꙅ	K L I: possessive tense (ie: words ending with " 's ").
	N			
	NG			
	O		**Suffixes:**	
	OW, OU		✗	W OO G: future tense
	OI			Y AR: -ing (action)
	OR		- -	Y a: ED (past tense for all)
	long OO			Y O : plural
	o			a: makes the word specific or referring to a specific group, etc.
	short oo or u			
	P			
	PS		**Separate words:**	
	R		)(	U M G: or, neither, nor
	AR			Z A D: because, cause, or then, or 'will' if used with future tense
	ARGH			
	S			G E N: with, and
	SH			M ÿ e: is (Mÿe-YO would then be 'are'); also used for 'am' as in "I am"
	SHK			
	TION			D a Z: if/but
	IR (as in 'ear')			Z a D: it/personal possession/ etc.; "it's" when *not* used as "it is"

Punctuation and modifier punctuation marks

     - -   : used over top of a given symbol, it draws out the sound of the symbol it's over and ends it in a "Ya" sound, but with no "a" on the "Ya", instead it ends in the next symbol.

     ፥   : used over top of a symbol, it's then pronounced long.

     ′   : put over top of a word, it signifies an accent on the symbol stressed.

     ( )   : put around a given symbol, it gives that symbol a rough sound (as if clearing one's throat); usually used with the "H" symbol.

     ⨯   : puzzlement question mark

⅄ : rhetorical question mark and others not meant to be answered, etc.

✕ : exclamation point (may also be used in mid-sentence; end sentence with this symbol would then be ✕ ⫻) .

⌇ = question mark (may also be used in mid-sentence; end sentence with this symbol would then be ?.).

╱ : a comma or other pause, like a ";" or ":".

⫽: quotation mark

⫻ : end sentence

✳ : combo of ✕ and ⌇

∴ A triangle of 3 dots, means a combo of ·· and ∶ , used over top of a given symbol.

There are *no* silent letters in the Maldene language; all are pronounced. It is read left to right.

APPENDIX B:
The Maldene Dictionary

The following is a dictionary of some of the words from the major native language of Maldene. The Maldene words are arranged alphabetically as per English, and spelled with English characters, but the Maldene words are given, and then their translation into English given as their meaning. Words are arranged by general types.

The words are spelled phonetically in English, with spacings between what would be each Maldene letter, as given in the previous Maldene alphabet. Long vowels are in upper case (like 'A'), and short vowels are in lower case (like 'a'). A "y" is always considered as pronounced long.

PREFIXES:

B I = offspring or son or daughter of -

B O = low, low elevation; used both as a separate word and as a prefix.

B o K = bad, indicating something that is bad; also used as a prefix to indicate such about that word (ex: bad odor, bad taste, etc.).

CH a = spoiled, as in a spoiled person who expects everything to be done for him, like a spoiled child- used as both a prefix and as a separate word

CH U (CH Y-OO) = rotten, spoiled (as in food); also used as a separate word.

D e B I = grand offspring or grandson or granddaughter of-

D e L = under, underneath; used both as a separate word and as a prefix.

F AUW = face of, or semblance of, or resembling such.

H AR = house of, or descended from, a given person; referring to one's ancestors, not of an actual physical building-type house.

J a N = place, stronghold, residence, or house (as in a physical house); as a prefix, indicates the physical home or stronghold of the word it's attached to.

K E S = high; not for height or tallness, but as pertains to something being elevated to a height above the ground where it's suspended or elevated; used as either a prefix and as a separate word for elevation.

R a N = signifies a kind of people that are a great people but also highly mystical, magical, and/or mysterious.

S e = to be something (so SeZOKaI would be "to be cursed" or "accursed")

S e K = short height (not necessarily small, just short height); used both as a prefix and as a separate word.

T a = high, tall, height, high as meaning for height or tallness; used both as a prefix and as a separate word.

T e = great (also used as a separate word for "great"), a great version of something

Z O = evil, bad; also used as a separate word.

SUFFIXES:

D e G = old or aged; indicates one who is old; used as a separate word or as a suffix.

e N = indicates one who does something (the something being indicated by the root word it's attached to), usually as a career or lifestyle. So a "consumer" would be KOSONeN.

K a = people(s), a kind of people; used as a suffix or a separate word.

L O = true, pure, the pure representation of something; also used as a separate word.

M AR = large; indicates something that is large; used as a suffix and also as a separate word.

M i NG = used to indicate the field of knowledge concerning the word that it's used with.

M O = added on to give a note of humbleness, etc., also used as the separate word "humble" or to be humble, etc

O T = the word "it"; something that is neuter; used as a suffix or as a separate word.

R e N = indicates that the type of creature given by the word is specifically of the *female* variety. Also used as a separate word for *female*.

R O N = as per R *e* N, but specifically of the male of the species; also used as a separate word for *male*.

S a = small or little; indicates something that is small; used as either a suffix or also a separate word.

S e a = indicates the utter essence of the attached word. Can also be used as a separate word meaning "utter and total essence/being/force, etc.".

S E a N = people(s) when speaking of a *race* of peoples; used as a suffix or separate word (in English, it may translate as being spelled as "cian").

S e ÿ a = indicates the utter lack of essence and even the antithesis of the attached word (i.e.: the opposite of 'sea'). Can also be used as a separate word meaning "utter and total anti-essence/anti-being/anti-force/unessence, etc.

S O = added on to give a note of hesitancy; also used as the separate word 'well' as in "well,....", etc.

S o L = indicates one who's a young one or child of the species; also used as a separate word for 'child' or 'youth'

S O M e = Added to give a note of coming from the heart; also means to come from the heart, etc.

T E = 'very' or 'extremely' something, in reference to the rest of the word (ex: very old, extremely skillful, etc.); also used as a separate word for "very" or "extremely".

T o N = indicates the practical physical application of something (usually a field of knowledge, etc.).

V a = Added to the end of a noun to make it into a verb denoting action as pertaining to the meaning of that noun, or the concept of that noun in action or as a verb; also can be used as a separate word for 'action' or 'act' or 'to act'.

The difference between this and the special symbol for 'YAR', is that 'YAR' can be used at the end of any type of word to denote the act of *doing* what it is that that word denotes, while this word ('Va') can only be used at the ends of nouns that denote a concept that can be directly put into action (no persons or things). 'YAR' can also be used to denote action in using the object given by the word (ex: chair => to use or sit in a chair, etc.). Some examples may make the difference clearer:

root word	with 'Va'	with 'Yar'
Dead, death	to die, die	dying, the act of dying
explosion	to explode, explode	exploding
Strength	to be strong	strengthening
work (noun)	work (verb), to work	working
chair	-	to use a chair for its intended purpose.

ÿ a = as a suffix, indicates the negation of the word it's attached to; as a separate word means "no" or "not", etc.

ÿ e a = as a suffix, means the opposite of that word; as a separate word, means "opposite".

GENERAL WORDS:

A eR G = slang cuss word, the pits in regards to a person, place, thing, event, etc.; also means things like F**K, D**n, Shalsbot, Frak, etc.

a L Ü V = everyone, everybody, all, etc.

a L Ü V a = referring to everyone/etc. from a specific group (usually implied from the conversation, etc.).

auGH U = anger, etc.

B e D a = some kind of ship, a prefix tells what kind of ship (sea, space, etc.).

B O D a L N = valley (low land)

B R auGH O = fight, battle, etc.

B R O M T a = strong, physical strength and might.

C a L Ü D = rules and guidelines, etc. (actually spelled like KaLÜD in the native Maldenese).

CH U T K R a = devious, crafty type of intelligence, sneaky, sneakiness.

D ä E = translucent pearly white color.

D a L N = land, landmass.

D a L N M AR = continent (large land)

D a L N S a = island (small land)

D a L N S a M AR = island continent (small continent); used for a land mass about the size of Australia or thereabouts.

D a L N T E M AR = planet (extremely large land).

D e K = counting, as in for numbers; refers to a numbering system.

D e K O = grandparent ("DeKOReN" and "DeKORON" for grandmother and grandfather); great grandparent would be either "D e D e KO" or "D e K O T E"

D e L B O D a L N = underground valley

D e L D a L N = underground (under land).

D e L N = a hole (as in, a hole in something)

DJU e V = The number '5' spelled out.

F AIR M = life, life-forms, etc.

F (auGH) R auGH = The essence, nature, and being of pure force of all types (gravity, electricity, magnetic, etc.), the definition of the various physical and energy forces of nature, etc.; pure force (not physical).

F au L T E Z = in English, spelled as 'Faltes', it's a major island, a land mass too large for a normal island and too small for a regular continent- about halfway between the two, etc.

words for thanks:

F AW ÏR = thank-you, thanks, to give such, etc.

F AW ÏR' M O = A kind of humble and self-giving thanks, etc.

F AW ÏR S e' = the kind of sarcastic type of thanks often given to mean the opposite of true thanks.

F AW ÏR S O = Thanks, to give thanks but with a note of hesitancy and/ or uncertainty.

F AW ÏR S O M e = the kind of true thanks, heart-felt thanks, which comes from the heart and can never be truly wholly expressed, etc.

F AUW S U = flower, etc.

F E = to; to do something, etc.

F O S a = air. If used as a separate word or a suffix then can indicate that "of the air"

G E O = world, planet, etc.

G L O M = ultimate strength (physical or otherwise)., force, mighty/great strength, etc.

G L O M i N = to boldly or bravely do something.

G O V = have, had, to have had, etc.; past tense of PIJ (although sometimes PIJYa used instead, mainly by upper class though).

H a Ï K L = a physical frontier (a place), etc.

H ÏR = forest, woods, at that thereof, etc.

HWEY AIR L O = Merry, happy, joyful, joyous, etc.

IR D O K = ocean, sea, etc.

J ä L = great ancient tome.

K a i = a (magic) spell

K a S e a N = people, society

K ar J O N = police, guards, patrols, etc., often thought to mean 'rip-necks' for how some town guards often treat the townsfolk.

K a' R U = a cry of triumph or victory.

K L AIR = explore, discover

K L AR = blood

K L AR Y O' N = The (Maldene) Red Death (a disease).

K L E U M = Wisdom

K L I M e' N = very smart genius type of intelligence (usually in one area but can be multiple areas, etc.).

K L O G M e N = Super-genius intelligence, the all encompassing all around super-genius type of intelligence, etc

K L OR M = death of ideas, dreams, etc.

K O = Parent; so mother is "K O R e N" and father is "K O R O N"

K O D e k = scholastic-use numbering system.

K O S O N = take, to take or consume (**not** eat)

K ÿ E = sky, the sky. If used as part of another word or as a suffix then it can indicate that "of the sky".

L O M = Memory (due to intelligence)

M a L D E N E =pronounced 'MaLdEN', the planet's name, the last 'E' is the only silent letter in the whole language.

M e N = mind, mental (as relating to the mind/mental, etc.).

M e N O M = smart, intelligent, intelligence, etc.

M e T = knowledge, concept thereof, etc.

M EUW M e N = scared kind of intelligence, meager, low minded, minor kind of intelligence.

M O N a S = monster, beast

M O N D E = the concept of a frontier, not a physical one, but a frontier of ideas, concepts, etc.

N AR L U = word for the UV color Ultra-Green.

N a T e R = nothing, nothingness, etc.

N eR D e K = death of one's true being/soul, etc.

N i K T O = death incarnate (as in a physical person or being).

N I M a = generalized excrement, bio-waste, urine, BM (solid organic waste, etc.).

N O = a *large* explosion (so N O V a would mean the act of exploding...).

N O Z = where, the question 'where', the asking of a place, etc. Where- a place.

Orain (OR A N) = word for the UV color Ultra-Orange.

O SH O = water, of water, etc.

P e K = phlegm, spit

P I Ë G O = insult: combination of pig (or worse), peasant (or lower, etc.), and dung pile all rolled up into one, etc

P I J = have, to have, has, etc.; present form of GOV (sometimes PIJYa used in place of GOV, mainly by the Upper Class).

P O = final, the last of something to be found or done, etc.

P O a K = the great finale, the great ending of something/one, etc.

R a Z E = to seek out, to go forth so as to find, to seek, to go, etc.

R e L = The period of 1 revolution of Maldene around its sun (or in general, the period of 1 revolution of a planet around its star). For Maldene, 1 rel equals about 3.6 Earth years. Note: Maldene people age by the rel the same way Earth people age by the year; so an 8 rel old Maldene child would be physically the same age as an 8 year old Earth child (this effectively gives Maldene types 3.6 times the life span of Earth people).

R E T O = illegitimate; so 'illegitimate child' would be "S o L R E T O"

R i K = fool, a fool, foolish

R OI = Stupid, idiotic, dump, etc.

R O = word (as in, a word)

R O D e N = language

S a H M O = secret or something that is secret or has been secreted, etc.

S a L = great ancient magical and highly mystical tome.

S a L ÿ e = beauty

S a L ÿ e N = beautiful, something that is beautiful.

S A S M O = (great) Secret or Mystery of Nature, the Ages, etc.

S a T M O = mystery or puzzle, etc.

S e' L e S a N = energy, light, heat, and the like, and the essence of such physical energies, etc.

S E M D O = strange, unusual

SH a K OO = An expression of astonishment.

SH I D OO = the great calling forth of the true inner nature of something or someone, etc.

S i L = slime

S o D = to put in the ground, to bury something (physically or figuratively).

S o D O T Ü V a = "sod it all", or "bury it all"- an expression, meaning to get rid of something, bury or trash the whole mess, etc.

S o L D e k = everyday-use numbering system.

S O M = space, as in outer space, the Great Unknown, the infinite space, etc.

S O M U V A = the stars, or of the stars (literally: that of space, etc.).

S OO D R a = magic, arcane powers, unknown forces (or forces unknown), powers of the universe, etc.

S o T = indicates something from the ground or of the ground; often used as a derogatory.

S P IR M a = life, the idea/concept of life and the living of it, etc.

S ÿ L V a' = the realm of the earth (including nature, etc.), etc., and everything of and from it.

S ÿ L V a' S e a = the utter essence of "SÿLVa'"

T a D a L N = mountains (tall land)

T AIR U = = word for the UV color Ultra-Yellow.

T a ÿ E = free, liberty, etc.

T a ÿ OR = free and mighty/strong, etc.

T e M e T = the term used for an ancient knowledge that combines various aspects of magic, technology, and psychic ability into one single field.

T e M e T o N = the practical physical use and application of TeMeT.

T E Y a' = spirit or spirit force (as in soul not undead)

TH ÏR = great and mighty City; used in front of another word (not a prefix, but a separate preceding word) to indicate City of -, etc., usually with a city's name.

TH ÏR e aR = civilization and the like, etc.

T O = pronounced like in 'toe'; new, newly found or discovered, new in concept.

T O V a K = mission, duty, entrustment, etc.

T R ü B = = word for the UV color Ultra-Blue.

T U = canine, dog

U V = 'of' in the sense of 'from', 'of', etc. (different from 'YOM').

V AIR U M = The not only belonging to something/someone, but more of the *being of* that something/someone else, etc. The 2 are 1 in the same thing. Also used to indicate a kind of extreme possession, etc.

V O = none, no one, no man, etc.

V O L D = the great Death, death of all, of dreams, ideas, physical existence, soul, death of all and more.

V O M O L = man/men, human, of man/men, man-kind, etc.

W i S = dry, absence of water and liquids.

W i S AIR = *extremely* dry and arid.

W i S AIR E = the utter and complete absolute absence of moisture, water, liquids, etc.

W OO M IR = before, before/ever, etc.

Y O M = 'of' in the sense of belonging to, being of, etc.

Y O N = death of life, the stopping of life's functions.

Y OR auGH U = great anger, but not YORa'ZauGH.

Y OR a' Z auGH = The great True anger that runs deep and true; also known as 'blood curse'- when nothing stands in your way to achieve your objective revenge, etc.

ÿ OR M = mighty, strength, great, etc.

Y U N D O = voyage, long journey or travel.

Z AIR = black, the color black

Z AIR Y O' N = the (Maldene) Black Death (disease).

Z O K a I = curse, a curse

Z OO L M e N = evil intelligence, evilly crafty, devious of intelligence, vile evil intelligence, etc.

SAMPLE CUSS WORDS AND PHRASES (assembled from the previous assortment of words, prefixes, etc.):

A eR G = slang cuss word, the pits in regards to a person, place, thing, event, etc.; also means things like F**K, D**n, Shalsbot, Frak, etc.

B o K CH U = used to indicate something that is *really* awful (like awful smelling, etc.).

CH U P e K : rotten phlegm

F AUW N I M a = face of excrement, or SH*T Face.

P I Ë G O = insult: combination of pig (or worse), peasant (or lower, etc.), and dung pile all rolled up into one, etc

S o D O T Ü V a = "sod it all", or "bury it all"- an expression, meaning to get rid of something, bury or trash the whole mess, etc.; sometimes a short slang version is used: SoTÜVa

T U - R e N = female dog (the "B" word)

Words For 'Death', Taken From Above: KLORM, N eRDe K, NiKTO, VOLD, YON

Words For Strength, Taken From Above: BROMTa, GLOM, ÿORM.

Other Composite Words Taken From Above:

DeLOSHO = underwater

GLOMSPirMa = lifeforce.

IRDOKMAR = great ocean

KÿESEaN = the name given by people of old to the race of Hawkmen; English spelling is often translated as Kÿecian

SeLO = truth

SOMYUNDO = combo SOM and YUNDO, travel through the great unknown

TeDeLNOSHO = name given to The Great Whirlpool

TEMAR = like 'MAR' but *very* large.

TESa = like for 'Sa' but extremely small.

YONSOODRA = death magic or necromancy.

Appendix C:
Maldene Time

This section gives the various time periods used in Maldene, and their Earth equivalent time periods. A capital letter means to pronounce it long.

Maldene Standard		Earth Standard Equivalent conversion
Name	**Time**	
Rel	1 Maldene year	3.608639440263 Earth years, or 1318 days + 1 hr + 20 secs
		times less than a day
tidon (tid)		1/2 sec
trIded (trId)	= 100 tids	50 secs
DIidlo (dIid)	= 5 trIds	350 secs, or 4 mins + 10 secs
nevor (nev)	= 20 dIids	83 mins +20 secs, or 5000 secs
Rise (day-rise, sunrise)	= 26 nevs	36 hrs + 6 mins + 40 secs
		times greater than a day
Kevey (kev)	= 9 rises	13 days + 13 hrs
fitay (fit)	= 2 kevs	27 days + 2 hrs
MOtab	= 6 kevs	81 days + 6 hrs, or 11 weeks + 4 days + 6 hrs

Rel	= 16 motabs + 12 Havar, or 876 rises
Havat Rise (Havar)	-one of 12 special in-between days (= 1 rise) not belonging to any given motabs.

other long- range time periods

Trirel (tril)	= 3 rels
Tricarel (TRIKaReL) (tricade)	= 10 tril = 30 rels
Tristurel (tristury)	= 10 tricaeds = 100 trils = 300 rels
Trilenirel (trilenium)	= 10 tristuries = 100 tricades = 1000 trils = 3000 rels
DOrel	= 5000 rels, the period between 2 Donjflou

Maldene Calendar

The following is the Maldene calendar. The motabs are given with their names and numbers, starting at the beginning of the rel, and the various Havar (not numbered, but denoted by an '*' in front of it). Each of the Havar are explained after the calendar is given.

-----beginning of calendar-----
---summer---

*Bejuïr (B e J YOO EEYR)
   1   Enterode (e N T er O D; spelled as *Enterod* in Maldenese): "The beginning of the sunny season"

2   Juxor (J YOO X OR): "The time to be jolly"
*Jee'dio (J e E' D i O)
   3   Heetar (H EE T ar): "The hot time"
   4   Extar (e X T ar): "The ending of the sunny season"

---fall---

*First Fatlaa'r (F au T L a ar')
   5   Planeop (P L a N e O P): "The time of the first planting season and the beginning of the season of Life And Death"
   6   Faleomar (F A L E O M ar): "The time of growing"
*Donjflou (D O N J F L ou): see extra note below
   7   Hevatluïr (H e V a T L OO EEYR): "The time of harvesting and joyous celebration"
*Kilio (K I L i O)
   8   Arüdwo (ar OOY D W O): "The windy time- of sun and wind (the windy season)"

---winter---

*Second Fatlaa'r
   9   Monwïr (M O N W EEYR): "The beginning of the cold season"
   10   Thüxor (TH OOY X OR): "The dreary time"
*Golndjïo (G O L N D J EEY O)
   11   Cthïrgo (K TH EEYR G O): "The time of the winter gods and the bringers of misery"... the coldest time of the rel.
   12   Dwïrgo (D W EER G O): "The ending of the cold season"

---spring---

*Third Fatlaa'r
   13   Radnïr (R a D N EEYR): "The Beginning of the rainy season"
*Bedfow (B e D F OW)
   14   Sadro (S a D R O): "The time of flowers"
*Noulow (N ou L O)
   15   Lomïr (l O M EEYR): "The time of mating and of love"

16 Enduïr (e N D YOO EEYR): "The time of the second planting and the ending of the rainy season and of the rel"
*Forth Fatlaa'r

------end of calendar------

Donjflou: An additional day that occurs only once every 5000 rels, kind of like the Earth Leap Year, except a lot less frequent. It is a day of omen and a time when mysterious, joyful, and/or dire things are said to come to the forefront.

Explanations of the Various Havar:

Fatlaa'r: Marks the transition from one season to the next; often a time of joyous celebration or dire preparation, as the case may be for the new on-coming season. There are 4 of these.

Golndjïo: Marks the middle of the cold season and the height of the cold season. A time to mourn over those lost in the winter (past and present) and to pray to the winter gods to make it easier.

Kilio: A period of 3 days for the celebration of the harvest (Harvest Celebration), the Coming Of Age for various peoples (becoming a man, etc.), and a time where witches, goblins, evils, undead, and dark forces reign (kind of like Halloween except longer, more so, and *real!*).

Jee'dio: A time of jolly celebration, marking the middle of the sunny season and often the hottest day of the rel. Also a time of practical jokes, etc.

Bejuïr: Marks the beginning of the rel; a time for renewals, treaties, etc.

Bedfow: A day of flowers; marks the beginning of the time of the flowers; a time of celebration for flowers and beauty in general. A time of happiness, beauty, and joyous celebration.

Noulow: Marks the beginning of the time of mating and of love, a day for loving, mating, marrying, renewal (of love, marriage, etc.), coming of age (for females, reproductive-wise), etc. A time of rituals for the above stated in some cultures as well.

Calendar history:

The present calendar puts its starting point at 10,000 rels before the coming Donjflou, at the establishment of the first of the Great Human Kingdoms, and dates from that point on in the form of " R.K. *rel #*", originally meaning **Rel of the Kingdom** (but it has lost its meaning since the fall of the last of the Great Human Kingdoms). Times before this starting date use the suffix of "O.T." (for Old Times) instead of R.K., and are dated as the number of rels that the time is **before** the starting date of "R.K."

Example 1: R.K. 9,990, 22 Juxor.

Example 2: O.T. 500, 23 Juxor.

Days of the Kev

The following, in order of appearance, are the days (rises) of the Maldene week (kev):

Name	part of the kev
Selerise	Forekev (beginning of week)
Sÿlvarise	
Metrise	
Mefrise	Midkev (middle of week)
Glomrise	
Myrise	
Orise	Endkev (weekend)
Naterise	
Volrise	

Times of Day

The following, in chronological order, starting at the Maldene equivalent of Midnight, are the various times of the Maldene day, given in terms of the *nev* of the rise, and if it's usually day or night around that time.

Nev	time of the Rise (Maldene name, abbreviation)	day/night
1-6	early morn (TEsolrise, tr)	night
7-12	mid morn (solrise, sm)	day
13	mid rise (LOnev, ln)	day (noon)
14-19	afternoon (degrise, dr)	day
20-25	early eve, eve (dr)	night
26	end rise (YOnev, yn)	night (midnight)

Time Notation

Like Earth time is written in the form of "7 o'clock AM" or "07:24", or "14:23:22", for hours:minutes:seconds, Maldene time is similarly written in a standard format, as follows.

The first format is: (nev number of rise) rise (time of rise abbreviation). This would correspond to the "7 o'clock AM" example for Earth.

Examples: 3 rise TR, 17 rise DR. Earth equivalent would be 3 o'clock AM for the first.

The second format corresponds to the "hr:min:sec" format for Earth. This format is: (number of nevs into the rise):(number of trideds into the nev):(number of tidons into the trided) (time of the rise abbreviation), where the nev is out of 26 per rise, the trided is out of 100 per nev, and the tidon is out of 100 per trided.

Examples: 03:92 TR, 25:03: DR, 19:24:73 DR.

Abbreviations for the times of the rise are the same as given in the previous table for "Times Of Day".

APPENDIX D:
Maldene Human-Normal Visual Spectrum

Due to the blue star of Maldene, the normal visual spectrum is shifted up into the ultra violet, as well as staying down at the normal red end of the spectrum. Because the natives can normally see up into the UV a bit, there are extra colors that they can see in this part of the spectrum. These extra colors would all be considered as UV to Earth-normal humans, but are considered part of the normal visual spectrum on Maldene. The native names of these colors are gives, as well as what they would roughly translate to in Earth-normal English (the translations are pretty much dummy names to designate these additional graduations of color). All colors in the UV range would appear as a very bright deep blue to a stark hazy white when observed by those from Earth. The names of the additional colors are given in the table below.

Maldene UV color name	rough Earth English translation
Orain	ultra-orange
Tairu	ultra-yellow
Narlu	ultra-green
Trüb	ultra-blue

Color Examples:

Maldene's sky: Orain (white to Earthers);

from ground: Trüb haze around the blue star (white haze around blue star to Earthers).

Plants: Chlorophyll (or local equivalent): violet, Orain, Tairu, and some

Narlu; a bit of green-blues through orange (a little bit of red) for some fungi, mosses, and other lower plants.

The below bar shows the range of Maldene human-normal visual spectrum as compared to Earth-normal, as well as showing the place on the spectrum of the Maldene UV-colors, and where the Maldene UV starts (anyone from Maldene said to have UV sight will have it for this *Maldene*-normal UV range, above the new UV colors given for standard visual range).

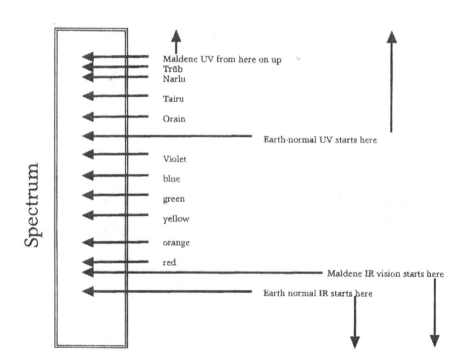

APPENDIX E:
Pronunciation Key to Character Names

The following contains the correct pronunciation to selected character names found in this story. The pronunciation is spelled phonetically, with spaces between the syllables, and long vowels are in upper case (like 'A'), and short vowels are in lower case (like 'a'). A "y" is always considered as pronounced long.

NAME	PRONUNCIATION
THE GOOD GUYS	
Baldegron	BaL De GRoN
Blag-ak	BLaG-aK
Bronto	BRoN TO
Candol	KaN DoL
Dwingale	DWiNG GAL
Eldar	eL Dar
Filmar	FiL Mar
Kilgar	KiL Gar
Lindel	LiN DeL
Lo	LO
Mov	MoV
Quickfoot	KWiK FooT
Sabu	Sa BOO
Sheil-Bor(h)	SHIL BOR(H)- the parenthesis around the "h" indicate that it is to be pronouced with a sound akin to a light clearing of the throat.
Shong	SHoNG
Starke	STarK

THE BAD GUYS

Beltor	BeL TOR
Krey	KRA
Miro	MI RO- an alternate (and possibly more phonetically correct) English spelling might be "Myro".

THE ???

Po-Adar	PO aDar
Kilinir	KiL iN EER
Kor-Lebear	KOR-Le BEAR
Lorel/Schanter	LOR eL / SCHaN TR
Mauklo	Mau KLO
Tauzy-Ril	Tau ZEE - RiL

Printed in the United States
202380BV00001B/22-39/A